A JEWISH STORY

Sheldon Cohen

authorHOUSE®

AuthorHouse™
1663 Liberty Drive
Bloomington, IN 47403
www.authorhouse.com
Phone: 1 (800) 839-8640

Published by AuthorHouse 03/30/2015

ISBN: 978-1-5049-0456-8 (sc)
ISBN: 978-1-5049-0457-5 (e)

Print information available on the last page.

Any people depicted in stock imagery provided by Thinkstock are models,
and such images are being used for illustrative purposes only.
Certain stock imagery © Thinkstock.

This book is printed on acid-free paper.

Dedication

I dedicate this book to Amanda, Megan,
Carly, Alexa, Ethan, Emily,
Derek, Rylie, Benjamin,
and the brave men and women willing to fight
terrorism, whatever form it might take

AUTHOR BIOGRAPHY

A graduate of the University of Illinois College of Medicine, Sheldon Cohen has practiced internal medicine, served as a medical director of the Alexian Brother's Medical Center in Northwest Suburban Chicago, and served as the medical director of two managed care organizations: Cigna Health plan of Illinois and Humanicare Plus of Illinois. The author taught internal medicine and physical diagnosis to medical students from Loyola University Stritch School of Medicine and the Chicago Medical School. Recognizing the fact that busy physicians are pressed for time and thus often fail to capture a thorough medical history, the author developed one of the first computerized medical history systems for private practice and wrote a paper on his experience with 1500 patients who utilized the system. This was one of the early efforts in promoting electronic health records, a work in progress to this day. Serving as a consultant for Joint Commission Resources of the Joint Commission on Accreditation of Healthcare Organizations, the author did quality consultations at hospitals in the United States, Rio de Janeiro, Brazil, Copenhagen, Denmark, and served as a consultant to the Ministry of Health in Ukraine, assisting them in the development of a hospital accrediting body.

Dr. Cohen is the author of 26 books.

AUTHOR'S NOTE

Having written non-fiction books on the practice of medicine, medical mystery fiction, short stories, terrorism and historical fiction, my favorite genre is historical fiction on the subject of World War II. This is my third book on the subject. The characters mostly are fictitious and I base their stories upon true events that occurred in the twentieth century, before and during World War I and II including the holocaust. I am a first generation American. In 1904, my mother, a three month old, came to the United States with her mother from Tykocin (Tiktin in Yiddish), Poland. All her life, she would claim to be born in Rochester, New York, her first residence in the New World. In her old age when America celebrated the centennial of Ellis Island, she changed her story bragging that she had passed through the famous island as an infant. My father, aged four, also arrived in 1904 from the same Polish location.

As a youngster, I heard stories about how my grandfathers "fled the Czar." They also came from Tiktin, an area under Russian dominance called the Pale of Settlement.

As I grew up I heard other stories about my heritage, including one told to me by my maternal grandmother about how she, as a young child, witnessed pogroms including the beheading of a Jew by a sword wielding "Cossack" on horseback. From my step-paternal grandmother I learned of her twelve brothers and sisters lost in the holocaust.

Later in life, my uncle's daughter told me that my maternal grandfather deserted the Czar's army rather than face the persecution of the Jewish soldier. Right before my grandfather was hoping to leave Russia-Poland and join his family in the United States, the Russians captured him, but a compassionate Russian guard said, "Let the young man go. His family is already there." I owe to that Russian guard my grandfather and two aunts and an uncle and six cousins subsequently born in the United States. The penalty for desertion was death by firing squad.

An interest in learning more about my heritage surfaced after I retired and had more time to reflect on such matters, so I studied the history of the Jews in Eastern Europe and their struggle with anti-Semitism, Hitler, World War II, the anti-Nazi partisan resistance in Europe and the Holocaust. After much study, I put together a fictional account, based on actual events, of Jewish and Soviet partisans that I hope will be informative and interesting to the reader.

Although the book has past relevance, in the present era of terrorism and rising anti-Semitism, it has current relevance as well. He who fails to learn the lessons of history is doomed to repeat it.

This historical fiction novel utilizes two fonts:
1. **Italicized *abcd* represents actual historical events**
2. **Times New Roman 12 abcd represents fictional events**

CHAPTER 1
PRELUDE
1904-1936
BERLIN, GERMANY

In 1904, Ben Frohman arrived in Germany with his Torah wrapped in leather; a Torah penned by his great-great-grandfather and passed down from generation to generation. He kissed it and stored it for safekeeping. He would breathe easier now, finally free of the pogroms that plagued the Jews of Eastern Europe.

The Frohmans. including Dr. Ben, his wife Leah, their son David and daughter Emily, represent refugees from anti-Semitism, fleeing from country to country in an effort to escape persecution.

In the late 1800's and early 1900's the Jews of Eastern Europe fled to Western Europe, South America, the Middle East, or the United States. In the 1930's the Jews of Germany did the same. If interested in more history, we can go back as far as the 1300's when Western Europeans blamed Jews for the Plague accusing them of "poisoning the wells." Those Jews that survived settled in Eastern Europe, principally Poland.

1

In my case and fortunately for my family, my grandparents fled from Russian-controlled Poland to the United States in 1904 where they lived in freedom and security.

Ben's father, also planning to leave Tiktin, Poland and follow his family was not as lucky, falling victim to the anti-Jewish violence.

Upon hearing the news of his father's death, Ben and his mother sat in mourning for the traditional seven days. Their grief knew no bounds, but they sought comfort based upon the knowledge that he would want them to survive and live in peace in their new country.

Although there was some anti-Semitism in Germany at the time, it was not government policy as it had been under the Czar. The early part of the twentieth century was a golden-era for Jews in Germany, and beside the occasional anti-Semitic rant, verbally or in print by individuals, there was no organized anti-Semitism affecting Jewish life and the ability to make a living.

As Ben grew up, his ambition remained to become a physician. His academic collegiate achievements allowed him to enter the University of Berlin medical school in an era when Germany and Austria were the world leaders in medical education and care.

When he graduated, he went to a dance with a friend and fellow male classmate at the Jewish Community center in Berlin. It was here that his life changed when he walked into the dance hall and caught a glimpse of a young woman sitting against the wall who took his breath away. She was short and slim with coal black hair fixed upon her head in a bun. There was not a hint of makeup on her beautiful face, nor was any necessary he thought. He was close enough to see her large, brown eyes. She was dressed in a long green skirt with a green sweater. Tremulously, he approached her. "Uh—excuse me, please. My name is Ben Frohman. Would you care to dance?"

She looked at him, a slow smile crossing her features, and as Ben stared back nervously, she said, "Why yes, I'd love to. My name is Leah Friedberg."

As they danced, she said to him, "Do I sense an accent?"

"Yes," he answered, and I thought I lost it all."

"Your accent is barely discernable. I'm good with languages," Leah said.

"That's a Russian or Polish accent you hear," answered Ben. "My mother and I came here in 1904. My father was killed in Russian controlled Poland during one of the pogroms many years ago."

"Oh, I see. I'm sorry to hear about your father," Leah answered sadly.

"Thank you," was all Ben could say.

Leah added, "We know all about the pogroms in Russia, and we've had many people flee to Germany. I'm sure that your life has been much better here."

"Yes, it has been; very much better."

They sat together after the dance, and as they did, he was relaxed and comfortable in her presence. Before he had to leave, he said as confidently as he could, "Leah, would you care to accompany me Wednesday evening to the Burgerstrasse Café?"

She smiled at him. There was a moment of silence as he could feel his heart thump in his chest. Then she said, "Why, yes. I'd love to."

A mutual interest was there from the start for the both of them. He learned that Leah was a nurse working in a private clinic. Her parents were Reform Jews and had arrived in Berlin from Byelorussia also fleeing the same events that forced the Tepper's exodus.

Both of them found that they had many mutual interests and they spent every moment together that he was free from his medical responsibilities.

This was their first love and every passing day brought them closer. They married shortly before he completed his internal medicine training. He started his practice and Leah continued nursing. They were on the threshold of a happy life, but worried as the newspapers told of Europe's unstable search to form alliances in preparation for the war that many feared would soon engulf the continent.

The assassination of Archduke Ferdinand of Serbia set the conflagration in motion that everyone had feared. In 1914, World War I started, and Germany called up many young physicians including Dr. Ben who had to turn over his developing practice to an older physician while he fought for the glory of his adopted country.

Germans, overcome with an intense patriotic fervor, gathered in street rallies to support the war. At one of these rallies on the Marienplatz in Munich, a young man stood in the sea of cheering faces. He screamed his support for the Fatherland. This twenty-five year old vagabond in search of a destiny would later describe the intensity of his feelings as he realized that he would soon be in a fight for freedom that would determine the future of the German nation.

His name was Adolph Hitler. Even though he was an Austrian, he joined the German army where he distinguished himself by earning the Iron Cross and after the war would enter politics, join and then lead the fledgling party, the National Socialist German Worker's Party (Nazis, for short), and, in the next twenty-five years, almost bring the world and the Jewish people to complete destruction.

Dr. Ben charged into the quagmire of World War I where destiny would take him far beyond his wildest dreams. His first wartime act was to pass through Liege, Belgium, an area the Germans felt they had to control before the invasion of France. The battle had begun.

The countryside had already become desolate, with ruined villages, fields pockmarked with shell craters and littered with the bloated corpses of men and horses and cattle. The soldier's uniforms were caked with mud, sweat and blood. In the first few weeks, they became battle-hardened veterans. Ben worked around the clock and the days merged into one utilizing his skills as a diagnostician on occasion, but mostly assisting in and performing surgery trying to save the lives of young soldiers with wounds of all degrees of severity on every part of the human anatomy.

The time was the time of the damned. The atmosphere of anesthetic agents and gangrene clogged the bronchial tubes like a thick, suffocating gruel. Breathing became .more difficult using surgical masks, so Ben often operated without them. Nothing prepared him for the volume and intensity of injuries, disease and death as both sides fought with dedicated fervor.

He kept thinking about the Kaiser's statement when the war started, that "The war would be over before the leaves start falling from the trees." But his never-ending emergency schedule necessitated continuous work, and as the leaves fell three more times he garnered more experience than he could ever have achieved in a lifetime of practice; there was no part of the human anatomy he didn't treat. He had learned to live on less than three or four hours of sleep a night.

Eventually, Germany and its opponents would be involved in the killing fields of a stalemated trench-warfare. Four years later in November 1918, by the end of the conflagration, eight million lost their lives and twenty million were injured. One hundred thousand Jews served in the German military, and twelve thousand died in battle. After years of battlefield stalemate, very little territory had changed hands. Hunger had become rampant on the home front. The

German people had been reduced to eating dogs and cats, or as they called them—roof rabbits. The country was war weary and clamored for peace. Revolutionary movements developed on the right and left of the political spectrum, and general strikes paralyzed the country. The troops began to mutiny, deserting in droves. Soldiers under their command attacked and killed officers that attempted to maintain discipline. The situation for Germany had become desperate and the country went down in defeat even though very little ground had changed hands and Germany had not been invaded.

It was Hitler's view that the German army did not lose the World War, but rather the civilian leaders who signed the armistice on November 11, 1918 and formed the new Weimar Democracy betrayed the military. Never mind that the German army was out of reserves and armaments to continue the battle, Hitler labeled the new Weimar Democratic government the "November Criminals" who stabbed Germany in the back. His view was that the world was in danger from Jews and Marxists who wanted to control the world. It was his mission to prevent that threat. With this in mind, while still a member of the German army, he was assigned to investigate a fledgling party the Nationale Socialistica Deutcher Arbeiter Partei (National Socialist German Worker's Party) Nazis for short. He was so enamored of the Nazi's philosophy that he joined the party and soon became its leader. By a combination of stirring oratory and ruthless, uncompromising leadership, Hitler and his party would strive to overthrow and gain control of the country. The world would never be the same.

After the armistice of 1918 ending the war, Dr. Ben was mustered out of the army and built up a busy practice as an internist in Berlin in spite of the raging street battles fought by the right and left of the political spectrum. In the attempt by these factions to wrest control of the new German Weimar Democracy established after World War I, many innocent civilians died. Through this all, Ben and Leah still managed to start their family: David, their first-born and Emily, their second and last child.

Germany, devastated by the war, had to endure the harshness of the Versailles treaty. Four hundred and fourteen clauses of the treaty dealt with German punishment:

Germany had to accept blame for the war.

Germany had to pay damages caused by the war.

German military was reduced to 100,000 men. They were not allowed tanks, nor submarines, nor an air force and only six naval vessels.

The Rhineland was demilitarized.

The treaty prevented German union with Austria, returned Alsace Lorraine to France, Eupen and Malmedy became Belgian property, Denmark received North Schleswig, Poland and Czechoslovakia received some German territory and the League of Nations controlled Germany's colonies.

By 1919, multiple problems beset the Weimar Republic including the crippling reparations of the Versailles Treaty, the violent opposition of radical parties (Communists and Nazis) and ten years later a world-wide depression and crippling inflation, which paved the way for Adolph Hitler to seize power.

The Frohmans could only stand by as post World War I political intrigues and world-wide economic conditions resulted in Hitler assuming power in Germany by 1933. Life for them and all the Jews of Germany would never be the same.

CHAPTER 2

REALIZATION

1936

BERLIN, GERMANY

Dr. Ben Frohman and his wife had been discussing their plight for several years, but now their decision was irrevocable; they had no choice.

Since 1933, when Hitler took over in Germany, anti-Semitic legislation was singling out Jews for 'special treatment' making it difficult for Jewish physicians to practice medicine. From the standpoint of medical ethics alone, it was becoming impossible to tend to patients, not to mention the financial inability to survive. Hitler's slow and deliberate attempt to eliminate Jews from German culture created hardships for the entire Jewish community.

Ben, whose past allowed him to understand through personal experience the evils of anti-Semitism, was frustrated and saddened that his children would have to experience what he went through in Russia-Poland as a youngster. Growing up in the anti-Semitic environment of the new Germany birthed by German Chancellor,

Adolph Hitler, was an emotional and mental harm he did not want his children to experience.

Ben was in excellent physical condition, obvious even through his clothing by well delineated muscles, broad shoulders, flat abdomen and an athletic gait all honed by recreational gymnastics. Although it was a young man's sport, he continued to pursue it on a tamed back basis even though he had little time to keep up. As good as it was for his body, it was also a welcome release from the pervasive and fearful thoughts that his mind had difficulty controlling. He knew that exercise was the perfect prescription and the words of Maimonides occupied a prominent place on his office examining room wall.

"As long as a person exercises and exerts himself...sickness does not befall him and his strength increases...But one who is idle and does not exercise...even if he eats healthy foods and maintains healthy habits, all his days will be of ailment and his strength will diminish."

He was fifty-one years old now in 1936, five feet and eight inches tall with brown eyes and pitch-black, wavy hair with a touch of gray on the sides.

Now would be a good time for discussion with his son, he thought. Dinner was over and he and David were in the kitchen alone.

"David, what are you doing for the next hour or so?"

"Not a thing. Why?" answered David.

"Good," nodded Ben. "Your mother and I made an important decision and you're old enough to understand what it's all about. Sit down. There are lots of things I want to go over with you."

Fifteen-year-old, five-feet-six inch David, like his father, was also slim and muscular with the same brown eyes and black hair like his father and mother. He had significant shoulders and upper body strength honed by ten years of gymnastic competition until the German sports club, directed by a Hitler edict, expelled him for being Jewish. David, bitter at the expulsion, found a Jewish gymnastic organization with a small gym where he could work out. The facility was not long enough for the vault, but adequate for a short tumbling matt, still rings, parallel bars, high bars and pommel horse.

His father was proud of David's gymnastic prowess—far in excess of his own—and proud of his prompt action in finding the club where he could continue with the sport that he loved. Although he would not admit it, he glowed with pride when his son scowled and said, "They're not going to shut me out." For Ben it was one of his son's first personal direct effects of Hitler's restrictions on Germany's Jewish citizens. David would be ready and receptive for what he was about to hear as he too was being influenced by Hitler's anti-Semitic legislation not only for present actions, but also restrictions that would affect his future.

If it was Hitler's plan to get Jews to leave the country, he was succeeding. As soon as he gained power in 1933, he did what he could to get Jews out of German government service:

In April of 1933, he started with the "Law for the Restoration of the Professional Civil Service, which stated that all Jews and others who were "politically unreliable" were henceforth excluded from any type of government post. There were random attacks on Jewish property as well as Jews themselves. Nazis publicly burned books written by Jews and anti-Nazis. They forbid Kosher-ritual slaughter of animals. They established a Department of Racial Hygiene.

In 1934, Universities could only have one and one-half percent of Jewish students, and Jewish activity in the medical and legal professions suffered to a significant degree. Jewish students were excluded from taking exams in medicine, pharmacy, dentistry and law. This edict would slowly eliminate them from these professions. If you were a Jewish physician, you were restricted from treating non-Jewish patients. Jewish student's prospects for medical school dropped, Jewish employees of the military lost their jobs, and Jewish actors found parts hard to come by.

From 1935 and 1936, the Nuremburg Laws were in place that restricted Jewish personal life and relationships with Aryans. The first law, The Law for the Protection of German Blood and German Honor prohibited marriage and intercourse between Jews and Germans. In addition, it prohibited the employment by Jews of any German female less than forty-five years of age. The second law, the Reich Citizenship Law, took German citizenship away from Jews, creating a distinction between Reich citizens and nationals. Jews lost the right to visit swimming pools, parks and restaurants. The authorities restricted their passports.

These laws, Hitler's first efforts to formalize the anti-Jewish measures taken to bring consistency with the program of Hitler's Nazi party demanding that Jews must no longer be citizens, would be his first efforts in the long process he envisioned to rid the world of Jews. The genocide would start later, but not while he was establishing his power base.

David sat down at the kitchen table in their three-bedroom apartment in central Berlin, an upper-middle-class neighborhood close to the doctor's office and hospital. He had a good idea what his father had in mind, but he respectfully remained silent.

In a firm, loud voice, Ben said, "I want to tell you everything, David. Your mother and I have been talking about this for at least a year and we agree. Emily will be okay with it; you know how she clings to her mother. For her, at her young age, the only thing she worries about is where momma is."

David smiled and nodded his head, understanding by his father's tone of voice that he would hear something important. He also agreed with his father's interpretation about his eight-year-old sister.

Ben continued, "From the time you learned to talk, the first punctuation mark that you understood was the question mark. I never knew a kid that would ask so many questions. Sometimes they were too tough for your mother and me to answer. We knew from the start that you were a brilliant boy and you proved that by your school grades. We're very proud of you."

David smiled and said, "Thanks, dad."

Ben continued, "When things got bad for Jews in Germany, you were just a toddler. I followed what was happening because of your grandparents, of blessed memory; they suffered from anti-Semites in Czarist Russia. You know about your grandfather and what happened to him. Since I was a kid, I heard about such things, so my antenna has always been up. After World War I there were former soldiers who blamed Communists and Jews for Germany losing the war..."

"Why did they do that, dad?" interrupted David.

"That's an easy one, son—I have no idea."

David laughed.

"Here's what I think, and this is just an amateur opinion you know. After the war ended in 1918, German Communists and German Fascists fought against each other to take over the new German government—the Weimar Democracy. There was blood in the streets. They hate democracy, you know, and they hate each other."

"Why do they hate each other, Dad?"

"Good question, David. They're similar in many ways. They both have a top man who runs things with an iron fist; a dictator. These dictator's words are law. I think they are both wanting to control the world, so if you have two powerful parties trying to control the world, you have all the ingredients for battle. It's a dangerous world, David,"

"I can see that," answered David.

"Anyhow, many of the Communists from Munich were Jews, but more were not. This latter fact did not matter to Hitler and his kind and so Hitler's Fascists said they would fight against the so-called Jewish-Communist plot. The Fascists lump Jews and Communists in one breath, you see. Communism got its first start in Russia about 1917. Before that in Russia under the czars, Jews lived under hard times. They suffered from discrimination—were even killed, so it is no wonder that some of them thought that Communism might be better than the conditions they were living with under the Czar. Anyhow, anti-Semitism didn't start then, it is as old as the bible. There's nothing new about it, but in early twentieth century times it probably came from the fact that Jews were trying to remain separate as far as their personal and religious life was concerned; they found it tough to become a part of non-Jewish societies.

"If we go further back in history when Christianity started, the Jews were blamed for rejecting Jesus and crucifying him even though the Roman authorities ordered and carried out the crucifixion. We became a convenient scapegoat, and it looks like we still are to this day."

"I think that we can discuss this for a year and never figure it out for sure," said David.

You're right, so let's stick to the point I'm trying to make: the fix we're in now and what we have to do to survive it."

This took David by surprise. After a period of silence and a crinkled brow, he said, "Survive it? Are you worried about us not surviving it?"

Ben nodded his head and punctuated it with a serious expression. "That's on the back of my mind. Yes, it's real for me. My own father didn't survive the pogroms in Russia. I don't mean to scare you, but you're smart enough to understand what's going on and what has happened and could happen again.

"Maybe my way of thinking comes from my training as a doctor. We always worry about the worst possible diagnosis every time we see a patient, because we don't want to miss anything for fear of not doing our job and not helping the patient. I guess that's what I'm doing; only I'm going from a personal level to a much broader one. What Hitler is doing and thinking is serious trouble for Jews especially. You understand?"

"Yes, I do," answered David.

"Anyhow, back to the history and the reason why I'm afraid of what's starting with Germany's Jews. Hitler fought in World War I and when the war was over he blamed Germany's defeat on the Jews."

"Boy, that's a stretch. Did you know him during the war?" asked David.

"No I didn't, but from his book, *Mein Kampf*, he was an anti-Semite long before the war ended—even before the war. Some day you'll read his book; he tells how he learned to hate Jews. He was a minor politician in Bavaria in 1922. No other Germans even heard about him, but a Jewish friend who was with me in the war and who lives in Bavaria told me about him and his anti-Semitism.

"In 1923, Hitler tried to take over the Bavarian Government with his famous Beer Hall Putsch. Thank God it didn't work. The Bavarian authorities stopped Hitler and his followers and killed some of them and put Hitler on trial. There was a lot of publicity and this made him famous in Germany and even around the world, but all he got for it was a five year prison sentence, which only lasted six months and that's when he wrote his book, Mein Kampf."

"It didn't sell many copies at first, but this same friend sent me one and I read it from cover to cover and it scared the hell out of me. I even took notes on his anti-Semitism. Here they are on the table in this notebook. I'm trying to unravel his brain, and I sure don't like what I'm coming up with."

"I know about his book, but I never read it," said David. "What are you coming up with, Dad?"

"Well, let me tell you. It's scary. He spelled out everything he planned to do. People thought it was the ravings of a maniac, but I read it as the ravings of a man who thought he was right about everything and everybody else was wrong. You had to agree with him, or else. He believed in a leader whose word was final. This to him was the only way to run a government."

"You mean a dictator like you said, right Dad?"

"That's it. Like Mussolini in Italy. He was Hitler's idol in the twenties when Hitler was building his party—the National Socialist German Worker's Party or Nazis for short. As far as the Jews were concerned, he accused them of ruining Germany. Plus, he says the Jews ruined all of civilization. To him, that means the whole white race. To Hitler, the Jews were the creators of the modern world that he hated and he claimed they would destroy the world as we know it."

"Why did he hate the modern world? I don't get it," asked a puzzled David.

"Because the modern world had freedom of speech and the press, a government of the people, freedom to do any job you want, no discrimination based upon religion, birth or wealth. Freedom to live your own life and go as far as it can take you as long as you work within the rules and follow the laws. Hitler blamed those freedoms on the Jews. He doesn't believe in them. He believed that only a super person could run a country, a 'great' man. A government of the people, a democracy was ridiculous in his mind. It could only lead to chaos. After I finished reading it, I thought that this book was a Bible of the devil and the man who wrote it would carry it out in every detail if given the chance. The fact that people laughed at it is proof that there is no better way to hide what's on one's mind than screaming it out in a book for the whole world to see. And to meet his goals, he had to get the Jews out of the way."

"You were right. He's starting to try isn't he?"

"Yes, he sure is, David, as soon as he became chancellor in 1933. He's not just trying, he's succeeding. We're seeing a chipping away for Jews of rights guaranteed all citizens, and I'm afraid it will get worse. He's been in control for three years now and if we can believe what he says, Europe and the world is his goal. This could mean war, and if it ever comes to pass, God can only know what will happen to the Jews. From my reading of Mein Kampf, I fear the worse."

"What do you mean by the worse?" asked a seriously alarmed David.

"If we're lucky we'll be sent out of Germany someplace. If we're not and if another World War starts it could mean—well, I hate to think about it," he said staring at the floor.

"He'll kill us?" said David without hesitation. Then in an ever-increasing loudness, he said. "Never, I'll take a bunch of them with me if that happens. Wouldn't you?"

"I would hope I would be able to. I would hope to fight back, but with what? People want to live; they hang on to hope up until the last minute. By then it might be too late. How do you fight back by yourself? How do you organize resistance? How do you get weapons? What about your family and reprisals? Your reaction is the reaction of the young. Fighting back is the thing to do, but you have to plan with people you can trust, with weapons, in secret. Where does one hide? What does one do?" Your enemies are powerful: an organized army with two-hundred years of experience. We have nothing."

"Yeah, I knew that was coming," said David. Some of my friends have already left Germany. Max and his family went last week." He slumped back in his chair.

Ben continued, "If worse comes to worse we have to be ready. The only one outside of the family I talked to about this is my friend in Munich who served with me during the war and sent me Hitler's book. I've tried to talk to a few others, but they look at me like I'm nuts. One minute into the conversation, it's clear to me how they're thinking, so that's the end of it; no sense going on. No one wants to believe there is such a possibility. The Russian Jewish and Polish citizens like my parents and relatives who lived in the Pale of Settlement in Russian-controlled Poland have known anti-Semitism that kills. Let's pray that we never experience what they have gone through."

"What's the Pale of Settlement?" asked a quizzical David

"That's a good question. I'll answer it as best as I can and it will give you an idea of what happened to Jews. So—let me think. Yes,

it was 1772 that they divided Poland between Russia, Austria and Prussia. They did this in three stages over twenty-three years, but the effect was that all of a sudden—bang—our ancestors from Poland found themselves part of Russia. The Russians now had a few million Polish Jews inside their boundary. Most of the Jews were poor, and some were in the middle class. The place where Jews had to live was called the Pale of Settlement, which was an area including parts of Poland, Russia, Byelorussia, Lithuania and Ukraine. As time went on, the Czar made different boundaries, and the population of Jews in the Pale increased to almost five million by nineteen hundred.

"At first the Russian government tried to ignore their new Jews even though it was against government policy to have them in their country, but then they found Jews handy for them because they could blame the Jews for the terrible position of the poor peasants. So what do you think happened?"

"I guess it got bad for the Jews?"

"You got that right. Russian citizens persecuted the Jews, and the government handcuffed them with all kinds of unfair laws. Jews lived in shtetls, the Yiddish name for small towns. There were certain places they could live and plenty of places they could not. The fact that the Jews kept to themselves and spoke a strange language, Yiddish, caused the other citizens to see them as foreigners. This caused a lot of tension between Jews and Christians, but in spite of the fact that the Jews lived under a Czar who hated them they had a democratic form of government in their communities. I guess this must be one of the reasons that Hitler blamed the Jews for that bad word—democracy.

"Christians in the towns beat Jews on the streets and Jewish homes were looted. I remember my grandfather telling me that Jews learned to stay behind locked doors during the Easter and Christmas seasons because armed and drunken peasants took revenge against the 'Christ killers.'"

"Okay, I get it," said David. How come you never told me about this before?"

"Well, I'm telling you now, because you might need some background to use for future decisions. May God see to it that you never have to think about such things." "This Hitler guy scares the heck out of you, that's for sure," said David glumly.

"Yes he does, and if you don't want to believe me then listen to his own words. I copied them down when I read the book. But first do you remember when I said that Hitler sees Jews and Communists as one and the same?"

"Yes."

"Do you know any Jewish Communists?"

"No."

"I don't know any either."

"Are there any Jewish Communists?"

"I'm sure there are."

"And I'm sure you're right. I suspect there are even Jewish Fascists. I'm certain that most Jews are democratic like the Weimar Republic was before Hitler overthrew it. So, as a doctor, I have to wonder if Hitler's thinking does not mean that he's paranoid, he feels that others are against him, or, if not that, then he is looking for a scapegoat to occupy the people's mind just like the Czars of Russia did to turn thinking in the direction they want. Anyway, here is what he said. I'll summarize it for you." Ben turned a few pages in his notebook, found what he was looking for, settled back in his chair and started talking.

The Jewish doctrine of Marxism—that's Hitler's word for Communism—he names it after Karl Marx, Communism's founder—says that Communism is a philosophy where everybody shares and it rejects the only way to run a country which is to be a strong leader that has all the power to make the decisions. The Communist philosophy spells doom for a country according to Hitler. He believes that the power and strength of one man is what countries need. Then he says that democracy is wrong because it does not want the strong man, it does see people as equal, which he does not, and that a democratic system will destroy a country and it could only result in chaos and the earth would end up with no humans left alive. Hitler goes on to say that anyone following the Jew would assist in that disaster, so he sees his mission as fighting for the work of the Lord by defending against the Jew.

"Wow, so God's giving him orders?" said David, shaking his head.

"No, not that, but in his warped brain he can read God's mind, so to speak. Is this a mad-man, or what? I hope you see now why I worry about this man. Anybody who can talk like this is a fanatic. He's laying out his plans for the whole world to see. He's telling us what kind of world he thinks people need in order to stay alive and do good—and that's a world either where Jews have no power, or where there are no Jews. I'm not sure which."

"I have a hard time understanding why Hitler thinks that Jews are so bad. What did we ever do that makes him think like that?"

"That's my son alright; he asks, asks, and asks. Never stop, David. That's how we learn. That's how we get answers, and we put those answers we get into our brain and we see if it makes any sense to us. I asked the same question myself, and even when I read his reasons, I couldn't come up with an answer, but I did come up with some thoughts that are mine that I believe in. I tried to peek into his head and I'll share my thoughts with you, but whether anyone, including me will have the true answers, I can't tell you. This was a fascinating study to me. I sure gave my brain a workout, and I got it all written down in my notebook, so here's what I think.

"He starts by comparing Jews in a good light to Aryans. In his mind, Aryans are the greatest people, and their descendants were the German people; none other. I thought that was interesting, because that to him is a compliment toward the Jews. He goes on to say that the Jews keep going and stay together and keep the religion alive for the last two thousand years in spite of the fact that they have so many enemies. But they still hang around and hold on to their religion in spite of all the enemies that have struggled against their species, as he says, throughout history.

"I never thought of that," said David. "He's right. What's funny to me is the way he calls Jews a species, like we're some kind of animal or something."

"Yes, he says crazy things, alright, but he doesn't discuss the reasons why the Jews have remained a single people," said Ben.

David stared at his father. "Do you know the reasons?"

"I think I do. First, Jews were the first to promote the idea of one God. We kept that concept alive for thousands of years from the days of Abraham to Moses and right up to now. We were one people then, in one location and when we lived in the area on the Eastern coast

of the Mediterranean about two thousand years ago, we built a great Temple in Jerusalem, a house of God. In that Temple was a Priest and the Ten Commandments that Moses received on Mount Sinai. We developed a Torah, the book of laws. With the Temple destruction, the Jews spread throughout the world. How would they stay alive? How would they remain a single people if they spread all over?"

"Let me think, dad. Hmmm—well, we're still Jews; we have a synagogue, we have a rabbi..."

"You've got it, David. We took the Temple with us wherever we went by building little houses of worship—synagogues. We kept the Ten Commandments and our rules, we kept our teaching over the centuries and we carried the Torah with us and always had a rabbi to guide us who replaced the one priest. We survived, but you'll never read any of this in Mein Kampf. Hitler will tell his people that we survived because our goal was to take over the entire earth; a Jewish plot. I can't get over the idea of his paranoia.

"Anyhow, he also says we're a smart people, but he says that's because the Jews get instructed by foreigners as he puts it. In this way he credits others for whatever brains the Jew has. From here on, you'll see that there's very little good he has to say about Jews. For instance, he says that the Jews have no culture, no art, architecture or music. He calls Jews parasites on other peoples."

"I guess now he's getting into it, isn't he?" said David.

"Yes, he is and he starts with a lie. Do you know what The Protocols of the Elders of Zion is, David?"

"No, what is it?"

"This was a bunch of documents that was written by the Ochrana, the Czar's Russian Secret Police. They wrote it just to get the minds of the peasants away from any thoughts of revolution against the Czar. I think they wrote it in the late eighteen hundreds. It was a proven

forgery. The Russians wrote this, and it said that secret Jewish world leaders wrote it and the Jews were planning to overthrow world governments, including the Russian government. In other words, it was a Jewish plot to take over the world—and all the brainchild of the Ochrana, blaming the Jews. The Jews would install an anti-Christ form of dictatorship. This got the people worked up against the Jews, turned their minds away from the Czar and was one of the reasons for the pogroms against the Jews.

That's how your grandfather, my father died. You can understand how important words can be in the lives of some people."

"Yeah, I remember what you and mom told me," said David. "But who were these Jewish world leaders?"

"There are no such animals. Jews don't have anything like that. Catholics have a Pope, but Jews don't have a single leader. We have famous Jews just like all other religions have famous members, and we have many rabbis, but there is no single Jew or group of Jews that control all Jews and want to take over the world. How stupid can anyone get? We're a fraction of one percent of the world. I remember my grandfather telling me that there were pamphlets spread all over Russia saying that the Jews were out to destroy the country. It was a firestorm for Jews. That's when plenty of them were killed. Now do you know why I worry, David?"

"I guess so, Dad, as he drummed his fingers on the kitchen table."

Ben noted the drumming. "Anyhow, Hitler mentions the Protocols, but only in a short paragraph. He even says that a Frankfurt newspaper often says it is a forgery, but he uses that as proof that the Protocols are true, because he says, 'The Frankfurter newspaper moans and screams once every week: the best proof that the Protocols are authentic.'

"I found this to be almost funny, because you remember when I said that the best ways to hide one's intentions are to publicize them for the entire world to see? Well that's what his book is all about; he's publicizing and therefore hiding his intentions. I can't help but think we are in great danger. This maniac has worked out his complete plan for how the Jews will take over the world. It's insane."

In an effort to throw some humor into the conversation, David said, "Tell me how we'll do it, Dad. When I'm older, I'll be ready to be the boss."

Ben's expression changed. He stared at his son without saying a word for ten seconds. Then, with a calm voice, he said, "David, you find this funny, do you?"

"Uhh, no dad." He looked at his father's stern expression, realized that his effort at humor had failed, and said, "I'm sorry, dad."

In a louder voice, Ben said, "You're doing what I told you the people I try to speak with about this subject do; they make fun of it. It stops me cold. Damn, David, I'm dead serious. You're my son and I love you. I believe we're in danger, but I have no idea what the future will hold, so I'm trying to prepare you and I want to give you options. This is serious. Do you want me to go on?"

With head bowed David said, "I'm very sorry, dad, please go on."

Ben sighed. "Ok, I love you and I accept your apology and understand that you were just trying to make a joke." He paused and then said, "Now where was I?"

"You were going to tell Hitler's theory about how the Jews will take over the world."

"Oh yes. It's a story that made no sense to me, but here's what he says. It goes on for pages and pages in Mein Kampf with all kinds of detail, but I'll make it short.

He starts with a single Jewish peddler who comes into a small town and the people accept him. This is a handy guy to have around. He's harmless and you can buy some nice stuff from him. Then the Jew becomes successful and other Jews join him. They settle in a separate section of the town, build a pretty good business and start to lend money, all the time building what Hitler calls a state within a state. Hitler never mentions that Jews had to make their own way in life because nothing was open to them. Nobody hired him because he was Jewish and there were quotas on him for schools that would only accept very few Jews. He had to fend for himself because that's all he could do. Then the population starts getting jealous of the Jew's success; he buys land, becomes a financier and charges interest. He becomes more successful and starts acting like a German, which makes Hitler angry. Pretty soon he takes over much of financing and starts having some influence on the highest levels of government becoming a 'court Jew'. Then he gets on the stock exchange and before you know it, he has lots of control and influence on big business and government. Then he overthrows the Monarchy, controls the unions, forms a Democracy and even goes so far as to poison the Aryan's blood by seducing the Aryan women. Not only that, but he also brings in all kinds of 'inferior human beings,' as Hitler calls them, to intermix with the Aryans and 'dilute their blood' as he puts it, so that the Aryans will all be made inferior and then the Jews will take over. You see, for Hitler, the Aryan German is the number one superior being. He goes so far as to say that they should be the masters of the earth, but the Jewish polluting influence will make that impossible. The last thing the Jew does is to turn the country Communistic. How's that for power, David, and all this coming from a little Jewish Peddler."

"Wow," said David. You're right, he is nuts."

"Well this nut runs a country, wants to conquer the world, and hates Jews, so where does that put us? That's all I'm asking."

"What kind of a weirdo thinks like that?" asked David.

Ben looked at his son who had a quizzical look on his face. He smiled and said, "That's an excellent question, David. Do you want me to give you a medical analysis—or at least what I think about him and his warped mind?"

"Yeah, that would be good. I want to be a doctor like you, you know."

"Okay, David, here's what I think. Did you ever hear of the word narcissist?"

"Uhh, no."

"Well, a narcissist is someone who has a personality disorder that gives one a feeling of great self-importance. They are preoccupied with themselves. They know it all. They know what's best for everyone."

"Well, that fits him alright," shot back David.

"Yes, and it can get dangerous," said Ben, "Because they create such a personality cult around themselves that the people are mesmerized. The narcissist is usually a great speaker and they can almost hypnotize their followers and give them hope. People become like putty in the hands of a pathological narcissist who tries to shape the world to his way of thinking. The bad news is that they can succeed. Their personality is so forceful that they will usually reach their final objective because they turn their admirers to their way of thinking. Power is all they are concerned about and it does not matter who is affected by their reach for power. Everything in a narcissist's life is about him and everything that is not about him and his goal is nothing."

"That's scary," said David.

"Scary is not the word for it. Dangerous is a better word because this narcissist has the Jews in his bulls eye and his main goal is to rid the world of them!"

"I don't know, dad, but I think all this is leading up to the fact that you're about to tell me we're leaving the country."

"That's right, David," said Ben smiling and nodding his head. "Let me get your mother and Emily in here. I want us all to be part of this discussion now. Leah," he called aloud.

"Yes," she answered from the living room.

"Can you come in the kitchen? I've just been talking to David."

"Be right there," said Leah.

Leah Friedberg Frohman was also a refugee from Russia arriving in Germany three years after her future husband. They both were one of the Eastern European Jewish refugees, or *Ostjuden*, (Eastern European Jews), whose families were fleeing the anti-Semitism of the Russian Czar. The *Ostjuden*, considered by the Nazis and even other Jews as inferior, would arrive in the early years of the twentieth century, but didn't know that they would have to deal with a future political party, Nazis, whose newspaper, The Voelkisher Beobachter, would damn the Jews by recommending that they be disenfranchised from every branch of government.

Hitler and his cronies, long before they came to power, had their plans all prepared— including future concentration camps—and published them for all to see. But who would notice and believe it? Indeed, as early as 1920, during the very early development of the Nazi party, the first few Nazis would establish their creed and future vision for Germany—a Germany free of Jews.

Leah, with Emily trailing behind, entered the kitchen and joined the two men at the table. Eight-year-old Emily looked just like her mother with a similar smile that could light up a room. She was sensing the tension in the household for the last six months, clinged closer to her mother and smiled less.

"What have my two favorite men been talking about?" asked Leah.

Ben answered, "David and I were talking about what we plan to do about conditions in this country. We got to the part that we're going to move."

"Yeah, but we didn't talk about where yet," interjected David.

"That's right," said Ben. "I was getting to that, but wanted your mother to be here first. We're going to live in Minsk in Byelorussia. Right now, Minsk is in Byelorussia in the Union of Socialist Soviet Republic (USSR), or Russia, Ukraine, Byelorussia and other neighboring countries organized together. Your mother was born in Byelorussia and I was born not too far from there in Northeast Poland under Russian control."

"Well at least there is no more Czar there," said David, "but what about anti-Semitism?"

"No matter where we would go around the world, we'll find people who hate, but in the Soviet Union as it's now called, it's better than here in Germany where now anti-Semitism is government policy and getting worse all the time. The good news is that when I went to Minsk to take a medical course, I lined up a good job in a clinic and hospital there for your mother and me. And I found a nice gym with good gymnastic equipment and a twenty-five meter swimming pool. It looked as nice as anything here does. I feel we should live okay. Your mother and I speak perfect Russian, which is the language there, and you and Emily do pretty well with it too. In no time, at all you will both be experts. You know how much your mother knows about history and current events and she too feels that we have to leave Germany. You smart kids understand Russian pretty well, so it'll be a good idea if we talk Russian from now on, so we'll all be better by the time we get there. We'll be leaving in three weeks as soon as school is over before the summer."

Emily sobbed, left her chair, sat on her mother's lap, threw her arms around her mother's neck and said, "Will we be able to swim, Momma?"

"You bet we will, Emily, and you know, you said you want to be a nurse like mommy. Well, daddy and I will be working in the hospital there, and I'll start teaching you about nursing, so by the time you're ready for nursing school, you sure will be ready. And don't forget what daddy said about the swimming pool. We'll both go there whenever we can, and I can take you there so you can swim with the other girls—and maybe you'll even swim with your old mommy sometime, even though you're so much better than I am. I'm sure they have a swim team you can join."

Emily smiled and hugged her mother.

Ben said, "And David, there's a good high school and university there and you'll be able to start next semester. When I was there and visited the gym, I spoke with the gymnastics coach. I told him about how good you were and he said he's anxious to check you out and it sounds like you'll be able to make the senior boy's team. They have competitions just like we have here in Germany. I watched the boys work out and I think you'll be as good as the best of them, maybe even better."

"Sounds good, Dad, as long as we're all there together—that's all that counts," said David.

"Perfect, David, that's the only thing that counts."

Leah nodded and smiled. "Okay, kids, go and finish your homework. Emily, get me when you're finished and I'll check it over."

"Okay, mom."

After both children left the kitchen, Leah said, "You did a good job with David, honey."

"Thanks. We've got smart and great children thanks to my brainy wife. Thank God for the Jewish Community Center dance where I saw this dazzling creature sitting against the wall. I just pray we're doing the right thing."

"We are, Ben. We must. For the last three years, we watched Hitler consolidate his power. The man is as ruthless as a human being can become. He's putting all his *Mein Kampf* ravings in place, and he's starting with you and me and all the Jews of Germany. He didn't waste any time. He wants us out and he's succeeding. It wouldn't be safe for any Jew in Germany any more and whoever doesn't leave is playing with their lives."

"That's what I tried to tell, David," said Ben.

"I'm sure you did a great job. David could understand. I just want to shield Emily a bit now. She's too young and it would worry her at this age. We just have to act as if we're moving to another country as a family with no deep reasons behind it. It will be easier there in Byelorussia where she will not have to hear about Hitler ranting and raving about the Jews."

"Is this madman going to bring another World War to the world?" asked David.

"A Nostradamus I'm not, but all the chess pieces seem to me to be falling into place. The world is worried about it and I have to agree. Don't you?"

"Yes, I do. Tell me, my genius wife, what do you think? You are my main teacher now that I don't go to school anymore."

Leah laughed. "Well, in this year alone three things have happened that in my mind, at least, all point in that direction…"

"What three things?" interrupted Ben.

"First, the Versailles Treaty demilitarized the Rhineland. This area is all German territory west of the Rhine with three big cities: Cologne, Dusseldorf and Bonn. In Hitler's mind, it meant that Germany couldn't use it. The effect was that it was no longer part of Germany. How long do you think he would stand for that? It took him three years, but he acted; he sent troops there. Shouldn't the French have kicked him out?"

Ben asked, "Why didn't they?"

"I wish I knew. I suppose they didn't want any bloodshed. Since the Rhineland territory was under treaty from Versailles, all the others who signed the treaty should have gotten together and kicked the Nazis out. So they didn't and that left the French on the border and they didn't want to act alone. That's my best guest. Anyhow, I'm sure it left Hitler feeling like a military genius. It just emboldened him. God knows what he'll do next."

"You got that right, but he doesn't need any more emboldening. He already thinks that he's a political genius," added Ben.

"Well, now you could add military to that list. I'm sure he's beginning to think that he's a prophet. God knows what a man like that is capable of."

"I agree. You said three things. What else is there?" asked Ben

"Another thing happened that had nothing to do with Hitler, but had to do with another Fascist dictator—Mussolini."

"Oh, you mean Abbysinia?"

"Yes, here was a great power and look what they did to a primitive country."

"So why do you use this as an example? Hitler probably never even knew that Mussolini would do this."

"You're right, I'm sure, but it's just an example of what Fascism can lead to when strong men think they can do what they want in the name of building their empire. This Rhineland thing was one of Hitler's first attempts to reconstruct his empire, and I'll bet you anything that it's only number one in what will be more grabs by this madman. There's plenty of talk about "The Great German Empire"—A Greater Reich. Don't you think that's his goal?"

"So, Hitler sees Mussolini in action, and it just wants to make him flex his muscles too," said Ben.

"Sure, Mussolini has been Hitler's idol. When Hitler tried his Beer Hall Putsch in Munich way back in twenty-three, he was trying to take over the government just like Mussolini took over Italy. But for Hitler, It didn't work. He wasn't ready. But he never took his eye off the prize. You got to give him credit for single-mindedness. I'm afraid the world will pay a price."

"The Jews are already paying that price. The world might later," added Ben.

"I don't think there's any later about it. It's already starting."

"And what's number three?" asked Ben.

"Number three is the big one, Spain. Their government couldn't govern. Left leaning socialistic parties competed against right-wing conservative factions; there was increasing polarization. When you have such chaos, here comes another Fascist group, a bunch of right-wing generals led by General Francisco Franco. And what do they do? They do what Fascists do best, they try to seize power. So what happens? A civil war. Who do you think jumps into that stew?"

"Yeah, Hitler and Mussolini."

"They made a pact with Franco, giving him military support in return for raw materials for their war machine. It worked. This enabled Franco to capture more and more territory. What do Britain and France and the United States do? You got it—nothing, but they did sign a Non-Intervention Pact thinking it would contain the war by not providing the government with armaments. But all it did was benefit Franco who conquered more and more territory."

"It sounds like Fascism is getting to be the wave of the future," said Ben.

"Pray it isn't. You can already see what it can lead to in Germany. Anyhow, Franco couldn't capture the north part of Spain, so he asked Hitler for the loan of his latest air force fighters and bombers. Hitler didn't hesitate; this would be the perfect opportunity to test his improved air force. He formed the Condor legion you read about. What a perfect chance for a dress rehearsal. Not only could he try out his military for the war he dreams about, but there were a lot of political reasons the war was tailor-made for him."

"What were they?" asked Ben.

"First of all, France had always been Germany's worst enemy. Now France had two Fascist states surrounding it—Germany and Italy. What better than to have a third one like Spain, on France's border.

"Second, there was a lot of political strife between the right and the left in France, which was being made worse by the Spanish Civil War; and the more strife in France the better, when it came to the relationship between France and Germany."

"Is that because all that political strife in France weakened her in her relationship with Germany?" asked Ben.

"Bingo. It was all to Germany's advantage. Another thing in Germany's favor was the third point: German collaboration with

Italy in Spain kept Britain and France in conflict with Italy thus driving Mussolini toward Germany. Hitler liked that."

"All I have to say is—thank you again, God, for the Jewish Community Center in Berlin, and thank God for my classmate who convinced me to go to a dance there."

"I thank him too," said Leah.

The stage was being set—a dress rehearsal of what was to ensue in the world conflict to come. Hitler, forged in the flames of conflict, was feeling invincible. He ordered his armed forces to prepare for war in four years; another promise he would keep.

The Frohman family was on the way to Minsk to seek a better life, but before thy left there was one more thing they had to do, a promise Ben made to his son that he would be sure to keep.

CHAPTER 3

BERLIN OLYMPIC GAMES

1936

Many months ago, David's gymnastic team's coach gave his boys two tickets each to witness the 1936 Olympics held in Berlin.

For Hitler, this was an opportunity to show off the new Germany and prove that his superior Aryans truly represented a master race. The games, handed to Germany by the Olympic Committee long before Hitler came to power, provided Propaganda Minister Joseph Goebbels the perfect opportunity to show case what Nazism did for downtrodden Germany, rescued from the ash heap of World War I.

In preparation, Hitler ordered the entire country sanitized of anti-Semitic posters, took Der Sturmer, an anti-Semitic newspaper edited by Julius Streicher, a fanatic Nazi anti-Semite, off the streets, took the "Jews not welcome here" signs off of store fronts and made sure that his construction workers completed the 100,000 capacity stadium on time.

Straining the Olympic definition of amateur athletic competition, the German athletes, given permission to practice full time, had an excellent advantage against the part time amateur athletes from the rest of the world. They proved this by taking first place in the team competition, winning more medals than any other country. The United States came in second, due in no small part to the efforts of Negro athlete Jesse Owens who won four Gold medals in track and field. In addition, nine other United States negro athletes also won Gold, Silver and Bronze debunking for all the world to see Hitler and Goebel's past pronouncements of the inferiority of the black race.

David's hero was a gymnast he had the privilege of seeing in past local competitions. Sergeant Alfred Schwarzmann was a member of the German gymnastic team preparing for the Olympics. Considered the best German gymnast, Germany pinned great hopes on this superb athlete.

Schwarzmann demonstrated his skills a few times at the gymnastic club that David belonged to before the club eliminated David because he was a Jew. David had not watched Schwarzmann in several years, but he could not forget his skills and was anxious to see him again before they moved to Minsk. So too did his father, Ben, and together they watched as

Schwarzmann won three Gold and two Bronze medals. David's former teammates were there as well, but they did not even acknowledge his presence. Joseph Schwarzmann, became a paratrooper, fought in Holland during World War II where he received a near fatal lung wound, fought on the Island of Crete and on the Soviet front earning two Iron Crosses for bravery. In March of 1944, his old wound acted up forcing him to spend time in a Munich military hospital. The British kept him as a prisoner of war from May 9 to October 29, 1945. In 1952, he won the Silver medal in the Helsinki Olympic Games at age forty, a remarkable accomplishment. The actual Gold medal winner protested by claiming that Schwarzmann

should have won the Gold, but did not because "he was German."
He died in 2000, age 87.

David's father noted these snubs to his son from former teammates, and in an effort to comfort him, he said, "You see how one man can change the thinking of people. Hitler has hypnotized an entire country. We don't belong here any more. He has become the law and whatever he says goes. Look what he's done to make it impossible for Jewish doctors to practice medicine even though Jewish doctors have been a large percentage of all German doctors and many have made great discoveries, but he ignores such facts that don't fit in with his thinking. It's insane when you think about it, but people can't put it to the test, because it would now fall under the heading of treasonous activity. Any opposition to him could mean death. I shudder when I think what one man can do to an entire country. We can't get out fast enough."

The track and field Olympics were a world-wide sensation with Hitler observing from the stands. Jesse Owens won Olympic Gold in the 100 meters, 200 meters, long jump and the 400 meter relay. His principle competition in the long jump came from Luz Long, the leading German long jumper. By the end of the meet, Owens and Long had become good friends as well as competitors. Luz Long, was wounded in battle in Sicily in World War II and, died three days later in a British hospital and was buried in the war cemetery of Motta Sant'Anastasia.

The torch-bearer who carried the torch into the stadium to light the Olympic flame was Siegfried Eifrig, a sprinter chosen for his height, blond hair, blue-eyed Aryan appearance. He did not compete in the games. During World War II, Eifrig fought for the Nazis in Africa and ended the war in a British prisoner of war camp.

With this last remembrance of Germany, Ben, David and family prepared to leave. They packed up their valuables including the family Torah and left for Minsk, Byelorussia.

CHAPTER 4
ASSIMILATION
MINSK, BYELORUSSIA
1936

The Frohmans arrived in Minsk and moved into a small three bedroom home. They used their German furniture plus a few new pieces to reflect the Soviet flavor of their new homeland. The location was close to the clinic and hospital where Ben would work as an internist and Leah would work part-time in the children's clinic as a nurse. David and Emily started school, made easier by their intense immersion in the Russian language over the last three weeks. Once acclimated to their new school, their parents would see to it that they became members of the local gym where David could continue with his gymnastics and Emily her swimming. To the great relief of their parents, the integration of their children into this new environment was going well.

The Minsk Jewish population was approximately 80,000 in 1936, representing about thirty percent of the population. For the most part, the rapport between the religions was a welcome improvement from what Ben and Leah remembered from their childhood, and what they had experienced in Germany since Hitler took over control of the government. They both breathed a sigh of relief; a heavy burden lifted from their shoulders, as fears for their children's safety resolved. Living in a country where anti-Semitism was government policy and had the force of law behind it cast a dark shadow on the psyche of the two of them and, worse yet, robbed the children of security. It was stifling and oppressive—but no longer, thank God, now that they were in their new home. Anti-Semitism was not dead in the Soviet Union, but not being government policy was the critical difference. Christians and Jews got along well in Byelorussia. The Frohman family joined the closest synagogue and enrolled their children in Hebrew school. It would be wonderful to live a Jewish life with a clear mind.

The history of Byelorussia was a centuries-long story of a country controlled by the neighboring powers of Poland, Lithuania and Russia. In October of 1917, the Russian Communist Revolution resulted in the establishment of a Worker's Soviet (council) in Minsk. The Treaty of Brest Litovsk between Germany and Russia ended World War I for Russia, and forced Russia to give up Poland, the Baltic States and part of Byelorussia to Germany and Austria-Hungary. After the treaty was in force, German forces occupied Minsk and made it the capital of the Byelorussian People's Republic, but this was short-lived. In December, 1918, after the armistice ending World War 1, the Russian army took over Minsk and proclaimed it the capital of the Byelorussian Soviet Socialist Republic. This too did not last as the city came under Polish control during the course of the Polish-Bolshevik (Russian Communist) War. Under the Treaty of Riga, Minsk returned to Russian control and resumed its position as the capital of Byelorussia SSR, one of the founding republics of the Union of Soviet Socialist Republics—where the Frohmans now hoped for a secure and better life.

After a week of settling in to their new home and adjusting to their new life, Ben started work in the Jewish hospital outpatient clinic. He had two small offices equipped to see patients and a consultation room for private discussions, paper work, medical record keeping, and just to relax.

He was busy right from the start what with many of the younger doctors serving in the military. Those patients requiring hospitalization, he admitted under his care and he would tend to his hospital patients first thing in the morning followed by outpatient office visits. He worked from 8:00 AM to 5:00 PM and was on call several times per week for emergencies.

For diagnostic purposes, he had at his disposal an x-ray and a small laboratory for blood and urine analysis. Not all of the available equipment was equal to the quality of German high-tech medical advances of the day and he missed them, but he prided himself on the best use of his own high-tech equipment: his eyes, ears, nose and hands. Trained as he was in the early days of the twentieth century, he considered himself a disciple of Sir William Osler, one of the first to teach at the bedside and promote the importance of the five senses: sight, hearing, touch, taste and smell. The complete physical examination was crucial and he had the necessary ancillary equipment he needed to perform this task. In addition, he promoted Dr. Osler's adage, "Let the patient talk, doctor, she's trying to tell you the diagnosis." He believed in this because he agreed that a thorough medical history and physical examination would establish, with a high degree of certainty, a correct diagnosis about eighty percent of the time.

He worked with Jewish, Byelorussian and Russian doctors and nurses. This was a welcome change from what he, as a physician, had experienced in Germany after Hitler's assumption of power.

As soon as Hitler took control, Ben was stymied and subjected to discrimination from surprising sources—those who had been friends. It was amazing to him how one man could change the thinking of intelligent people and turn neighbor against neighbor; proof of Hitler's narcissistic power as he reminded himself.

He did not make a great deal of money in his new position in Minsk, but his income, as well as his wife's, made them comfortable—and that's all that counted after what they had just been subjected to.

Although medicine was rewarding from the professional standpoint, it was also frustrating because there was so little that doctors of internal medicine could do. In actuality, there was so little that they knew. There were many maladies of unknown etiology. The most common question he had to answer was, "What causes it, doctor?" "We don't know, but there's a lot we can do to help," was his standard answer. He wished that medicine would advance to the extent that the answer to the questions about "cause" would roll off his tongue with ease and confidence.

Even the known infectious diseases like pneumonia and strep throat were not treatable with a specific agent to cure in all instances. At this time, the treatment was to make the patient comfortable, follow them with frequent vital signs and be sure that their hydration and nutrition was adequate. This was to support the patients own ability to heal; a little understood mechanism. Perhaps the day would come soon when specific treatment would be available and scientists developed a full understanding about the exact mechanism of self-healing. In the meantime, the young did well, but infants and the elderly had a high mortality rate.

Leah got right to work as soon as they arrived in Minsk. Because of the closeness of work and schools for their children, Leah would be sure to walk to Emily's school with her little girl at least until she felt confident in her new surroundings and also until Leah was confident. She and Ben would go to work together as they both had to be there at the same time. Leah only worked until 2:00 PM, which would give her plenty of time to be with her children when they arrived home from school. All the logistics were falling into place.

Leah worked in the clinic and was responsible for immunizations. At the time, there was only immunization against Small Pox, Diphtheria, Pertussis (Whooping cough), and Tetanus. In addition, there was Rabies vaccine available for the occasional child bit by a rabid animal, and Typhoid vaccine as this disease was still a threat.

She also did clinical nursing working under the direction of the attending doctors. This included taking vital signs and doing triage to determine the severity of the problem to prioritize the sicker children and occasional adult to the front of the line. Enjoying nursing practice as much as she did, it was a labor of love.

The time came to take Emily and David to the gym to sign them up for swimming and gymnastics. Although they had passed by the facility, they had never entered, so they both viewed the visit with great anticipation.

They visited the gymnastic section of the gym first. When David entered, his eyes opened wide. The first thing he noticed was that there was a long vault run. He breathed a sigh of relief because the Berlin gym where he practiced was too small to accommodate this event. All the standard gymnastic events were available for practice. He looked at his mother—a wide smile on his happy face. There were many gymnasts there varying in age from three to adult. Their skills were evident to a nervous David.

The Russian gymnasts were some of the best in the world, so David was apprehensive and his mother could tell. "Don't worry, David, you'll show them a thing or two. My son is the best."

Ben had visited the gym when he made his trip to Minsk and had introduced himself to Coach Anatoli Stepchik. Stepchik appeared to be in his early thirties, but still looked like the typical gymnast: firm and fit with the muscular definition of a prepared anatomical specimen, each muscle well delineated from its neighbor.

Leah approached him. "Good afternoon, Mr. Stepchik, my name is Leah Frohman. I hope you remember my husband, Ben, who spoke to you about six weeks ago. We're the family who moved to Minsk from Germany, and my son David has been in gymnastics for eleven years. This is David, sir."

Coach Stepchik approached David with outstretched hand, "Pleased to meet you, Mrs. Frohman. Hello, David, your father told me all about you. Welcome to our gym."

"Thank you, sir."

"My, you both speak such good Russian," said the coach.

"My husband and I were both born here," answered Leah.

"Oh, I see. Welcome back." Turning to David, he said, "How old are you, David?"

"I'm almost sixteen, sir."

"Good, David, do you want to show me what you can do?"

An alarmed Leah said, "Oh, Mr. Stepchik, with all the moving that we've done, David hasn't practiced for about three weeks."

David interjected as soon as the last word was out of his mother's mouth. "I can show Mr. Stepchik some things, mother. I've been doing strength exercises almost every day by myself to keep in shape."

Stepchik added, "If your mother's worried, David. We can wait. There's no hurry."

"Please mother. I'm pretty sure I'll be ok. I won't do anything tough, I promise."

Observing the pleading expression on her son's face, Leah said, "Well, Mr. Stepchik, I don't know much about gymnastics, but if David's confident, I guess it'll be okay."

David leaped up.

"If it's good with your mother, it's fine with me," said the coach. "Just do some simpler exercises. Pick your best stuff."

With his coach watching, David warmed up with some stretching exercises, ran in place and then did a short tumbling run followed by a stint on the pommel horse and parallel bars. He kipped up on the high bar and launched into a series of giant swings, then dismounted with a one and one half twisting somersault. It looked perfect to Leah. "Ten," she shouted.

The coach clapped his hands. "I like what I see, David, We'll keep an eye on you for the first couple of weeks, but I'm pretty confident you'll be on the senior team."

The smile on David's face could have lit up the gym at night.

"Let's sign your son up, Mrs. Frohman. I look forward to working with him."

"Thank you, sir."

Emily had been sitting in complete silence, observing and showing patience, but smiling now because it was her turn; she could not wait to see the swimming pool.

The twenty-five meter pool was in excellent shape. On both long ends of the pool, there were three levels of wooden benches for observers. The swimming coach was a young woman by the name of Tamara Shebrianovich. Like most swimmers, she was slim and supple with loose flexible muscles. She asked, "How long have you been swimming, Emily?"

"Four years."

"Can you swim all the four strokes?"

"Yes, I can, and I was going to start practicing the 100 meter medley," said a wound-up Emily.

"Very good, can you show me what you can do?"

Emily looked at her momma who nodded her head.

Emily dove in and did all four strokes, with the coach watching in rapt attention. Then she leaped out of the pool with a broad smile.

The coach turned to Leah and said, "That's very good, Mrs. Frohman. She shows promise at such a young age. It will be a pleasure to work with her."

When Emily heard the news, she let out a whoop and jumped backwards into the pool.

Leah was ecstatic. As long as her children were happy, she was happy. She could not wait to share the good news with her husband. They were on the threshold of a happier life—and she thanked God for this new start and her children's happiness.

The last quarter of 1936 brought a personal peace to the Frohmans, but anxiety to most of the countries of the world. Since Adolph Hitler and his Nazi Party had assumed control of Germany, major European countries, as well as other world powers, embarked upon far-reaching diplomatic activity to form alliances to counter this new threat to world peace. Smaller countries were quick to declare neutrality, stating that their countries' policies would remain independent of any great power. This was naiveté to the extreme, and they knew it, but that is about all a minor power could do. In the minds of many, there was no doubt that Hitler was preparing for war, and the announcement of Hitler's four-year economic plan in October of 1936 did nothing to alleviate that concern.

In the same month, Germany and Italy announced the Rome-Berlin Axis. This would result in a close collaboration between Italy and Germany, something that the Italian leadership (Mussolini) avoided during the first three years of Hitler's takeover of power, as he was fearful of Germany's territorial goals.

As Leah had surmised, when Italy invaded Abyssinia in October of 1935, the relationship with democratic countries of the world suffered. When Hitler and Mussolini aided the Fascists during the Spanish Civil War, that relationship with the democratic countries worsened. The strained relationship between Mussolini and the democracies prompted Italy's rapprochement with Germany. Mussolini at first did not identify with Hitler's anti-Semitism, but, as Germany's strength increased, he too issued anti-Jewish edicts.

The next important geopolitical development occurred in November of 1936, when Germany and Japan signed the Anti-Comintern Pact. Japan was concerned about the fact that they were not a force in the Pacific and they did not trust Russia. Germany was fearful of Soviet Communism, in Hitler's mind the direct antithesis of his Nazi dictatorship.

Lenin formed the Comintern in 1919, two years after he overthrew the Czar and established a Communistic state in Russia. Russia and many of the Socialist, Communist and left leaning organizations and countries of the world worked toward the establishment of Communist parties to "aid the international proletarian revolution," or—spread Communism throughout the world.

The Anti-Comintern pact of Germany and Japan was to be a counter-weight to Communism.

With a month passing since their arrival in Minsk, the Frohmans continued to adjust well to their new life. The children's language skills were increasing at a pace that astounded their parents. Best of all, Emily became less clingy with her mother as she integrated well at school and started her swimming lessons and practice. Leah would accompany her to the pool at least twice a week. It was a welcome release to swim with her daughter, watch her progress and, at the same time, get some relaxing, healthy and fulfilling exercise.

David was fully engaged in gymnastics and made the senior team. This honor depended only on one's skill set; age was not a factor. Seniors competed with other seniors from other clubs. He made good friends with one of the gymnasts who also helped him improve his skills. This young man, Valery Gregov, was a year older and lived close to David's new home, so they also spent time together away from the gym. Valery was a Christian, and other than telling David that he had had one pair of Jewish great grandparents, their difference in religion was never an issue. This was very different from what he had experienced in Germany. David took up the name of Val for his new friend.

Val took David home with him on one occasion and he met Val's parents. The mother was at least a head shorter than her tall and well-built husband who stood six feet, weighed 200 pounds, and was forty-eight years old. He worked as an engineer responsible for the upkeep and smooth functioning of the Minsk civic building, the site of government for Byelorussia and the Minsk district, which housed the mayor of the town and other civic functionaries including Communists representatives beholden to Moscow.

Mikhail, Val's father, said to David, "So you're the new friend Val told me about. He said that you were a very good gymnast, and now the senior team has a chance at the title in the district. I'll come to the gym some day and watch you guys work out."

"That'll be fine, sir," said David, but I wish I was as good as Val."

"Ah, a modest boy; I like that. Val told me that your family all came here from Germany."

"Yes, sir."

"Welcome to Minsk."

"Thank you. We like it here."

"Val says you have a sister?"

"Yes, sir, her name is Emily."

"How old is she?"

"She'll be nine soon, sir."

"Do you have a telephone at home, David?"

"Yes sir."

"Here, write the number down on this of piece of paper. We'll call your parents and have a get-together here some time. I already talked about this with Val's mother. I still have old Jewish artifacts from my Jewish grandmother who got it from her ancestors. They're very old. I'm very proud of them, and I would like to show them off and meet your family."

"Thank you, sir. I know my mother and father would sure like to see them and meet you all too."

When David returned home, he told his mother that he met Val's mother and father. "They're very nice," he said, "and they want to have us over to their house sometime. The father said that he had Jewish grandparents and had some of their old Jewish stuff that he wanted to show off. He asked for our phone number."

"That's nice, I hope he calls. What kind of Jewish stuff did he say he had, David?" asked Leah.

"I don't know. He called them artifacts and said they were very old. His grandmother got them from her ancestors. I bet they're from the eighteenth or nineteenth centuries."

"That would be very nice; I'd love to see them. I hope they call."

Within a few days, Leah received the call from Mrs. Gregov, Val's mother, Sonya, and Leah accepted her invitation to dinner at their house.

"I'll have my husband's sister's nine year old daughter here to keep Emily Company, Mrs. Frohman."

"Oh that's thoughtful of you. I'm sure Emily will like that."

"We'll have a light dinner and then we'll talk. I don't know how religious you are, but you can be sure we won't have any ham or pork—or milk with meat for that matter."

Leah laughed. "We're not super religious, but we never eat those, so thank you."

"My husband has told me all about his Jewish grandmother. He has such fond memories of her," said Sonya.

"That's wonderful. I'm anxious to learn all about your family. David and Val have become good friends. He tells me that Val's the best gymnast on the team."

"That's nice of David. He's a fine boy," said Sonya smiling.

Leah said, "Thank you again for the invitation and we'll see you Saturday evening. We look forward to it."

The Frohmans arrived at the Gregov home anxious to establish a good friendship with the family. This was the first hoped for close relationship with other than fellow employees at the hospital and clinic.

The Gregov family, Mikhail, Sonya, and Valery represents those non-Jews, free of bigotry, who befriended, collaborated with and in many instances gave shelter and protection to the persecuted Jews of Europe. Many of them are enshrined as righteous gentiles in Israel's Yad Vashem, a world center for holocaust research and education.

They received a very warm and cordial greeting from Val's parents and had a typical Russian dinner including two varieties of pickled herring, potato salad with chicken, hard-boiled eggs, pickles and beets, and for dessert, cake with loose-leaf tea. They engaged in small talk while the children were present.

After dinner, the children went off to do their own thing while Ben and Leah, and Mikhail and Sonya viewed Mikhail's grandmother's beautiful and very old Jewish antiques including a collection of dreidles of all sizes, a kiddush cup, two menorahs, a set of candle sticks, and four wine glasses and a wine bottle. They discussed each in turn. "Those are absolutely exquisite," said Leah, "and you've kept them in such good condition."

"Thank you, I wouldn't part with them for the world. They remind me so much of my grandparents," said Mikhail.

"I know what you mean," said Leah.

"When I told my sister that you were coming and that I would show you our grandparent's things, she gave me something I would like to show you." He took it out of a drawer and gave it to Leah. "I never even knew about it. She remembered packing it away years ago in her attic, so she gave it to me to add to what I already had and said I should ask you what it is. Neither one of us knows for sure."

Leah held it and turned it eying every centimeter. "Oh, this is beautiful," she said. "It's called a Yad—that's Hebrew for hand. When the rabbi, or anyone, reads from the Torah, like we do on Sabbath, the reader can hold this and point to the part he is reading with the little hand and little index finger at the end of the long handle. It isn't a requirement that one uses it, but the idea is that the Torah parchment is considered sacred and it doesn't absorb the ink, so if the Torah is touched with the fingers, it could damage the letters. Look, Ben, did you ever see such a beautiful Yad?"

"No. That is truly exquisite," he said with genuine admiration.

"What is this chain at the end opposite the finger?" asked Mikhail.

"That's what is used to hang it from the Torah for safekeeping after the Torah is read and covered up and put away until the next time."

"Ah, that's good to know," said Mikhail. "Thank you so much. Now we know all about everything my grandmother left us. I showed this collection to someone years ago, without the Yad, and they wanted to buy it. But I will never sell it."

"I wouldn't either; never in a million years," said Ben.

Mikhail added, "I was thinking that when Sonya and I are old we might donate it to a Jewish museum, so that people can always enjoy it."

"That is a great idea and very thoughtful," said Leah.

"Thanks for the information. I'll tell my sister," said Mikhail. "I have another question, if you don't mind."

"Sure, what is it," said Ben.

"My guess would be that the condition for Jews was not good in Germany and that's why you moved to Byelorussia."

"Not good is an understatement," said Ben. I believed our lives were in danger; not only the Frohmans, but all the Jews of Germany. Hitler and his Nazi Party's hatred know no bounds."

"You were wise to run from that madman. People who hate like that can never change. If they ever feel threatened, they'll do whatever it takes to get rid of the threat. How did Hitler handle the threat from Roehm and his supporters in '34? It wasn't a problem for him. He killed them; simple as that. That's how dictators work. We have our own dictator here—Stalin."

"He's someone I know so little about," said Sam. In Germany all we read about is how great Hitler is," said Ben, "Tell me something about Stalin."

"Well, when Stalin was a young man and an early member of the Communist Party, the Czar put him in Siberia twice. When Lenin overthrew the Czar in 1917, Stalin became part of the organization. He was too clever, though. He took advantage of his position and built up a power base. When Lenin died, there was a fight for power between Stalin and Leon Trotsky. Well, you know who won that battle. Stalin's in charge and Trotsky was clever enough to flee for his life. Nobody even knows where he is today. And if he's smart, he'll never show his face again—if he wants to live that is."

"Dictators seem to be all alike, don't they?" asked Ben.

"That's the nature of the job. It's kill or be killed the way I see it. Look what Stalin did with the Ukraine."

"What's your take on it?" asked Ben.

"Ukraine was one of the only parts of the Union of Soviet Socialist Republics that resisted Stalin's collectivizing all the peasants; they like their own independence—they always have. Stalin said, no chance, so he made the peasants turn over most of the grain quota to the state. That's why there was massive starvation there. Millions died."

"You are giving me a real education, Mikhail, I appreciate this. He turned to Leah, and Ben said, "I hope you're taking this all in, Leah."

"Yes, I am."

"And I haven't mentioned those who died in the Gulags, all to cement Stalin's dynasty," answered Mikhail. "And when he had finished, he turned on opposition within his own party. Talk about paranoia—he wrote the book on it. If you offered opposition to his leadership you disappeared."

Ben turned to Leah and said, "Did you hear that, Leah; just what I said about Hitler. Paranoia and narcissism must be a trait of all dictators."

"I don't doubt it at all," said Mikhail. "All they see is enemies 'of the State.' And 'enemies of the State' cannot live. They have a single minded purpose in life—power and Control is all they live for; it's all that drives them. Nothing must get in the way. Stalin is getting rid of opposition as we speak."

"Have you heard about Hitler's Mein Kampf, Mikhail?" asked Ben.

"I heard about it, but I haven't read it."

"I read it about ten years ago. I got it from a friend of mine. I read it from the standpoint of his anti-Semitism,

but he also talked about what he called the German need for Lebensraum, living space, and he meant the Soviet Union. On top of that, in his mind all Communists are Jews. In fact, he doesn't talk about Jews separate from Communists. He refers to them as the Jewish-Communist menace. So with him hating Communism, and his opinion that his country needs more living space in the Soviet Union, what does Stalin think about that?"

Mikhail quickly responded, "There were a few attacks on Hitler in the press, but beside that you don't hear much about it. You're right though, the conversations I have at work tell me that they view Hitler as a threat. You know that we helped Germany after World War I by setting up some military training sites for them in Russia, so they could dodge the Versailles Treaty, but when Germany signed a Non-Aggression Pact with Poland we terminated the German military training sites."

"What did Hitler have to say about that?"

"I don't know. I'm sure he wasn't happy and it strained our relationship with him further. I do know that Litvinov who is the Russian People's Commissar for Foreign Affairs, and also a Jew, considers Hitler to be the greatest threat to the Soviet Union and he worries that we don't have a strong enough military, so he's trying to contain Germany by working with other countries and the League of Nations. This is a chess battle for the world."

Ben laughed, "Poor Hitler. Doesn't he know that the Russians are the greatest chess players in the world?"

Mikhail laughed. "Let's hope he doesn't have to find out. By the way, the Jews aren't the only people Hitler would like to get rid of."

"Well, in his Mein Kampf he wasn't too keen on the Slavs," said Ben.

"That's it. He views the Slavs as all Central and Eastern Europeans, and he refers to them as the masses put on the earth to serve and obey" answered Mikhail

"Serve and obey him, I suppose," said Ben.

That's right, him and his Aryans who are destined to control the world as far as he's concerned."

"We ran from him once. I sure hope we don't have to run from him again," said Ben.

"I doubt that will happen. He'd have to be insane to war against us. Let him read about Napoleon."

"I sure hope you're right, Mikhail. Well, Leah, I think we should round up the kids and go home. Mikhail and Sonya, we can't thank you enough for your hospitality."

"It was our pleasure," said Mikhail. "By the way, have you visited the forests around Minsk yet?"

"No, but I heard they're beautiful," answered Ben

"They sure are. You'll come with us the next time we go for a picnic."

"Sure, Mikhail, that sounds like fun. When do you go?"

"On a weekend, so we'll probably go pretty soon before it gets too cold."

"I have to take call on certain weekends, but if I'm off call, I can make it. The whole family would love it."

"It's a date then. I'll be in touch," said Mikhail.

It took them two weeks to get together and they found themselves in one of the many forests for which Byelorussia was famous. The Frohman family, who never visited the forests of Germany, stared spellbound as they viewed their surroundings. The forest was thick with trees blocking much of the sunlight. There were birds in great flocks flying over the treetops and landing as one on the swaying branches. Small animals scurried over the blanket of fallen leaves.

Mikhail had picked a location with a flowing shallow stream where the water was so clear you could see the rocks lying on the bottom and fish competing for the spaces between them. On the other side of the stream were shallow hills thick with trees and brush as far as the eye could see. There were pine trees by the thousands. The quiet, the solitude, the beauty almost made the Frohmans forget why they had come.

Val taught David about the trees and the streams. On the other side of the stream, David found a fairyland of light and dark, shadows and sunlight, trees and brush, and what seemed like millions of chirping birds. Frogs croaked a duet with the chirping birds. David's eyes widened, his mouth opened, his breathing deepened. He felt like an ancient explorer discovering the New World. He stopped adjacent to the stream and stared into the water. "Look at all the fish in the stream," said David, "there must be a hundred of them."

"That's why we pick this place," said Val. "Right before we go back home we all fish here."

"Do you catch any?" asked David.

"We sure do. In fact, my dad brought plenty of fishing poles and bait. You'll be able to fish too. We always go home with about ten or fifteen fish and we eat for weeks."

"That's great. I never fished before," said wide-eyed David.

"All you do is put the worm on the hook, stick it in the water and wait. I'll show you what to do when the fish bite."

"Okay, I'm ready any time."

"Did you see that picture in my house of a tree knot hole?" asked Val.

"Where was it?"

"It was hanging on the wall over the small desk in the corner of the dining room where my father does some work sometime."

"Yeah, I did," said David. You mean the drawing?"

"Yep, my father drew it."

"I wondered what that was," said David, "he's a heck of an artist."

"Well there it is," said Val pointing into the thick of the forest."

"Where?"

"Let's go, I'll show you," said Val.

David followed Val and they stopped before the largest tree in any direction, standing straight up perpendicular to the forest floor higher than any tree within sight.

"Yeah, this is King Tree," said Val. "That's what my father calls it."

"Wow, that is something," said David with neck extended. "Where's the knot?"

"On the other side, about six feet off the ground."

David walked around the tree and stopped in front of the knot. "It's big enough to put your hand in there. How deep down does it go?"

"Only about twenty centimeters."

"My father thought that it was so beautiful that he did a chalk drawing of it and then he did a water color. He's a great artist, I think. Too bad he doesn't have enough time to do it more, but he does have a few pictures."

"Sounds like a great hobby," said David.

Val said, "It relaxes my father. He draws every chance he gets, which isn't too often though. We better get back to camp. I'm sure we'll go fishing soon."

When they arrived back, the families were already fishing. David smiled as he watched his mother, father and sister intent in their new adventure.

"Come on, Val, set up David and lets get some dinner for the next few weeks," said Mikhail.

CHAPTER 5
EVALUATION
1937-8

"Ben, I have some interesting news for you," said Mikhail via phone call in February 1937.

"What is it, Mikhail?"

"I have a translation of the Hitler speech that he gave before the Reichstag on the fourth anniversary of his taking over Germany. I'd like to share it with you sometime."

"Sure, I'd love to see that. Where did you get it?"

"At work. Don't forget, I'm pretty close with my co-workers. The government officials share things with me all the time even though I have nothing to do with politics. I know you would be interested in what Hitler has to say. Who knows better than you what can happen to people he considers enemies? I'll tell you the truth, my bosses are worrying more and more about this madman."

"Come over to my house, Mikhail, anytime some evening that's handy for you, and, if you don't mind, I'd like my wife to be involved. She's really the one who's followed what's going on a lot better than me. In fact, I rely on her to keep me up to date."

"That's great. Would Thursday evening about 7:00 be okay?"

"We'll see you then, Mikhail, and thank you so much."

Mikhail arrived on time, and together with Ben and Leah sat down at the dining room table that Leah had prepared with some delicacies. Mikhail passed copies to each one and said, "I thought that we would start reading from page one. I'm curious to hear what you think. After all, you were one of his subjects, so to speak."

"And what a nightmare it was," said Ben with a shudder.

They started reading in silence together. Leah was the first one to comment. "The first thing that strikes me is that he says he will be speaking about his 'successes' for the German people. What one has to understand is that he has defined who the German people are. We Jews are not included even though many Jews, including my husband, fought for Germany during the Great War, and most of the Jews have been born in Germany and have been citizens all their lives. People of color—black or yellow—are not included in his definition; neither are gypsies, or mental and physical defectives and anyone not pure white or not descended from Aryans, whatever that means."

"He extends that out to the world," said Ben. "He doesn't just deal with those that live in Germany. Look what he thinks about Slavs."

Mikhail asked, "Do you think that, in the future, if a Slav moved to Germany they could ever become a citizen?"

"I would doubt it," said Ben.

"Why do you think he has this fixation on Slavs?" asked Mikhail.

"Because they live in territory he's interested in for his lebensraum, or living space for the German people. Mikhail, you'd just have to serve him as a slave if he had his way," said Leah

"He'd be in for a surprise, if he tried to implement that policy. Is he so stupid that he thinks anyone would sit still for that?" asked Mikhail.

"No, not stupid, just blinded by ambition and by his own belief in Aryan superiority and the Aryan's destiny as the world leaders," added Leah. "Also if we go on to the next page he explains how he answered the question from some people about why a revolution was necessary and why there was no collaboration with parties in Germany that were already in existence," said Leah; his answer is lame and makes me sick."

"What do you mean?" asked Mikhail.

"He says that the old ways never helped the people. This comes back to his hatred for parliamentary democracy, which in his mind is a sure recipe for paralysis in government. Never mind that it works in many countries. It can't work in Germany because it counters his own thoughts and beliefs that only a strong man can run countries. Nothing else can work. Look what he says here. 'It doesn't work and it must be eradicated.' And, believe me, that's just what he did. In his mind only a revolution can change it, and that is a revolution patterned after his thoughts."

Mikhail added, "He and Stalin think alike. We have a megalomaniac here just like the Germans do."

Ben added, "He also says that during a parliamentary democracy, the people are not considered, because the politicians jockey for position for their own benefit. On the other hand, he's quick to point out that he considers what's best for the people in all his decisions. What a joke."

Leah said, "If we go on further in his speech, he states that the old government is incapable of making changes that benefit the people. It will take a radical transformation, a revolution as he keeps calling it, and one that will sacrifice life and blood. He's proven that to be the case because that's just what he's done—shed blood to cement his power. It's all justified to bring him into control. Only he knows what's best for the people. God knows how many will have to die to keep this maniac in power."

"To me, everything he says is to justify his grab for power. Such people who live to control others will bring ruin to the world," said Ben.

Leah added, "Further in his speech he also justifies everything on the basis of—let me summarize what he's saying. Yep here it is; it all boils down that each racial species has to conserve the purity of the blood that God gave them."

"It's all about his obsession with racial purity, agreed Ben. "With that one statement, he damns everybody and everything that could pollute the super race. He goes so far as to say that anyone who is not interested in preserving racial purity is going against God's gift and God's handiwork."

"Quite a way with words, huh? It's amazing what crazies will do and say to justify their own warped thinking," said Mikhail.

"Amen," added Ben. Leah, do you think that, in his blaming the Jews for everything, it would be possible for a man like that to be ever talked out of such folly?"

"That's an easy one. Not a chance. When you have a crazy man whose whole belief rests upon a conspiracy theory, such as the Jews are out to take over the world, anyone trying to talk him out of it would run up against total and blind opposition."

"What do you mean?" asked Ben.

"I can think of two reasons," said Leah. "First because a believer such as Hitler, and I suppose Stalin too, have to believe that any contradictory evidence against their way of thinking has been placed there by the conspirators themselves to mislead the world. That's how they explain any opposing thought away. They have to think of such contradictory evidence as nonsense. Second, and even if others besides Jews try to debunk Hitler's conspiracy theories, their thoughts are explained away by saying they are secretly allies of the conspirators, the Jews."

"That's good thinking, Leah, I'm sure you're right," said Mikhail.

"You were talking about Hitler's ideas of racial purity, Leah," said Ben.

"Yes, back to that," said Leah. "And look here, on the next page he states that Germany is now doing research justifying the doctrine of racial purity. And further, he says that the whole world needs to adopt this creed, so as to prevent the Jews from their attempts to control the world by destroying racial purity."

Ben smiled, turned to Mikhail, and said, "This is all so beyond common sense that one almost can only make a joke out of such folly. I pledge to you, Mikhail that I have no desire to abolish the concept of racial purity in order to take over the world."

"I'm glad, Ben, and I am pretty confident that my grandfather and grandmother also were not part of such a plot," said a smiling Mikhail shaking his head.

"We just have to pray that the power that Hitler now has will not lead the world to ruin," said Leah, "also, I like the way he says that since he came from the people, the future leaders of Germany will also come from the people. Never mind that the selection depends on his way of thinking. This is racial purity at its best. They will have to adopt Hitler's thoughts. If not, they will be lucky to be allowed to resign rather than getting a bullet or a knife in their hearts, just like the Night of the Long Knives when he had his best friend Roehm and his followers killed."

"No doubt," said Ben. "Look at the next part. It's a bit confusing to me. It speaks to what I believe is his concept of the law and the judiciary. "It looks like he's saying that the system has led only to confusion in Germany since it didn't reflect German character.

Translated into Hitler-speak, I think he means it didn't reflect his way of thinking."

"Like everything else in his brain," added Mikhail.

"Right," said Leah. "I think I get what he's saying.

Whereas, in the past, the law has been set up to protect individual rights and property, under Hitler's realm, that thesis does not fit in with Nazi philosophy, and now that he is in power, he will place the nation above any person and property, and to ensure that is the case, there will be one legislator and one executive.

Does that mean that he is taking on the responsibility for the legal system himself? Sometimes I think he deliberately engages in double talk to confuse everyone."

"Here's the sentence that maybe clears it up," said Ben. "I'll sum it up.

He wants to set up the German penal code so that German justice will be placed for the first time on a basis which ensures that for all time to come its duty will be to serve in maintaining the German race.

"There we go again. That's his underlying theme," said Mikhail.

"I think he has another one," said Leah.

"What is that?"

"His anti-bolshevism, his hatred of what he calls the Jewish-Communist, or Jewish-Bolshevik menace. For him, the word Jewish and Communist is the same. He doesn't separate them at all. His hatred of Communism is a nebulous one in the minds of his people, but his hatred of Jews puts a face on the German people, to see and touch. Dictators need that to focus their people. The Czar of Russia was no different. He did the same. Hatred killed my husband's father. We know it first hand," said Leah.

Ben added, "Yes, that's why I worry about his relationship with Russia. After World War I, the control of Germany was a battle between Hitler's fascism and German Communism. There was blood in the streets as they both tried to take over the Weimar Republic formed after the war. Hitler won that battle as you can see. What is the feeling here in Byelorussia, Mikhail?"

"We're a little country never strong enough to have its own independence. Neighboring powers control us all throughout our history. Right now, we're a member of the Union of Soviet Socialist Republics with all the strings pulled in Moscow. That's the reality of it. In Byelorussia though, the people have differing views. We have Byelorussian nationalists who want their independence from any foreign powers and we have Byelorussians that have no problem working and living under the Communist system. My family is not Communistic and if I could have my wish, I guess I would prefer that we could live under our own system, but realism takes over. That is not possible now. We do what we have to do to survive and raise our family. I'm not political and always have been that way. It is the safest course. So far, my position is secure and I am able to raise a family in peace. I am lucky to have such good friends at work.

"I do worry though because I'm afraid that Hitler has ambitions far beyond his borders, and that is the greatest threat to us. As I said before, Litvinov, the foreign minister, insists that Hitler is a serious threat. While Molotov believes that Russia can contain him. I hope we never find out who's right."

Ben added, "He sure spends a lot of time on the Bolshevik menace, as he calls it, and contrasts Germany's personal experience with it as opposed to Britain that has no experience with it and thinks of it only as a Russian phenomenon. In fact, Hitler thinks that his fight against Bolshevism is saving all of Europe and maybe the world."

"You're right," added Leah. He says that 'Bolshevism is a terror no one can tolerate.' What can that possibly mean for any German-Russian relationship in the future?"

"We can only hope it will not lead to war. Hitler would be crazy. It would unify the entire Soviet Union and spell doom for Hitler," said Mikhail.

Leah added, "Well I don't think we've solved the world's problems here today, but I sure enjoyed our discussion. Thank you so much, Mikhail for sharing his speech with us."

"It was my pleasure and thanks for your hospitality. We must get together soon. There is a gymnastics meet coming up next week and I hope we can all attend so we can go watch our two prospective Olympians: Val and David."

They all laughed. "We'll be there, you can be sure, Mikhail," said Ben.

The gymnastics competition took place at the University where the gym was much larger and had the ability to accommodate many hundreds of spectators. There were representatives from a dozen teams who had made the finals. Val qualified as one of the top ten all-around, and David, one of the youngest competitors, placed within the top ten in the pommel horse, his favorite event. Ely, Leah and Emily felt great pride in their son and brother's accomplishment at such a young age. The Olympics took place in Berlin in 1936 and Val was in the running to represent The Union of Soviet Socialist Republics in the 1940 Olympics. However, the war to come would cancel it and have a devastating personal impact on the two families.

The Parliaments of Europe were all concerned about Hitler's intentions. In France, in an effort to prevent German aggression, they constructed the Maginot Line. This "impregnable defense," built in five years in the early thirties at a cost of seven billion Francs, and stretching between Luxembourg and Switzerland along France's border with Germany, would prevent any attack along the border. Three fortified lines with anti-tank emplacements and pillboxes were considered impervious to tank warfare and impenetrable by the German army. Such thinking was to become folly and a monument to the idea that fixed emplacements could deter any would-be modern aggressor. When Hitler embarked upon his Western offensive in 1940, he swept into France through the Ardennes, North of the Maginot Line. In one fell swoop, he destroyed the concept of fixed defensive emplacements and proved the French wrong when they found it unnecessary to include the Ardennes forests, because, as they maintained, 'tanks would find it impenetrable.' This bold sweep, led by Generals Heinz Guderian and Erwin Rommel, reached the Meuse River at Dinant and caused the French to abandon Paris. Warfare would never be the same.

In late 1937, Italy joined the Anti-Comintern pact. This was the third nation, along with Germany and Japan, to join. There were now two factions competing for world control: the extreme right and left of the political spectrum.

In early 1938, the pressure on Austria to merge with Germany had reached its climax. For years there had been many Austrians, both Nazi and non-Nazi, who pursued a "Heim Ins Reich" (home in Germany) movement. German Nazis had provided support for the Austrian Nazi Party by lobbying for German-Austrian unification. The pressure on Austria's Chancellor, Kurt Schuschnig was rising. Although he was committed to remaining independent, he tried to hold a referendum to ask the Austrian people what they preferred: independence or merge with Germany. His expectation was that the Austrians would vote to remain independent, but they cancelled the vote when the Austrian Nazis staged a coup d'etat on 11 March, 1938. With power transferred to Germany, German troops entered the country and took control. Austrian citizens had awakened to an Anschluss (union) with Germany.

The treaty of Versailles had prohibited the union of Germany and Austria, but there was no reaction of the World War I allies. Hitler was being progressively emboldened.

Under the Treaty of Versailles, Britain and France governed the Saar region for a period of 15 years, and its coalfields ceded to France. At the end of that time, a plebiscite was to determine the Saar's future status. The plebiscite took place and the great majority of the citizens of the Saar voted to return to Germany. This was the first peaceful result for Germany in regards to the Versailles Treaty. The next, of course, was Hitler's success in remilitarizing the Rhineland, and now the take over of Austria. His Mein Kampf predictions played out one at a time, albeit in an increasing order of difficulty.

Ben arrived home from work one evening and Leah greeted him with a Russian newspaper that had written a full report on the Austrian situation. "They're a full part of Germany now, and it all happened without Hitler firing a shot," she said. He's gobbling up Europe and what's interesting is the reaction of England."

"What do they say about it all?" asked Ben.

"Well, they start out by registering a strong protest against the Nazis for their—let me see—yes, and I quote—'their use of coercion, backed by force, against an independent State in order to create a situation incompatible with its national independence.'"

"Wow, how tough can they get?" said Ben with biting sarcasm. "What else do they say?"

"Well, then they add that 200 years ago Scotland joined with England and that wasn't much different than Germany and Austria now."

"Aha, now the appeasement starts," said Ben.

"Chamberlain says that there was not much they can do unless they were prepared to use force, which they were not. But then he says that they will review their state of defense preparedness," said Leah.

"Oh, that'll make Hitler quake in his boots, won't it."

"We just have to pray that he will eat enough to give him a full belly."

"Well, I hope he gets that full belly long before he decides to act on his lebensraum in the East. That is my worst nightmare," said Ben.

Another Hitler target in 1938 was the Sudetenland. This area, along the Northern border of Czechoslovakia had been a part of Germany in the 1800's, and after the First World War, it became part of Czechoslovakia. Hitler, with an eye to restoring the Greater German Reich, wanted the Sudetenland back in Germany even though most Sudetan Germans had been content to remain part of Czechoslovakia.

When Leah heard the news, she said to Ben, "It looks like his belly hasn't been filled yet."

A Sudetan-German Nazi-like political party, formed in 1935 and financed by Nazi Germany, began to complain of discrimination by the Czechs. That was enough of a pretext for Hitler who wanted to invade Czechoslovakia, but his generals resisted pointing out that Czechoslovakia's powerful army could offer formidable mountain defenses in the Sudetenland, and if Britain, France, or the Soviet Union came to Czechoslovakia's defense, Germany would not prevail. One group of generals made plans to overthrow Hitler should he ignore their advice. The Czechoslovakian situation set in motion a four-nation great power conclave.

In a hoped for resolution of the Sudetenland question, the British Prime Minister, Neville Chamberlain, met with Hitler at his Berchtesgaden home. Hitler was looking for British support in his planned takeover of the Sudetenland, going so far as to tell Chamberlain that Germany would invade Czechoslovakia if they did not receive British approval to return the Sudetenland to Germany. After discussing the situation with Edouard Daladier of France and Eduard Benes of Czechoslovakia, Chamberlain told Hitler that Britain could not accept his proposals.

Hitler felt that Chamberlain's refusal was a bluff, because he knew that neither Britain nor France were willing to go to war over the Sudetenland. Nor were they willing to make an alliance with Russia since both democracies hated Communism and viewed it as an international threat.

Mussolini came to Hitler's rescue when he suggested a four-power conference on Czechoslovakia to include Germany, Italy, Britain and France without including Russia or Czechoslovakia. In Mussolini's mind, this would enhance the possibility of an agreement over the Sudetenland and undermine opposition to Germany.

The meeting took place in Munich on 29 September 1938. Britain and France agreed that for the promise of no further territorial demands in Europe, Hitler could have the Sudetenland. Two days later, Hitler marched in and took over this critically fortified area, which included all of Czechoslovakia's mountainous defenses. Czechoslovakia now found itself defenseless against any further aggression.

Ben and Leah remained keen observers of the geopolitical chess game played out for the world to ponder. Who would make what move and what were the ramifications? Leah was fearful while Ben prayed that, by some miracle, Hitler had reached the end of the line as far as his ambitions were concerned.

"He would have to have a death wish to try and go any further. You can only spit in the face of your enemies so long, before they spit back," said Ben.

"If you're talking about Chamberlain, I don't think he's the spitting type. I rather think that he'd continue to appease while Hitler takes over Europe," answered Leah.

"You get no help from newspapers," said Ben. One day you read that Hitler has made up his mind to invade the rest of Czechoslovakia while another source says the opposite."

"I can only wonder how Stalin feels about being left out of the Czechoslovakia discussion. If this doesn't make him worry about Hitler's intentions, I don't know what will," said Leah

Ben nodded his head in agreement and said, "Hitler thinks that he's Germany's new Bismarck. If he had a brain in his body, he'd rest on his laurels now and solve the issue of Czechoslovakia peacefully and be content to leave the rest of Europe alone. That's what I'd like to believe, but every time I think of his Mein Kampf, and see how fanatical he is, an inner voice tells me that a man like that will not rest until he has all of Europe and the world. It is very depressing because you and I and our children are our world."

"So far," said Leah, I believe England and France are giving him slack, because all he has asked for is the return of those areas that used to be German or where there is a German majority. I mean like the Saar, the Rhineland and the Sudetanland. He got what he wanted because neither Britain nor France was willing to go to war over those territories. Even though the Sudetenland has become part of Czechoslovakia, it does have a German majority and used to be part of Germany, you see. He'll get whatever he can peacefully—and the rest he'll go to war for."

Ben countered, "I believe you can never forget what he said in his Mein Kampf about his master Aryan race and their need for lebensraum. He's gained plenty and if he would stop now the world could breathe a sigh of relief. Taking Czechoslavakia would be the first time that he would set out to conquer non-German lands. What's the world to think then?"

"Don't you see the contradiction?" asked Leah.

"What do you mean?"

Leah answered. "You yourself have said that in his book he always makes the point that racial purity is the ultimate goal for his superior Nazis. Jews and Slavs just defile Nazis so they should never be a part of Germany."

"Not exactly," said Ben. "Yes, he makes that claim all the time, but that does not mean, as far as Slavs are concerned, that they can't be used as slaves of the German masters once he has taken all their lands for his so-called lebensraum. And maybe he means the same fate for the Jews."

It would not take long for Ben's words to become prophetic. In late autumn on November 7, 1938 a German Jewish refugee by the name of Herschel Grynszpan shot and killed an employee of the German Embassy in Paris named Ernst Vom Rath. He did this in retaliation for the Nazis deporting ten thousand Jews, including Grynszpan's father, to Poland. The Poles refused them. Grynzpan had meant to kill the ambassador, but shot a third secretary sent out to see what he wanted.

Goebbels wasted no time issuing instructions that "spontaneous" demonstrations should break out all over Germany. The true organizer was Reinhard Heydrich, the number two man after Heinrich Himmler of the SS. His instructions were specific:

- *Burn down Synagogues only if certain there would be no fire danger to adjacent property*
- *Destroy Jewish businesses and Jewish residences, but do not loot*
- *Police will not interfere*
- *Jews, especially the rich, are to be confined to concentration camps*

These crimes took place all throughout Germany and Austria.

They arrested twenty-thousand Jews, looted 7,500 shops, burned or destroyed 195 synagogues, killed thirty-six Jews and wounded thirty-six. This "night of the broken glass" resulted in a backlash from a world horrified by what had taken place.

"And what do you think Hitler said about the fact that the world was shocked at this all-out pogrom against the Jews?" asked Ben.

"I don't know. What did he say?" answered Leah.

"Can you guess?"

"Hmm—not a clue really—probably he said something about the damn Jews and their ability to get sympathy from the world?"

"Well, that's logical thinking, but no, he said that the sympathy of the world was proof of the scope of the Jewish world conspiracy."

"Oh, I see, The Jews have the whole world in their pockets, and all for the purpose of being against Hitler and Germany and for world control You're right—paranoia to the extreme. It means to me that he is determined to act against Jews in one way or another. We were lucky to leave when we did," said Leah.

"Yes, but I live with the feeling that he's trying to get you, me and our children," said Ben.

CHAPTER 6
PRELUDE TO WORLD WAR II
1939

At breakfast, one morning after the children had left for school, Leah said, "We've got a few minutes before we have to leave for work, so let me summarize this for you, Ben." "Summarize what?"

"Hitler's speech to the Reichstag—his first 1939 speech."

Ben nodded with interest. "More bad news, I suppose."

"He says Europe will not have peace until the Jewish question has been disposed of... "Oh, my God; more of the same?" interrupted Ben.

"Yes, right. Listen to the whole thing," said Leah. Here's my summary. He says that the Jews are parasites feeding on the productive work of all other citizens of whatever country they live in. He keeps suggesting that rich Jews are out to start a world war, and if they don't stop, the outcome will be annihilation of the Jewish race.

"This is scary, Ben. He's doing what all dictators and fanatics do: he's already casting blame away from him for a war, which if it comes can only be his fault."

"They all need their scapegoats, and we're it," said Ben, banging his fist into the table.

In March of 1939, Hitler played out the second part of the Czechoslovakian drama. The first in October of 1938 was the takeover, by Germany, of the Sudetenland with its majority of German inhabitants. In the second act, Hitler invited the president of Czechoslovakia, Hacha, to Berlin. He kept him waiting for hours and then advised him that the German army was about to invade his country. The takeover of the Sudetenland had eliminated the Czech defenses and Germany had surrounded the country on three fronts. Hitler pointed out to Hacha that he had two options: cooperate with Germany to assure a peaceful occupation, or face war including Goering's threat to bomb Prague to ruin. Hacha had no choice. Hitler took over the rest of Czechoslovakia. Hacha remained as president, but had to swear an oath of allegiance to Hitler. Germany took over local control offices, the Gestapo assumed police authority, Jews had to leave civil service jobs and Nazis banned political parties. Communist party leaders fled for their lives to the Soviet Union. The German occupation started with a peaceful tone, but became harsher in time as Czech opposition stiffened.

"Another country taken over without firing a shot," said Leah.

"I think that this will be the last one," said Ben, but he was wrong:

Memel was a Baltic port with forty thousand German inhabitants that the allies ceded to Lithuania after World War I. The take over of their tiny town was a cakewalk by Hitler who just ordered that it be "annexed."

"You were wrong, Ben, he needed a fast dessert."

"Will this be it, I wonder?"

"I don't think so."

"I hope you're wrong," said Ben, "because I'm sure this is the last conquering he'll be able to do without war."

Shortly after Memel, the Spanish Civil War ended with General Franco in control of the Country. Britain and France had learned their lesson: they made a pact with Rumania and Greece should Germany or Italy attack and they submitted formal guarantees to Poland. The world was lining up and taking sides in the event of the feared war that many felt would soon sweep over Europe for the second time in twenty-five years.

It all reminded Ben of pre World War I days.

The summer of 1939 was ending. Ben and Leah decided to have one more picnic before the weather changed. "I'll call Mikhail and invite all the Gregovs," said Ben. "That sounds fine," said Leah. "I look forward to it."

"How about you, David, we expect the whole family to be there. This will be the last chance for a picnic. You know how fast the weather changes."

"Okay, Dad. Can I bring a friend?" asked David.

Ben looked at Leah. "Val will be there, I'm sure, if you're talking about him."

"Nope, not Val. I'm talking about a lady friend."

Ben again looked at Leah and she at him before Ben asked, "A lady friend. That's news to us."

"Who is she?" asked Leah.

"Her name is Hannah Brunstein, and I met her at a student dance."

Hannah Brunstein represents a young Jew who fell in love with another Jew during a time of great peril. Their trials and tribulations before and during World War II typically faced surviving young Jews during this period.

"Did you hear that, Leah. Your son met a girl at a student dance. What better place to meet a woman."

"Can't think of any," smiled Leah.

"Please bring her," said Leah, "We want to meet her. Is this serious, David?"

"I like her a lot," nodded David.

"How long have you known her," asked Leah.

"About two weeks."

"She lives in Minsk, I presume."

"Yes, and I'll answer your next question before you ask it. She's in pre-med like me."

"I can't wait to meet her," said Ben.

The Frohmans and the Gregovs met together at the same forest location where the Gregovs invited them. While Leah prepared the table with food and goodies, David and Hannah and Val and another young lady walked further into the forest to see "King Tree" with its beautiful Knot Hole that had been memorialized on canvas by Mikhail. Then they fished, hoping to add some protein to Leah's table.

"While the ladies are at work, Mikhail, bring me up to date on your take on what's going on in the world. I appreciate your thoughts on it. You seem to be right on the mark all the time," said Ben.

"Well, as I already mentioned, I have the perspective of being the good friend of many of the politicians at work, so I can tell you what they think and try and add some of what I think. And it doesn't look good."

"How do you mean, Mikhail?"

"Have you read some about the troubles we have with Japan along the border between Manchuria and Mongolia?

"I have to confess that, yes, I've scanned it, but I don't pay much attention because it seems unimportant to me when there is so much going on in Europe."

"What's happening along that border may well have great relevance to what's going on in Europe," answered Mikhail.

Really?" said a puzzled Ben. "Clue me in, please. That's an area of the world I know nothing about."

"Let me start with some background," said Mikhail as Ben poured himself a drink of water.

"You know that Japan whipped us in 1904-5 during the Russo-Japanese war."

"Yes," said Ben.

"Stalin has done a good thing. He's strengthened our military near Japan so that will never happen again. But the Japanese keep testing us ever since they occupied Manchuria and Korea. There's a problem with the border between Manchuria and Mongolia; we disagree where it has been all these years. We have a strong military there and so does Japan."

"I get it. You don't hear much about this in the press, do you?"

"Nope. Hitler is the big news now. No one pays much attention to what's going on near Japan. There's just the two armies snarling at each other and shooting and invading over the border—wherever that is. But things became interesting in May of this year. One of our cavalry units from Mongolia crossed what the Japanese believe is the border to find some grazing land for their horses. That didn't last long because the Japanese cavalry attacked them and drove them back across the Khalkin Gol River right in the middle of the contested

territory. This made our side kind of angry and we returned to rejoin the battle. The Manchrians now couldn't budge us, so they came in with a much bigger force, which caused us to withdraw at first, but then we returned with an even bigger force than theirs and wiped out the Japanese and Manchurians. It was decisive. They had enormous casualties, so they struck back with their air force and attacked one of our air force bases and caused considerable damage."

"And this is all an undeclared war, it sounds like," said Ben.

"Exactly, but plenty died—declared or undeclared," said Mikhail.

"So what happened then," asked Ben, spell bound by all this new kind of information.

"The Japanese got super serious and put together a large force to drive us the hell out of there. But a new man for us, a Lieutenant General Georgi Zhukov, came on the scene and they fought like cats and dogs for several months reaching a stalemate until General Zhukov put together almost five hundred tanks and several hundred planes, and artillery plus about 50,000 troops and beat the Japanese back in a decisive battle. It was a great victory. The Japanese got whipped. Believe me, they'll think twice before they ever decide to come back."

"And to think I never even knew about the details," said Ben. "You mentioned at first that that battle could be important to Europe. Tell me how," Ben asked.

"I'll give you what I hear from the office which seems to be the consensus of the discussions. If there ever is a war in Europe involving the Soviet Union and Germany, Stalin will be better prepared, because he will not have to worry about Japan and could concentrate all his forces against Hitler. That's bad news for him. Remember Napoleon."

Ben responded, "I see what you mean, Mikhail. The Japanese got a lesson that one could only hope that they learned well. If there is a war in Europe, with all the resources in industry and manpower that the Russians have, would Hitler be nuts enough to attack Russia when Russia can concentrate everything against him?" asked Ben.

"He probably would. He is crazy after all," answered Mikhail.

"You're right, of course. I can't forget about his desire for lebensraum. He speaks of the Ukraine breadbasket for the German master race in his Mein Kampf, and I've always said to my wife that Mein Kampf is his bible and he plans to carry out what he wrote. God help us, sighed Ben."

They were pausing to conjecture about their discussion when David and the group returned to the base camp. "Mom, we struck it rich," said David.

Leah turned from her table to see the youngsters returning from their fishing adventure with eight fish. "Look at the size of those fish. We'll all eat like kings today," Leah said.

"Hannah caught three of them," said David.

"Good job, Hannah."

"Not bad, I guess for only the second time I ever fished," answered Hannah.

"She got the knack alright," said David.

"I have a good teacher," replied Hannah, smiling at David.

The both older Frohmans grinned with happiness as they noted how the two youngsters looked at each other.

"You better filet the fish, Mikhail. My husband is no surgeon. That's why he became an internist," said Leah.

Mikhail laughed. No sooner said than done."

"He's great at that," said Sonya, he always does that at home."

The picnic went well. The friendship between the Frohmans and the Gregovs grew stronger, as did the relationship between David and Hannah.

In the meantime, when Hitler marched into Prague, Stalin authorized his foreign minister, Maxim Litvinov, to propose a conference with the Soviet Union, Britain, France, Poland, Romania, and Turkey. The purpose of the conference was to forge a united front against Hitler. Britain, under Chamberlain, never accepted the idea of a conference. Some, like Winston Churchill, urged that Britain accept the concept of a multi-nation united front against Germany, but Chamberlain would have none of it.

Stalin, therefore, concluded that Britain and France were encouraging Hitler's drive in his direction. He now felt that he needed an agreement with Germany. After extensive negotiations between Joachim von Ribbentrop of Germany and Vyacheslav Molotov of the Soviet Union, a non-aggression pact was forged. It hit the world like a lightning bolt. Here were two political ideologies from opposite ends of the political spectrum joining forces.

"I don't believe this," said Leah. Two guys who hate each other and each others politics? Communism and fascism in bed together? Oh, my God!" She shook her head.

"At least, if they signed a treaty, they won't go to war with each other," said Ben.

"Since when would a piece of paper ever stop either one of these tyrants," countered Leah.

Hitler and Stalin agreed to settle all differences by negotiation, never join forces with any third party attacking each other, maintain continuous contact, and never participate with any grouping of powers aimed at the other party. Hitler got what he wanted: an agreement from the Soviet Union not to join Britain and France if they came to Poland's rescue in the event of war between Poland and Germany. He could now invade Poland with impunity. The Soviet Union, no longer a potential foe, would allow Hitler to call Britain and France's bluff.

The von Ribbentrop-Molotov pact also included a secret unpublished protocol. The Soviet Union and Germany would carve up Eastern Europe. In the Baltic, the dividing line would be the northern frontier of Lithuania. North of this frontier was the Soviet's sphere of interest. South was Germany's. This meant that Lithuania, in the event of war with Poland, would fall into the hands of the Nazis.

The rest of the world was unaware of this secret protocol. As was their intent, Germany and the Soviet Union kept this plan to themselves.

Last-minute frantic negotiations between Britain and Germany were to no avail. Hitler's intent, declared only in secret, was to invade Poland on September 1. These wartime preparations occurred almost at the same time as the Russian-Japanese adventure. The pieces were falling into place that would affect the next years in the history of Europe. With the news of the pact, Leah and Ben tried to figure out the rationale for it. "Why do you think these two dictators did this?" he asked.

Leah thought for a short time. "I think that both of these monsters feel that it won't be long before they are both at war with each other. How can Stalin not believe that Hitler has his eye on the Ukrainian breadbasket? But, right now, the last thing Hitler needs is to become involved with Russia while he has his mind on Poland. As far as Stalin is concerned, his main concern is to avoid war at this time. He tried to do it with a pact with England and France, but they weren't interested."

Ben added, "You could add that Stalin was suspicious of England and France. I think he feels that they both are interested in getting Russia and Germany slugging against each other so that they will both weaken and leave England and France alone. Don't you agree?"

"Yes, I agree" said Leah. "A pact with Germany would enable Stalin to buy some time at the expense of Poland. The time he gains plus the territorial advantage he gets gives him a bit of an advantage should the day ever come that Hitler would invade. He gets time to build up his strength."

Ben added, "And don't forget that the German pact with Russia would isolate Poland and make it difficult for England and France to interfere. I'm sure that interests Hitler."

Leah sighed and shook her head. "Dictators have got to be chess players," she said.

"I love the part of the pact that says they will not attack each other for the next ten years...a non-aggression pact," added Ben. "Fat chance, huh?"

"From Molotoff-Ribbentrop to God's ears," she added.

Prior to the Polish invasion, the Nazi propaganda machine went into action. Hitler told the German people that Polish troops were preparing for invasion and making forays into German territory and terrorizing German citizens. Then the Nazis reported that Polish troops had opened fire and seized the radio transmitter in Gleiwitz. On September 1, 1939, the Nazis struck "in self-defense." Almost two million German troops invaded on three fronts: from East Prussia in the North, Germany in the West, and Slovakia in the South. A new form of warfare was unleashed, and a new word would enter the world's vocabulary: blitzkrieg or lightning war.

The true story surfaced years later during the Nuremburg trial after the second World War finally ended. Reinhard Heydrich, head of the Sicherheitsdienst, the Nazi security service, developed a plan that Hitler approved. Nazi prisoners were dressed in Polish uniforms, killed and presented to the world as attacking Poles who had invaded Germany. This would be Hitler's "provocation" for his attack.

Twenty-six hundred German tanks and two thousand aircraft stormed across the border. Dive-bombers rained destruction on defenseless towns and refugees. This was the first time that such a massive assault struck any country. Civilians were a legitimate target. Warfare had changed forever. Mankind would henceforth face the threat of utter extinction.

The Poles were unprepared, and within two weeks, Warsaw fell. However, Hitler's campaign was no walkover. The Poles offered surprising resistance, and the Nazis lost fifty thousand men, almost one thousand tanks, and seven hundred airplanes. On September 3, Britain and France declared war, but no help was forthcoming for Poland. They stood alone.

On September 17, the Soviets invaded across Poland's East border. Already beaten by the Nazis, the Poles were helpless to resist. The next day, the Soviet troops met the Nazis at Brest Litovsk. They carved up Poland. Britain and France remained at a distance but were relieved that Germany would not get all of Poland.

Stalin became uncomfortable with the pact's secret protocol that carved up the Baltic States, giving Lithuania to Germany. He believed that the three Baltic States of Lithuania, Estonia, and Latvia constituted a single entity and that their division would create difficulties between Germany and the Soviet Union. Therefore, he proposed an exchange: he would give some Polish lands to Germany and include Lithuania in the Soviet sphere of influence. In that way, all the Baltic States fell under Stalin's yoke. This included Vilna, and the Jewish population in Lithuania received an influx of Polish refugees from a fallen Poland, and, for the time being, breathed a sigh of relief.

But Russia had another worry—Finland. Russia invaded on November 30, 1939.

Ben asked, "Why, Mikhail?

"Because Finland has been part of Russia since 1809, but they have always wanted independence and they saw their chance during the Communist Revolution in 1917 and proclaimed their independence in the same year. But things have changed now and Stalin is fearful of invasion from the West. Leningrad is only about thirty kilometers from the Finnish border. This is within artillery range, so Stalin tried to get Finland to station Russian troops within their borders. Finland said no and fought back, but as expected, numbers prevailed and Russia won. Stalin signed a peace treaty and got thirty-five square kilometers of Finland. That was enough to ensure Soviet defenses, but it exposed two important points for the rest of the world to contemplate. Stalin had some strategic smarts and the Russian army was not well trained and equipped."

"So Stalin, being a quick learner, figured out that he had some work to do to bring his army up to standards," said Ben.

"That's right," agreed Mikhail.

CHAPTER 7
JOZEF ASKENAZY
THE FIRST EVIDENCE
1940

The suspense was over. The Nazis conquered Poland. The Frohmans could only stand by and continue to evaluate the world stage, a task they took with great seriousness wondering if Russia would be next on Hitler's list.

David and Hannah's relationship was flowering in the direction of loving intent. As it turned out, Emily knew Hannah, because she was an assistant coach at Emily's swim club. Swimming had given Hannah a slim muscular figure. She was five foot four inches with blue eyes and black hair, cut short as an accommodation to her favorite sport. Emily was overjoyed with David's new relationship. So were David's parents, amazed by Hannah's sophistication; fluency in four languages and knowledge of any subject. She spent time at David's house, as did David at Hannah's house. Both families got to know each other. Hannah's father, a tailor, and her mother, a homemaker, were also delighted with Hannah's choice. Ben and Leah could not help but notice this dedication to family.

They're too young," said Leah.

"About two years younger than I was when I saw this dazzling beauty sitting against the wall in the Jewish Community Center in Berlin," said Ben.

Although David was nineteen and Hannah was eighteen, they grew up fast in a changing world where young people were confused because of an unstable and uncertain future.

"Don't let that stop your dreams," said Ben as he tried to reassure his son and his son's girlfriend. "You can't let a possible cloud overlooking the future stop your future plans. Never lose sight of the prize. If you can't reach your plans because of circumstances beyond your control, then stop, do what you can do to bring back the good days, or vow to get through the hard times waiting for better days, which will surely come. Keep busy. I hope you understand."

"We will do that, dad. We promise."

In the meantime, Poland's Jews were quick to learn what was in store for them. Before the start of the Second World War, 3,500,000 Jews resided in Poland representing ten percent of the population. Most of them lived and worked within the larger cities.

The Nazis invaded Poland with their new blitzkrieg form of warfare including a rapid tank onslaught followed by a massive infantry assault. They won the war in short order overwhelming the tough Polish defenses.

Initially the Nazis confiscated Jewish property and other valuables and herded Jews into ghettos where they forced them to work for the benefit of the Nazi war-effort. These ghettos were required to have Jewish councils (Judenrate) whose responsibility it was to carry out their Nazi master's orders. Conditions in the ghetto rapidly deteriorated resulting in deaths from starvation and disease, a fate only escape from the ghetto could alleviate. By the end of the war, The Nazis liquidated 90 percent of Poland's Jews.

Jozef Askenazy, a Polish-Jewish laborer was one of the first to feel the lash. He was divorced from his wife before the war. She moved out and took her two children with her to Bialystok where she eventually remarried. Jozef rarely saw his children, a source of deep sorrow for him. He worked in construction as a foreman for a construction company that built homes and other buildings in and around northern Poland, but with the onset of the war, that all ended. Escape was on his mind.

He was a large man, standing six feet two inches and weighing 220 pounds with upper and lower arms and chest muscles reflecting his occupation. He wore a bushy mustache, a bit gray in spite of his young age of forty-five. His hair, partially bald, also showed signs of gray. Dark brown eyes, a hawk like nose and a cleft in his chin added to his appearance, an attraction for unattached women of the community. He used that to his advantage.

Not long after Poland's surrender, German soldiers belonging to an artillery regiment rounded up Jozef and forty-nine other Jews. The men were taken off city streets and marched to a position near the border between Poland and Lithuania. The angry soldiers barked out orders telling their captives to repair a bridge.

I don't like the feel of this, thought Jozef. These men are drunk. They'll have no use for us when we're finished. I don't want to be one of the first Jews sacrificed for Hitler's dream of a Judenfrei (Jew free) world. Escape! How? That's what I better do, but now is impossible. They surround us on all sides. We are in their sites and they are all armed.

After working for ten hours and when their task was complete, the soldiers walked them back to town. Armed with their automatic weapons at the ready, when they arrived, one of the soldiers asked, "Is there a synagogue here?"

"Yes, the small wooden building over there," pointed out one of the laborers.

"That's perfect. You've had a hard days work. Get in there, wash up and get a good night's sleep."

Jozef did not like the chuckles coming from many of the soldiers. I wont stay in there he thought. I must escape. He was familiar with the synagogue and knew its entrances and exits.

The men walked into the synagogue in single file. When they turned down a corridor heading for the room where they could lie down, Jozef slid out of a corridor door leading to the rear of the building. He sprinted into the adjacent forest with what remaining strength he had left and kept on going until the rat-a-tat-tat of multiple machine guns stopped him in his tracks. Like the World War 1 combat soldier he had been, he hit the ground, turned around and looked back through the trees of the forest and saw the flashing lights of the machine guns through the synagogue windows keeping rhythm with the noises of the gunshots. They're killing them—the bastards—the bastards. My God! He crawled away until hidden by some large trees, then leaped up and ran as fast as his legs could carry him to get to the Soviet zone of Poland. At least escaping into the Soviet zone would take him away from the accursed Nazis. After about 100 meters, he stopped and looked in the direction of the synagogue. What he saw horrified him even more. Where the synagogue stood, there was now a wall of flames stretching as high as the highest tree and casting an eerie light, which bounced off the low hanging clouds. My God in Heaven, they torched the synagogue!

My friends. They've cremated them! He pointed his fist toward the heavens. Revenge, he whispered under clenched teeth.

Jozef Askenazy undergoes an experience that actually happened after the start of World War II. The S.S. took fifty Jews to repair a bridge in Poland. With the Jews work complete, they then took them to a synagogue where they were all shot and killed and the synagogue torched. Jozef Askenazy represents those Jews who witnessed or learned about their friends or relatives death at the hands of the Nazis and/or their collaborators. This prompted in them an intense desire for revenge driving them to join and or lead partisans in dedicated anti-Nazi activity.

Jozef Askenazy now knew what he had to do. He would leave Poland forever. My children, he thought, I'll never see them again, but they should be safe. My ex saved them without realizing it. She married a non-Jew; one good thing she did in her life. It'll probably keep her alive for our children. It's just a short distance from the border with Byelorussia and then about a week or so trek to Minsk where I hope I can find Tante (aunt) Rosa. She's lived there all her life. I'll travel at night and live off the forest. I'll sleep during the day. I must get there to tell what just happened. Will anyone believe me?

Late at night, exhausted as he was, he still managed to get in about seven hours of walking after he crossed the boundary between the Nazi and the Soviet zone. He drank water from some of the fast running streams. When it turned light from the approaching morning, he lie down under some thick shrubbery and fell asleep as soon as his head hit the leaf pile he used for a pillow. A full sleep plus the ample supply of water, leaves, berries, roots and raw fish from the streams sustained him. He did not want to take the chance of anyone seeing him even though he was in Byelorussia. When I get to Minsk, I'll find a hospital, he thought. That should be the safest place to go to tell what happened. The world needs to understand what they're facing.

Within thirteen days, he had reached the outskirts of Minsk. He washed his clothes and himself in a stream, redressed and walked through the city. He asked the first person he saw for directions to the nearest hospital, and when he arrived there, he asked to see a doctor. A nurse signed him in and the nurse was Leah Frohman who took him to Ben.

Ben asked Jozef the reason for his visit and Jozef answered, "I escaped from a slaughter of forty-nine Polish Jews by Nazi soldiers in Poland."

A startled Ben could only sit back and listen as Jozef told his story from beginning to end. He told it with such sincerity and emotion that Ben had no doubt as to its veracity.

Stunned, but calm and thoughtful at the same time, Ben said, "There are some things I'd like to do, Mr. Askenazy. First, I want to give you a complete examination and make sure that you're in good health after this ordeal you've been through. Second, I want to tell your story to a good friend of mine that has contact with Byelorussian government officials. What you have told me is too big to end with my ears. This is news for the world to hear. I am a Jew also, sir."

"I am glad then that you are the first to hear my story," said Jozef.

"Why did you come to Minsk?" asked Ben.

"I have an aunt who lives here and there is no way I will ever remain in Poland after what I just went through."

"I understand, Mr. Askenazy. I and my family ran from Hitler in '36."

After hearing Ben's story, Askenazy said, "It looks like I came to the right place."

Ben examined his new patient and found him to be in excellent health.

Ben, said, "Mr. Askenazy, I..."

Jozef interrupted, "Please, Doctor, Call me Jozef."

"I will, Jozef, and call me Ben. I wanted to ask that if you are not in a hurry to find your aunt, I would like to invite you to my home to recuperate for a few days. I want you to meet the right people who need to hear what happened to you. Then you can get hold of your aunt and surprise her."

"Sure, Ben, I appreciate that. I will cooperate any way that I can."

"Good. The nurse you met is my wife. She'll be going home soon and we'll follow a few hours later. It'll be a pleasure to have you as our guest. In the meantime, I'll call this friend of mine. He needs to hear what happened to you. He probably will want to arrange other meetings with you and his associates."

"Whatever you say, Ben, but I'm a mess as you can see."

"Well fix you up. You can take a shower here and I'll lend you some clothes until you get settled with your aunt."

"I'm lucky to meet you. Thank God. I can't thank you enough," said Jozef.

"You're an important figure in the world now, Jozef. You need to stay in good shape."

As it turned out there were more Polish-Jewish refugees fleeing the Nazi excesses in their native land. Many thousands had arrived in Byelorussia; the great majority of these refugees were Jews.

Once Jozef settled in Ben's home, Ben called Mikhail and told him, "I have an amazing story for you, Mikhail. I met a man at the hospital. He walked to Minsk all the way from Poland after surviving a massacre committed by Nazi troops on forty-nine Jews. You'll find it hard to believe, Mikhail. I would like you to meet him. You need to hear his story and maybe the people you work with should hear it also. This is a story for the world to hear. Could you come to my house Saturday? I'm putting him up there for a few days before he surprises his aunt who lives here in Minsk."

After a short period of reflective silence, Mikhail said, "I'll be there, Ben."

CHAPTER 8
A TEAM ASSEMBLES
1940

On Saturday morning, Mikhail arrived and Ben introduced him to Jozef. Mikhail sat in stunned silence as Jozef told the entire story with great emotion interspersed with choking pauses as he remembered some of his good friends, amongst the first victims of Nazi terror. "It is starting. The massacres are starting. They are rounding up Jews and Polish officials and God knows who else."

"Are you sure," Jozef, do you have proof that these acts are widespread?" asked Mikhail.

"I have my own personal experience and eye-witness accounts from people I trust who saw executions carried out in the public square."

"My God," said Ben.

"And these are the people who Stalin has allied himself with, who Stalin has split up a country with. This period of history will forever be a stain on the Soviet Union," said Mikhail.

"This is getting too close for comfort," worried Ben.

Mikhail asked, "Tell me Jozef, you speak perfect Russian, better than most Poles I ever knew."

"Yes, I speak Yiddish, Polish and Russian I grew up in Russian controlled Poland, and I fought in the Russian army during the Great War 1914-1918."

"You are lucky you survived that disaster, Jozef," said Mikhail.

"Don't I know it," said Jozef, "in 1914, I was a nineteen-year-old kid thinking I was in a great adventure." He paused, obviously reflecting back before he continued.

"At first, we advanced close to Krakow in Galicia, but they beat us back, and about all we did after that is retreat until we had another battle around Gorlice. I lost all my friends. Why was I spared, God only knows. Anyhow, we had to retreat again, this time with orders to destroy everything—scorched earth. By the time we finished near the end of the war, there wasn't much left of Poland. In 1916, we had another battle in Galicia, but never were able to take advantage of some of the gains we made. About the only thing that happened in that war was that Poland was destroyed, the Czar was finished and the Communist revolution happened in Russia."

"But after the war at least, Poland became its own country," said Ben.

"And how long did that last—a little over twenty years and now divided again between Soviet Russia and Germany. It's hell being a little country between two great powers, isn't it," asked Mikhail. "By the way, Jozef, what are your plans?"

"My plans are to surprise my aunt who lives here in Minsk and who I have not seen in more than twenty years. Then I will try and figure out what I might do here. I hope she can help me."

Mikhail stroked his chin and said, "If you you're going to live here, you'll need identifying papers. I can help you get those where I work."

"Thank you, thank you. I am very grateful for that."

"And speaking of work, what kind of work do you do, Jozef?"

"I have always worked in construction. Twenty years has turned me into a handyman. I can do anything and will do anything."

"After you get settled, we will see what I can arrange for you. We have some construction projects going on all the time where I work."

Jozef grasped Mikhail's hand with a force that made Mikhail wince. While shaking it vigorously he said, "I don't know what to say. I am so grateful. And you too, Ben. I promise that you will have the best out of me that I can give."

"If your work is as powerful as your handshake, Jozef, I'm sure it will be the best," smiled Mikhail waving his crushed hand in the air. "I have to go now, but I expect to hear from you in the next few days. We have to start things going for you."

CHAPTER 9
PHONY WAR
1940

"And what do you think of our new friend, Jozef?" Ben asked Leah.

"I look at him and it makes me sad," answered Leah.

This response came as a surprise to Ben who, after a short pause, asked, "Why is that, Leah?"

"Because he is a man growing up in a cruel world under circumstances beyond his control. He fought and no doubt killed as a teenager. As a man, he almost died, just because of his religion. To stay alive he had to leave his own country. I'm sad because we have a son growing up in that same world, and I can't visualize his future because we are in another war now with all its uncertainties. It is so depressing."

"That's true, but we can't let all these uncertainties rub off on David from us."

"Yes, that's right, but he is too intelligent not to know what's going on. I've heard him and Hannah talking about the world situation. You can't hide anything from them. They know exactly what's happening."

"I know, but maybe there's some good news on the horizon."

"Good news?" asked a surprised Leah. "Tell me about that, please. Good news from the original gloom and doomer? You're kidding. What happened?"

"I don't blame you for that, but—where's the war?"

"What do you mean where's the war?"

"Well, think about it," said Ben, "there hasn't been a bullet fired in anger for months. Every now and then, I have a dream that Hitler will mend his ways and tame down his mein Kampf ambitions by realizing he has added territory to his pre-war 'Greater German Empire.' I keep hoping a miracle would be thrown down at him in the form of a lightening bolt from God saying, 'Stop Hitler, That's enough.'"

"You're a dreamer my dear husband. You're living in a delusional state and you know it. Even the newspapers are calling it the Phony War, or Sitzkrieg. True, Hitler hasn't invaded France as expected, but the British navy is fighting to keep supplied from the Atlantic. What is going on is that both sides are trying to negotiate and end to the war that won't embarrass either side. Do you think that will ever be possible since Hitler is so intransigent?"

"Not a chance," answered Ben. "Hitler's ego will not allow him to stop his Mein Kampf road map until it's all finished."

"And don't forget that Britain's terms for ending the war is that Hitler withdraw from Poland. When do you think he'll start?"

"Okay, lady, don't rub it in, he'll withdraw the day the sun doesn't rise. You got me back to reality. Here I am."

"Welcome home.

There was a naval battle that took place in Uruguay, of all places. Three British cruisers chased the German Battle ship, Graf Spee, into Montivideo harbor and the German commander, rather than surrender, scuttled the ship after landing all the sailors on shore.

Here was a British victory," reported Leah.

Ben answered, "Where do you learn all this stuff? A bit of good news, I guess. What about France. Do you think they'll do anything? Germany didn't invade. France didn't attack. They're staring at each other over the border. Heck of a war."

"A military genius I ain't" started Leah...

Ben interrupted, "You would have been if you served in the military a few weeks."

"Ha ha," laughed Leah, "anyhow, France feels safe because they think that the Maginot line is impenetrable. Whether that's true or not, I have no idea."

"Let's hope it'll make Hitler think twice," answered Ben.

CHAPTER 10
ALL OUT WAR
MAY 1940

Germany's economy relied on a steady supply of iron ore from Sweden. The Swedes sent their ore over land to the port of Narvik on the Norwegian coast. The Norwegians then shipped the ore to Germany. As a neutral country, anxious not to anger Hitler, the Norwegian government continued this pre-war approach. This was fine with Hitler who preferred that Norway remain neutral, so as not to involve his troops on another front. This tenuous relationship between Germany and Norway remained until the Norwegian government allowed a British destroyer to board the German transport Altmark carrying British sailor prisoners captured by the Graf Spee in Uruguay. The Norwegians searched the boat and found nothing. The British, not deterred, boarded the boat without Norwegian opposition and found the prisoners. This episode changed Hitler's strategy regarding Norway— he would have to occupy Norway to safeguard this supply route from British interference.

In the meantime, the new British Prime Minister, Winston Churchill, recognizing the vital strategic importance of Norway to Hitler, wanted to take Norway before the Nazis. His government refused, but did allow a mining of Norwegian waters to prevent the iron ore boats from reaching Germany. This act ended the Phony War. The Next day, April 9, 1940, Hitler invaded Denmark and Norway. A helpless Denmark succumbed immediately and by June 10, 1940, Norway capitulated.

At the Same time, Hitler struck at France, Holland and Belgium. He bypassed the Maginot line by outflanking it with a massive panzer (tank) assault through the Ardennes forest, a task thought impossible by France. The Nazis caught the French flat-footed as they raced through Belgium and into France behind the Maginot line. The campaign was a spectacular victory, a repeat of the blitzkrieg or lightening war that forced Poland to surrender.

The second spectacular part of the campaign was the battle of the Belgian Fort Eban Emael, considered by military experts to be impregnable.

Belgium has always had a military disadvantage. Situated between two historic rivals, Germany and France, its fate depended upon the geopolitical vagaries of the times. Germany had always feared a French, British, and Russian military coalition. Therefore, before World War I, the German general staff developed a plan to cut through Belgium. The flat Belgium countryside offered ideal terrain for this purpose. This move would enable them to encircle the French from the rear and prevent the British from rushing to assist the French. At the same time, the necessary units were available to defend the Soviet Eastern front.

When World War I started, Germany demanded that Belgium allow its forces to pass through unhindered. When Belgium refused, Germany struck, smashed through a ring of weak forts, and defeated Belgium in less than two weeks.

In the 1930s, after Hitler assumed power, rejected the armistice and conscripted millions of men for military duty, Belgium decided that they would build an impregnable fortress to prevent the German encirclement strategy through Belgium. The site chosen was at the junction of the Albert Canal and the Geer River. In 1935, after five years of construction, everyone agreed that this was the most impregnable fortress in Europe. A full strength, there were 1,200 officers and men on duty, but on the fateful night of the surprise attack, there were 780 men stationed within the fort.

German paratroopers in gliders landed on the roof of the Fort. It was a surprise precision attack and after 27 hours of vicious fighting, the Belgians surrendered.

The way was now open for German Panzers to surge through the gap created by the fall of Fort Eban Emael. The defenders of the fort became prisoners of war. The fall of this impregnable fortress created the myth of the invincibility of the German army, and Belgian morale sank. The nation soon capitulated.

In Holland, the onrushing Nazis decimated the French Seventh Army and destroyed Rotterdam with a massive German air force (Luftwaffe) terror attack. Thousands of bombs gutted the center of the city. Twenty-five thousand people became homeless, and thousands died. The Dutch commander surrendered his entire army, and Queen Wilhelmina and the Dutch government took refuge in London.

German General Heinz Guderian, attacking through the Ardennes, smashed the French defenses, entered France, and sped through that country as they had through Poland. They cut behind the British, separating them from the French. Britain and France were helpless against the Hitler juggernaut. France was defeated. The day of fixed military forts and defenses ended.

Winston Churchill, the new Prime Minister of Britain, was the only voice that had foretold all that had happened. The appeasers said nothing more. There were those in the British government who had a fear of Soviet Bolshevism and thought their security would be strengthened against this threat if they sidled up to Hitler's powerful Third Reich. With their eyes open, they had sought accommodation with a criminal regime. They had ignored the Nazi excesses, the brutality, the torture and murder, the anti-Semitism and the racism. They had sold out those countries that tried to stand with them in the name of peace. With the fall of France, Britain now stood alone. Would history learn from this experience? Churchill offered his country only "blood, toil, tears, and sweat."

CHAPTER 11

INTROSPECTION

JUNE 1940

Western Europe burns, the future is hazy and uncertain. What better time to have a picnic, meet with friends, hike, fish, relax. There was comfort in association. Even serious discussion went down easier when friends provided input. Ben, Mikhail and respective families were in the forest again and this time they invited Jozef who by now had reunited with his aunt, received identity papers, and worked part time at the Civic building. He never stopped showing gratitude to his two friends who made it all possible. Never in his wildest dreams would Jozef imagine such a smooth transition into a new land. He rather envisioned a partisan-like existence in the forests of Byelorussia. There was peace here, but it was a peace because of a mutually beneficial relationship established between bitter enemies with opposing philosophies—Nazis and Communists. A house of cards is what it was. This thought plagued him on an ongoing basis.

"I thank God, that at least we are living in peace now while the rest of Europe burns," said Leah. "I propose a toast to England in its valiant fight against the Nazis. God grant them victory and an end to this madness." She raised her glass of water.

Ben, Mikhail and Jozef raised theirs. "The phony war was too good to be true, wasn't it," said Ben.

"We have to be realistic," added Mikhail. "This war has barely started. We are in for a long struggle."

"We," said Ben. "You said we, but we are not in this war yet. Are you sure we will be in one?"

Nodding his head yes, Mikhail said, "I am sure, and so are you, Ben, unless you choose to forget Hitler's Mein Kampf and his longing for the East that is such a prominent part of his writing."

Ben smiled and nodded. "Touche, Mikhail, you are right. That's what I said, but every now and then I catch myself in wishful thinking and hope for peace, which every so often rears its beautiful head and drowns out reality—so sad."

"What about you, Jozef?" asked Mikhail.

"What about me?"

"Will we be pulled into this war?"

Jozef's face turned somber and serious and then evolved into anger as he said, "I don't know, But I do know what I will do if there is war that reaches us here." He banged his fist on the table and the glasses shook.

Everyone stared at Jozef. Ben broke the silence. "What is it that you'll do, Jozef?"

Jozef's voice rose to match the fire in his face, and he said passionately, "In 1914 to 1918, the Germans chased me all over Poland. I lost all of my friends. How I survived bombs, shells, bullets could only be by the grace of God. Everything changed for me. Twenty years later, they set out to kill me again. I am alive only through another miracle. I feel as if God has given me a mission. If they come again—I will not move. I stay here and fight to the death. This menace must end for all time. Enough."

In stunned silence Leah, Ben and Mikhael stared in admiration at this impassioned statement made with a voice of determination such as none of them had ever heard. Finally, Leah broke the silence and asked calmly, "How will you fight, Jozef?"

"How? I have no plans now, but I will make my plans day by day depending on the circumstances. For me, every German soldier will be a mission to destroy. My brain will have only one thought and the planning will revolve around it. How can I stop them? How can I kill them? They will understand me loud and clear. They will know who I am."

Silence reigned again until Val, a girlfriend of his, Hannah and David walked up with their collection of fish.

"Good work. Another good fishing day I see," said Mikhail. Then, after a short pause he said, "Val and David and girls, why don't you take Jozef for a little tour of the area here. He hasn't seen any of it yet. We'll prepare the fish." Then he turned to Jozef and said, "Go with them, Jozef, take in the beauty. Show him King Tree and the Knot Hole, Val."

"Sure, dad, we will."

Jozef stood up, nodded his head. "Thank you, Mikhail, I'll do that. I have spent much time in Poland's forest. Let's see if Byelorussian forests are as beautiful."

After Jozef left, the three of them set to work on preparing the fish. Mikahil said, "God in heaven that set me to thinking. Have you ever heard anyone speak with such emotion as Joseph?"

"You're right," said, Ben, "but can you imagine what he just went through, barely escaping death and watching the Nazis annihilate his friends. We might all react like that."

"Leah said, "You can't speak with such intensity and not mean it. He will fight to the death."

Mikhail added, "I agree, Leah. As Jozef was talking, I was thinking—what will I do? How will I react?" The thoughts make me dizzy. I'm not a Communist member of the party. The Nazis will kill Communists just like they will kill Jews. As one who wants Byelorussian independence, the Nazis may see me as someone they would want to collaborate with. As a collaborator, I then have the option of working with them or I could work as a double agent. In either position, I will have enemies and if the Russians win, I would end up on the end of a rope as a collaborator. If the Nazis win, I will end up on the end of a German rope as a spy. These are my options. But there is no doubt, if the Nazis invade Byelorussia, they will have me as an enemy. How and in what way I can be the best enemy is what I have to figure out."

"We have an easier decision in the Frohman family," said Ben. We have no choice. I have no reason not to believe that what Jozef said is happening in Poland will not happen here. So, as a Jew, we face death. I can't imagine any other way to think. God forbid, if the Nazis ever try and conquer the Soviet Union, they will eliminate us. Thinking like that leaves us no choice. My family would have to flee. But that brings up another problem. Where do we go? We have no place. This leaves us taking to the forest where we try to survive by living off the land. I would need help with that. I am not a forester and neither is my dear wife here. This needs to be an organized effort. Can we find any others who will think like this while we are at peace and while the enemy has signed a nonaggression pact with the Soviets? I doubt it. If we resist we will resist one at a time. Then we will have to organize. My head spins at such thoughts. Who could lead such an effort?"

"Perhaps Jozef," said Leah immediately without hesitation or change of expression. Ben's eyebrows lifted at the suddenness and certainty of his wife's words. He said, "Jozef is a fighter. You heard him. He wants to fight."

"He can fight better with other fighters," answered Leah.

After a long thoughtful pause and a nod of his head, Ben said, "There she goes again. One thing I've learned, Mikhail, is to listen carefully when my wife speaks. Wisdom flows from that mouth like a waterfall. I agree that if it would come to opposition from the forest, hit and run tactics, logistics, weapons, Jozef fits the bill better than any of us. Four years in the military fighting bloody battles, a forester, a handyman; what more could we want. We need to talk more—with Jozef."

The German juggernaut rolled through Western Europe. Belgium, Holland and France fell. Denmark capitulated rather than subject their population to aerial destruction, Norway surrendered after a valiant struggle. The Nazis succeeded in cutting off British, French and Belgian troops leaving them surrounded in Dunkirk, France, on the shore of the English Channel. Winston Churchill labeled the war in Western Europe a "colossal military disaster." German forces could have easily wiped out the entire British army, surrounded on three sides with the sea to their backs, but they did not—and some suggest that this failure was the reason Germany eventually lost the war.

The rapid success of the Nazi army was due to the success of Blitzkrieg. In this success, however, lay the seeds of the failure at Dunkirk to remove the threat of the British army. For when the Nazi tank corps completed their headlong rush to the sea and surrounded the British, they arrived exhausted and out of fuel and supplies. They outran their own infantry. They had no choice but to halt, rest, resupply, wait for the infantry to arrive and slowly prepare to finish off the British.

In one of the great stories of warfare, the British mobilized their navy and their citizens with commercial and private boats to launch an amazing sea-born rescue of their stranded troops. It succeeded before the stunned eyes of the Nazis and remains as one of the greatest rescues of all times, saving the British army to fight another day.

CHAPTER 12
GERMAN CONSOLIDATION
BRITISH CONSOLIDATION
1940-41

The "Blitz," starting September 7, 1940 was an effort by the German air force to bomb Britain into submission. The 76 consecutive nights of London bombings resulted in heavy civilian casualties. They also bombed other British cities. Hitler thought he could destroy British morale, forcing them to sue for peace, but a combination of dogged determination, Churchill's leadership and young British pilots turned the tide causing Churchill to make his famous speech..."Never have so many owed so much to so few." Hitler would have to turn his attention elsewhere. Britain survived and stood alone.

As the German juggernaut rolled on, the Soviets, in an effort to establish military defenses against Germany, gave ultimatums to the three Baltic States of Lithuania, Estonia and Latvia. The Russians entered these hapless countries, set up puppet governments, arranged rigged elections and then welcomed the three Baltic countries as members of the Russian consortium of nations, the Union of Soviet Socialist Republics. The chess game was on.

After France fell, the British, worried that the intact French fleet would fall into German hands, gave the French ultimatums: join the

British in the fight against Germany, hand the ships over to Britain, disarm all their ships, scuttle their ships. The French refused all these options. The British then asked that the French sail the ships to the French West Indies and turn them over to the United States, but the French refused this option as well, so the British surrounded the ships and opened fire destroying most of the French fleet as it lay anchored in Oran, Algeria.

Shortly after this episode, Italy invaded British Somaliland, marking the beginning of World War II in Africa. Five weeks later, on September 13, 1940, Italy invaded Egypt and two weeks after that, Germany and Italy signed the Tripartite Pact with Japan making them part of the Axis Powers. The war expanded.

Historians postulate that Mussolini, jealous of Hitler's conquests, wanted to prove that he too could succeed militarily. In an effort to reassert Italian interests in the Balkans, he invaded Greece after the Greek government rejected Mussolini's demand to occupy some Greek territory. Mussolini's army could not cope with a Greek counter attack, forcing an infuriated Hitler to rush to Mussolini's defense. Nazi blitzkrieg was too much for the Greek forces and they surrendered. This operation may have had an influence on the eventual outcome of the war, as it delayed Hitler's secret plans to invade the Soviet Union (Operation Barbarossa) subjecting the German forces to one of the harshest Soviet winters on record and preventing the capture of Moscow.

In the meantime, the war in Africa between the Italians, Nazis and British raged on and by the end of 1940 British troops captured two Egyptian cities from the Italians. At the Same time, Hungary and Romania became a part of the Axis powers by signing the Tripartite Pact, further expanding the war.

CHAPTER 13
OPTIONS OF YOUTH
1941

Their gymnastic practice complete, David met Hannah and Val. The plan was to have some coffee in a local café, enjoy some camaraderie and discuss whatever came up. Gymnastics was a welcome respite in dangerous and uncertain times, and God knows these were such times. The atmosphere in the café was noisy as usual, but the three were lucky to get a somewhat noise protected side corner booth in the short leg of the L-shaped bar. The last months saw the development of a true friendship between them enjoying each other's company molded by clear thinking about the threat facing the country from the perspective of their common ages and an uncertain future.

"Your father has the ear of the Byelorussian officials, Val, what does he have to say about the war? Do they think we'll be in it?" asked David.

"It's mixed," answered Val. Some of the officials say no because Hitler has put his Germany together now and will leave well enough alone. They say he's had a pretty good meal already and if he tries to swallow the Soviet Union, he'll choke to death just like Napoleon did. Others say that he'll definitely attack us and my father says that's based upon intelligence from Poles who sneak over the border between the German and Russian zone of Poland and warn of the big build up of German troops and tanks."

Hannah entered the conversation. "That sounds like pretty good evidence of Hitler's true intentions, don't you think?" David agreed.

"My father says that Stalin is aware of the buildup and he already confronted Hitler with it," said David.

Val quickly added, "And my father said that Hitler explained that he was moving his army out of range of the English bombers. You know that England is fighting back by bombing Germany with their air force."

"Thank God for the English Channel, I guess, because if it wasn't there I'm sure that Hitler would have just continued his march into England and taken it over without much trouble," said David.

"As weak as the British were then, I'm sure you're right," agreed Val. "What do your folks think, David?"

"They're very worried. They fled from anti-Semitism twice already. My father left Russia when he was young because of the pogroms that killed his father. He went to Germany and had it good until Hitler took over. Then he fled again, this time back to Byelorussia. Now the pressure is on because there is talk of Hitler following him again, only now to the Soviet Union. He's beginning to feel paranoid. I hear him talking to my mother. Where could we go now? He says Germany and all Western Europe is out. If Hitler invades here, do we go to Siberia? As a Jew, if he stays where he is, he's sure our lives will be in danger. So I think that he thinks we should stay here and hope it never happens, but if it does, he plans to go into hiding and just try and stay alive until the war would end, hopefully in our favor."

"How about you, Hannah? What does your father say?" asked Val.

"I never hear him saying anything about it. He never likes to talk about the future, but he's the kind of man who will act suddenly when he has to. My guess is he will go in hiding and try and stay alive and keep his family alive, but if he has to fight—I know he will."

"What about you, David. What would you do if the Germans came?" asked Val.

"Right now I think I would hide in the forest with people who know how to live off the land as long as it takes until the end of the war. Whatever happens, I hope all of us will always stay good friends and act together," said David.

"We will," answered Val."

As the young people pondered their options, the British and Italian's war in North Africa continued. Much of Libya came under British control and they captured Mogadishu in what then was Italian Somaliland.

The war centered on who would control the Suez Canal with its access to oil from the Middle East. Britain became dependent on oil the more their military became mechanized.

When Italy invaded Ethiopia in 1935, Egypt, wary of Italian plans for Africa, granted Britain permission to station their troops in their country. This also included Britain and France using Alexandria, Egypt, as a naval base allowing them to control the Mediterranean.

With the onset of World War II, Britain was concerned about Italian intentions in the Mediterranean and Africa. When Hitler invaded Poland, Italy did not declare war, relieving British concerns, but when Germany invaded France, Mussolini, anxious to participate in some of the spoils, declared war against Britain. The equation changed. Britain and Italy were now enemies at war in North Africa and it did not take long for it to heat up. The North African war did not go well for Italy and this forced Hitler to commit his forces. Under the direction of General Erwin Rommel, soon to be known as the Desert Fox, Hitler invaded and confronted the British in what would be a long two-year back and forth struggle until Germany withdrew after their military situation and supply problems across a British-controlled Mediterranean became untenable.

CHAPTER 14
PLANS FOR RESISTANCE
1 JUNE, 1941

"Ben, this is Mikhail, I'm calling you to ask that you meet me as soon as possible, because I have some information that you need to know. It's very important."

"Sure, Mikhail, can you tell me what it's about?"

"Not on the phone, Ben. I need to meet you tonight at 6 o'clock at the café. Jozef will be there too. He was working here today and I already asked him to come."

"I'll meet you there," said Ben with a feeling of dread.

When they all arrived, they sat at a corner table and Mikhail said, "You haven't heard much about the war lately. Things are quiet. Hitler has gotten all he ever wanted in Western and Central Europe. In fact, he got more than he expected—Greece, Yugoslavia, the Island of Crete in the Mediterranean. I believe it has all been to protect his flank for his real prize—the invasion of the Soviet Union."

"You believe or you know, Mikhail?" asked Ben.

"It's not just me talking. This is information that has come to the civic building where I work and it comes right from the mouth of German soldier deserters who escaped from the German controlled part of Poland into the Russian controlled part. They say the next step is an invasion of Russia."

"It is no surprise to me," said Jozef.

"Nor me either if I'm honest with myself," said Ben. "Lately I've been living in a hopeful dream world. Will my family escape this time? How I wish. Then I remember what I told my son, why we had to flee from Germany and come here. I am ready for whatever it takes. I want to keep my family alive and I will do anything to make that possible. We're all in the same boat."

Mikhail added, "You're right about that. Most of the citizens working in the Civic building in Minsk are Communists. They are already making plans. If the Nazis break through, they'll motor to Moscow as fast as their wheels will carry them."

"Like rats leaving the sinking ship," said Jozef waving his fist in the air."

Mikhail answered, "They will tell you they are leaving to get to Moscow to help in the fight. They will tell you they know the Nazis will kill them if they stay."

"In that they are right. That's just what they did in Poland," said Jozef. "Jews, Communists, government officials are all doomed. So they have to run or stay and fight. I say stay and fight. As far as motoring to Moscow to organize against the Nazis, that'll work only if they get to Moscow first before the Nazis do. If they don't, they'll have a nice reception when they find the Nazis there; a bullet in the heart as they stand against a wall, or the hangman's noose." Jozef laughed.

Mikhail nodded his head and smiled. He said, "I thought that in the event the worst happens, we should be making our plans now."

"I agree," said Ben, "What do you think, Mikhail?"

"Well, I'm in a different situation than the two of you," said Mikhail. "You are both in danger. If the reports from Poland are true, you would be lucky to stay alive once they get here. In my case, I'm not a Communist, I'm a Byelorussian independent. The Nazis have no reason to do away with me. In fact, they may want to collaborate with me. Minsk is a big city. The Civic building will be mostly empty if they arrive, and I'm sure the Nazis would use that as headquarters. They'll find many Byelorussians that hate the communists especially in the countryside and it wouldn't surprise me if some of the citizens greet the Nazis as liberators. I can do that too. In that position, I can be a double agent and provide intelligence to you and others in the forest. There will not only be Jews there, there will be other Byelorussian patriots and Soviet army groups. The Nazis will know they are in a fight, but they'll be so busy with the Soviet army they won't have the reserves to deal with partisans. This is not just me talking; this is the consensus of the Minsk leaders in headquarters. I think that could be my role—a double agent. I may be able to learn things that could help the partisans."

"Yes," said Jozef, smiling and nodding his head. "That's a great idea and you could be a valuable source of intelligence for us, but wow, Mikhail, that would be dangerous."

"Nowhere near as dangerous as what Jews will have to go through," answered Mikhail. "How about your role, Jozef," he added.

"I go to the forest the minute I hear that the Nazis have stepped across the border. There I'll wait for all those who will follow, and there will be many. I've been talking to Jews all over the area. Some will stay, some will travel east to stay ahead of the Nazis and some will follow me. There will be hundreds if not thousands, some ready to contribute any way they can, some ready to fight. Those who go with me will need to be ready for all-out war. I envision two things:

one, to fight them with all our strength, and two, to help Jews escape; all kinds of Jews, those who can fight and those who cannot."

"I like your philosophy. We count on you for leadership, Jozef," said Ben.

"You will have it," said Jozef with a fierce look of determination.

"And what is your contribution, Ben?" asked Mikhail

"I and my wife can contribute the most by providing medical care. We'll try to keep us as healthy as possible living in primitive conditions. My children will help. My son is a pre-med student and my daughter who is a teenager will also help. Her mother has educated her in nursing techniques to prepare her for nursing school. We'll contribute in any other way that Jozef believes will be necessary. In how we plan to resist, there can only be one boss. Someone must have the final say." He looked at Jozef and said, "That's you, Jozef."

"My job will be easy," said Jozef, "the job description will have only two sentences: keep us alive and kill Nazis and their plans."

"So, is it settled," asked Mikhail, "you both will go right to the forest?"

"Yes," Ben and Jozef answered together.

"Have you thought about how we will communicate," asked Jozef of Mikhail.

"Not much yet. Do you have any thoughts, Jozef?" answered Mikhail.

"As a matter of fact, I do. The day you had your son show me around the forest near where we met and had a picnic and the youngsters fished and then introduced me to King Tree and the Knothole, I got an idea."

"What was that, Jozef?" asked Mikhail.

"I identified a good location in the forest about a mile or two west of King Tree. It's very dense with very little light getting through.

There's a small crystal-clear spring, which should be enough for water supplies. This may be a good location to stay. We can't communicate by radio because that can always be intercepted, so we need another system. Every few days someone can make the short trip to King Tree and pick up messages placed in the Knothole. How does that sound, Mikhail? Is that possible?"

Mikhail pondered for a moment and then said, "That is a damn good idea. If I learn something of interest, I can bring the message there, put it in a water-proof container and drop it in the knothole."

"If you can do that for sure, Mikhail, we have a way to communicate. We can leave messages in there for you too."

"A two way post office and everything can be mailed for free. Brilliant," said Ben, "Mikhail, I'm reminded about the picture you drew of the knothole that hangs on your wall."

"Yeah, what about it?" asked Mikhail.

"After we set up the post office, that picture in your home is evidence. We can't take any chances."

Mikhail nodded his head and a sly smile crossed his features. "Damn, Ben, you think of everything. What a mind for minutiae. You are right. What I'll do is destroy the picture, and hope that the day will come that I can visit the Knothole and redraw it after we've beaten the Nazis. We'll memorialize it. That will be a day to celebrate. God grant that we will all be around to witness it." He looked toward the heavens. "This was a good meeting. We're as one. I pity the poor Nazis. If they knew that the three of us were organizing resistance against them, they would never dare to invade."

They all laughed. "I like that," said Ben, "a little humor in a threatening situation can never hurt."

"Let's meet here in two days, same time to continue planning," said Jozef.

"One final thing," said Mikhail, "you must be the only two people in the world besides me who know about King Tree and the Knothole. If I'm to have a clandestine role in this, and believe me, I insist on doing it, the three of us must be the only human beings on earth that know about it. How you receive your information while in the forest must remain a mystery forever. I trust you two with my life. As long as I stay in that role, my wife and children will never know. And the same must be true of you, Ben, and you Jozef."

I pledge my life on it, Mikhail," said Ben.

"May Adonai strike me dead if I break this pledge," said Jozef.

Hitler intended to attack the Soviet Union ever since 1923 when he wrote Mein Kampf. For him, the Ukraine breadbasket was the ultimate source of grain that could feed his entire population. He envisioned large well-run farm complexes where the Nazis would live in fortress-like, luxurious enclaves while harvesting and sending the fruits of their labor back to the fatherland.

Hitler knew that the invasion of the Soviet Union had unique problems. The size of the country made blitzkrieg less effective than it had been in the smaller countries of Europe. Supply lines would be longer than any other country. He reasoned that if he could attack in late spring or early summer of 1941, he would have plenty of time to encircle Russian armies and prevent them from retreating into the interior to fight another day. He hoped that a three-pronged attack would capture Moscow, trap the Russian armies in place and end the war long before the vicious Russian winter would stop all forward German movement.

For Joseph Stalin, it was inconceivable that Hitler would attack before 1942 and certainly not before England and France surrendered. France went down to defeat in June of 1940, but England became a bitter pill to swallow as the English Channel and the British air force and Navy stood between conquered France and the White Cliffs of Dover. The British, under the determined leadership of Winston Churchill remained in the war as a prickly thorn in the German foot.

CHAPTER 15
FURTHER PLANS FOR RESISTANCE
8 JUNE 1941

David and Hannah met in the same café after school. He said he wanted to speak with her on an urgent matter. They sat at a table for two, had tea and Hannah said, "What is it, David, you look kind of sad."

David looked at her, smiled and said, "You know me like a book, don't you. I need to tell you about plans my parents made."

"I think I know what you want to tell me," Hannah said. "That's the main topic of the Jewish community nowadays. What are we going to do? Everything comes from rumor and mouth to mouth. You don't see anything in the papers about what the Nazis are doing to Polish Jews, but many Poles who escaped from Poland have plenty to say about it and it isn't good."

David continued, his voice tense; anxiety written on his face. "My father says that the reason you don't see anything about it in the papers is because of the pact between Stalin and Hitler carving up Poland like they did. How would it sound if Stalin announces the friendship pact with Germany while at the same time tells the people what killers they are? He can't do that, and in a country with a dictatorship if he says no word in the newspapers, that's it—nothing.

He speaks the gospel and what he says goes. It's a mess; a chess game between two madmen one of whom knows that war is imminent and is just waiting for the best time to strike while the other one knows the same thing, but wants to stall war as long as possible so he can be better prepared."

"I agree with that. So what were you going to tell me about your parents?" asked Hannah.

David sat back, the anxious expression gone from his face as he explained, "If the Nazis attack, my parents made the decision to hide in the forest and stay there until the war ends. My father met with Jozef Askenazy last week here in the café and they agreed to that. Jozef will head up a Jewish partisan group. He's the one with the most military experience and he's as tough as nails. I'd hate to cross him. Don't forget, Hannah, that news is top secret and not for anyone's ears but ours."

David sat with eyes riveted on Hannah. He took her left hand in his. Hannah stared back and squeezed his hand, her face a sad blank.

"So much for that, Hannah, has your father made any plans?" asked David.

"Not that I know of. I told you how quiet he is. He hasn't said a word about it to me. If he spoke about it to my mother and made any plans, they haven't shared it with me yet. A few weeks ago, I did hear him say that the Nazis would have to be insane to attack us. The Soviet Union is too big for anyone to conquer. He keeps talking about Napoleon who marched in with a half a million men and by the time he completed his march out, he had 20,000 men left."

A sad look crossed David's features as he squeezed Hannah's hand and said, "Remind your father that Hitler will not only march in, he will truck in, tank in, fly in, glide in, parachute in. Times have changed, Hannah, if we're invaded you can't stay here. You and your family put your life on the line if you do. Please, talk to your father. Tell him that if the worst happens, you will all have to follow us into the forest. Your lives are at stake. He must understand. I can't bare the thought of not being with you. I would worry every day wondering if you were alive. You must leave with me, Hannah; I love you with all my heart." And then, after a short pause and unchanged expression, he said, "Marry me now."

The suddenness of David's proposal brought tears to her eyes as she sat up straight, stared at her beloved and choked out sobbing words, "I love you as much, David, but if my parents stay in Minsk, I'd have to stay with them. I know you would understand. Knowing you as I do, I'm sure you would do the same. I have to know what the future will bring first before we marry."

"Yes, I know and you're right, I would do the same, but please try and talk some sense into your father if he's planning to stay. It's all up to him. You know Mr. Gregov; Mikhail, who works in the Civic building, he has information from the top. They are all sure that Hitler will invade soon. The day the Nazis cross the Russian border is the day we'll leave and hide out until we see what happens. If the Nazis win, we stay in the forest. If they don't, we go back home. You and your family come with us. As soon as we set up camp, we'll know our future. Then we'll marry. I'll protect you. We've already got bags packed with clothes and food just in case. Tell me that you and your family will come with," and his voice cracked as he choked on his words, took her hand and kissed her palm.

That same evening, the three men, Jozef, Ben and Mikhail met again at the café. They were there to discuss any progress and further plans. Jozef came prepared with a notebook filled with initials and numbers only he could understand. He showed the notebook to his two associates. Ben commented, "Jozef, I hope you know what this is, but I sure don't. I just see initials and numbers."

"Let me take a look," said Mikhail. He took the notebook, turned the pages and agreed with Ben.

This is all the work I've done in the last week or so. I didn't get much sleep. I understand every initial and every word. I just don't want an enemy to understand it in case they capture the book. I visited about fifty Jewish families I am sure I can trust, most I've met before, some I haven't, but I advised them all to flee with us if the Nazis attack. After I told them what happened to me in Poland, I got about thirty of the families to agree. I spoke with many and if they all keep their promise, we will have plenty of talent to help us build our shelters and defend us, cook, sew and whatever else we need. I collected eight rifles, lots of bullets and even some explosives. I spoke to a pharmacist who told me he'll come with plenty of medicines and medical supplies."

"That's great, Jozef, we have some too," interrupted Ben.

"Bring all you can," said Jozef.

"I will. And I'm hoping to build a little area in the forest where I can examine patients and do some medical and surgical work in private," said Ben.

"That should be no problem, Ben, we'll have plenty of wood to work with plus I know at least one carpenter with all his tools who will be with us."

"It just occurred to me that I know where the army garrison has their munitions," said Mikhail.

"Is it possible to get in that facility?" asked Jozef.

"I'll ask some questions of some good friends and see what I can find out," said Mikhail.

"Are you sure you can do that without arousing suspicion," asked Jozef.

"Yes, I'm sure because these are Communists who have the same plan we have, and that is to get the hell out of Minsk. Only they will go to Moscow while we squirrel in the woods. I'm sure they would rather that partisans get the weapons if the Russian army fails. They already told me that if Germany invades and gets close to Minsk and forces us to retreat, they plan to leave some soldiers here who will do just what we plan to do, flee into the forest, set up a resistance movement, harass the Nazis all they can, interrupt supplies, blow up trains, blow up bridges, and kill, kill, kill to quote them. I said, don't you think that the Jews should do the same thing? Their answer was, 'they better, because their lives won't be worth a kopek if they don't.' Then I said, would you help the Jews if they become partisan fighters too? They said if the Jews are serious and they plan to fight and prove it, sure we would help. The enemy of our enemy is our friend you know. I thought that was encouraging. What do you think, Jozef?"

A smiling Jozef said, "That's good news, Mikhail, but I will be wary at the start. We have to concentrate first on organization and planning." Then he paused and spoke almost in a whisper, his face showing no emotion, his head down. "Once we're ready, believe me we'll show them what we can do. I have forty-nine friends in Poland and all the Jews to avenge who have suffered and died so far. That is my life's work now." Then he picked his head up, looked at Mikhail and said to him, "Do you think that those who believe in Byelorussian independence will take to the forest and fight the Nazis?"

"Some will and some will wait to see and some will greet the Nazis as liberators, because they like to believe that the Nazis will allow independence as long as there is no Communism," answered Mikhail.

"Have any independents approached you to join them?" asked Jozef.

"Never. They know I have a close association with Communists where I work, so they stay clear of me."

"That's good, Mikahil." And with a broad smile Jozef added, "You are the perfect double agent. And King Tree and the Knothole will be a great help too."

When Ben arrived back home he never expected to hear what he heard from his son. David, after gathering his mother and father around the kitchen table, said, "I asked Hannah to marry me today."

Ben and Leah looked at each other in shocked surprise. Ben responded after accepting the fact that what he heard from his son was the truth even though the timing of David's proposal was beyond comprehension. "David—now when we are facing what may be a struggle for our lives."

"Yes, mom and dad, that's exactly why I did it. It will be a struggle for Hannah's life and her family's life too. As long as I will struggle and she will struggle, I feel it's my duty to struggle with her and protect her. I love her and she loves me."

"Oh my God, oh my God," moaned Leah, head bowed and hands in front of her face. When she regained her composure, she looked up at David over her fingertips and said, "What did she say when you asked her?"

"She didn't answer because she doesn't know what her parents have planned. She said her father never talks about it and she doesn't know what they will do if the Nazis invade. I tried to tell her that if there is an invasion, their lives will be in danger, something you know, Dad, through personal experience and for sure, Jozef knows. She said, as much as she wants to marry me, she couldn't abandon her family if they decide to stay in Minsk. That's the kind of woman she is. I could do nothing but agree with her and understand, because I would do the same thing. But how could I let her stay here, how could I leave without her?" he said holding back tears.

Leah went over to her son, put her arms around him and hugged him.

David said, "Dad, do you think you know Hannah's father well enough to talk to him and let him know the danger his family faces if they stay here."

"I know him, but not well and I think it will be too obvious if I just went over there to speak with him about leaving Minsk if the Nazis invade. It would be better maybe if we invited the Brunstein family over to our home as part of a social gathering where we would let him know our plans to leave, and try to put the same idea in his head. What do you think, Leah?"

"Yes, I like that. It would be a better approach."

"Could we invite Jozef here too?" asked David. He could convince anyone."

"I'm sure that's true, but I think that might be too obvious. I would rather this be for our two families because of your serious relationship with Hannah. We all know that you two will marry some day. What no one ever figured is that you would ask her now while we are facing the problem of our lives. I don't say that in anger, David, I understand what you did and I sympathize with it. I can only hope that it will turn out to be a brilliant move on your part that will end with her father making the right decision."

"Let me call Mrs. Brunstein," said Leah. "I'll invite the whole family to come for dinner. "We'll get to know them better and tell them about our plans. That might draw out what he's thinking. After dinner, keep Hannah and Emily out of the room, David. We'll leave it to your dad to speak with Mr. Brunstein alone."

"I will, mom, I love you both."

Leo Brunstein and his wife Miriam were both orthodox Jews—
not in their dress, except for the constant Yarmulke (Yiddish for
skullcap) perched upon his head, but in their religious practices. Leo
was forty-five years of age and had been a tailor all his adult life.
His wife, Miriam, three years younger, was also orthodox. Hannah
initially offered opposition to her parents' orthodoxy, but decided that
for the sake of household harmony she would keep her opposition to
herself and go along with her parents sincere, unchangeable heartfelt
beliefs.

David warned his mother that the Brunstein family was strictly
kosher. This was no problem as she already kept two sets of dishes,
one for dairy products and one for meat and never mixed the two in
one meal. He told his mother to be sure and tell the Brunsteins that
this was indeed the case in their household. To make certain that
Hannah's family would show up, he told Hannah to be sure and tell
her parents that the Frohmans kept kosher.

Leo was a short, somewhat stocky man with a salt and pepper
beard and olive complexion. His wife was the same size with pitch-
black hair covered with a babushka. She had a light complexion in
sharp contrast to her husband. Void of any make up, she needed none
on her clear blemish-free attractive face. Her daughter, Hannah,
looked just like her, words they heard often from stranger and friend
alike.

Leah called the Brunsteins and spoke with Leo's wife, Miriam.
Together they made arrangements for the get-together.

The Brunsteins arrived and when they sat down at the dinner table,
Ben said, "Leo, will you give us the honor of saying the Hamotzi?"

Leo nodded his head, stood up and sang in a voice that startled
the Frohmans with its rich baritone, "Baruch Atah Adonai Eloheinu

Melech Haolom Hamotzi Lechem Meen Haaretz—Blessed are you oh God King of the Universe who brings forth bread from the earth."

"Leo, that was beautiful. Now my children know how the Hamotzi is supposed to sound," said Ben.

"Thank you," answered Leo.

"You could have a career as a cantor. I'm amazed," declared Ben.

"The cantor we have in our synagogue makes me sound like a chicken," answered Leo.

They laughed.

Ben was sure to have a plentiful supply of red wine available. He wanted his guest loosened up, as he hoped to speak with him alone and see what he could learn about his intentions in the face of a possible German invasion. It was clear to Ben that Hannah had never mentioned David's proposal probably not wanting to influence her father. Leah and Miriam sat around the kitchen table, Ben and Leo sat in the dining room with a small bottle of wine.

Ben said, "I'm glad that you and your family could make it here tonight, Leo. In this day and age, with the threats we face we may not see each other again and I wanted to get together at least once so we can say our goodbyes."

A surprised Leo looked at Ben in a quizzical manner for a few seconds before he said, "Goodbye? Are you going somewhere?"

This was his lead. It was easier to get to the subject than Ben thought. He sighed and said, "We don't want to go anywhere, Leo, we love it here, but we believe the Nazis will invade us soon. In our case, we have run from anti-Semitism two times already: from Russia-Poland to Germany and Germany to now Byelorussia in the Soviet Union. This time we will not run, there is no place to run anymore, but we will hide. Yes, we have decided as a family to hide, because if we stay, to put it bluntly, they will kill us. They are already killing Jews in Poland, you know."

"Yes, I have heard that too, but I have also heard that Jews that can be useful they will not kill. You are a doctor. Why would they kill you? They need such talent. I am a tailor. I have heard that they have set up tailor shops to make and repair clothes and uniforms." Then Leo's face tuned even more serious and he said, "But where will you hide?" "We'll go into the forest where we'll stay alive by living off the land. This war will not last forever."

"It will if the Nazis win," said Leo raising both hands in the air.

Ben countered, "That's why we have to hide. Many of us will fight the Nazis. We have to do everything to make sure they don't win. I for one, even if they guaranteed they would keep me and my family alive, would rather die than work for them as a privileged Jew while they are killing other Jews." This was blunt and perhaps a snub against Leo and Ben knew it, but he wanted to make certain that Leo understood where he was coming from and also he hoped to influence him to go into hiding.

Leo, taken aback by this thought remained silent for a time, but then said, "Hide? Can you hide from the Nazis? They will come into the forest and wipe you out."

"We've discussed that. We think they'll have enough on their hands with the Soviet army, so they won't waste resources hunting a bunch of civilians in the forest," said Ben. Besides, I'm told that with their style of fighting they are comfortable in the wide-open spaces. That's where they excel. They are not comfortable in unknown forests where partisans will be used to the land and built their defenses."

Leo nodded his head, a slight smile on his face. "How does one eat kosher in the forest?" Then he laughed.

Ben smiled. "Under such circumstances, God will forgive you, Leo, just like he forgives the sick who can't fast on Yom Kipper. Seriously, have you thought about it? What will you do?"

Leo answered, "I think I will do what I have always done, and that is to pray everyday that we are not invaded. What lunatic will invade a country that stretches from one end of the world to another? Even Hitler isn't that stupid."

How do I break through such resistance, thought Ben? "But what will you do if he does invade?"

"I don't worry about possibilities," said Leo without looking at Ben.

Hannah was right, thought Ben. How will I ever tell David? What'll he do? It was clear to Ben that Leo was uncomfortable about the questioning. He would change the subject. "We love your daughter, Leo. She is a beautiful and brilliant girl. Our David is a lucky man."

"Thank you, thank you, we feel the same way about David."

After the Brunstein family said their goodbyes and left, David asked his father, "What did you learn, Dad? Did Mr. Brunstein say anything about their plans if there is an invasion?"

"I couldn't get anything out of him. He doesn't think there will be an invasion. He said only a lunatic would dare to invade a country that 'stretches from one end of the world to the other.'"

David struck his left palm with his right fist and said, "Damn, Hannah was right, he never makes plans in advance. He only acts when he's pushed. What can I do?"

"I don't know what to tell you. I only know that I couldn't budge Mr. Brunstein. If they don't come to the forest with the other Jews, you may have to wait until after the war to marry Hannah"

David's anguished look matched his voice as he said, "Who knows if we will be alive after the war."

The next morning, anxious to speak with Hannah, David showed up at her home. Hannah's father was at work; her mother was at home. David accompanied Hannah to a neighborhood grocery store, a weekly chore for groceries, one of her many responsibilities.

David said, "I wanted to talk to you about what happened yesterday at my house."

"I think I know what you're going to say, David. My father told us about your father's decision to leave for the forest if the Nazis invade."

"What did your father say about it?" asked David.

"He said that he thought that your father was basing his decision on bad past experiences and he could understand that, but at the same time he thought that he was too hasty because the Nazis, if they come, will be too busy with the Soviet army to deal with civilians. He thinks we would have plenty of time to decide the best course of action."

"Time will tell who is right," said David. "If I'm in the forest and you stay in Minsk, maybe I can come visit you every so often."

"We better see how things sort themselves out, before we make any plans," answered Hannah.

"I know. You're right as usual. We play it by ear at the start, but you can be sure I'll figure out a way to keep in touch with you," said David.

"Where will you be? Have you all decided yet?"

"You know the location of King Tree and the Knothole. From there if you walk about a mile or two north. That is where we plan to set up. We may have thirty families there to start according to Jozef. If the Soviet army has to retreat, they'll leave soldiers to form partisan detachments to harass the Nazis. By the way, don't say anything to anybody about the Forest location."

"I will not, David, you can be sure. I guess our plans to be doctors will have to wait, won't they."

"Yes, we'll have to wait while we concentrate on trying to stay alive and doing what we can to help defeat our enemy." Then he stared at her lovingly, saying, "I want to spend the rest of my life with you, Hannah."

She looked at David with tears welling up in her eyes, and put her arms around him and hugged him tight. "And I want that too, David."

CHAPTER 16

BARBAROSSA AND THE FALL OF MINSK

22 JUNE, 1941

German Generals were fearful of a two-front war and counseled Hitler against taking such action, but Hitler, always mindful of his Mein Kampf plans, launched Operation Barbarossa on April 22, 1941. At 3:00 a.m., three million men in 140 divisions, 3,400 tanks and 2,770 aircraft poured across the Russian border in three groups: Army Group North, Army Group Center and Army Group South. Army Group North included Finns, anxious to recapture the territory taken by the Soviets in 1940. The Soviet army was ill prepared, therefore the German assault sped forward as Army Group North headed for Leningrad, Army Group Center charged toward Smolensk and Moscow, its purpose at this early date was not to reach Moscow, but was to protect the flanks of North and South. Army Group South with Hungarian and Rumanian elements headed for Kiev in Ukraine.

There was joy in Berlin as the onrushing Nazis and their allies overran the unprepared, uncoordinated Soviet army.

Early in the morning of 22 June when the Frohmans awakened, they heard the news on the radio: the Nazis invaded. Shocked, but not surprised, Ben told his family to collect all the pre-packaged supplies they gathered for this contingency and get ready for their exodus to the Minsk forest.

"I'll go to the hospital, orient Doctor Vorashilov to my hospitalized patients, and tell them we're leaving. This should take about an hour and when I get back, we'll leave. The hospital administration already knows of our plans to go in hiding. They already heard it from many of the Jewish employees and they understand."

Leah, David and Emily tended to business with wordless efficiency, getting ready for the long trek. If the Nazis succeed and capture Minsk, the Frohman's will be ready to do Jozef's bidding. If the Nazis were defeated, they would return. Better safe than sorry was the byword for this exodus. Their life made a sudden drastic turn. They had no choice. David tended to his assigned responsibilities, all the time thinking of Hannah and holding back tears while wondering if he would ever see her again. He could not let this saddest day of his life interfere with the course of action his family decided to take. Emily, who had grown into a much more stable and confident teenager, silently went to work. She completed all her assigned tasks and pronounced, "I'm ready Momma."

The Brunstein family heard the news as well. Surprised by the rapidity of this German decision, Leo said nothing prompting Hannah's question, "What will we do, father?"

He answered without hesitation, "We stay here and see what happens. The Nazis may take many months to travel through Poland and much of Byelorussia. We have plenty of time to be able to know if they make any progress."

"David told me his father said they sped through Europe with their Blitzkrieg in days, so why won't they do that now."

Confidently, Leo answered, "Because our army has the advantage of knowing the German tactics by now. I can't believe they would not have figured out a defense to stop them."

He's not ready to make a decision, Hannah thought, but she said, "I pray you're right, father."

Jozef heard the news on the radio and with his aunt's blessing packed his aunt's horse with munitions and supplies, his backpack with clothes and miscellany. He had asked his aunt to go with him should it be necessary to leave, but at age seventy-two, chronically ill and a widow, she deferred rather than be a burden to her nephew. "You've got important work to do, Jozef, I will only get in the way and I couldn't make the trip if I wanted to. What would the Nazis want with a sick old lady?" she laughed.

Jozef kissed his aunt and said, "After we kill them, I will come back for you, Tante Rosa. May Adonai watch over you."

"I will wait right here with one of Adonai's angels," she smiled. As it turned out, Tante Rosa's angel took her to heaven within a few weeks, thus sparing for her the horror of the drama that would soon play out for Byelorussian Jews.

Twelve of the thirty other families Jozef contacted joined him on the trek to the forest. The others will follow, he thought. Jozef and his group were the first to arrive followed in two hours by the Frohman family. Within six hours the other families, who promised Jozef they would join him, arrived. The Jozef partisan group started existence with thirty-one Jewish families or 122 individuals, including sixteen children less than ten years of age. My work will not be easy, Jozef thought. There's enough food for about a week. What happens in the war will determine how we will get more.

Just as Mikhail had said, as soon as the Minsk Communist government officials learned of the German attack, they fled north to

Moscow in their automobiles to join the war against the 'Fascist dog.' This left an empty building with Mikhail the only one remaining. Mikhail's first task would be to start their communication scheme known only to the three of them: Jozef, Mikhail and Ben. He printed, in bold letters, GOD GRANT US VICTORY, put the note in a small waterproof metal box, took the long walk to King Tree after dark and placed it in the Knothole.

Unbeknownst to the Brunsteins,

the German army raced toward Minsk. On 24 June, two days after the land invasion, three waves of forty-seven aircraft each bombed Minsk. The bombing damaged the infrastructure with the center of the city suffering massive property destruction and loss of life.

The Brunsteins were lucky. Their home, at the periphery of the town center, escaped damage, their lives spared.

A frightened Hannah said, "Does this change your mind any, father?"

Leo, visibly shaken, said, "I had no thought of airplanes. I should have though. This is a different war. Death can come to you out of the sky in an instant."

"Everybody in Minsk is leaving," said Hannah. "We should go too, or better yet, we should follow the Frohmans into the forest. They won't bomb the forest." She hoped that the realization of the bombing, which seemed to come as a surprise to her father would change his mind, but his answer told her otherwise.

Leo, in a slow and deliberate voice, answered, "We will not live like squirrels in the forest. We will go with all the others and find the Soviet army. They will give us protection and shelter."

An exasperated Hannah, knowing her fathers intransigence, dared to say with ever-increasing emphasis, "The Russian army won't give us shelter. They have one job now and that's to fight the Nazis to the death. Civilians just get in their way. They won't help us. They can't help us."

This only increased Leo's resolve. "You will listen to your father, girl!"

Hannah stiffened. Her first thought was, I'll go to David, but no sooner had she thought it, than she realized she could not leave her family. "Yes, father," she answered and picked up her backpack.

They joined a long column of Jews escaping the Nazis. They were alone on a dirt road. It was a long and difficult trek. They marched six hours and rested one. By midnight, they slept in the fields out of sight of the road. After several days, they stopped when in the distance they could see troops marching toward them. When the distance closed, the troops stopped marching and stood with automatic weapons at the ready. They realized finally—the troops were the enemy, a large detachment of paratroopers who had jumped in East of Minsk! Their uniforms were clean suggesting that they had not been in combat. One would have thought that they were ready for a parade. The commander of the troops marched toward the standing line of Jews, one arm holding his weapon pointed at them. He stopped when he was within ten feet of Leo who stood spellbound at the realization that Nazi troops were already past Minsk and this far into Byelorussia. The commander approached as the Jewish column stood trembling and silent. The commander saw Leo's Yarmulke, turned, looked at his troops, pointed to Leo and then pointed to his own head.

"Where from?" the Nazi officer asked in a pleasant conversational tone, albeit a broken Russian.

"Minsk," answered the trembling Leo.

"Go back Minsk. The war is kaput. No more Soviet army. We treating you good."

The standing Jews stood spellbound, looked at each other, turned around and walked back in the direction from which they had come. Leo and Hannah did not look back, but wondered if they would hear gunshots marking their last day on earth. The seconds passed without bullets and Hannah braved a glance back and could see smiling Nazis looking at them as they retreated.

We treating you good, thought Hannah. What could this mean? Were these men making a macabre joke?

CHAPTER 17
REALITY
JULY, 1941

A veteran of World War I and the Russian Civil War, Dmitry Pavlov had a distinguished career in the Russian Army. As a military advisor, he also fought in the Spanish Civil War in 1936-37, earning the honor of the title Hero of the Soviet Union. In 1940, he became commander of the Byelorussian front, receiving the rank of General of the Army, the second highest army rank possible. None of this would come to his rescue, however, after the Nazis defeated the troops under his command and captured Minsk in six days. Stalin ordered him to stand trial. Found guilty on July 22, 1941, justice was swift; Pavlov was shot and buried the next day. This was Stalin's way of letting his generals know that cowardice in the face of the enemy meant death

After Stalin died in 1953, the army exonerated Pavlov in 1956 due to 'lack of evidence.'

The Jews that marched with the Brunsteins were the exception in Byelorussia the year of 1941. Under Godless Communism for many years, Byelorussia prevented organized worship and promoted integration of the Jewish Community into Byelorussian society. Most Jews followed this secular path, living fully integrated amongst their Christian neighbors. Some, like the Brunsteins, did not take this route, but kept to themselves and adhered to the orthodox Jewish tradition. Many of them had personal experiences with anti-Semitism in other countries and were more wary about the potential of a German invasion. Others were naïve, never believing that Hitler would break the pact with Stalin. The World War that was raging in Western Europe would never reach them and was a matter for others to be concerned about. Some of the older Jews remembered World War I German soldiers who treated the civilians with kindness, and could not believe the horror stories that rumor presented as real.

The Brunsteins returned home exhausted after their long trek. Their home was still intact, spared the destruction of central city property lost to the indiscriminate bombing. They were alive and together, having avoided the fate of many Minsk citizens with the onset of war. They hoped that the worst was over, but it was not to be, as the

Nazis and some of their Eastern European allies, anxious to prevent resistance, incarcerated all Minsk area men ages fifteen to forty-five. The men, Jewish and non-Jewish, knew what could be in store for them. They had lots to think about, surrounded by barbed wire in a large open field exposed to the hot sun with no food and water.

Leo Brunstein, one of the prisoners, had plenty of time to relive the errors of his thinking, but still clung to the hope that this was temporary until such time that the Nazis would learn of his usefulness as a tailor. What he did not understand was that the Nazis were intent on weeding out Jews that were useful tradesmen, intellectuals or professionals, for these were sources of an intelligent opposition, a dangerous threat to the occupiers.

Miriam Brunstein and Hannah, plus other relatives of the imprisoned men could visit, so they smuggled food and water to the men behind the wire.

The prisoner's frustration knew no bounds. The reason for the imprisonment, and the future fate of the men remained a mystery, as their questions were unanswered.

By the fourth day, the Nazis separated Jews from non-Jews in their barbed wire enclave. One day the visiting relatives found only barbed wire surrounding an empty field. The absence of her father sent Hannah into a controlled panic. What no one knew was that the non-Jews were sent back to their families, and the Jews were put on trucks and driven to the outskirts of Minsk where they were taken to pre-dug pits, told to stand on the edge and shot.

Leo was one of those driven there by truck, heard the shots in the distance and when he arrived and saw the pre-dug pits half filled with bloody bodies, he understood the errors of his thinking and knew his fate. With sorrow, emotion and his mind filled with images of his wife and child, he looked toward heaven, a rich baritone ringing out over the pit. Shema Yisrael Adonai Elohenu Adonai Echod—Hear Oh Israel The Lord Our God The Lord Is One—the last words a pious Jew said before death. At least he had time to sing the Shema, he thought, as the shots rang out and he fell dead into the pit.

Mr. Brunstein represents Jews who were shot to death and buried in a pre-dug pit, and there were many.

A friend of the Brunstein family, Abel Stolar, was also in the barbed wire enclave. Placed on the same truck with Leo, he arrived at the pit where he listened to Leo singing when the shots rang out. He felt a burning pain on the right side of his neck and fell conscious into the pit. Several men landed on top of him making conditions ideal to hide the fact that he survived. Still as death, he looked out of the corner of his eyes at Leo lying with mouth and eyes open with a bullet wound that shattered the rear and side of his head. Daring not to stir, Abel feigned death and felt himself half covered over with dirt by men shoveling on the rim of the pit. He lay there surrounded by dead bodies until well past dark when he crawled out of the pit into a grass-covered field and back to the outskirts of Minsk. This twenty-year old man would make two stops before he would flee into the forest. He knew now that remaining in Minsk was a death sentence for Jews.

Abel Stolar represents some fortunate Jews who fell wounded into the killing pits, feigned death and miraculously escaped.

Abel had always been in perfect health, but this near-death experience, preceded by four days of dehydration and starvation, weakened him considerably. His dark blue eyes shrunk, his tongue was dry and an attempt to say a few words aloud was difficult. What he would give for a drink of water. He found walking had changed; light-headedness forced him to pause, get on his hands and knees for a time before he could get up. He had large musculature on a five feet six inch frame, but they ached and for the first time they did not seem to follow commands. The Brunstein home was on the path toward his house, so he stopped there first. He knocked on the front door, awakened the family and Miriam Brunstein came to the door. When she saw who it was she said, "Abel, what's wrong? What happened? Look at your neck."

"It's just a flesh wound. I came here to give you some news, but would you please give me a glass of water," he said as he stumbled to the kitchen table."

He downed it almost in one gulp and asked for more. When he finished, Abel said, as Miriam and Hannah stood nearby, "They've killed many Jews. I was shot and played dead and managed to escape, but not before I saw what happened to Leo."

"What?" screamed Miriam. Hannah stiffened and she felt as if her head had disconnected from her body as she waited for what she knew she would hear; her father was dead.

Through tears and a cracking voice, Abel said, "They trucked in loads of Jews to pre-dug pits. They shot them all. They killed Leo while he was singing the Shema." He broke down in uncontrolled sobs, the tears flowing down his cheeks.

"Oh, my God," Miriam wailed. Hannah stood stone faced with eyes closed and fists clenched staring at the floor.

After a moment of silence, Abel said, "If I could just rest for a few more minutes, then I'll go home, get my parents and hide in the forest. I know partisans are there. They'll fight to stay alive. You can't stay here. We have to join them."

"I know where there is a group that is already there," whispered Hannah still staring downward.

This seemed to wake Abel up. "Where?" he said.

Feeling it was safe to give Abel the location—Hannah did just that. "When will you leave, she asked"

"It'll probably take a few more hours for my parents to get ready. I'll rest, eat and drink more. We'll go tonight while it's still dark. If I were you, I'd also go. The rumors from Poland were all true. They're doing the same thing here."

Hannah continued, "When you meet the group in the forest, please ask for David Frohman, tell him what happened to my father, and tell him that Hannah and family will be joining them soon." No sooner had she finished than she looked at her mother. Her mother looked at Hannah without saying a word. Hannah knew that her mother's silence meant agreement.

"David Frohman," said Abel. "Yes, I'll give him the message. I'm sorry I had to be the bearer of such bad news. I have to go now. God bless you and I expect to see you soon."

After Abel left, Hannah said to her mother, "When will we leave, mother?"

Miriam, her face like a death mask, did not answer.

"Mother," repeated Hannah, we have to go now."

"You have no papa anymore," she moaned, "no papa—anymore." They cried and huddled together for solace.

They had a restless sleep and it was 10:00 a.m. before they awakened. They had a small breakfast. Their plan was to pack food and other valuables and leave for the forest after dark late in the evening when the streets are empty. Before they could start packing, a loud knock on the front door startled them. When they opened the door, their hearts sank, for standing there were armed Nazis and others who announced that they had one hour to pack no more than five liters of hand luggage apiece because, "You have to move." These four words, said in a loud, authoritarian voice, left no room for questioning or stalling.

By sundown that day, they became residents of a Jewish square-mile ghetto in a small home with a dozen strangers all marked, as they were, with a yellow Jewish star on the left upper front and back of their clothes. Hannah was torn with double grief: she was at least with her mother in their hour of need, but her hoped for meeting with David at this time was not to be—and would it ever?

The days passed, and as the conditions deteriorated, escape was always on Hannah's mind. It soon became evident that there would not be enough food to sustain life. Her mother became depressed. Those who attempted to escape from the ghetto did so at the risk of their lives. The guards shot any ghetto resident found outside of the barbed wire that surrounded their prison.

In a matter of weeks, meager provisions ended. They bartered clothes and shoes for whatever food was available. The struggle for existence became all encompassing. Some banded together for emotional support, while others retreated into their own thoughts. Those who chose to isolate themselves did not last long. Some of them would sit in a corner, staring, not eating, not thinking and unmoving until death.

Weight loss was slow and steady. They began to notice changes in their bodies. Bone surfaced through diminishing muscle. Ribs became easily palpable. Shoulder blades poked out of thinning skin, and backbones took on the appearance of a row of beads. Desperate need cried out from the sunken eyes of children who would wait in stony silence for watery soup. All one could do was work and struggle to stay alive. There was nothing else. No recreation, no music. A book was a treasure passed on from person to person. At least one could enter another world in the written pages.

Surely if we stay here any longer, we will die. Escape, in spite of the risk, became an option, thought Hannah. There were areas under the barbed wire that ghetto residents would crawl through to barter or beg for food with outside residents. Guards killed some who left and killed others when they returned. Others succeeded in their mission. It became a game of Russian roulette, but since a slow death was inevitable, especially as Typhus became a risk in the ghetto, more inhabitants made the attempt. We must get to David, she thought.

CHAPTER 18
PARTISAN BEGINNINGS
JULY, 1941

Abel Stolar left the Brunsteins feeling better after the short rest and fluids. He arrived at his home, greeted his worried parents, told them about his narrow escape, and convinced them to leave with him for the forest. Thanks to Hannah, he knew where to go. His parents, already worried about the deteriorating conditions for Jews, were easy to convince, now that their beloved son was well. His mother tended to the flesh wound on his neck, thanking God, that the bullet missed vital structures. "God has a mission for you," she cried, "he guided the bullet so you wouldn't be killed."

They packed as large a supply of food and clothes as they could carry and set their sights on joining the partisans. Leaving at 2:00 a.m. in the pitch dark of a cloud-filled sky, they arrived at their destination eight hours later, exhausted but grateful for their successful journey. They knew when they reached their destination because a large black bearded man dressed in knee high boots, pant bottoms within the boots, a beat-up khaki jacket and armed with a rifle pointed at them stepped out from behind a tree and said, "Halt. Identify yourselves."

"I have a message for David Frohman. Is he here?" asked Abel.

"Yes, he is, but my instructions are to bring any new recruits or anyone who comes here, to the commander first."

"That's fine. It's good to be among friends."

The guard led the Stolar family to Jozef who was sitting on a large rock talking to three other men. The Stolar's, looking in all directions, noted the various stages of construction of shelters and other unknown structures. No doubt, the occupants were organizing for the long haul. Jozef asked the same question he asked of all new recruits, "Why are you here?"

"I speak for myself," said Abel, "I want to fight against the Nazis. They're killing Jews now." Then Abel told his story about his miraculous escape from sure death. Jozef and the three men, with faces of stone, listened in rapt attention as Abel's mother rung her hands with eyes closed, silently thanking God.

"You've come to the right place," said Jozef. "We're growing. We plan to fight and give refugees shelter. With your experience, It sounds to me like you want revenge, and you'll get every opportunity here."

"After what I witnessed, all I have on my mind is revenge," answered Abel.

"You'll have your chance if you're a good student willing to learn."

"I'll do my best, sir. As long as the Nazis do what they are doing, I'll fight them to the death." Then he paused before he asked, "Is there a David Frohman here? I have a message for him?"

A happy David received the news that Hannah and her parents would arrive soon, but the happiness turned to sorrow when he learned of Hannah's father's fate.

Turning his attention to the subject of Hannah, David said, "If you saw her yesterday, then she should be here today,"

"That's what I believe," said Abel.

Neither one of them knew at this time that Hannah, her mother and all other Jews were behind barbed wire in what would soon become a struggle for life itself.

As time passed, other Jews joined the partisans, but not Hannah and her mother. David became distraught. The arriving Jews brought with them word of the ghetto with its imprisoned Jews. That's why Hannah never showed up, thought David. He gave his parents the bad news.

When Jozef retrieved messages from King Tree and the Knothole, he found two of them: The first saying GOD GRANT US VICTORY and the second with the news of the Jewish ghetto, its location, the gradual disappearance of Jews, its size, the number of ghetto inhabitants, the barbed wire, the guards, and a warning of a ghetto genocide in progress. Mikhail was very detailed with his information.

David asked that his father accompany him to speak with Jozef. Ben said, "Why do you want me to go with you to speak to Jozef? What are you thinking, David?"

"I'm thinking of Hannah and her family and all the other Jews and what can be done to rescue them."

"I'll go with you, David, but were just a small organizing group. I know we're not ready for any military-like action yet."

"I know, dad, but I can't rest until I find out if there's anything I can do."

Granted an audience with Jozef, the information only served to depress David and Ben. Jozef said, "A rescue in the ghetto at this time is out of the question. There are 100,000 Jews in a square mile of space. They're living like sardines in a can and are starving to death. Every so often, some of them disappear. They take them out and shoot them all, men women and children. The Jews are fenced in with barbed wire and they shoot on sight anyone caught trying to escape. Only the army could help, but they've retreated to fight another day—at least we all hope. Right now, we're concentrating on growing and collecting supplies and ammunition to get ready for the day when we can start killing those bastards. Not only the fate of the Jews, but the fate of the world is at stake. In short, David, we aren't ready to help you with a rescue. If we would fail, it would set us back or even end what we are trying to do. I hope you understand."

Ben thought how hard it is to forget the individual for the sake of a greater goal. David, his mind racing, said nothing, but the next day he sought out Abel only to discover what he feared: Abel met Hannah in her home, but now she was in the ghetto living with others and Abel had no idea where in the square mile she was.

David's thoughts of a solo rescue offered obstacles to success that he could not overcome. In the next few days, while his mind was racing with the mixed emotions of depression and hatred, Jozef came to him and said, "There are two new recruits who came in about 5:00 a.m. and they want to talk to you."

"About what?" asked David.

"Come with me. I'm not sure, but they seemed anxious and they're beat from escaping from the ghetto—some of the lucky ones."

When Jozef and David arrived, he was shocked to see one brother who was a classmate of his and the other brother, younger, who he knew of, but never met. The younger brother, exhausted, was already asleep on the ground. David said to his classmate, "It's good to see you, Eli." Jozef said, "You wanted to talk to us? What's it about?"

"I escaped from the ghetto, but I have news of Hannah," said Eli.

David could see the rapidity by which Eli's facial expression changed from the excitement of meeting an old friend to the anxiety of being the bearer of bad tidings.

"What is it?" asked David with an expression matching his friends.

"Before I escaped I saw four armed men collect four truckloads of Jews and drive away with them. Hannah and her mother were loaded on the last truck."

"Are you sure, are you certain?" asked a frantic David.

"Yes, I saw it with my own eyes."

David asked, but knew the answer. "How about her father, did you see him?"

"No, he wasn't with them. Maybe he was on another truck."

"No," David said glumly, "he's already dead. The bastards killed him first. And now they've come for the rest of the family." He cried out in anguish.

Eli, observing all this said, "All I saw was them taking her away. I didn't see them killing her. Maybe she's alive. Maybe they took her away to work someplace. I've heard of that happening."

David didn't answer, his head bowed with eyes closed.

Jozef, a witness to this human tragedy thought—poor David, he loved that woman with all his heart. Like his father, he wanted to stay alive, learn from his father and mother and help them medically. We'll encourage him to keep thinking like this, but now he has a very personal reason to see how he can avenge. This will change him. I'll have to keep my eye on him.

CHAPTER 19
FIRST STRIKE
SEPTEMBER, 1941

As the weeks passed, the obvious anti-Semitic excesses of the Nazis and their collaborators in Byelorussia had the effect of swelling the ranks of Jozef's partisan Jewish group. He now had to plan for two divisions of his expanding empire: the needs of his people, and military force. The military would depend on Mikhail, soon to be busy at work ingratiating himself toward his new masters.

Mikhail was correct, the Nazis established their headquarters at the now, almost empty Civic Building devoid of its Communist masters who, true to their word, motored to Moscow the instant they received news of the invasion.

Mikhail was there to greet the first German troops who took over the building. The commander was Colonel Gunther Klee, an SS officer who appeared after the Nazis captured Minsk. He was not surprised at Mikhail's warm greeting, for there were some in Byelorussia sympathetic toward the invaders: principally non-Communists who hated the Communist system; anti-Semites with a blind hatred for Jews or anything Jewish; and anti-Semites who hated Jews based upon their perception that 'too many Communists were Jews.'

Colonel Klee pulled up to the civic building in his chauffeur driven military scout vehicle seven days after the invasion. Mikhail was the only employee left in the building. The Communist functionaries had gathered up their papers, valuables and secretaries and by this time were safely ensconced in Moscow—as long as that would last.

Mikhail met Colonel Klee at the front door. He extended his hand and said, "Welcome Colonel Klee, it's a pleasure to meet you."

"And you are Mikhail Gregov?" They shook hands

"Yes, sir, I am."

"My adjutant said you would be here. We have much to talk about. Shall we go in, Mikhail. May I call you Mikhail?"

"Of course, sir."

They entered the building and Mikhail took Colonel Klee to the office occupied in the past by the Minsk mayor. "This was the office of the mayor," Mikhail reported, "he's gone to Moscow along with everyone else."

Colonel Klee laughed. "At least they had the sense to know that nothing was going to stop us."

"Yes, sir, they as much as said so," answered Mikhail.

"There are no Communists left here, I presume," said Colonel Klee.

"No sir, none."

"How long have you been here, Mikhail?"

"I started working here as a young man, before the Russian revolution and the takeover of Byelorussia that brought the country into the Union of Soviet Socialist Republics. I was here long before the Communists came."

"And you are not a Communist, I presume," said Colonel Klee.

Mikhail shook his head vigorously and said, "No sir. I am not and never have been."

"So how is it that you worked here all this time," asked Colonel Klee.

"Sir, because I know every brick, every piece of lumber, every wire, every pipe, every inch of this building. It is old, and like anything old, it needs tender care. I am the doctor for this building. When it is sick, I fix it. Without me it will die and my previous employers knew that."

"I like your dedication, Mikhail. We are taking over this building as headquarters for the invasion through the center of Russia."

"All I need to know is your requirements and it will be done, sir."

"We could use your talent. How many of you are still here?" asked the Colonel.

"Just me, sir."

"Were there any Jews here?"

"No, sir, never." He was quick to add, "There are Jews in Minsk, sir, as you know, but I and my family have nothing to do with them. We go in different circles. I don't ever socialize with Jews," he lied with a straight face.

Colonel Klee nodded his head. "Good, Mikhail, we will help you with the Jewish problem. What do you think of our occupation?"

"I'm optimistic, sir. Anything is better than Communism, but as for me, I have no control of the political system, Men with guns control that. I built a good occupation and make a decent living and can care for my family, and that's all that counts for me. I'm lucky to be able to do this in Communism, because the only ones who live in luxury are the Communist bosses. The little man scrapes the bottom of the barrel. It's a wicked system and I'm glad to see it over. For the masses of people, there is no incentive in such a system."

"How do you think you'll do working for us?" asked the Colonel.

"To be honest with you, sir, I don't know. It's all up to you. All I know is that if you asked me what I would prefer, I would say I would like to see Byelorussia as an independent country, but I understand that a little country like ours with no army of its own that lives between great powers can never achieve that goal. I hope that we can be friends with Germany and Germany can grant us some degree of independence. I'm not a politician. I will just be content if I can continue what I'm doing and make a living for my family."

Colonel Klee smiled, nodded his head and said, "I like your attitude, Mikhail. My staff will be here tomorrow. I will need housing for some of my officers. Is that a problem, Mikhail?"

"None, sir, we can make arrangements either in this building or we have some abandoned homes that you can use. All I need is your decision on what you would choose for your officers and I'll get the locations ready according to your specifications."

"That sounds good. I'll see you tomorrow, Mikhail. We've got more things to talk about."

"Yes, sir," Mikhail said, trying to slow the anxious pace of his mind and the rapid pace of his heart as he prayed that he had passed the first test in gaining the confidence of these war criminals. As unsure as he was of his countries union with the Socialist Soviet Republic, living under the invader and their murderous philosophy was almost more than he could stand. He prayed he had taken the first steps in assisting in its destruction. He needed to gain their confidence. We will see what tomorrow brings, he thought. He would send his coded message to King Tree and the Knothole and alert his allies to a possible future action if everything worked out over the next few weeks as he hoped they would.

Deep in their enclave in the forest, David continued assisting his father, although he was quieter and his smile had become a memory.

Time passed at a snail's pace and the news continued to worsen. All he knew about Hannah and her mother was that the enemy took them away along with a truckload of ghetto Jews to an unknown fate. He could only keep the very faint hope alive that somehow Hannah and her mother, spared the heartless killings for whatever reason, would show up some day. Until he had proof of their deaths, that thought would sustain him even in the face of the mass killings, now common knowledge.

Abel Stolar, once he had settled in to his partisan existence, approached Jozef. "When will we see action?" he asked.

Jozef, recognizing the impatient voice of a young man, knew he had to lay down the law in a way that would bring control to a man who had every right to desire and every right to be impatient about an urge to carry out the revenge that was consuming him.

"I like your desire, Abel. You'll have your chance, but hear me loud and clear now. We're all anxious to get revenge, but one thing we can't do is each act alone with his own plan. This will be a coordinated effort. We work as a team and the team has one coach, and I am the coach. Do you understand me?"

The strength of Jozef's voice and words lined up Abel as a subordinate under the leadership of one man whose responsibility was to make such decisions. Abel was a cog in a wheel, one of many that saw to it that the wheel turned with an efficiency that guaranteed arrival at their destination. Jozef had the oil-can and used it to keep the wheel turning. "I understand," Abel said.

Jozef added, "Be patient, we're organizing and doing well. I'll put you to work soon enough. When this war ends, you'll feel good, because we'll see to it that you helped end it. That's the reason why we are here. We do it as a team. Understand one thing though, I don't want to squash good thoughts; you get an idea, you bring it to me. I guarantee you will be heard, but remember, the decision to act is a decision I make and if it is a good plan, we'll discuss it and perfect it and then and only then will we carry it out. Notice I say we. Knowing what I know about you, I will guarantee that we will bring you into the discussion, and if the role is right for you, I will see to it that you get it. I have reason to believe you'll hear good news soon."

Abel nodded his head. He got the message as loud and as clear as a powerful leader could make it. "Thank you," he said wiser in the ways of partisan organization.

The next day, Mikhail met again with Colonel Klee who told Mikhail that he would need some accommodations overnight for a very important General with his staff who would arrive at the Minsk airport in five days for 'important local business.'

Wondering what the words 'important local business meant, but wise enough not to ask, Mikhail said, "Yes, sir, would you want me to get rooms here ready or would the General and his staff perhaps want to use one of the empty houses I mentioned that are nearby."

"How far away are these homes, Mikhail?"

"A short walking distance, sir."

"Well then, let's take a look at them. They will need permanent arrangements, but we'll worry about that later."

"How many in the party, sir?" asked Mikhail.

"There will be four counting me."

"The largest home has three bedrooms, so…"

Colonel Klee interrupted, "That's fine, Mikhail, the General and his two staff can use the bedrooms to sleep. Can you set me up with a comfortable cot?"

"No problem, sir."

"Let's go take a quick look," said Colonel Klee walking toward the door.

Colonel Klee found the accommodations satisfactory. "This is a nice home, Mikhail. Why is it empty?"

"It was owned by Jews. They fled when the invasion started. That's all I know, sir. I spoke with a neighbor who has no idea where they went."

"That was smart of them," said Klee. "Are the neighbors Jewish?"

"No, sir," but one of the problems we have had in Byelorussia is that the Jews have managed to mix in with the Christians."

Klee laughed, "Soon all Jews will have their own accommodations—all together."

Mikhail read the sarcastic note in Klee's voice.

"My adjutant will be here later, so the both of you can get these offices and home ready for the staff. These two jobs will keep you busy, Mikhail."

The note that Mikhail left in King Tree and the Knothole detailed the critical news about the German General and his staff staying at the abandoned home in Minsk with the information that the date would follow.

No sooner did Jozef get the news, he sprung into action. His plan was beyond his expertise, but he knew how to accomplish it nevertheless. There was no time to lose. He needed men anxious for revenge: David and Abel were perfect. He rounded them up immediately, sat them down and said, "I have a mission and I need two men who want to kill Nazis. Are you interested?"

"Yes," they both said simultaneously, their eyes lighting up.

"Come with me," he said.

"Where are we going?" asked David.

"We're going to the Russian partisans," he answered, and as a confused David and Abel looked at each other, Jozef added, "no more now, you'll learn all about it when we get there. Just say nothing. Let me do all the talking. You'll both have your chance for revenge."

"How do you know the Russian partisans?" asked Abel.

"I know the commander. I met him right after we started to set up. That's enough. Follow me."

They walked through the countryside past small towns and farms finally entering another forest filled with swamps and small lakes. In the thick of the forest, they heard words, but did not see the person who spoke them. "Stop—hands up," the voice said. David and Abel followed Jozef's lead, and did what the voice asked.

Jozef said, "We are not armed."

Then three men, dressed in a combination of Russian army uniforms and civilian clothes stepped out from behind dense undergrowth.

"Who are you?" they asked rifles pointed.

"I am Josef Askenazy, partisan commander. I have urgent business with Major Kalemnikoff."

Andrei Kalemnikoff represents a Soviet army officer left behind the lines by the retreating Soviets after the Nazis invaded the Soviet Union. Their task was to help organize civilian partisan resistance against the Nazis, collaborate with and direct other partisan groups.

The three men approached, searched a calm Jozef, a frightened David and Abel, and satisfied that they had no weapons, said, "What is your business?"

"That's only for the ears of the commander. He knows me."

With two men following and one in the front leading the way, they walked to the Russian encampment where they met the Russian commander, one of many Russian soldiers left behind during the retreat whose job it was to harass the German army in the rear.

They found the Russian commander in a small hut with his Russian aid, a buxom Russian female army officer left behind as a personal "aide-de-camp" for the commander. Dressed in Khaki from top to bottom, with a half grey beard and bushy, pure black mustache, when he saw Jozef, he waved his hand holding a glass of clear liquid, and said, "Jozef, it's good to see you. To what do I owe the honor of this visit?"

"A very important item just for you, Andrei."

"Not for Lieutenant Brushka's ears? She is my second in command," he said as he slapped her on the rear. David and Abel took note of this interplay. Brushka's raucus laughter accompanied by massive breasts bouncing under her khaki jacket distracted Jozef momentarily, but then he quickly answered, "I leave that to you to tell her later if after you hear what I have to say, you think you can share it with the good lieutenant."

Andrei, now serious, said, "Jozef, Lieutenant Brushka must know everything I know in case I'm killed. You understand? I trust her with my life."

Brushka represents military or civilian women of many nationalities who also served as valuable partisans in many roles including combat.

Jozef could tell by the expression on Andrei's face that there was no give in that statement."

"Sure, Andrei."

"First, Jozef, let me ask you how things are going since I first met you when you started up."

"Things are doing well. We got the organization up and running, but it's a little difficult because the Nazis and their allies keep killing Jews, so we get more and more escapees who come to join us," answered Jozef.

"Well, the more the better. You know, the army told us to discourage Jewish partisans from forming, because some crazies in the population will not know who to kill first, Jews or Nazis, and the army wants the people to concentrate only on Nazis," answered Andrei.

Jozef quickly responded. "It doesn't matter to us who wants to kill us. We will fight back and beat them to it. Anyhow, back to your question of to what do you owe the honor of my visit?" said Jozef

"Yes, what is it that is so important that it is for my ears alone?" asked Andrei.

"We need your help, Andrei, we want to blow up a house with four high ranking German officers in it, including one commanding general."

David and Abel turned and looked at each other and then moved closer to Jozef. They didn't want to miss a word.

Andrei's eyebrows lifted. He picked up his glass again and said, "Ahh, a noble enterprise for a bunch of Jews." He looked at Brushka and smiled. She smiled back, nodding her head. "Why do you need our help, Jozef?"

"For one, we have no explosives, and two, we don't have the expertise even if we had the explosives. So, if we pull this off, we can only do it with your help."

"And who are these two young men you bring here?"

"These are my two assassins. They will have the honor and pleasure of pushing down the plunger that will send the German officers to Nazi hell."

{

David and Abel looked at each other and smiled, then looked at Jozef and nodded their heads.

"Lucky boys," said Andrei, "why do they rate the honor?"

"Because Abel here was shot by the Nazis, and fell wounded into a pre-dug pit with dead Jews all assassinated. He crawled out from between the dead bodies and escaped to fight another day. David here lost his fiancée, perhaps the same way. I think they deserve the honor."

"By all means, Jozef, wise choices. Are you sure you know what you are talking about with the four German officers? How do you get such important intelligence?" asked Andrei.

"That information about my intelligence source, I take to my grave," said Jozef.

Andrei laughed as did Brushka again accompanied by her mammary side-show. "Wise, Jozef, wise. I accept that for the time being, if you promise that after the war you will give me the secret."

"No, Andrei, I will never give anyone the secret until all the participants are dead including me."

Andrei nodded his head. "You are too wise for words."

"Can you help, Andrei?" asked Jozef.

"I can and I will. I'll provide you with an explosive expert, enough explosives to do the job, and if this one is successful, you will have all you need in the future. We can get enough to blow up the whole German army. My bosses are always happy to give me whatever I need."

"Andrei, I believe we have the start of a beautiful collaboration. I pity the German army."

"Let me shake the hands of your two assassins. David and Abel is it?"

"Yes, sir," they both said.

One at a time, Andrei grasped the right hand of David and Abel, who both winced under Andrei's power.

"Easy, Andrei, they need their hand. They've got a plunger to plunge."

Andrei laughed. "Before you meet your new partner, we will drink to our combined mission with a small shot of Vodka."

Andrei, Jozef and Brushka downed theirs and smacked their lips. David and Abel downed theirs with mutual grimaces, the first such taste for both of them. This was their introduction to partisan warfare. They puffed up their chests.

Three men started on the trip to the Russian partisans; four headed back to the Jewish partisan encampment. Joseph, David, Abel and Sergei looked like pack mules weighed down by explosive paraphernalia for the soon to be implemented first strike against the hated enemy.

Sergei, a career Russian army sergeant was the last person one would expect to be an explosive expert. Standing five feet and two inches with thick glasses, a baldhead and a booming voice— something no one would expect to hear coming out of that tiny frame— he had been in the Russian army for twelve years and witnessed Stalin's high-ranking officer massacre of the thirties.

Sergei represents a Soviet army enlisted man who also played a role in partisan resistance.

On the trip back, Jozef oriented him to the mission. Mikhail, in his previous King Tree and the Knothole message, advised Jozef that the next message would include a full description of the accommodation chosen to house the officers while awaiting their orders about their behind the lines assignment. Sergei would need this in order to plan the explosive placement that would guarantee the Nazis their final sleep before they would awaken in Nazi hell. Sergei was grateful for this mission, as all previous missions involved blowing up structures, such as bridges and railroad tracks in order to prevent or delay the delivery of vital supplies for the German war effort. Now, for the first time, he would be killing people, the same people responsible for the loss of some of his family, victims of the indiscriminate bombing of Barbarosa's early blitzkrieg.

Growing up in rural Russia, this would be the first time Sergei saw civilian Jews, much less work with them. He knew of Russian Jewish soldiers, but had only a rare personal contact with them. So far, he liked what he saw in Jozef, David and Abel, three men with every reason and desire for revenge, and more importantly, he received a direct order from Andrei to work with them, follow orders, take charge of and answer to no one regarding the explosives, their placement and detonation. It would be a labor of love.

After they arrived back at the Jewish partisan encampment, Jozef left for King Tree and the Knothole fully expecting to receive Mikhail's specific instructions regarding the location, address, inner floor plan of the home, the date when the officers would be sleeping there and a back-door key to allow entry. He was not disappointed. Mikhail also included a portion of a map about a mile square surrounding the home.

Jozef was pleased. "Study these, Sergei. This attack will have to take place in four days. When you've developed your plan, let me know and you, I, David and Abel will meet to plan the next step."

"It won't take long, said Sergei.

"How long?"

"I'll meet the three of you here in two hours," answered Sergei confidently.

"Good we'll be here."

True to his word, the four of them met in a location sure to prevent any interruptions. Sergei said, "Look at these drawings. Setting the explosives is not a problem. I'll fix them to the basement ceiling under each of the beds that are on the first floor where the Nazis will sleep. The explosives will be three times more powerful than we need to kill them. I'll see to that. The wires that lead to each of the TNT bundles will connect up to one wire that will exit the house through this basement window. We have to extend this wire, and camouflage it in the back yard to go under the rear backyard fence and into the field and forest behind the house at least 100 hundred meters away. I'll also set up a second and extra powerful TNT site in the basement on the floor also with a wire that I'll attach to the same plunger. This one will have a two second delay. If one batch of explosives doesn't go off the other will. More than likely, they will both go off two seconds apart. There is no way anyone in that building will survive. That's the easy part. Now comes the hard part..."

"What's that?" interrupted Jozef.

"If I can go to the site so I can get in the house, check out the first floor and the basement and also the back yard and the area beyond the back yard fence, I can be more sure of myself that what I just told you makes sense."

"Then we better go, Sergei. I worked in the Civic building not to far from the house, so I'm familiar with the area. We leave tomorrow early in the morning at 1:00. We'll get there in a few hours. How much time will you need to check the place out?" asked Jozef.

"No more than one-half hour."

"David and Abel, you didn't hear anything—understand?"

"Yes, sir," they both said.

"We'll see you both tomorrow afternoon at 2:00 o'clock."

"We'll be here," said David.

David went back to his mother and father. They had both noted his absence. Ben asked, "Where do you disappear to?"

"I've been helping to get food," lied David uncomfortably.

Anticipating such a question, David had his answer already prepared.

"With who? Where do you go?" asked Leah.

"I go with Jozef and a few others into the countryside. They've figured out a whole route they go to where they get food from people who support the partisans."

"Is it safe, David" said a worried Leah.

"You don't have to worry, mother, Jozef has worked this all out. He knows who's friendly and who isn't. It's not a problem. He needs some young guys to help carry supplies, that's all. Anyhow, the medical business, thank goodness, is pretty sparse now, so I need something to do to make a contribution."

"Alright, David, be careful please."

"Nothing to worry about, mother, there are no Nazis who go in the countryside." They're too busy with the Russian army."

Jozef and Sergei left at 1:00 as planned. "Just follow close behind me," said Jozef. They armed themselves with pistols safe within a hip holster. They took a back route offering much less chance of discovery. Josef stopped at the location he thought would be where they would set up the plunger about 100 meters to the rear of the target home and he told Sergei this.

"You see that fence ahead?" asked Jozef.

"Yes," answered Sergei.

"That's the rear fence in the back yard of the house where your targets will be. Crawl there, climb over the fence, crawl to the back entrance, open the door and do your thing, Sergei. I'll lie here and wait for you. If you can do it all without lighting a match for light, you'll be safer."

Sergei went to the house, opened the back door that led to the first and main floor. He found three bedrooms and measured the distance of the bed from the walls. He also measured the distance of a cot in the living room from the walls. Then he went down stairs to the basement and placed marks on the ceiling under the beds and cot. There was one small window in the basement abutting the back yard. There's where the wires will exit, thought Sergei. Completing this task in less than ten minutes, he left the basement and went to the main floor, exited the back door and crawled back to Jozef.

"It'll work, Jozef," said a smiling Sergei. "Let's get the hell out of here."

When they could speak, Sergei said. "When you find out what date the Nazis will come to the house—for their final rest, I'll be able to wire everything in plenty of time to set up the blast, get out and watch our two young men work on the plunger and enjoy the boom and light show. I may need the help of one of them to carry in the explosives."

"No problem, Sergei. Take David. I know him better than Abel. He's a genius and a fast learner. Work with him tomorrow to help you streamline the operation. It should just be a matter of days before we act."

Good, Jozef. Just give me a little notice when we're ready to go."

"That I'll do."

Mikhail received the information about the German officers, their time and date of arrival. He readied the home for the overnight sleep and transmitted all the information via King Tree and the Knothole in the waterproof metal container. Josef picked up the container late that evening and early the next morning he met with Sergei, David and Abel to work out the details of plan "Lullaby," so named to reflect the lullaby they plan to present to the German officers to promote a permanent sleep. Sergei oriented an enthusiastic David on his role in the explosive placement. David and Abel's actions reflected their glee in what they perceived as a "crushing blow" soon to be levied on the accursed enemy.

"Who knows?" said Jozef. Killing this German general and his staff may win the war for us, and you young men will be written up in the history books. I can see the headlines now—Two Jew Boys Win War." A good laugh was a tension easer as they left for their mission.

The idea was to wire the home about 3:00 in the morning with the explosives, extend the wire out of the back basement window, bury it or hide it for 100 meters, mark its end location and return early the next morning with the plunger when the Nazis were asleep. Then David and Abel could do their thing.

They arrived back to the partisan camp and Jozef said, "Okay, everyone get a good sleep. We need to be alert when we go back. Not a word to anyone. I'll meet you here at ten tonight. When we get there by 2:00, we'll only go as far as the end of the wire, attach the plunger and let our two assassins get to work. By that time, the Nazis should be snoring in their beds. See you then."

The trip back was uneventful. About all they would run into this time of darkness was an occasional forest creature that would scamper away at their presence. They crawled the last several hundred yards to reach the wire's end. Jozef whispered, "You have the honor of attaching the wire, Sergei."

"This is a labor of love," he said as he attached the wire to the plunger.

Next, Jozef said, "David, put your hand on the plunger." He complied with a wide eyed smile. "Abel, put your hand on top of

David's. Don't push down yet. I'll count to three and when you hear three, you both push down, then fall flat on your belly with both hands over your ears. Ready...one...two...three." The explosions came in the hoped for two second interval. The house disappeared in flashes of light, flame and smoke. No one could survive. They all got an instantaneous glance before beating a hasty retreat crawling on their knees until trees surrounded them, than they ran and walked back to camp.

David thought, that was for you and your mother and father, Hannah. That exploding house is a vision I'll never forget.

Abel thought, take that, you bastards.

Sergei thought, finally, Nazis, not railroad tracks.

Jozef thought, number one and more to come.

As soon as they arrived back, Sergei pulled out a small flask filled with Vodka. "We drink to a successful mission." David and Abel, exhausted from the tension and fear of their first partisan operation, winced again.

CHAPTER 20
SECOND STRIKE
OCTOBER 1941

The unprepared Red Army managed a fierce fight, but could not cope with the German onslaught. Many cities including Minsk fell to the onrushing German army. The Nazis captured or killed Russians in ever-increasing numbers: 290,000 in the Minsk operation alone; in the north, the Baltic States fell to the Nazis with many greeting them as liberators; in the south, Kiev was in jeopardy.

The German advance was so rapid and Russian casualties were so vast that German military headquarters confidently told Hitler that the only thing left to do was mop up. Hitler felt he won the war, but Stalin had other ideas; he appointed himself head of all political, military and economic activity and for the first time tried to rally his people by urging a scorched earth policy and appealing to the ideals of Russian Communism and Russian nationalism.

In time, the Nazis were ready to capture Leningrad in the north, Kiev in the south and Moscow in the center. Then the rains, mud, freezing weather, and the vast Russian territory caught a German army ill prepared, ill clothed and overextended as far as their supply lines were concerned.

As the Nazis stalled, the Russians had an opportunity to rebuild their army.

Jozef retrieved a message from King Tree and the Knothole that said an order has gone out to local police to round up Jews. Why and for what purpose was not part of Mikhail's letter. Jozef would inform his contacts in Minsk and surrounding area to keep their eyes open and report back as soon as there was any information on the subject. All Jozef assumed was that the round up was not for any good purpose, and if any Jews failed to return that would be enough for Jozef to mobilize and take action, for it meant that they were either killed or subjected to forced labor, both crimes that in Joseph's mind demanded capital punishment. Involving local police in any action harmful to Jews, regardless of who ordered it, would not grant the police immunity; anyone collaborating with the Nazis would meet the same fate as the Nazis themselves.

Nineteen year-old Avram Rosenovich, a six-foot soccer player, muscular with brown hair, brown eyes and a large nose visited friends in a small suburb of Minsk. He returned home to find his mother and father not at home. Wondering if they were visiting the elderly next-door neighbors who they often would help with chores, he went to the neighbor's home. He did not see his parents and asked, "Were my parents here?"

"No, Avram, they took them," the woman of the house said with an apparent sadness that Avram detected.

"Who took them?" Avram asked with tremulous voice.

She answered, "The police."

"Police—what police?"

"Byelorussian police. They came here too, but they left us alone because they were only looking for Jews," she answered. "They said they had orders from the Nazis to round up Jews. I know some of those men. They are from the Gramensky Avenue police station"

"Round up Jews for what?"

"We don't know, Avram. They didn't give any reason, but they did say the Nazis need the Jews to work. They were laughing about it. Just last week they took the whole Glickstein family away and then a few days later they came back and emptied out their house of all the furniture and clothes. You better run away, Avram. They're killing your people. I wouldn't go out there now. They might still be in the neighborhood. Stay here for a while. They already left here, so they won't come back."

Avram sat down. "When did this happen?" he asked with a feeling of doom.

"About two hours ago. Stay here tonight. It'll be safer for you. Then you can go into the forest. I hear that your people are going there. That's what we would do if we were young and Jewish."

Avram appreciated the concern of this friendly elderly woman, and said, "That's kind of you and I appreciate it, but I'll go back home and wait. If they don't come back by tomorrow evening, I'll go to the forest."

"You better not take the chance, Avram, if they know that you live there too, what if they come back for you?"

"You're a brave lady. You know the Nazis said they'll kill anyone who helps Jews, but you still want to help me."

"Look what your folks do for me and my husband who doesn't even know me anymore."

"It's a blessing that they do it," Avram added, "but you're right, if the police come back, they might get me at home. I'll stay, but I'll sleep in your barn, so if they find me there, you just didn't know I snuck in—that's all."

"Whatever you want, Avram, and God be with you."

The crow of a rooster awakened Avram at dawn. He went to his home and his parents were still not there. Nothing had changed since yesterday. Would he ever see his parents again? He knew he had to get into the forest and find Jewish partisans, but he had no idea where they might be. At least the forest would be an escape. It was too dangerous to stay where he was, surrounded by enemies and friends: the friends he knew; the enemies he did not. So armed with layers of warm clothing and supplies to last about a week, he waited until dark, left the neighborhood and wandered the woods. After three days, a sudden harsh voice stopped him in his tracks, "Stop, state your name and business. I have a gun pointed at you."

Avram choked out, "My name is Avram Rosenovitch and I'm looking for partisans."

The voice stepped out from behind a tree, still unseen by Avram. "Walk straight ahead. I'll be behind you and tell you where to go."

In thirty minutes, they arrived at an encampment. Several other men joined the party and surrounded Avram. Avram's guard entered a hut, was in there about a minute, opened the door and said, "Avram, come in."

Sitting before him were two scruffy looking strangers: Major Andrei Kalemnikoff, commander of the Russian partisans and a woman dressed in a tattered Russian army uniform. Andrei said, "You are looking for partisans, Avram?"

All Avram knew was that these men were not Jewish partisans. He gulped. "Yes, sir,"

"What kind of partisans are you looking for, Avram? We are partisans. There are all kinds of partisans in these forests," Andrei said with an emphasis on the Avram while staring at Avram's nose.

The emphasis on his name told Avram that this man, whoever he was, most likely a Russian army man, could tell he was Jewish. He would brave it and said, "Jewish partisans."

"Oh, you're a Jew," said Andrei in mock surprise.

"Yes, I'm a Jew," Avram said.

Andrei asked, "How do I know you're telling me the truth? How do I know you're not a spy?"

This surprised Avrom who said, "My name is Avram Rosenovich. The Nazis ordered the Byelorussian police to round up Jews including my mother and father. I don't know where they are. I'm alone and I want to fight back."

"That's what I like to hear, Avram. Now if I can just prove you're Jewish, I'll help you. Pull your pants down."

This shocked Avram who stole a glance at the woman in the room.

"Oh, I see, you're a modest boy, you're worried about Brushka" He laughed. "Brushka, have you ever seen a Yiddish schmuck?"

"I did, but the Jew was only three weeks old," she smiled.

Andrei laughed, "Brushka, tell me if you think it grows when a Jew baby becomes a man." Then he looked at Avram and said sternly, "Pants down, Avram."

Said with such a firm voice, Avram did as told and Andrei nodded yes. "That's all I need," Andrei said. Brushka, what do you think? Does it grow?"

"A little," she said, holding her thumb and index finger about an inch apart."

After a good laugh at Avram's expense, Andrei said, "Brushka, would you get me Sergei, please."

When Sergei appeared, Avram had to relate the entire story for Sergei to hear.

Andrei said, "Sergei, don't you think that this is a job that Jozef would love to take on. A perfect task for Jewish revenge in my book."

"Yes, perfect," said Sergei as Avram stood by wondering what and whom they were talking about. Then Andrei added, "Sergei, I've got a job for you." Then he turned to Avram and said, "We're going to put you right to work, Avram. Sergei here will take you to the Jewish partisans. Once they hear what the police did to your mother and father, I'm sure they'll let you work with them and see to it that the police never again take orders from the Nazi bastards to round up Jews. Anyone who works with Nazis, we kill, you see, so thanks for coming to us with this news. We've got all the work we need, so we'll turn this over to the Jewish partisans where it belongs. They're doing good work. Help them out please."

Finally understanding what all this was about, a more relaxed Avram said, "Yes, sir, I will."

"Sergei, deliver Jozef some explosives. Work with him. After you take care of the police, do the same to the police station as the other house we lit up." He laughed, "You like that Brushka?"

"I love it," she smiled.

Carrying explosives and extra rifles, Sergei and Avram walked to Jozef's encampment. There Sergei introduced Avram and told him to tell Jozef the same story that he told Andrei. Jozef listened intently and slapped his thigh when Avram finished. "An amazing coincidence," Jozef said. "We had just heard about the new Nazi order to the local police to capture Jews. Now we know for sure there are families taken away never to return. When Andrei heard about it from you, Avram, he knew who should take care of it. Well, he sent you to the right place. With a little training, you'll join us and we'll get you some revenge."

"Did they kill my mother and father?" asked Avram whose face reflected a combination of sadness and anger.

"I can't tell you for sure, and I hope they didn't kill them, Avram, but to me it doesn't matter. Your parents are either dead or they have lost their freedom as prisoners or slave labor. Nobody has the right to kill innocents. Nobody has the right to make another person a slave. What those police did is a crime, but they'll never stand before a judge, so I am the judge, and I declare them guilty as accessories that made it possible for the Nazis to take your mother and father. The Nazis will pay the ultimate price and we'll all carry it out just like they carried it out on forty-nine of my friends in Poland and just like they tried to carry it out on Abel here. In this business, it's an eye for and an eye and a tooth for a tooth. That's how we work. Where did you say this police station was, Avram?"

"Gramensky Ave Police station outside of Minsk."

"You know how to get there?"

"Oh, yes."

"Let's have a little something to eat, I'll round up about four others and we'll make our plans," said Jozef.

Jozef, Sergei, Avram, David, Abel and two others met to plan the attack. Jozef said, "Avram, tell everybody what happened to your parents; bring everybody up to date."

Avram told what happened, everyone listening in rapt attention to his emotional presentation.

"Now you know why you're all here," said Jozef, "we're going to take revenge." He left it at that, avoiding any further details for the time being.

It took David to break the silence. "What do you mean by revenge?"

"All those police, or at least those we find, are going to die by our hand."

More silence.

"Any one of you who would rather not participate, tell me now," said Jozef.

After a period of silence, David raised his hand. This was no surprise to Jozef—he expected it, for David was the kind of brilliant youngster who needed justification for all his actions. "Yes, David, what is your question?"

"Don't get me wrong, I'm not against your action, but there are some things I'd like to talk about before I join."

"That's good. You all need a clear mind before you decide to kill. What is your question, David?"

"Why do you think these police rounded up Jews and turned them over to the Nazis?"

"Why do you think, David?"

"I don't think they did it on their own. Why should the police bother making Jewish enemies on top of German enemies?"

Jozef laughed, "Who says the Nazis are their enemies? The Nazis are their friends. Most of the police prefer the Nazis over the Russian Communists, so they want to get on the good side of them."

David quickly answered, "So getting on the good side of them means sending Jews to their deaths?"

"Let me turn this around for you, David," said Jozef, who rocked his chair back on the two back legs. "Let's suppose you were a Jewish policeman and an invading army took over your city and told you to round up all the Christians and turn them over to the invader. What would you do?"

David stood up straight, shoulders back. "I would refuse."

"But what if they said they would kill you if you refused?"

"I would still refuse."

"Do you think that the Nazis told the police to round up Jews, David?"

David thought for a few seconds, nodded his head and said, "I suppose they did."

"And if the police refused, do you suppose that the Nazis would kill them," Jozef asked.

"Yes, I believe they would."

"That's where you're wrong, David, They would not and they do not."

"How do you know this," asked David.

Jozef said, "Sergei, what do you think?"

"You're right, Jozef, they assign them someplace else," answered Sergei.

"Right. No army would kill their own men except for desertion and becoming a proven traitor. No army can be in the position of harming their own soldiers who refuse a known criminal act. So why didn't these policemen refuse? They didn't, and they will pay the price—from us. Knowing all that, David, the option is yours to join us or not."

As he thought of Hannah and her family, he said, "I join."

"Any other questions?" asked Jozef of the others. No one had any.

Jozef turned to Avram and said, "Avram, can you describe the police station for us?"

"Yes, it is a wooden building about twenty-five meters square. It is only one story high. There is one big open room where each policeman has a desk. There are two rooms in the back where they can keep prisoners for a short time and there are some storage rooms on one side."

"Where are doors?" asked Jozef.

Avram, without hesitating answered, "Two big ones in the front and a smaller one in the back that leads down a short hall before it gets to the main room. The front doors also enter into the main room. There is one toilet off the hall in the back."

"What's around the building?" asked Jozef.

"Not much for about a block away. Then there are mostly small homes and some small farms."

"Is it a wooded area?"

"Yes, the whole area is wooded."

"What do you think, Sergei?" asked Jozef.

"I think we have to get there after sundown late in the afternoon. We all barge in with our guns, round them up against a wall and shoot. The faster the better and since this will be a fast job, we can't stay around wiring the place for explosives. We kill them; pour petrol on the bodies and on the walls and set fire to it all. Since it's mostly wood it will go up fast."

Thinking of the Synagogue in Poland, Jozef stroked his chin, lifted his eyebrows and said, "I like that, Sergei, except we don't give them any time to think by rounding them up. We kill then when we charge in."

"What's the possibility of seeing the place before we make final plans?" asked Sergei.

Avram immediately said, "I can do it. I have a place I can hide there with no problem, and I can check it out late every day and see if the police meet there at a certain day and time."

Interested, Jozef asked, "Where can you hide and not be found, Avram."

"When I came home one day, my mother and father weren't home, so I thought they might be at the neighbor's house and I went there. They weren't there and the old lady who lives there told me the police took my mother and father, and she said I better not go home because maybe they'd come back for me. Then she said I could stay there with her and her senile husband, but since I knew that the Nazis would kill anyone who shelters Jews, I told her I would stay in her barn, so at least she could say she didn't know I was there if anyone found me."

"I see. That might work. Good thinking, Avram. I'll give you five days to see what you can find out. Report back here if you find out anything. If you're not here in seven days, we'll pick a day and get the job done without you. That'll give us some good planning and training time." Then he turned to Sergei and said, "I don't know how long you can stay, Sergei, but your idea about torching the place rather than blowing it up is a good one, so if you need to go back to Andrei, that's fine. We'll know what to do."

"Yeah, I'll go back. This is a Jewish job. Keep the explosives, put them in a water-proof box, wrap them and bury them away from the camp, and when you need them use them in good health." With that, he shook hands all around and started his walk back to the Russian partisans.

This would leave Jozef, David, Abel, and the two other men to plan the action. Josef wanted to have at least seven men involved, so he recruited two more. If Avram joined them, that would be eight; plenty to do the job, especially since they had two machine guns—one for Jozef and one for Avram—if he returned. If Avram did not return, he would train Abel to use the machine gun.

But after five days, Avram did return, armed with detailed drawings of the police headquarters and the surrounding area. He reported to Jozef.

"That's great, Avram," said Jozef. We're all going to meet tonight, so I'll study these drawings, Be sure you come and we'll bring you up to date and see if we have to make any changes after we all review the drawings you made."

"I'll be there," Avram said.

When they got together that evening and after introducing Avram to the two new members of the assassination team, Jozef had Avram describe the police headquarters as they passed his map around. Jozef said, "Look at the map, study it and see if anyone has any changes to the plan. Avram, we made a decision to all charge through the front doors. I will be first and you will be second. We will both carry machine guns, and don't worry; I'll teach you how to be an expert before you use it. The others will charge in behind us, three lining up on our right, and three lining up on our left. They will all carry rifles. We all fire simultaneously and kill every man in sight. Two of the men are carrying petrol. As soon as the firing is over, they spread the petrol on both sides of the room and the floor. We set it on fire and disappear in to the forest through the back door."

Avram listened intently and said, "I had the idea that we would talk to them first and let them know why they're going to die before we kill them."

"Believe me, Avram, they will know the second their body is ripped to shreds by your bullets. We can't give them time to think or time to act. Boom, we do the job. They are dead. They know why. But it isn't important that they know. It is only important that every still alive Byelorussian policeman in this country knows what's in store for them if they round up one more Jew." He banged his fist on the table.

Avram smiled and nodded his head. "I understand," said Avram.

"Alright, does anyone have any thoughts after looking at the map?"

There was a period of silence before David said, "Looks good to me."

The others agreed.

"Okay, it's a go. Avram, when is the best time do you think."

"There are two times when the police are all there. About 8:00 in the morning, they report for work and they stay there about a half hour before some of them leave and some stay. The next time they are all there is about five-thirty to six."

"What do you think would be the best time?" asked Avram.

"In the evening, because even though the area does not have many people near by, they're starting to stir in the morning, but after dark, I never saw anybody around."

"Does everyone agree?" asked Jozef.

It was unanimous. They all agreed on the evening.

"Avram, let's learn about machine guns. All of you—we go Wednesday."

David received rifle instruction all the time wondering whether he would be able to shoot at a human being. Were these enemies human, he questioned. He talked himself into believing that they, and their allies, were not, and anyone who could kill Mr. Brunstein and possibly Hannah and her mother were a menace that needed to meet their maker before they kill others. He needed to let that sink in to his mind so that it became a part of him; then it would be easier. One thing however concerned him. He lied about his activities to his parents and felt guilt. Certainly, as an adult, he did not need to get their permission to be involved in Jozef's missions, but some of his absences, recognized by his parents, were a cause of concern for them. He decided to tell them all, going into detail only about the past mission when they dynamited the home with the German general and his staff.

His mother, Leah, said nothing, although the look on her face said volumes. His father, Ben, said, "I was starting to get suspicious,

David, but I can understand. Anything we as Jews can do to destroy this menace facing us is a blessing the way I see it. Of course, we'll worry, but you don't need to ask permission of us anymore to do anything. We're very proud of the way you turned out, so we're confident that your decisions will be wise ones. We'll pray for you every day."

Leah, still silent, hugged her son.

This weight now lifted off David's shoulders freed up his mind to be able to concentrate all his efforts working with Jozef and the others.

Jozef had three meetings with his group of assassins, as they called themselves, and under Jozef's direction, they planned every step, confident that if they attack after dark, a majority, if not all, of the police will be in their cross hairs.

Wednesday they gathered and discussed the plans one more time. Led by Avram, they left for the police station so they would arrive after dusk. When they got close, Jozef looked through the rear window of the police station with binoculars and could see police sitting at their desks. "They're in there," he whispered. They tiptoed down the side of the building, arrived at the front door, congregated in a preplanned line and entered one at a time with guns blazing. The shocked police had no time to go for their weapons. Some of them did not even see who killed them. The operation lasted about ten seconds principally carried out by Jozef and Avram with their machine guns and aided by rifle fire directed at individual police. No one would know whose bullet killed whom. As soon as the firing stopped, two partisans took off their backpacks, retrieved the petrol cans and emptied the contents. Two other partisans dropped matches on the petrol. Flames shot up as they all escaped through the back door and ran to the forest—all except Jozef who spent a few seconds pushing a very sharp stake into the ground upon which there was a sign in bold print BETRAY JEWS AND DIE. This time as Jozef looked back, he was reminded of when he looked back to see his forty-nine friends going up in smoke in the Polish Synagogue. His face was a stone mask. Revenge at last.

CHAPTER 21
GHETTO SURPRISE
NOVEMBER 1941

Within one month of the invasion of the Soviet Union, the Nazis hung up notices ordering that all Jews move into a restricted area of Minsk with defined boundaries (ghetto). Prior to this announcement, they established a Judenrat or Jewish council to govern the area. The terse announcement added that any Jew found outside of these boundaries faced death on sight. Those who lived in this area and were not Jewish had ten days to move out. Jews moving in registered at tables set up in front of the Judenrat building. Once they moved in, the Nazis forced them to help construct a barbed-wire fence along the exterior boundaries of the ghetto. This area remained undamaged during the initial bombing as the German air force concentrated on and destroyed the center of the city.

Food soon became a matter of life and death. Those Jews of the ghetto, assigned to work details on the outside received some food at work. Jews who did not leave the ghetto received rations that could not sustain life for long. Starvation necessitated dangerous trips outside of the ghetto wire. Many returned to the ghetto, but others did not and no one knew their fate, but feared the worse.

This volume of living space was too small to handle the massive number of Jews required to live there. Several dozen people forced into one home or apartment made for difficult and unhealthy living conditions. Jewish police organized to guard the inside of the ghetto gate, controlled exit and entry, while German soldiers and Byelorussian police patrolled the outside of the ghetto to prevent anyone from leaving or entering by crawling under the fence. It soon became evident by direct eyewitness testimony, that Jews, for the slightest of "offenses," died by German and or Byelorussian police hands. It also became common knowledge from escapees that those Jews transported out of the ghetto in trucks went to their deaths, shot while standing over pre-dug pits.

The instant Hannah and her mother heard the knock on their front door and saw who was standing there they knew their fate. "Get on the truck," said a German sergeant with a harshness that demanded rapid compliance.

With rifles pointed at them, they climbed up a small hanging ladder on the back of the truck. "If we stay on this truck we'll die," said Mrs. Brunstein to Hannah. "Right before the truck turns the next corner we jump. First you, Hannah, than me. It's our only chance."

Hannah said nothing, nodding in agreement. As they approached the corner, Hannah jumped and when she landed on the ground, her right foot went into a depression on the road resulting in instant excruciating pain. She saw the truck turn around the corner, but she did not see her mother jump before the truck passed out of view.

Hannah thought—she got around the corner before she jumped. That's why I didn't see her. These were instantaneous thoughts and they were good enough to block out the pain for a second, but then she felt the agony, looked down and saw her foot grotesquely twisted. She knew enough to realize that her ankle was dislocated and maybe fractured. She started in a slow, agonizing, painful crawl to the closest house. When she arrived at the front door, Hannah, looking back to see if her mother was coming, knocked on the door. Hannah's mother was nowhere in sight.

The door creaked open a bit and an old face with a white beard and gray hair peered out and looked down to see Hannah, He called to others who came to the door. Immediately, an argument ensued amongst the residents of the wooden home as to whether or not to grant entry. "We can't get enough food for us," one said. "We can't turn away a fellow Jew," said another. The latter opinion prevailed, and the residents helped Hannah crawl in on her belly. When she was in the house, three men picked her up, and Hannah, clenching her teeth so as not to scream out in pain, found herself on an old couch in what once served as a living room, but now looked more like a dormitory.

"She needs a doctor," said one of the residents.

"No, no," said Hannah. They were taking us away on trucks. Please, will someone look out the front window and see if there is a lady there on the street."

The old man with the white beard looked and said, "There's no one there." Hannah groaned.

"You need a doctor to fix your foot. It's all twisted. We'll get one for you," said the man's wife.

"No doctor, please, no. Don't trouble anybody. Don't risk it. If they catch you trying to help an escaped Jew, they'll kill you all. If there are three men here, I'll tell them what to do to try and straighten out my foot."

"But what do you know about it?" one asked curiously.

"Only a little. I was studying to be a doctor. Please, I'll risk you helping me."

The men stared at each other before one of them said, "Go ahead, tell us what we can do?" said the old man.

She looked at the crowd around her and pointed and said, "You, sir, stand behind the couch, reach over and hold my lower right leg with both hands. Hold it solid in one place, so it doesn't move. Then I need two more men to kneel on the front side of the couch, one to hold my heel and the other to hold my foot around my toes and the front of my foot." The men went in position and did as she told them. As Hannah winced in pain, she said, "Listen, please. I'll count to three and then you, sir, behind the couch, pull my lower leg toward yourself while the two men in front of the couch holding my foot pull it toward the end of the couch and at the same time push it toward you. I don't know how I'll stand the pain, but if it goes back into place, it needs to be wrapped with lots of layers of cloth and splinted with two pieces of wood and wrapped again."

One man took two old shirts out of a drawer, while another went into the back yard and brought in two pieces of lumber about thirty centimeters long. "Will these do?" they asked.

"Perfect," Hannah said.

"Okay, if you're ready," said Hannah through clenched teeth, "one…two…three."

The men felt Hannah's foot slip into place with a loud crack while Hannah kept her grimace, but temporarily lost consciousness. A woman standing nearby felt for her pulse. "It's okay," she said. The men wrapped her foot in place with the shirt, two splints and the second shirt.

When Hannah awakened, she asked half-delirious, "Is my mother here?"

"No, they said." Hannah groaned again as tears flowed. Then she looked down at her foot and nodded yes.

The severe pain kept Hannah couch ridden except when she had to use the toilet. Then with two homemade crutches, she was able to hobble there. This was difficult because when she tried to stand upright and hop to the bathroom, the pain worsened.

In time, the black and blue marks gradually faded, the swelling slowly diminished and the pain lessened a bit each day. These were all signs of improvement. Housemates shared some food with Hannah, but there was never enough although water was plentiful.

Living under such conditions was stressful. Most of the inhabitants of the house met at the front gate every morning, showed their passes and traveled to their daily "jobs." As long as they were capable of work, slave labor though it was, the trucks that took ghetto inhabitants to their deaths never picked up workers.

Two of the non-working older men felt vulnerable and made plans to escape to the forest to join the partisans. They were the ones who suggested that Hannah leave the living room and stay in one of the bedrooms, because should the Nazis or the Byelorussian policemen enter the house looking for the two men, they would see Hannah immediately, and she was not registered there. That would be the equivalent of a death sentence for all.

Hannah moved into the bedroom as suggested, and as the days passed and she continued improving, the men confided in her that they were going to try to escape by crawling under the barbed wire under cover of darkness and go into the forest to find partisans.

"Better to die trying than to sit here hiding waiting to die," one of the men told her.

Hannah knew what was on the men's minds. She had similar thoughts. If they left, and if they agreed, she would go with them. She knew where to go whereas these men did not, but she would not share the information with them because if the Nazis caught them and they knew the Jewish partisan location, there was the danger that the Nazis would torture it out of them.

She answered, bluntly asking, "You're right. I agree with you. Would you consider taking me with you?"

"You feel the same way?" he asked.

"Yes," she answered with unchanged expression

He continued, "We have no idea where to go. We'll have to live off the land and it's cold out there now. We don't know if we'll make it, but at least we'll have tried."

Hannah, knowing her present location and knowing exactly where David was, said, "We can make it with three or four layers of clothes and socks and a hat or wraps around our neck and head. Will you take me?"

"How can you be sure we'll make it? You sound confident."

"I trust in God," she said trying to get them off the track.

Both men laughed. One of them said, "That's very funny. You trust in a God to help one Jew while that same God allows the killing of thousands, maybe millions of Jews?" "Trust me, that's all I ask," she answered.

"What about your leg?"

"I can make it, especially if I can wrap the whole foot with some kind of padding. Don't forget the great doctors I had." She managed a weak smile.

They laughed.

"The time to go is as soon as possible," said Hannah.

They lived in one corner of the ghetto not far from the barbed wire, so once ready they slipped out of the house. Fortunately, the absence of a full moon made it darker than usual outside, but when they approached the barbed wire and heard voices, they quickly crawled back to a nearby home and hid behind a storage bin out of site of the Byelorussian Police who were making rounds outside of the wire. When the police disappeared around a corner and their voices were no longer audible, the younger man of the two ran back to the barbed wire and started frantic digging with a hand shovel. When finished, he waved his hand. The idea was that Hannah would go first and the digger would go last and then reach under the fence to put the dirt back in place.

Still located in the city and outskirts, they followed Hannah who knew the direction she had to travel to get out of the city and to the edge of the forest. She did so mostly by traveling down alleys. The two crutches she used increased her speed by enabling her to keep her injured foot off the ground, albeit with great difficulty.

Still pitch dark, after several hours they entered the forest. Hannah sat down and leaned against a large tree. "I need ten minutes to rest," she said while trying to bear the pain in the ankle and foot exacerbated by the stressful and difficult escape from the ghetto. The other men lay down beside her. "Where do we go now?" they asked.

She answered, "Just follow me, but now at a slower pace if you don't mind. We won't find Nazis here, just animals, snakes, frogs, birds and partisans. The worst is over for us."

She knew where the stream was where she and David fished. From there she also knew how to get to King Tree and the Knothole, and then the location of the Jewish Partisans and David. She started crying.

"What's wrong?" asked one of the men.

"Nothing," she said, "these are tears of joy," but she thought— mother where are you?

Anyone they might see in these thick forests would be partisans, or people looking for partisans. Byelorussian police and German soldiers avoided any forest where they were like fish out of water with a short survival time.

So the two men and Hannah felt as if they had achieved freedom, but the men wondered if Hannah was really a lucky charm. She exuded confidence where they had none, so they followed wherever she went and did not ask questions.

Then Hannah saw it; the stream. David, she thought will I see you soon? Again, the men noticed a contradiction—a smile with tears.

Hannah identified the direction where dawn was just poking its head above the landscape. She picked the point where David crossed the stream and took them all on a trip through the thick forest to King Tree and the knothole. When she found it, she stopped, put her hand over her face, looked up at the heavens and knew that their journey would bring them to the partisans. Without a word about the identification, she said to the men, "Let's go. It won't be long."

The men looked at each other. They both simultaneously thought that she knows where she's going. They followed her without a word.

It took about forty minutes when three men with rifles pointing said, "Stop, who are you?"

"We're looking for partisans," said Hannah.

"Put up your hands," they said while approaching.

They complied, were searched, and one of the riflemen pointing his hand said, "Walk that way, we'll follow and tell you where to go."

After a short time, they arrived at the partisan encampment. The guards took Hannah and the two men right to Jozef. Hannah recognized him immediately, sped up her crutch walk, and when she reached him she dropped her crutches and threw her arms around his neck. "Mr. Askenazy," she cried.

A startled Jozef, had to stare at her for a few seconds before he recognized her. "Hannah, thank God," said Jozef.

"She introduced Jozef to her two companions.

The two men who traveled with Hannah now knew that finding the partisans had been a predetermined destination. They looked at each other and nodded. One said to the other, "God gave her a dislocated ankle so she would come to us and save our lives." The other, saying nothing, looked askance at his friend, but then shrugged his shoulders.

"Jozef said, "Hannah, tell me all that happened. We were all thinking the worst."

She emotionally related the entire story. Jozef listened in fascination.

"Hannah, let me take you in my hut where you can lie down. It looks like you're having pain in that foot."

"Thank you, Mr. Askenazy. That would be nice."

"I'm Jozef, Hannah, please."

"Yes, Jozef."

When she had settled in the hut lying down with injured foot elevated, Jozef said, "Here Hannah, drink this. Then just rest for a while. You've had some tough times. I think I'll get hold of a friend of yours," he smiled.

She nodded, smiled, said, "Thank you, Jozef," and drifted off to sleep in seconds.

Jozef came out of the hut, arranged for some of the partisans to orient the two new members, and told one of the partisans to tell David that Jozef wants to talk to him about an important matter. "If he asks what it's about, tell him you have no idea."

Twenty minutes later, David arrived. "What do you need, Jozef? What can I do for you?"

"We have a new project I want your opinion on. Go in the hut and see what you think."

"What's in there? What should I check out."

"You'll see, just go in."

David walked in and within fifteen seconds, he walked out. "Jozef, there's a sleeping woman in there."

"I'm aware of that," said Jozef.

"I didn't want to wake her," said David.

"Okay. Just go back in and take a closer look at that sleeping woman."

"Alright, Jozef." What's this all about I wonder, thought David.

This time David did not come out for a full two minutes. When he did, his countenance changed. With an ecstatic expression on his face, he said, "I had to look more than once. She's lost so much weight, I didn't recognize her at first. Hannah. It's Hannah, Jozef… I…I…she's still asleep and must be exhausted. What happened?" and the tears rolled down his cheeks.

"Jozef said, She's had it tough, David. I'll let her tell you all about it later. Go back and tell your parents. I'll send for you when she wakes up. This is a happy day for all of us."

David nodded his head, turned and walked back to his parent's field hospital where they practiced their primitive medical and nursing mission. When David told them about Hannah, Emily jumped for joy and they all hugged.

"You'll all come back with me when Jozef tells me to come back," said David.

Ben said, "No, David, get her yourself, meet her again, talk to her and then bring her back. She'll stay with us until you two decide on what you want to do with your lives."

Hannah was exhausted. She slept ten hours before she awakened and then Jozef got David who promptly came back to see her. He walked into Jozef's hut. Neither David nor Hannah said a word as they fell into each other's arms, grasping each other for a full minute. "Thank God, I thought for sure you were dead," said David.

"And I was sure I would be soon," she replied.

They sat there for a time long enough for Hannah to tell her recent story plus the disappearance of her mother.

"I'll talk to Jozef and see if there's anyway he could find out what happened to her. He's got a web of spies all over."

"Thank you, David. I love you." And she thought and prayed silently that her mother would be found alive.

"I love you too, Hannah. Now let's go and see my mother and father and Emily. They know you're here and they can't wait to see you. My father needs to check out that ankle and see what kind of a job Dr. Brunstein did on herself."

Jozef gave them his horse for Hannah to use and David guided her to his family. Emily rushed to her side and hugged Hannah, as did Ben and Leah. Ben unwrapped her foot, examined her ankle and said, "You did a good job, Doctor Hannah. Most dislocations are accompanied by a fracture, but it seems that the ankle is healing well although unstable yet, but that's to be expected. I'll put on an elastic wrap for better support. It should help, but keep using the crutches."

After Ben applied the wrap, David and Hannah sat alone and David said, "You're a partisan now, Hannah. You stay here with us. And you and I have some unfinished business to discuss."

"And what is that, David?" she asked, but had a good idea what he would say.

"I hope we'll have the first Jewish partisan wedding in the forest." He held her in his arms, stared into her eyes and lovingly asked, "Will you marry me, Hannah?"

She nodded her head. "Yes, I will, David, but I want to wait a while. I've got my mother on my mind and I need to clear it up. Right now, I don't know if she's living or dead. I never saw her after she jumped off the truck—if she jumped—I don't know. If she didn't, then they took her away to her death." She started crying.

"Do you know what street you were on when you jumped?" asked David.

"Yes, I was on Zaslavskaya Lane when I jumped right before the bus turned left on the corner on Ratonskaya St. My mother was supposed to jump right after me, but the bus turned the corner and I didn't see it anymore. When I landed, I dislocated my ankle. I don't know if she jumped around the corner or not. I kept looking back as I crawled to the house and I never saw her.'

"Ok," said David, "I got it all down. Jozef has contact with some people in the ghetto who leave every morning and work for the Nazis. I'll get right on it and talk to Joseph and see what he can find out."

"Thank you, David. I love you."

"And I love you, Hannah."

The next day, David spoke with Jozef and told him the entire story including the address where Hannah jumped and her mother disappeared.

"Here's what I know, David. According to Mikhail with one of King Tree and the Knothole messages, the Nazis make a sweep through the ghetto every Thursday evening and round up Jews who don't work. They put them on trucks, take them out of the ghetto into the countryside, and kill and bury them. They're slowly eliminating Jews—plain and simple. Let me first get hold of one of my contacts who can check with the people on Ratonskaya Street and see if anyone knows what happened to Hannah's mother."

"Who's your contact?" asked David.

A surprised Jozef responded, "The less people that know that, the better. There's only one who knows, and that's me and that's the way it stays, David. You should know such things by now."

"Yes. Sorry, Jozef."

Jozef said, "Let me get back to you in a few days after I see what I can find out. If Hannah's mother jumped, there's a good chance some one saw her, because every Thursday the ghetto Jews know to look out the window and watch the trucks go by. They may have seen something. I'll have my contact look into it, and if I find out anything you'll be the first to know, David. The amazing thing is that many of the ghetto Jews still don't know or they refuse to believe that the Nazis are killing them. It's unbelievable."

"Thanks, Jozef, I'll wait to hear from you."

It took five days before Jozef got back to David. His direct contact, a Jewish guard at the ghetto gate, spoke with the residents of Ratonskaya Street. Indeed, the residents saw a lady jump from the truck. She was hesitant as the bus rounded the corner and sped up. On jumping, she failed to realize that her body was going the same direction as the truck, so when she landed, her momentum took her backward and she fell striking the back of her head on the pavement causing unconsciousness. The people in the closest house carried her to safety and took care of her. The ghetto guard confirmed she's still there, having regained consciousness with no major problems. As it turned out, Mikhail had mentioned, via King Tree and the Knothole, the recently started truck removal of ghetto residents, so Jozef was contemplating some action against them. This was his opportunity.

When Jozef told David about Hannah's mother, David was anxious to tell Hannah, but Jozef told him, "No, David, I have a plan I'm working on. Don't tell Hannah yet. How would you like to join us in a rescue?"

"What kind of rescue? Are you talking about Hannah's mother?"

"Yes, as well as others in the ghetto. We need a German speaker for this plan. It may not be necessary, but it might. We have to be ready."

"Well, I can fit that bill." Knowing how secretive Jozef was about all his plans, David asked, "Can you tell me about it now?"

"Only if I'm sure you'll join us. And before you'll answer, you need to know that it's possible you will have to kill. I'm hoping it won't be necessary, but it might."

"And who do I kill this time?" asked David.

"They will be Nazi soldiers or Byelorussian police, but it doesn't matter because they will be guilty of criminal activity," answered Jozef matter-of-factly.

"And that crime is…," asked David.

"Driving Jews to their death, and they know it, said Jozef through clenched teeth." "Consider me in," said David.

"There will be three of us; me, Abel and you, David. Be here tonight at 6.00. We'll work out the plans. Remember, say nothing to Hannah. When she sees the surprise that you're going to give her— you'll need all your strength." He laughed.

That evening, the three men met to hear Jozef's ideas. They sat on large boulders around a table outside of Jozef's hut.

"Here's the plan, "said Jozef. "First, the trucks start out about a kilometer away from the ghetto gate. They leave one at a time for the ghetto to round up Jews. We concentrate on the last truck. There are two men in each truck armed to the teeth, and if there is any opposition to Jews leaving, they shoot them on the spot. I have in mind a location where we can hide close to where the trucks leave. Here's what Abel and I do. I approach the truck from the driver's side, jump on the running board and put a bullet in the head of the driver. Abel mimics me on the passenger side. Abel and I put the bodies in the back of the truck and cover them up. Abel stays in the back. You, David, have been watching this from the side of the road. You run to us and sit in the passenger side and I drive the truck. You'll be wearing a German Sergeant's uniform and just in case it's necessary you'll sprech Deutch if you have to when we go through the ghetto gate. I hope it won't be necessary because the Jewish gate guard already knows to let us pass. He'll recognize me, but in case he doesn't, or anything happens to me, you'll just say Kol Nidrei. That's the password and he knows it. We all need to know where we're going. Here's the address of the house in the ghetto and directions how to get from the gate to the address. Memorize it. There's also directions of how to get from the ghetto to the forest with our passengers including Hannah's mother plus whoever else from the house decides to go with us. That's the general idea. We'll rehearse this in our minds every day until it's automatic and then we go on Thursday."

There were at least a dozen dry runs until the process became automatic. The three of them left on foot with plenty of time to reach their destination. David had a backpack with his German uniform and a small tarp carried within. They all carried pistols with extra ammunition. The Nazi trucks came from a depot staffed by the Nazis and local supporters. The short truck drive by the Nazis to the ghetto included a one-block area with a dirt road and no homes. This was the sight chosen to apprehend the truck, which had to drive slowly because of the poor road conditions. As the truck passed, Jozef and Abel emerged from behind trees, leaped on the running board and killed the driver and passenger before they knew what was happening. David, now attired in his German sergeant's uniform joined them, put the dead men in the back of the truck, and, according to plan, drove toward the ghetto gate. There the ghetto guard, immediately recognizing Jozef, waved them on. From there it was a short drive to the address on Ratonskaya street.

In the meantime, the homes inhabitants watching the trucks through the front window, were surprised when two men, not in uniform, approached the front door. David, in his German uniform, stayed outside in the truck. The home's residents opened the door and an impatient Jozef asked, "Is a Mrs. Brunstein here?"

A hand raised, and a shaky voice said, "That's me. What do you want? Who are you?"

With the quick answer, "Hannah sent me," Ms. Brunstein's hands went up in front of her face. "Oh, my God," she said.

"You come with us, Mrs. Brunstein. Anyone else who wants to come, make up your mind in three minutes. That's when you leave this ghetto forever."

As Jozef led Mrs. Brunstein to the truck, she spotted David in the front seat. Her inclination was to go to him, but Jozef stopped her. "Not now, later please. You'll see him later."

With a truckload of ghetto Jews, they passed back through the gate and drove their pre-determined path to the forest where they now felt free to bury the bodies of the men they killed, abandon the truck, and took the long walk back to their encampment. They arrived late in the evening. Ms. Brunstein cried and hugged David. "My Hannah is okay?" she asked.

"Yes," he answered, "you'll see her tomorrow." Then she and the others sat down and fell asleep within minutes. Ms. Brunstein was still smiling as she slept.

The next morning, David arrived early and reunited with Hannah's mother. He told her about Hannah, her escape and her recovering ankle injury. She listened in rapt attention, not saying a word as David talked. When he finished, Hannah's mother started to cry and hugged David. "These are tears of joy," she said.

"Let's go and see Hannah," he told her.

Hannah was with Ben, Leah and Emily and had no idea where David had been all day yesterday, but David's parents explained that he often goes on missions for food and other miscellaneous items.

Then David and Ms. Brunstein walked into their encampment. The shock on Hannah's face turned into unrestrained joy when she recognized her mother. As the tears flowed she buried her head in her mother's neck and while doing this, she lifted up her eyes, looked at David with a gratitude that he would remember forever, and said, "Yes, David, you have my answer now. I will marry you." He smiled and he joined them, holding them both in his arms. To Hannah, he said, "I love you, Hannah, you have made me the happiest man in the world." To Ms. Brunstein, he said, "We owe your rescue all to Jozef, he planned it all."

Leah Frohman smiled with happiness as she heard David say this. It reminded her of the time when they were thinking about partisan resistance and she recommended Jozef as the natural leader in any such undertaking. She felt good. To her husband Ben, she whispered, "We must help them make a glorious wedding under the stars."

CHAPTER 22

MAZEL TOV—A WEDDING

DECEMBER 1941

"We want you to marry us, Hersh," said David to Hersh Rosansky, a rabbinical student turned partisan fighter.

"Mazel tov," said Hersh, "I guess I'm the closest thing here to a rabbi what with one year left before my postponed ordainment, but it will be my pleasure. If it's okay with you, it's okay with me," he said.

Hersh, a young man of twenty-three with a thin black beard, a skullcap attached to a full head of black hair, and close-set brown eyes, knew what awaited him if the Nazis invaded. One of the first men Jozef spoke to when he was making contingency plans before the war, Hersh agreed that staying in Minsk was a death wish if the Nazis struck. He left with Jozef the instant he heard the news about the Nazi invasion of Russia. Hersh was single and he convinced his family to join him in the forest. His mother, father, and teen-aged sister were all forest dwellers now.

"What do we have to do, Hersh?" asked David.

"I'll give you a streamlined version because that's about all we can do here in the forest. First, you need to understand that you marry for two purposes: companionship and procreation. And what do you both think of that?"

David said, "I agree to both, but as to the procreation part—that will have to wait."

"For better days," added Hannah.

"Good thinking. Just keep that part of the bargain. You know, marriage is a holy contract, a *kiddushin* or sanctification, a fulfillment of God's commandment. It is a legal contract, with rights and obligations known as a *Ketubah*. As long as you have the Ketubah, you don't even need a rabbi to marry you, but everybody does it, of course to put religion and faith into the marriage."

"We want a *Ketubah*," said David, "where do we get one?"

"I'm afraid you'll have to write it yourself."

A shocked David said, "I wouldn't know where to start."

"It's easy. Just sit down and write what you feel are all the obligations a man should have to his wife. The more you think about it, the more you'll come up with."

Hannah asked, "What about the wife's obligation to the husband?"

"Do it, Hannah. You write it. That's preferable in my opinion. Since the modern way of thinking is that marriage is a fifty-fifty proposition, I never could understand why the *Ketubah* was so one sided. I suggest you write your part first, David, then you, Hannah. Just don't get into any fights, please. If there is any chance of that, just do it the old-fashioned way—husband's obligations to wife. We don't want a divorce before the marriage." He laughed. "Oh, and by the way, you need two witnesses to sign it."

"Anything else we have to do?" asked Hannah.

"Once you get the *Ketubah,* I'll take care of everything else. Tell me four men you would like to hold the canopy over you during the ceremony. David, the Saturday before the wedding, I'll bring you up to the Torah to bless it. That's just to remind you both that the Torah will be a guide to your marriage. We'll go through a ceremony."

"I have a Torah, a family heirloom," said David. That's what I want to use. It's from a grandfather of mine going way back."

"Perfect," said Hersh. "Get a ring—anything will do. I'll say my words, you'll do as I ask, and I'll tell David when to step on the glass and break it. Then you'll kiss and be man and wife under God. Give me the date of the big day, and we'll get you there. We shouldn't waste time. We don't know what could happen here one day to the next."

'Rabbi' Hersh and the happy couple planned their wedding in all the details possible under such adverse conditions. Held on a cold evening with all appropriately attired for the weather, the entire partisan group attended. The smiling groom, David, accompanied by his parents, Ben and Leah, marched down the 'aisle' to Hersh. The crying bride, Hannah, walked down the 'aisle' accompanied by Jozef in lieu of her assassinated father, while Hannah's mother, crying as well, stood near Hersh.

When they came together, Hersh said, "We are here today in the forest under stars, in the cold, and under adverse conditions made bearable by a happy occasion to share the marriage ceremony of David and Hannah. The *Ketubah*, signed and witnessed, legalizes this marriage ceremony before God. David and Hannah, as I wrap this *Tallit* around your shoulders encompassing you both, let it stand for a symbol unifying you as one in the Laws of Moses and Israel under God for all time to come until death do you part. David, take Hannah's hand in yours."

David took Hannah's hand, looked lovingly into her eyes and said from a carefully prepared and memorized speech, "Hannah, I love you with all my heart and for all eternity. I pledge to you that I will keep this love for you as my prime mover, sharing life with you and protecting you until the end of our lives. I do this today and forever as one small effort on my part due to personal love of a man for a woman and overall love for the Jewish religion, today facing the worst peril of its long history. We agree that although our obligation is principally to each other, we both understand that Judaism, as a way of life, must continue. Let us never forget, in these days of great peril, that our obligation to protect Judaism will never end. With that in mind, and as long as threatening conditions remain unchanged, we also pledge continued struggle against the terror that we face, for if that battle is lost, our personal pledges to each other will be meaningless. We will promote unity and cohesiveness with our partisan brothers until we emerge victorious against the threat we face and save our way of life for future generations."

"I understand and pledge the same to you my darling David," said Hannah.

Hersh said, "David, do you take this woman to be your lawfully wedded wife, to love and cherish her in sickness and in health for better or for worse until death do you part?"

"I do," said David.

"Hannah, do you take this man to be your lawfully wedded husband, to love and cherish him in sickness and in health for better or for worse until death do you part?"

"I do," said Hannah.

"David, place the ring on Hannah's finger."

Starring into Hannah's eyes as she stared back, David, by touch alone placed the ring on her finger. Then he broke the glass by stomping on it with his foot as the guests all shouted Mazel Tov.

"I now pronounce you husband and wife. You are now one soul in two bodies. You may kiss the bride," said Hersh, shortening the ceremony due to a sudden increased wind chill. After more Mazel Tovs and congratulations all around, the bride and groom retired to one of the underground shelters, built by the partisans where they would spend their first night as husband and wife.

CHAPTER 23
MINSK FINAL SOLUTION
FIRST QUARTER 1942

The Nazi officers who first occupied the Minsk headquarters where Mikhail Gregov worked were part of an elite group; a second army, so to speak. Only this army, not part of the regular German army (Wehrmacht), reported directly to Adolph Hitler through his intermediaries, Heinrich Himmler, head of the SS (Schuttzstaffel or defense echelon) and Reinhard Heydrich, head of the Reich Security Main Office (Reichssicherheitshauptamt RSHA).

This second army, the Einsatzgruppen, first formed in 1939 was to follow the German army into Poland, round up Jews and place them in ghettos. Two years later, at the start of the Russian campaign and with an agreement with the German army, they were now to implement phase one of the "final solution," the elimination of Eastern European Jewry and other enemies of the state. Four groups of Einsatzgruppen (A, B, C, D) formed for this purpose, did their job with ruthless efficiency in Poland, Russia, Byelorussia and the Ukraine.

The handpicked officers, trained at a top-secret location, were PhD's., lawyers, teachers and other professionals. Assigned to one of the four special task forces, the officers' instructions from Hitler were simple: follow the army, pacify the rear, get rid of all enemies including Communists, commissars, priests, intelligentsias, officials, Jews, and anyone conceived as being against Hitler's way of thinking. The philosophy of these murderous groups was war is cruel but simple, and if Germany is to avail forever, there must be no potential enemies left to organize future resistance. The Einsatzgruppen knew what Hitler expected and they fanned out following the three German armies that swarmed into Russia, Byelorussia and the Ukraine.

The German invasion of Russia was very successful in the early months: the northern invasion force surrounded Leningrad; the center group raced toward Moscow; the south group placed Kiev in the Ukraine under siege. Russian losses were considerable. Germans captured and killed many hundreds of thousands.

The Russian Chief of Staff, Georgi Zhukov, advocated that his troops defending Kiev should retreat and take up stronger defensive positions. Stalin would have none of it and insisted that Zhukov defend Kiev at all costs. The Germans inflicted massive casualties on the ill-prepared Russians and captured Kiev, but the delay may well have prevented the capture of Moscow. In addition, the approaching winter slowed the Germans as they went further into Russia, Byelorussia and the Ukraine. The longer supply lines, Stalin's retreat tactic of leaving nothing standing before the advancing enemy (scorched earth), plus behind the line attacks by partisans, and the freezing weather created unsolvable logistic, military and health problems that forced the Germans to stop, thus ending the blitzkrieg.

By October and November of 1941, the German troops came within fifteen miles of Moscow. Stalin ordered all of Moscow's citizens to head out of range of Nazi guns. He stayed in an underground bunker, took control of the war, made patriotic speeches, rallied his forces, brought a new German offensive to a halt and forced a

320 kilometer German retreat before the gates of Moscow—the first
German retreat of World War II.

The central Einsatzgruppe ran into trouble in the form of a
Jewish partisan group led by Jozef Askenazy assisted by a Russian
soldier explosives consultant and two young Jews who dynamited
the Einsatzgruppe leaders in their beds one night. But not before
the terrorists started their dirty work by organizing police and local
anti-Semites to help them kill prominent locals and especially Jews.

Now the Einsatzgruppe was leaderless, and the drive toward
Moscow in the central zone faced some problems unless a new
leadership group could continue their vital work.

"Assign one of your best men to head this group," said Hitler to
Himmler. "The center is too vital to the Russian invasion to take
any chances. There seems to be a well organized behind the lines
resistance movement around Minsk. Get rid of it."

"Yes, Mein Fuhrer. I have a perfect man for the job—Oscar
Hoffman."

"I'm counting on you, Heinrich."

Colonel Oskar Hoffman was one of those German men born in
the late 1800's whose accident of birth would cause them to have to
serve their country in two world wars. He joined the army in 1914
as a lieutenant and fought in World War I. Many would not survive
one war or the other. The experience would affect their lives, more
often than not in an adverse manner. Hoffman was very intelligent
and insanely brave, always leading his troops from the front. This
assured him multiple wounds, but also multiple decorations including
two iron crosses.

Colonel Oskar Hoffman represents an actual Nazi Einsatzgruppe
leader by the name of Oskar Dirlewanger (1895-1945). In a group

famous for barbaric cruelty, Dirlewanger stood at the top. An intellectual PhD in political Science, a rapist who served prison time for molesting young girls, he fought in World War I, then with the Freicorps after that war and in the Spanish Civil War and World War II where he was responsible for destroying many villages including killing women and children in Byelorussia. While recovering from his twelfth wound in Bavaria after the war, he was beaten and tortured to death by Polish guards working for French occupation forces.

After World War I, during the political crisis of the Weimar Democracy, Colonel Oskar Hoffman (I will start italicizing now because the life of Oscar Hoffman exactly parallels that of the real Oscar Dirlewanger)…

fought as a Freicorps (Freecorps) officer. Freicorps officers were right-wing anti-Communist soldiers used by the Weimar Democracy in a strange democratic and fascist collaboration to preserve the fragile new German post World War I government against the Communists.

After the struggle, Hoffman (Dirlewanger) returned to school, completed his PhD in political science and joined the Nazi party, but was expelled when he was caught seducing a young girl from the BDM (Bund Deutcher Madel), the female counterpart of the Hitler Youth.

Years later, in 1934, the lure of another BDM was too much for him and earned him two years in Dachau concentration camp. Released when he volunteered to fight in Spain in the newly formed Condor Division in 1939, he suffered several wounds, which required a return to Germany. When Hitler disbanded the Condor Legion in 1939, his superiors assigned Hoffman to the SS. It seems his compulsion for young girls kept him out of a career in politics and kept him in the military.

After the start of WWII, the idea of the Einsatzgruppen came to fruition, and for such a fighting force, the Nazis needed the dredges of society, so who better to be one of the leaders than Hoffman (Dirlewanger) Recruiting like-minded soldiers from the prisons of Germany completed the force.

Himmler gave Hoffman his new assignment—Minsk. He told Hoffman about the setback experienced by the first Nazi Einsatzgruppe leadership in Minsk and advised him—although he would not have needed such advice—that cruelty was to be his hallmark and that his job was to 'dispatch' all enemies of the state, especially Jews, as rapidly as possible. By now after three wars, four if you count his *Freicorps* experience, and in spite of his advanced education—or perhaps because of it—his mind was full of the Nazi creed. Hitler's Mein Kampf, which he read from cover-to-cover, guided his very existence.

Mikhail experienced a cold chill when he first saw Colonel Hoffman. He was the tallest German officer he had ever seen, standing well over six feet. There were several fine, and one thick, ragged scar on the right side of his chin that forced him to speak out of the left side of his mouth. Mikhail thought, and time would prove him correct, that he would never see a smile from the face of this man whose very being radiated cruelness. The less I say the better, thought Mikhail.

"Take the four of us on a tour of this building," Hoffman gruffly ordered.

"Yes, sir." answered Mikhail.

They started in the basement where Mikhail tried to impress upon his new bosses the complexity and age of the heating equipment stressing that after many repairs he would be able to ensure them comfort even during the coldest weather. In this way, he wanted them to understand that he was indispensable to the smooth functioning of the building. The three other floors were all office and meeting space most of which now lie empty since all the Communist functionaries had fled to Moscow. With the tour complete, they sat in the former Mayor's office on the first floor.

"I want you to set up four living and sleeping quarters on each of the second, third and fourth floors," said Hoffman.

"Yes, sir," said Mikhail. He was determined to use these two words as his sole means of communication with the Colonel whom he recognized as one who would be likely to find ulterior motives in any question Mikhail would ask. To continue to serve as a double agent, this philosophy would be his best chance to keep this status alive. Mikhail thought, why twelve sleeping quarters? There are only four of them. Maybe they plan to sleep in different locations each night, or they will have visitors on a regular basis. Whatever the reason, with a man such as the colonel any why question would be like playing Russian roulette.

Mikhail, aided by German enlisted soldiers went to work moving furniture and beds to four rooms on each floor. They finished the task that day. When told, Colonel Hoffman's only response was a non-smiling nod of his head. With that response, Mikhail left the room and went to the basement where he continued his inspection of the heating equipment.

That evening at home he prepared a report for King Tree and the Knothole.

Three days later, Jozef read the report:

New Nazi commander for Minsk...Colonel Oskar Hoffman... Very tall...about fifty years old...scarred face...mean bitch...three other officers and troops to follow...will keep you posted.

Jozef would keep that in mind awaiting any further information. He thought, what could this mean? Elimination of the Minsk ghetto was progressing. There was the start of Nazi forays into the countryside where they started to kill Jews, so it appeared that a systematic war on Jews was starting to heat up. He felt helpless in the face of overwhelming odds. He needed to get this new head of the snake, this Colonel Hoffman. What a brave man Mikhail was, thought Jozef. At least Hoffman, a big man, might be an easy target. What I wouldn't give to get him in my sights. We'll see what Mikhail says.

The Germans faced a new reality in December 1941 when the Japanese struck Pearl Harbor, Hawaii. Hitler, finally honoring an agreement with another country (Japan), quickly declared war on the United States. The Pearl Harbor surprise attack unified America as nothing else could. At the same time, many German generals realized that a sleeping giant could slowly, out of reach of German attack, build up its industrial might and be a very formidable enemy. Coupled with the German inability to destroy Russia in the weeks Hitler predicted it would take, these two factors were an unexpected roadblock into Hitler's plans for a glorious and rapid victory of Nazism over Europe and perhaps the world.

Now that Roosevelt and Churchill were allies in the struggle to defeat Nazism, Both leaders met together in Washington D.C., agreed on a combined Chief of Staff to lead the war effort and made their first priority victory over Germany in Europe followed by victory over Japan in the Pacific.

With Hitler's plans for a rapid defeat of all his enemies stymied, he would at least carry out his second major goal: the destruction of the "Jewish race." With that in mind, the Wannsee conference in Berlin was set to find a "Final Solution" for the Jews.

The Wannsee, a public lake with beautiful gardens outside of Berlin was a tranquil setting in sharp contrast to the nature of the meeting's topic: review progress already made in killing Jews, define who was a Jew, and plan the "Final Solution," the total annihilation of European Jewry. Reinhard Heydrich was there, Eichmann was there, as where other functionaries representing the Security Police, politics, administration, the Nazi Party, and the Race and Resettlement Office of the SS.

After the German invasion, the rapid advances of the Germans through Russia emboldened the Nazi leadership who realized that four million Jews of the Soviet Union (Eastern Poland, Russia, Byelorussia and the Ukraine), would fall under German hands. This made the solution of the Jewish question an imperative.

In addition, if a German "Garden of Eden" arose west of the Ural Mountains, pacification of the entire region was a priority. This meant that the area must be Judenfrei, and all potential enemies eliminated immediately.

Such was the order that came down from Hitler.

If the Soviet territories were to be the killing field of Jews and others, than the Nazis would transport German, Austrian and Czech Jews to the Soviet Union, working to death those who could serve them in some capacity and killing immediately those who were of "no use."

Oskar Hoffman was to be an important cog in that wheel. He and his three underling officers got right to work planning while they awaited the arrival of Nazi troops to carry out the final destruction of the Jews, and once that was completed—local partisan destruction as well. No one must be left that could offer opposition to Hitler's final plans for his *Judenfrei* Nazi Utopia.

With a man like Hoffman looking over his shoulder, Mikhail vowed to keep a low profile and do his work keeping the heating system of the old building in working condition, a formidable task.

Hoffman and his fellow officers met every day in the meeting room on the first floor. A different Nazi officer or officers stationed in Minsk would attend the meeting and then they would leave to an undisclosed location, which Mikhail interpreted to be an inspection trip of some sort. They were obviously making plans for some actions and whatever it was, it could not be good. They would be gone for a few hours and then return to continue with the meeting. This was a daily ritual.

On one occasion after they left the building, Mikhail was on the first floor inspecting some heating ducts. He saw the Nazi officers drive off and he opened the door of the meeting room, caught a glimpse of the long rectangular table where the meetings took place and noted a typewritten sheet on the table in front of each chair. This must be the agenda of the meetings the officers held or some other type of information. Mikhail quickly closed the door, thinking that if caught even looking in that room, God knows what they would do to him. Stepping in that room would be enough to label him guilty, and the Nazi system of justice is guilty unless proven innocent, but they had no time to prove anyone innocent so they rendered the verdict on the spot and carried out the sentence concurrent with the rendering—a bullet in the head.

On the other hand, the information on those papers might be vital, and in the corner of the room on a table was a mimeograph machine possibly used to produce the papers that were on the table in front of each chair. So armed with the knowledge that the officers had driven off and never returned before at least two hours, Mikhail dashed into the room, heart pounding, headed straight for the mimeograph machine, turned the crank and produced a quick copy that a rapid glance told him had the same general configuration as the papers on the table. Written in German, he had no idea as to its contents, but King Tree and the Knothole would know.

Jozef retrieved the copy, removing it from its waterproof container accompanied by a note from Mikhail stating 'from a Nazi officer meeting.' He opened the paper and as soon as he saw the German script he went to Dr. Ben, called him aside, made sure that no one else was within earshot and said, "This is from Mikhail. I need a quick translation. They sat down on a fallen log and Ben unfolded the paper and translated.

"This is a letter to a Colonel Hoffman. It's telling Hoffman that a 190-man army company would be arriving at the Minsk train station on the twentieth late at night. They're fully armed and ready to carry out Hoffman's orders to rid the area of Jews and other undesirables."

"Does it define undesirables?" asked Jozef.

"No," said Ben. I guess it assumes that Hoffman knows what that means. Also, it says that the military equipment the company carries with them will be light arms plus all the usual equipment of a fully armed company."

"I guess that means they mean business."

"What are you thinking, Jozef?" asked Ben.

"I'm thinking that we can't go toe to toe with a fully armed company of 190 men, but we can try and disrupt and delay their plans. I'll talk it over and see what the consensus is, but my thinking is that we can dynamite the train while they're on it, slow them up and maybe injure or kill some of them."

"That would be a great accomplishment if you can do it, nodded Ben."

Jozef continued, "More than one track comes into Minsk from many directions, so we have to know the right track. I think we can rule out a track coming from the east because that's where the troops are that invaded. I'm sure they'd be using troops from Germany for this mission. From what I understand, they've got specially trained troops who work in the rear behind the Nazi forward lines."

"That makes sense," said Ben. Maybe you'll get more news from Mikhail."

Jozef nodded. "That man is a hero in my book. If they catch him, he's as good as dead. What else does it say?"

"The last part of it orders them to destroy the partisans once the Jews are out of the way."

"Hmm, I was expecting that. Are there any specific instructions?"

Ben silently read the letter and said, "No, it sounds like the high command will leave it to Hoffman, or maybe instructions will come later. God only knows. Mikhail also says that this Colonel Hoffman is the meanest, angriest man he has ever come across who is capable of anything. He feels the Jews are in their greatest danger ever. Good luck, Jozef."

Jozef tried to envision what Colonel Hoffman looked like. He conjured up a picture in his mind and envisioned it with a bull's eye on the Colonels forehead. Save that for later. Jozef reasoned that destroying the train would be only a three man job. The less the better, he thought. Stealth would be important. He envisioned three of them carrying enough dynamite to blow a large hole on and under the train tracks, derailing the train. With preliminary plans in his mind, he sought out David and Abel who had previous experience with dynamite when they blew up the home where the Nazis officers were sleeping. He spoke with Abel first and told him to be at his hut in the morning on the seventeenth. Then he went and sought out David and found him with Hannah working at the medical compound with Ben and Leah. "How are the newlyweds," Jozef asked.

"We're fine," answered Hannah as David smiled and nodded in agreement.

They engaged in small talk until Ben diverted Hannah's attention for a moment. Jozef grabbed David's arm and quickly said in a whisper, I need to talk to you. Be at my hut in an hour." Then before David could say anything, Jozef bid farewell to Hannah, Ben, and Leah and walked back to his hut.

When David arrived, Abel was already there. Seeing Abel, David knew that Jozef had an important motive in mind. He waited for Jozef's words.

Jozef did not disappoint. "Do you remember the explosives Sergei left us?" Jozef asked.

"Yes," they both replied.

"We're going to put them to good use," Jozef said with a wide smile on his face. Jozef's expressions spoke as loud as his voice, and David and Abel knew that with that wide a smile, the 'use' would be an important one and they knew not to ask.

"We're going to blow up a train filled with Nazis." He paused for effect. "Doesn't that make you feel good?" he asked, the smile never leaving his face.

"I don't feel good, I feel great when I can do that to Nazi bastards," said Abel.

"David smiled and nodded. He was continually amazed at the information that Jozef could come up with, wondered as to its source, but again knew better than to ask. "The three of us are going to carry dynamite and everything needed to rig up an explosive around and under train tracks. We're experts after all; we watched it done once, now we do it once, then we teach. That's the partisan way. There's a shipment of Nazis coming to do us harm and I want to arrange a greeting for them even before they get here. The idea is to find a location where the train is on a straight track and going fast, so when we blow their asses to kingdom come, we derail and cause the most damage. I hope we find a location where we can watch our handiwork from a distance. Then, after we do the dirty deed, we run like hell away from there and come back home like nothing happened. You like?"

"I like," said Abel

"I love it," said David.

"There's one fly in the ointment," said Jozef, "and that is I don't know what time at night the train arrives in Minsk, so I want us in a location in the forest ready to blast about thirty or so miles from the Minsk train station where we have the best hideouts while we do our thing. We'll get there the evening before, get some sleep, hide out the next day, set up the explosives in five meter increments and wait for the train to come. As soon as the locomotive is over the dynamite locations, we blow it and watch the train fall into the holes and get the hell out of there. Okay?"

David and Abel both nodded yes.

"Be here at noon on the nineteenth. Remember, as far as anyone else is concerned, you're just leaving for the usual supply trip."

Abel went back to his family and told his parents that he would be going on a supply trip in a few days that would be a bit longer than the usual. They accepted his explanation without comment.

David told Hannah the same. She said nothing for a short time before she said, "I know you like an anatomy text, David, and I know when you're lying. What are you really going to do? All I needed to hear was your wedding speech to tell me about your mind set. You're going to continue the fight aren't you?"

David stood speechless for a moment and then said, "Jozef swore me to secrecy. I have no choice. I promised and so I can't say a word to anyone, not even my brilliant wife who knows my every thought. Someday, if we survive this mess we're in, I'll tell you everything. I love you so, and that's why I have to fight back and do everything I can to save us all."

Hannah looked at him lovingly and nodded her head. "I understand, David. I love you too."

On the eighteenth, Jozef, Abel and David met to discuss plans for their latest mission. Jozef's face reflected the seriousness of their new adventure. They gathered up Sergei's dynamite, wires, plunger, and placed them in back packs along with three days of sparse provisions and left late in the evening planning a thirty-kilometer march outside of Minsk that Jozef laid out in advance. This would take them to a spot in the forest where the railroad track was straight line. They gave themselves plenty of leeway planning to arrive on location on the nineteenth. After a good evening of hoped for sleep, they would awaken and station themselves close to the tracks. The plan was to lay the dynamite just after dawn and lie in wait for an evening train heading for its destination in the central Minsk station on the evening of the twentieth.

What happened next shocked both Abel and David. Jozef said, Abel and David, you're free to leave now."

David, who at the time of this verbal bombshell was watching a rabbit scatter over the landscape, turned his head toward Jozef and in shocked surprise said, "What the hell are you talking about, Jozef, where's the adhesion in this group of three? I thought we were unified." Abel listened in shocked surprise.

"We three are unified, but you need to know that there are those among us who are not."

Abel asked with angry emphasis, "What are they saying? What do they want to do?"

"Let me start from the beginning," said Jozef. "When we first came to the forest there were only thirty of us. You both knew my philosophy then. There would be one leader and I was it. My philosophy is to stay alive and kill Nazis. That will be our contribution to this awful war and the Nazi Jew killing blood bath. Everyone in the group must agree. As it turns out, as the Nazis tighten the screws, more Jews manage to escape and come to us. Some of them want to fight. Some of them don't want to stir things up and all they are interested in is survival and have no courage for a fight. They say they are afraid of the reprisals which will follow and why stir the Nazis up."

David asked, "How do you handle them? What do you say?"

With a rising crescendo to his voice and with increasing emotion, Jozef said, "I tell them in no uncertain terms that this partisan group is a fighting group. Our reason for existence is to fight and kill Nazis before they can kill us. I tell them that yes we are outnumbered, but that means we fight all the harder, and if we die we will at least have died striking the bastards who want to kill us. Then I look them in the eye and say if this is not your philosophy then you are free to go and set up your own partisan pacifist group and die like sheep surrounded by a wolf pack. That's not for my group and anyone thinking like that has no place with us. To stay with us, they have to be willing to fight, at least in self-defense, and they will be watched like a hawk watches for potential enemies."

Then Jozef stayed silent for a few moments, regained his composure and said, "That wasn't meant for you two. I trust you both with my life. I just want you to know what we are up against now. Mikhail assures me that the new commander, this Colonel Hoffman is a man that he tries to avoid at all costs. He is a fanatic and ruthless and we can expect the worst."

This only steeled Abel and David to the mission. "Were with you to the end," said David.

"That's what I want to hear. Never let these pacifists influence you."

"Not a chance, Jozef," said David noting that Jozef was more relaxed now that he had gotten that off his chest.

That evening at dusk, after surveying the railroad tracks and finding a straight long run where their binoculars would allow a good two-mile line of sight, they laid the dynamite around the tracks, wired it up in four locations and set back to wait the train's arrival. "I still have a nagging question," said Abel.

"What's that?" asked Jozef.

"How do you know that this is the right train?"

"I don't," said Jozef nonchalantly.

David and Abel looked at each other, before staring at Jozef speechless.

"It's no mystery really. I can't come up with perfect intelligence before this act of war we are about to commit today, so I do my best. Who could be on this train arriving from all areas controlled by Nazis? Are they Jews going on vacation or visiting relatives or on a business trip? Not a chance, since all Jews are now prisoners of war, locked up in ghettos or killed as we speak. Are they gentiles? Maybe if the gentiles are allies of the Nazis, and in that case they will get what they deserve. Are they Byelorussian soldiers or Russian soldiers? Not a chance at this time. There are no trains other than trains carrying Nazis or other enemies, so I don't give a shit who's on it."

David and Abel listened in rapt attention, but Jozef had more to say.

"Just remember, we are planning war and as with any war plan, the best made plans end when the first shot is fired. All hell breaks loose. Everything may change. Our best chance is to blow the tracks, and get the hell out of the way. If the train is over the dynamite, it'll stop right there you can be sure. Just follow me and run like hell back to camp. We'll probably get separated; you're young pups and I can't keep up with you, but I'll see you back in camp and we'll get ready for the next mission, which as long as I'm still alive will never end."

After dusk, they wired the tracks with dynamite. Most of the rest of the time they spent in silence, each with their own thoughts, a minute passing as if an hour. Finally, at nine-twenty p.m., they heard the train off in the distance. Rushing into position, Jozef, the closest to the action, held his hand high in the air. When the train drove over the explosives, his right hand dropped down, David and Abel pressed the plunger. Four blasts lifted the train off the ground before a smoking wrecked heap fell into fiery holes. The three saboteurs fled as fast as their feet could carry them.

CHAPTER 24
BILATERAL REVENGE
FIRST QUARTER 1942

"Who did this?" screamed Colonel Hoffman at a special meeting called to discuss the issue and plan a response.

"Partisans, who else?" answered one of the men at the meeting.

"Of course, partisans. What kind, damn it"

"We can't answer that for sure, sir, but a trace of explosives turned up, one bit with a Russian letter on it."

"That tells us nothing, but I'm going to make an assumption and that assumption is that Jews did it. The bastards will pay. What's the casualty report?" asked a tremulous Hoffman.

"Sir, eight are dead and twenty-eight are wounded, some seriously."

"Captain, you will organize a further round up of 100 Jews for each of the men killed. That's in addition to the usual round up. Get to the remaining company and have them get busy involving local police to help collect 800 Jews. You know what to do. After that you keep track of all our wounded and as soon as one dies, get another 100 Jews and kill them. We're going to have to get to work and finish the job on these criminals. Then it's all out war on the partisans. Those are our orders and they will be carried out."

No one had any doubt that Hoffman's words were law.

"Yes, sir."

"I want some intelligence about where the partisan camps may be. We need some scouting expeditions out in the forest and some surveillance planes to find their location or locations. Look for smoke, look for any signs of activity. Let me know every step of the way what you're planning."

"Yes, sir."

The sudden influx of Jews into the forest brought the news of the increased killings that alerted Jozef to expect trouble. The Einsatzgruppe troopers were in a full offensive mode with part one of their jobs—getting rid of Jews. The increased rapidity of this activity alarmed the "useful Jews" who now felt their days were numbered as well. The many Jews who now found their way to Jozef's encampment made security impossible. Some of them would return to Minsk attempting to see relatives. Doing so resulted in their capture. Under extreme and novel forms of torture followed inevitably by death, a few gave up the location of the Jewish partisans. Mikhail confirmed this and sent a message via King Tree and the Knothole. It said, 'hectic activity here. Hoffman barking orders. Kill more Jews. One hundred to one. Teach them a lesson. Danger. Danger. Get the partisans now.'"

Jozef knew that it was just a matter of time before they'd have to flee to another location; but not yet. If there was to be a battle for survival let it come, and there might be a way to turn it to a Jewish advantage. With that in mind, he decided to see his good friend, Andrei Kalemnikoff, a vital cog in his hoped for wheel. It all depended on Andrei.

When Jozef arrived at the Russian partisan camp, he quickly met Andrei with the ever present Brushka at his side. A smiling

Andrei said, "To what do I owe the honor of this visit, Jozef. When you come, there is always excitement. Big things happen. What's on your mind?"

Jozef said, "How would you like to kill more Nazis in one day than you ever killed before?"

Andrei slapped his hand on his thigh and said, "I knew it, the man brings more excitement than a barrel of monkeys. Right, Brushka. Kill more Nazis? That is my Raison d'etra," he said in perfect French. "tell me more."

"Raison de what?" said Jozef.

"Reason for my existence. It's French."

"You speak French?" asked a surprised Jozef.

"Sure, and Russian, Byelorussia, Ukranian, English and German. Tell me more, Jozef."

"Do you know about the increased killing of Jewish civilians lately?"

"So I've heard," Andrei said nodding his head.

Jozef continued with his serious facial expression that both Andrei and Brushka recognized. "According to my sources, the Nazis are going to rid the area of all Jews and once they've finished that they will go full blast against the partisans, which to them are a pain in the ass, but which so far they want to avoid because they're not at home in the forest."

"Ah, those mysterious sources of yours again, Jozef. As I said, and I'm holding you to it, after the war, you'll tell me all about it. You are sure they're coming after you Jewish partisans soon?"

"No I'm not sure they're coming after us Jewish partisans even though they're probably a little pissed off after we killed some of their reinforcements."

Andrei interrupted, "Aha, I knew that might have been you. Good work, Jozef."

"Thanks. That was a three-man job."

Andrei whistled. Brushka nodded in admiration.

Jozef continued, "I only know they're coming after the partisans. If I had to bet, I would say the Jewish partisans first, because Jews are their first target, but they never said which partisan group is first in their cross hairs. I think they'd like to kill us all. And you are a bigger partisan threat than we poor Jews are who have to scrounge for food and arms and can barely defend ourselves. I figure this: if they're coming after partisans they don't expect the Jewish and Russian partisans to work together. We have a common enemy now and I think that together we can give them a party they'll never forget."

"You are a wise man, Jozef. I'm glad you're not in the Russian army. You would probably be my boss if you were. Do you have details?"

"Just an outline at this stage."

Andrei reached for a pencil and paper. "Let's hear it, but remember me teaming up with Jews will raise a lot of my superiors eyebrows, so it better be good. No, it better be great."

"Even better than great," said Brushka whistling the Russian Kozatsky.

"It is," said Jozef. "Okay, I agree with you that they will come for Jewish partisans first. After all, their orders are to kill all local Jews and then concentrate on partisans. That's us on both counts. I'm sure they'll take their company of men and head to our camp. They know where we are now and they're armed to the teeth. This will be the first time they will risk attacking us in the forest. We can't defeat them alone and we know it, but we can hold them off for enough time to have you strike. They had about 290 men; a full German company, but after our attack on their train, there are about thirty less. They'll never expect your force to hit them, so with us from the one direction and you from the other we will have them in a cross fire. With good planning and enough fire-power we can kill them all. Then you and I, Andrei, will send a letter to Der Fuehrer thanking him for sending us these pigeons to eat and request that he send us more."

Andrei stood up and stomped his feet. "You hear this, Brushka? Hitler is right: these Jews are going to take over the world and Jozef is the head of the world-wide Jewish conspiracy that Hitler talks about. Brilliant, this is brilliant. One detail I need though, my genius friend."

"What's that?" asked Jozef.

"When does this happen?"

Jozef, stroking his chin said, "That's the one detail I haven't found out yet. Give me time. You will be the first to know when they plan to attack—after me, of course."

Andrei nodded. "I'll need about three days notice to beef up my forces and make us invincible. We will chew them up like a lion on a zebra."

They shook hands and Jozef said, "Collaboration; there's nothing like it. With the world lining up against Hitler, how can we lose? You'll hear from me the moment I find anything out."

On the way back, Jozef stopped at King Tree and the Knothole and left a note of four words: must have attack date.

Mikhail retrieved this note and recognized the urgency. The Nazi military activity in headquarters was at a frantic pace since the attack on the train "by the Jews." Colonel Hoffman and his group started their day in the meeting room where Mikhail could hear the colonel barking out orders. Mikhail avoided the room since he had retrieved the orders that announced the imminent arrival of the Nazi company of reinforcements, but he understood that Hoffman's daily meetings no doubt included planning for a final retribution against the perpetrators of the attack. If only he could get in that room again. With this in mind, he hatched a plot. Before the Nazis awakened on the upper floors, he entered the meeting room, went into a side room where the heating controls were and turned down the heat. Then he made himself scarce.

As expected, within ten minutes after Hoffman and his men entered the room, Mikhail received a call to come and "fix the damn heat. It's freezing in here." Mikhail entered, went directly to the side room, turned up the heat and came out and put his right hand in front of a heating vent and announced, "It's fixed colonel, sir. A loose wire is all. You see the heat is flowing again." All the time side-glancing about the room and on the desk where he saw type written notes in front of each officer and the mimeograph machine still in its usual location. He left the room as quickly as he had entered. The less interaction he had with the colonel, the better. He would have to risk it again and get a copy of the document on the desk hoping it would reveal the timing of the expected assault.

After the Nazis left the building, he ventured into the room and within seconds had turned the mimeograph crank producing the duplicate. The next day, Jozef retrieved it from King Tree and the Knothole, sought out Ben and asked him to interpret. "Does it say anything about an attack on us and if it does, is there a date?"

Ben read and translated simultaneously. "The next target is the Jewish partisans as soon as the Nazis get all their replacements and munitions. It describes our location in detail. They've zeroed in on us, Jozef. What are you going to do?" said an alarmed Ben.

"I'll get to that, Ben, please continue. We have to know the date. Is there a date for the attack?"

Ben read the rest of the document and said, "No, it just says the attack will take place as soon as the troops are battle ready."

"Damm," said Jozef.

"This will give us a chance to get away. Right?" said Ben with fear written on his face.

Jozef noted the tremor in Ben's voice and calmly said, "Trust me now Ben. I'll give you all the information within forty-eight hours. Please keep this confidential. Just know that I've got a plan and am not working alone. I'm confident that we will all come out of this okay. We may have a big surprise for our Nazi friends."

Ben, his brain going a mile a minute, remained silent, but thinking how Jozef always came through, nodded his head and said, "Okay, I'll wait. You've taken us through tough times in the past and my confidence still holds. Please let us know as soon as you know something."

"That's a promise."

The next morning, Jozef sought out David, took him aside and said, "Whatever you're doing, David, drop it and come with me. I need you to translate from German to Russian just in case the man we're going to see can't read German as good as he brags he can."

"Who's that?"

"Andrei Kalemnikoff of the Russian partisans. I'll tell you the whole story on the way there. Big things are going to happen."

David listened intently as Jozef told him every detail about the pending Nazi attack including the collaboration he started with his Russian friends.

When they arrived, Jozef reintroduced David to Andrei and said, "I brought him here to translate a message I got from the Nazis written in German."

Andrei laughed, "Did you forget I told you that I can speak German?"

"No, I didn't forget, but you didn't say how good you can speak it. I didn't want to take any chances."

"Good, Jozef, you are a careful man. Let me see the message. When he looked at it, his first comment was, "Jesus and Jozef, this is an official German military document. I knew you were good, but not that good. I know better than to ask where you got it, but my opinion of you just climbed up a notch."

David stood by dumfounded at this interplay between two partisan leaders.

Andrei kept reading and said, "You were right, they plan to kill every last one of you first." He started to laugh and said, "But they didn't know who they were dealing with. In fact they didn't know that you had a friend in high place—me. What a party we will have. I can't wait. Let me go on and finish this epistle. Yeah, just as I thought, no date. Brushka, this is going to be such fun that I think I'll take you with us. You haven't killed any Nazis for a while."

"I'm ready, liebchen, and she launched into some more German speak."

Jozef, amazed at German coming out of Brushka, said, "Right. I guess you weren't kidding when you said you can speak German, Andrei."

"Like a native, and I taught Brushka too." And he rapid-fire spoke German to David and the two of them carried on a conversation for a few minutes while, Jozef stood by dumbfounded.

"Okay enough of that," said Andrei, "Let's go back to when you first came to me about this problem. Great plan—I loved it. You want to kill Nazis but realized you can't do it alone, so you sought me out. I viewed that as you kicking the ball to me and now I needed to dribble it and score a goal, and that's just what I did; score 1 to 0. I have friends in high places in the Russian army. That should be no surprise to you, Jozef, because, after all, the Russian army set us up. But now I had to put on my political cap because your idea was so good, they had to know about it, but if they knew it was a rescue of Jews, there are some who would say okay and there are others who would say who gives a shit, we're not going to risk men on saving Jews. We discussed this once before as I remember. Anyhow, I had to convince them that the Germans, since they killed all the Jews already, are now going after the Russian partisans. And that's not bullshit either, so when I asked them for support, I got all I need. We're making plans as we speak. They think I'm in charge of this because the Russian high command has given me the order to organize all local partisans so we can act together just like you are attempting to do, Jozef. You're ahead of your time, my friend. Anyhow as long as my superiors know I have a part in this, they're behind it 100 percent. We're ready to fly, Jozef. But the date—we need the date. What do you think?"

"I don't have the date yet. I hope we'll get it soon, but until then, I'm with you 100 percent too. You can do it without me and I can't do it without you. I don't care who gets the credit along as the job gets done. You can have all the credit. Without you there is no mission. So, be my boss, take charge and tell me what to do, Andrei."

"What a team," said Andrei. "Just use your sources and keep trying to get the date. I'm going to give you a radio. If you learn the date, radio me immediately in code. As an example, if the date should be March 10, you'll send a message saying March 20. That's all you'll say. I"ll know that the true date is March 10, ten days earlier. Do you both understand?"

"Yes, ten days before," said Jozef and David. Jozef added, "We've purposely never used a radio before afraid that we could be traced."

"That's wise, and if you learn the date with plenty of time then send a runner. We'll do the same, but if, by chance, you find out the date at the last minute, we'll have to use the radio. Got it?

"Yes."

"By the way, I'll be sending you 100 modern rifles and two machine guns and plenty of ammo."

"Hallelujah," whooped Jozef.

"Hallelujah is right. I had to pull teeth to get them." Andrei added, "I know you've got your sources, Jozef, but we're not just sitting around eating borsht. We've got spies getting us information right in Minsk. It wouldn't surprise me if they come up with the attack date first, but either way it doesn't matter. We're working together on this. Expect to hear from me tomorrow. I'm coming to your camp with all the plans I've laid out. Tell your lookouts to expect me. We're going to put 'em in a vise and we'll both turn the screw." He laughed and slapped his right knee with his right hand.

On the way back to camp, David said to Jozef, "I'll never forget this day. You guys are both the greatest."

"Thanks, David, but even if we teach the Nazis a lesson, we'll have to take up camp and move to another place. Too many Nazis know where we're at now. We can't kill them all. When we get back to camp, we'll get everyone together and let them know what's happening. Are the Nazi Einsatzgruppe in for a shock or what? I can't wait."

The next few days saw frantic activity at the Jewish partisan camp. Representatives of Andrei's Russian partisans arrived and worked together with Jozef preparing a defensive position approximately two miles south of the camp's location. As best as can be determined from the terrain, any Nazi attack on the Jewish partisan camp would require a specific route leading directly north from Minsk. Andrei and

Jozef both agreed that the Jewish partisans would interrupt the Nazi march two miles south of Jozef's camp, and fight a holding action. In the meantime, the Russian partisans would rush into position with all the cooperation that the Russian army could supply, and together with the Jewish partisans surround the Nazis from two directions and open up a withering fire with rifles, machine guns, mortars and artillery. If all went as hoped, combined forces of the armed Jewish partisans and Russian partisans would decimate their enemy and kill them all, unless they realized the hopelessness of their position and surrendered. As Andrei said, "I'd like to see them surrender, but who could trust the bastards. If they give up, I don't think my men, in the heat of battle, would be able to stop firing. Anyhow, why take a chance; might as well finish them off. It's perfectly legitimate to kill in battle. We'd do them a favor. They won't last long in one of Stalin's Siberian gulags."

A few days later, not only Mikhail noted when a large force of Nazi's and local police gathered outside of the civic building, but Andrei's civilian spies did as well. This sudden development left no time for Andrei to leave a message at King Tree and the Knothole, although he did later that evening after the gathered Nazi force left to attack the Jewish partisans. When Andrei received a coded radio message from his spies that the Nazis left for the attack, he promptly sent Jozef the information in their previously agreed code.

The respective forces swung into action. Jozef and his near one-hundred men partisan force, armed to the teeth, took up their positions, while Andrei's large force rushed into position from another direction. They were ready and eager to surprise the hated enemy.

As soon as the Nazis came within site of the Jewish partisan line, all the Jewish partisans opened fire simultaneously taking the Nazis completely by surprise. The first to fall was Colonel Hoffman leading his men, as was his custom in two World Wars. Shot in both legs by machine gun fire, he lay helpless on the ground, but attempted to crawl to cover as did the rest of his men still alive after the initial barrage.

But as they lay under cover from the north where Jozef's men kept up the barrage, Andrei's men opened fire from the east. With the combined fire of the two defensive units, they decimated the Nazi troops; many killed and many lying wounded cried out in anguish. Those who survived the onslaught fled south if they could, but Andrei, recognizing this possibility, had about forty of his well-armed group take up a position behind the Nazis and they stopped their retreat with more raking fire.

The entire battle was over within ten minutes. The Colonel was not finished off. The great majority of the men were, a few were still alive although gravely wounded. Jozef, holding a machine gun and David, holding a rifle led the Jewish partisans and cautiously approached the fallen men. The first one they reached, a good ten meters in front of his company, was Colonel Hoffman who lay on the ground without saying a word, a stunned expression on his face, both legs covered with blood.

"David, you see, we have the honor of gunning down a full Colonel of the invincible Nazi army. Talk to him and see what you could find out."

Surprise registered on the Colonel's face and replaced the grimace of pain when David asked him his name in perfect German. There was no response as the Colonel switched his gaze back and forth between Jozef and David.

"The silent type, I see," said Jozef.

At that point in the one-sided conversation, Andrei arrived and asked, "What have we here, Jozef?"

Sheldon Cohen

"We have the leader of this pack of murderers. A full Colonel of the invincible Nazi army. An Einsatzgruppe member too proud to talk, dazed that a pack of Jews could do this to him. Poor bastard. He's the silent type. He doesn't believe what just happened.

"Well, that's what I would expect," said Andrei. "He has nothing to say. I'm sure he thought that he would be killing a bunch of Jews today for his Fuehrer. Instead, a bunch of Jews came near killing him and wiping out his entire company. At least that's what he thought before I came and he saw that the Jews and Russians worked together. The poor man has fallen into a state of depression; must be because of the sudden realization that he's going to lose this war." With that, Andrei lapsed into his own perfect German, asking the Colonel if he would like to spend the rest of the war in Siberia as a prisoner. The Colonel, more dazed by what had just transpired, again did not answer and Andrei said, "Hmm, nothing to translate for you, Jozef. So you see, our Colonel has left the decision to us. That's the only conclusion I can come to by his refusal to answer the question. It looks like we will have to make the decision for him." He turned to the Colonel and said, "Do you want us to decide your fate, Colonel?" Again, no response, this time accompanied by a scornful look.

"Oh, our Colonel looks a bit disturbed, Jozef. What do you think?"

"Just leave him to me, Andrei. I'll give him the same fate as his fellows gave 49 of my friends in a synagogue in Poland."

I take that to mean he's caput."

"It'll be my pleasure," said Jozef with increasing anger.

Andrei, noting the change in Jozef's expression along with an obvious increasing agitation, said calmly, "You forget one thing, my Yiddishe friend."

Jerking his head toward Andrei, Jozef said, "Don't tell me you speak Yiddish, too? And what do I forget, Andrei?"

A smiling Andrei said, "You agreed that I was the boss, so as long as I am, you'll do exactly as I say. You won't kill this man. He is, after all, a prisoner of war entitled to all the privileges of the Geneva Convention. Some joke, huh? He'll be my prisoner and I'll turn him over to the Russian army, they'll try and save him, so that he can spend his remaining time in Siberia, where I can assure you his chance of surviving is about as good as my flying to the moon tomorrow."

Jozef, recognizing himself in Andrei's assertion of power, realized that yes, he had agreed that Andrei would be the boss of this mission and he, Jozef, was in a secondary role. The look on Andrei's face conveyed the same message. Calming down, Jozef said, "Yes, Andrei, you're right, you're the boss. Take the bastard away before I shoot him by mistake."

"Good, Jozef, I hate to see you become a war criminal. Granted, the Nazis don't seem to give that a second thought, but that doesn't mean that we follow suit. When this war ends, your conscience will be clear."

David, listening carefully to this verbal interplay learned a great deal from the conversation between two older and much more experienced and wiser men.

Andrei's men carted the Colonel and a few wounded off on makeshift stretchers.

"We'll come back soon with power equipment, dig trenches and bury the whole mess of them before they stink up the forest," said Andrei.

"I suggest we take a load of Nazi uniforms first. They may come in handy some day," said Jozef.

Within two days, the Colonel was in the hands of the Russian army.

When the Colonel and none of the troops returned from their mission to eradicate the partisans, the two officers remaining in the Minsk Civic Building reported to Berlin that no Einsatzgruppe or police troops returned from their Jew killing mission in the Minsk forest. Why they did not know, but Mikhail, who retrieved a message from King Tree and the Knothole, knew.

He would continue his very low profile and see what happens next.

CHAPTER 25
NAZI'S PURIM PLOT
2-3 MARCH 1942

The Biblical Book of Esther relates the story behind the Jewish holiday of Purim. A Jewish orphan girl, Esther, raised by her cousin Mordechai, matures into a beautiful woman who marries King Ahasuerus and becomes queen. The king favors Esther over all his other wives..

The villain of the story is Haman, the king's advisor. He hated Mordechai because Mordechai refused to bow down to him. Haman advised the king "there are people scattered throughout your kingdom that do not follow the king's laws as all others do and they should not be tolerated." "Do as you wish with them," said the King to Haman. Haman planned the Jews extermination.

Mordechai urged Esther to speak with her husband, the king, on behalf of the Jews in his kingdom. Esther, taking her life in her hands by approaching the king unannounced, told him about Haman's plot to kill her people. In deference to his favorite wife and remembering that Mordechai once saved his life, King Ahasuereus saved the Jews of his kingdom. As was the custom of the time, Haman and family paid with their lives for his treachery.

The book of Esther is the only biblical book that fails to mention God. There is only a vague reference made when Mordechai states, "Esther or someone else will save us." This suggests that God may work in unexpected ways: fortunate luck, chance or coincidence.

Purim is a festive holiday. Jews celebrate and perform Mitzvot (good deeds) by reading the Book of Esther in the evening and the following morning, partaking of a good meal, giving food to friends and charity to the poor. When reading the Book of Esther, loud noises, boos and rattling of gragors (noisemakers) accompany the name of Haman.

What better time than Purim to organize a massacre. The Minsk Einsatzgruppe advised the Judenrat that 5,000 Jews in the Minsk ghetto were due for resettlement and ordered them to assemble at a specific location. When asked if this included children and elders, the Nazi Einsatgruppe answered, 'what's the difference.' This nonchalance alerted the Jews to the fact that the Nazis and their collaborators planned a massacre. Word spread throughout the ghetto and panic set in. The order went out to, "Save yourself, tomorrow is Purim. We will be saved and our enemies will suffer the fate of Haman."

The Jews did not assemble, dispersed and took refuge wherever they could. Some escaped the ghetto. The Einsatzgruppe did not find a single Jew when they arrived at the designated location.

As revenge, an orgy of murder by bullet and grenade ensued. Eichmann, the Nazi in charge of Jewish transportation and extermination, watched his first 'Jewish executions.' This was one of many massacres hastily organized and carried out by the Einsatzgruppe in Byelorussia until very few Jews remained alive.

CHAPTER 26
DOUBLE HEADER
SECOND QUARTER 1942

As soon as the battle against the Jewish partisans ended, Jozef announced that the time had arrived for them to move. Their new location was approximately three miles northeast of the first location directly north of a swampy area making any direct approach difficult. The cooperation of the all the Jewish partisans was exemplary, as they knew that the move was necessary since the enemy now knew their current position. After their resounding victory over the Nazis, they felt more secure.

The Nazis were beginning to have more problems on the Russian front than they had ever bargained for.

The Nazi army, unable to function well due to one of the worst winter in Russian history, spent considerable time on re-supply and reinforcements readying themselves for the spring offensives and the hoped for end of the Russian resistance. In addition, Italy, Rumania, Hungary, Slovakia and Spain sent military contingents to help the Nazis.

They had fought for five-hundred miles to come within fifteen miles of Moscow. Hitler was confident of the final victory, but the "one final push" which brought them close enough to be able to see the spires of the Kremlin was as far as they got before an inspired Russian resistance ended all hopes of capturing Moscow. For the first time since September 1, 1939 when they invaded Poland, the vaunted Nazi juggernaut met its match.

The entire situation began to change for the Nazis. The myth of their invincibility received a shattering blow as the stubborn Russians rallied. None of the final Russian targets fell to the onrushing Nazis. Moscow did not fall nor did Leningrad in the north or Stalingrad further south or the Caucasus oil fields. In addition, the supply lines from the United States and Britain stayed open and the Russian factories moved east of the Urals and, uninhibited, mass produced war material on an around-the-clock schedule.

The heads of the commanding German generals began to roll as Hitler, in his fury, took supreme command of all German armies and carved out a niche for himself that no previous president, prime minister, king or emperor ever conceived of holding.

The law, in essence, stated that Hitler's dictatorial powers were ramped up to an extent never before seen in Germany. Hitler had the power of life or death over any German citizen regardless of rank or station.

Hitler had indeed become the law.

The second quarter of 1942 saw some Nazi victories that would be short-lived: They began an offensive in the Crimea; they besieged Sevastopol and began to plan a drive toward Stalingrad hoping to conquer the oil resources of the Caucasus.

In the meantime, the murder of Jews took on a new dimension as the Nazis began gassing Jews to death at Auschwitz concentration camp in Poland. This was the first location, but by no means the last. Work began on Birkenau, the main Auschwitz killing center,

Chelmno, near Lodz, followed by Belzec, Sobibor, Majdanek and Treblinka.

The Nazis were rethinking their position; Russia was too bitter a pill to swallow and America had just entered the war convincing many of the higher echelon Nazis, perhaps even Hitler, that the war may have become a lost cause. At least the systematic murder of the Jews could shift into high gear, for with the focus of hostilities in the Baltic, Poland, and Russia, six million Jews came under German and their allies' control. It was time to implement Hitler's 'final solution.' If he could not win the war, he could, at least rid the world of Jews.

Back in Berlin, Ernst Kaltenbrunner who had taken over leadership of the Einsatzgruppen when Hitler assigned Heydrich the job of *Reichsprotecktor* of Czechoslovakia, was astounded when he heard the news that the entire company of his Einsatzgruppe plus their police allies never returned from the attack on the Minsk Jewish partisans. This could mean only one thing—a possibility too horrendous to contemplate—that the Jews defeated his men. A pack of hiding, cowardly, sniveling Jews! He knew that he would have to tell his superior, Himmler, and God knows what that would mean.

The next day he dropped the bomb. Himmler sat stone-faced for good ten-seconds while contemplating the ramifications of Kaltenbrunner's words before he stammered out, "What are you trying to tell me? They didn't come back! Where are they? What happened?"

"They don't know. Not a single man returned to headquarters. It's like they disappeared off of the face of the earth."

"Colonel Hoffman?"

"He didn't come back either."

Himmler sat quiet, eyes closed, head bowed, both hands clasped and resting on his lap, deep in thought. Finally, he said, "We'll have to wait longer. You don't know Hoffman like I do. For all I know he wiped out the Jews and then went after the Russian partisans. He did things like that in two World Wars. Nothing would surprise me with that man. We don't know if he's dead. As long as we have no proof, we keep our mouths shut. You hear me, Ernst."

"Yes, sir."

"I wouldn't even think of giving the Fuehrer bad news unless I had proof. He just sacked all his generals, for God's sake. He took over control of the Russian front himself. Nothing's going like he planned in Russia. Six weeks! That was his estimate of how long the Russian campaign would last. Well, you see what happened—a quagmire. I wouldn't want to be responsible for giving him bad news unless the proof was in my hands. That goes for you too, Ernst. Keep your lips sealed. Say nothing, you hear."

"Yes, sir. In the meantime there are only two officers in the Einsatzgruppen in Minsk. What do I tell them, sir."

"Find out who they are and send three more high ranking officers. Tell them to investigate and send us a report within ten days about Hoffman and the rest of the company."

"Right away, sir."

The two Einsatzgruppe officers remaining in Minsk were confused. Colonel Hoffman told them that they would return from their anti-Jewish partisan liquidating mission within two days. The fact that not a single man returned left them with the impossible conclusion to contemplate that the Jews killed Hoffman and his men. Who would have ever believed such a result? Everyone's impression was that, yes, there were partisans and, yes, they caused some mischief, but destroy a company of trained soldiers and police?

"There's no way," said one to the other, "Hoffman kept going, that's all. He's still out there looking for more partisans. Maybe he's even planning attacks on the Russian Partisans. You know how he is."

However, time passed with no return of any troops or police and so they reported the disappearance to Berlin. Then they received the news that Kaltenbrunner was sending three more Einsatzgruppe officers to assist in determining the reason why Hoffman and his company failed to return.

Mikhail learned the reason when he received a King Tree and the Knothole message from Jozef detailing their "success." As long as this war is far from settled, he hoped his mission could continue.

One of the Nazi officers told Mikhail to prepare living quarters for three more officers who would arrive at the Minsk airport in four days. The officer would arrange to have them picked up and brought to the Civic Building. Mikhail's response was yes, sir. That evening Mikhail advised King Tree and the Knothole about the arriving officers, hoping that Jozef might be interested in planning an encore with three more Einsatzgruppen. Jozef responded with a one-word answer—yes.

With his mind full of pre-planning, Jozef then sought out David and said, "Now that we're settled in our new location, David, are you ready for an encore?"

"Always, Jozef. What's happening?"

"I have it on good authority that our Nazi friends in Berlin are wondering what happened to their Einsatzgruppe they sent to Minsk to polish us off."

"I thought you would send them a telegram telling Hitler that they're in Nazi Hell now," suggested David.

Jozef nodded and smiled. "Good idea, but I'd rather keep them guessing. I know that they're sending three officers to try and find out and report back home. The Berlin brass has steam coming out of their ears to say the least."

"Aw, what a shame. You want to arrange a welcoming party for the three officers?"

"You got it, David."

"Anything planned? Knowing you, I'm sure you already got it all figured out."

Nodding yes, Jozef said, "They'll arrive at the airport on Thursday. To get from the airport to the Civic Building they have to take Komsomolskaya Street. One part passes next to the forest. There are very few cars on the road so an open Nazi staff car will be easy to spot, especially filled with uniformed officers. There will be six of us going dressed in Nazi uniforms and we count on you to speak German to them..."

"What am I supposed to say?" interrupted David.

"We'll be on the side of the road. You and I will be carrying machine guns; the others, pistols. As they come down the road and spot us in our uniform, you step out on the road, get in front of their oncoming car, lift up your hand, welcome them, and tell them to stop in German. They'll wonder what it's all about, but they'll stop. As soon as that happens, you raise up your gun and fire. We join you from the side of the road. The bullets will be coming at them from two directions, and from so short a distance, we can't miss. It'll all happen so fast, they'll be dead before the shots stop echoing through the forest. Don't you love it?"

"Yes," said David, "I. Thank you for the opportunity, Jozef."

"I'll pick the other men and let you know who's going with us. After we've done the dirty deed, we slip back into the forest, pack away our Nazi uniforms and beat a hasty retreat. Got it?"

"Sounds good, Jozef, I look forward to it," said a smiling, nodding David.

David returned to his wife. Hannah said, "You don't even have to tell me. Anytime Jozef calls you, I know there's something dangerous going on. How long will you be gone?"

"A few days at the most, but don't worry, Jozef knows how to keep things safe for us."

"And here I was, hoping now that we're in a new location we can live out the war in peace." She paused, looked at David and said, "Don't say it. I know we have to help. That's our mission."

He took her in his arms.

Mikhail prepared three more rooms as directed. So far, his mission was going well, but he couldn't help but worry. How long would he be able to carry on with one success after another? When would suspicion turn in his direction? He did his job on the physical plant to perfection. He kept a low profile, but was always available for whatever job his superiors had for him and he only spoke to them when spoken to. He said nothing about the fact that Hoffman and his company never returned. It was, after all, none of his business. He wanted his superiors to think that he thought they were on a mission somewhere and they could come back at any time.

Then a breakthrough; one of the officers asked Mikhail whether the three living quarters he ordered to be set up were ready for the arriving officers.

"Just about, sir," answered Mikhail.

"Well, make certain that they're ready by 11:00 am Sunday. That's when I expect them. Also, make sure that the meeting room is ready. As soon as they come in and stow their gear in their rooms we're all going to meet."

"Yes, sir, no problem."

That evening, King Tree and the Knothole received its message: Expected officers time of arrival at 11:00 am Sunday.

That should make Jozef's planning much easier, thought Mikhail. If they're going to be here at 11:00 am, they'll arrive at the airport about 10:00 or so.

Indeed it did. Jozef made plans according to the reported arrival time. Now they just had to pray the Nazis would keep to their schedule. Jozef oriented the six men and he and David and the six left for their mission. They had to travel around the city from north to south where the airport was located. Most of the trip would be in the forest, so they backpacked their Nazi uniforms. Their destination was Komsomolskaya street south of the airport on the way to the Minsk Civic Building. They arrived at about 9:00 am before the expected arrival time of the plane and took up a station in a large clump of trees not far from the road. Donning their Nazi uniforms, they nervously awaited their prey. David was the key. The road at this point was a straight shot for several miles, so they had an excellent opportunity to see any expected car a good distance away and get ready for the mission.

David, carrying binoculars, kept a vigil down the road and was able to give ample warning time when he recognized an open Nazi staff car in the distance driving toward him. He alerted his men to follow him along the side of the road as he walked down the center of the road toward the approaching staff care. As the car approached, he smiled, raised his left waving hand in a signal to stop while his right hand carried the machine gun, his heart pounded as his brain thought of the swift retribution soon to be deservedly meted out to these murderers intent on their killing mission.

The car slowed, stopped before a still smiling David who suddenly raised his machine gun and opened fire, as did the five others, including Jozef. It was over in ten seconds leaving a heap of bloodied, dead bodies. Two seconds would have been enough, but once the men squeezed the trigger, it was difficult to release. Eight more seconds were in memory of the relatives and friends of the men on the mission.

Certain that they had completed their task, they quickly entered the clump of trees, took off their Nazi uniforms, placed them in their backpacks and one by one started the long trek back home satisfied by a job well-done.

Mikhail was home Sunday when the officers were supposed to arrive. When he showed up at work Monday there was a strange silence. The two officers nodded in his direction, but with grim faces had nothing to say. Mikhail had already noticed that the three rooms he prepared for the arriving officers remained unoccupied, so he understood that Jozef had succeeded again.

Byelorussian citizens soon discovered the dead bodies. They stopped and stared, but did not take any action. Local police then came across the blood-covered corpses and called the Civic Building to inform the Nazis of their deaths. Within minutes, the officers stationed at the Civic Building notified Berlin who interrupted Kaltenbrunner at home. "It has to be the partisans," they told him. Kaltenbrunner immediately informed Himmler who called a meeting for the next day at headquarters. Minsk was becoming a suppurating boil they had to lance.

Jozef and David and their crew arrived back in camp. Hannah fell into David's arms. "We did our job," is all he said.

CHAPTER 27
GERMAN OFFENSIVE
MID 1942

Joseph Stalin made a stirring speech to his countrymen on November 7, 1941 when the Germans stopped their forward progress due to exhaustion and freezing weather and while they regrouped for the next phase of the battle to "finish them off."

Now the time approached.

If the German generals had their way, they would have attacked Moscow, but since Hitler took over full control of the army, he turned his attention to the southern front and elected to take the Crimea, the Port of Sevastopol and Stalingrad. He took this approach after Russian planes taking off from Sevastopol attacked the Rumanian oil fields at Ploesti, Rumania, destroying eleven thousand tons of oil. This was a threat that in Hitler's mind could not wait, so the capture of Sevastopol became a priority. Hitler assigned General Erich von Manstein to this task. He brought to bear the most overwhelming concentration of artillery seen to that point in the war, air bombardment, and frontal infantry assaults and captured Sevastopol.

Stalingrad was a major industrial city and a gateway to the oil rich regions of southern Russia and the Crimea. Hitler's plan was to neutralize this city's industrial might, control the Russian oil source of the Caucus and weaken Russian ability to fight.

The news of the massacre of the three men sent to Minsk to investigate the disappearance of Hoffman and his company of Einsatzgruppe, threw Kaltenbrunner into a frenzy. This had never happened before. He would have to report it to a furious Himmler in all the detail he could muster. He told Himmler the bad news and was surprised at his reaction—silence. Himmler said calmly, "I'm dumbfounded, Ernst. The Minsk partisans are making fools of us. I can't risk any more men by invading the forests around Minsk. It looks like they know what we plan to do before we do it. The best approach at this time will be to leave them alone and let them rot in the forests. Our offensives have started all over Russia. We should finish them off soon. That's the Fuehrer's thinking right now and I can't disrupt his planning by bad news especially when he's leading the offensive. He wants to eliminate the threat to Ploesti by taking the Crimea and then the rest of Russia. The Russian campaign could be over in a matter of a few months. Arrange to send another company of Einsatzgruppe there, but do not tell anyone in Minsk. Understand? When they arrive, it will be a complete surprise"

"Yes, sir."

Mikhail was shocked when another company of Einsatzgruppe arrived unannounced. The two officers left in the Minsk Civic Building likewise were startled as well. There was still some work necessary liquidating the remaining Jews of Minsk and its environs. The fact that this group of Nazi soldiers arrived unannounced caused some concern for Mikhail especially as he got wind of the surprise on the faces of the current Nazi occupants of the building. It was clear to Mikhail that they must be getting suspicious in Berlin.

In spite of the slow-down in military activity in Russia brought about be the cold Russian winter, Hitler saw success around the corner. The Crimea was under Nazi control. He had alleviated the threat to Ploesti and its oil and now controlled the Russian oil source, although all the Russians left for the Nazis was a wasteland of scorched earth and wrecked oil facilities.

Hitler was enjoying great success with submarine warfare, sinking more British and American ships then they could replace. Since Hitler had conquered Western Europe, he was able to transfer his troops, arms, tanks and planes to the Russian front. Nothing suggested to Hitler that Britain and America could launch any attacks. It was time to finish off Russia. The Mediterranean was a German and Italian lake. Hitler was confident that a decisive victory was close-at-hand. After his forces neutralized Stalingrad he had thoughts of advancing on Moscow. His delusions of grandeur had reached the point where he felt Russia was doomed, and Britain and America would sue for peace.

His generals, however, were fearful of the German lack of resources, men, tanks, transportation facilities and planes to do so much on so many fronts. They had to rely on foreign troops, Italians, Hungarians, Rumanians, Slovaks and Spaniards. Hitler, however, felt that the Russians "were finished" and these deficiencies would not matter. His generals pointed out that simultaneous efforts to capture the Caucasus as well as Stalingrad would put the German army in great danger, especially as intelligence reported the vast numbers of Russian troops that Stalin was able to make available, a figure that Hitler refused to accept. Hitler's answer was to sack more generals.

With Hitler's mind fully occupied with the Russian front, he received a blow from another source. General Rommel's Africa Corps was in trouble.

"Are you all settled in to your new digs, Jozef," asked Andrei who played a surprise visit to his friend.

"Yes, good to see you, Andrei. We're all settled in and this place is more secure than where we were before because of the swamp between us and Minsk."

"Good thinking, Jozef. After the trouncing we gave the Nazis, I don't think they'll be interested in coming after us here in the woods. Hitler's too busy 'finishing us off.'" Andrei laughed. "Army intelligence thinks his taking the Caucusus will be a bitter pill for him to swallow. He had an opportunity to take Stalingrad, but he couldn't. Now we're rushing in more reinforcements, and if we hold there we think that he'll be thinned out too much and we're going to chew him up and spit him out. Sometimes I feel like just dancing for joy."

"I'll join you, Andrei, I can do a mean Prisvodki."

"You mean Prisyadka, Jozef." As Andrei laughed, Jozef could tell by his demeanor that his actions were in line with the good cheer and confidence that Andrei was showing.

Jozef asked him, "What do you think we should be doing to help slow the bastard down?"

Andrei had the answer right at his fingertips. "The army tells me that he'll let his rear troops finish their job of getting rid of all Jews and future enemies while he concentrates on his army finishing off Russia. He needs the Russian army out of the way so he can make slaves of us serving his master race. We're dealing with a mad man, Jozef, but he bit off more than he can chew. He's in for a surprise.

We're going to save the world from this bastard. Our job now is to do everything we can to disrupt his supplies. Blow up every train track you can find and keep on blowing them up. We'll deliver you more dynamite soon. Anyhow, it looks like I don't have to worry about you doing the right thing with this magic source of yours."

"I'm a little worried that my magic source is drying up, Andrei. I haven't had any information for a while now."

"Hmm, anything I can do to help?"

"I don't think so. Not yet, anyhow, but if you give us those explosives, you're going to need earplugs because we'll blow up any train tracks we can find for fifty miles between here and Germany."

It took a week before the Russian partisans delivered the railroad explosives to Jozef. He assigned the project of destroying railroad tracks to Abel who developed four teams of four men each and trained them all in explosives. With the help of railroad maps, they embarked upon late night expeditions to disrupt as many rail lines as they could that headed toward Minsk. It was just a small effort by one Jewish partisan group, but it added up to an impact which had a negative effect on the German effort to launch their spring of 1942 offensive.

CHAPTER 28
WIPE AWAY THOSE TEARS
SUMMER 1942

One week after the rail and transportation disruption assignment, Andrei again showed up at Jozef's partisan encampment requesting another favor.

"Always good to see you, Andrei, what can I do for you; do you have another assignment for us?" asked Jozef.

"Not exactly, but I need to ask you some questions."

"Shoot."

"I know you have a doctor here, and I need to know if he's doing good work for you and your people?"

Jozef did not hesitate and said, "For sure he does the best with what he's got to work with. His wife is a nurse and their daughter helps too. He's set up a good sanitary system and keeps us free of contagious diseases, plus he made sure that we would never pollute the small water supply we have access to. He does what surgery he can on the injured or wounded and treats us for whatever ails us. We're lucky to have him, that's all I know."

"Very lucky," said Andrei. "One thing we have trouble with in all the partisan groups is that we lack doctors. Most of the groups don't have any medical help at all and just do the best they can. It's giving me problems because I have to see to it that the partisans are supplied with what they need and that's just not only arms and munitions. They need medical care too. We're trying to do a better job coordinating all the different partisans in the forest and the army assigned this district to me."

"Do you want our doctor to work with other partisans too," asked Jozef.

"We might need him in an emergency, but the partisans are spread out all over Byelorussia, Ukraine, Poland, Russia and more, so we can't expect him to handle all that. I'd like to talk to him now because we have another doctor I want him to meet that I'm trying to convince to practice medicine with us. As a matter of fact, Jozef, this other doctor is on his way here. My men are bringing him. He should arrive soon."

"Alright, let me go get Dr. Ben. I hope he can help."

Two hours later, Jozef, Andrei, Dr. Ben and Dr. Yeheskiel Atlas gathered and sat under the trees in the shade.

Yehezkiel Atlas was an actual young Jewish physician who saw his family wiped out by Nazi forces and dedicated his life to anti-Nazi resistance as a partisan. Wounded in battle, he succumbed to his wounds in December 1942. His partisan comrades buried him in an unmarked grave in the forest.

In November 2008, Byelorussian patriots finally brought Dr. Atlas to a traditional Jewish burial when they unearthed his body, provided a religious ceremony and the Byelorussian army performed a gun salute and provided a guard of honor.

Before the meeting, Andrei brought Dr. Ben up to date as to what he wanted him to accomplish, and that is to convince Dr. Atlas to assist the partisans as a practicing physician. The two men, Dr. Ben and Dr. Atlas had some things in common. Dr. Ben told Dr. Atlas about his experience as a youngster in Czarist Russia: the killing of his father in a pogrom; he and his mother fleeing to Germany where he received his medical education during the good times; and then the rise of Hitlerism and state-sponsored anti-Semitism necessitating that his family flee again, this time to Minsk in Byelorussia. Dr. Ben noted Dr. Atlas' serious demeanor, his excellent eye contact, black hair, almost blink-free eyes and silent attention reflected on a young masculine very handsome face. Atlas was a striking twenty-nine year old man. Ben couldn't help but feel that there was something about his demeanor that told him from the start that convincing Dr. Atlas to do anything may well be folly.

"You were wise to flee that madman," said Dr. Atlas. Too many Jews stayed behind only to die. In Germany, you at least were able to see and hear Hitler speak. He made no bones about what he was going to do, but you listened first hand. We did not. We here in the Soviet Union had the tendency to view it as a German problem, never understanding what might happen, always hoping for the best until it was too late. We were naïve fools," He said with an ever-increasing volume to his voice and anguish on his face. "They killed my whole family. I have simplified my life—I seek revenge."

Passion to the extreme, thought Ben; another Jozef.

Dr. Atlas continued. "You want me to practice medicine with the partisans? I will answer you, but first let me tell you my story." He paused as his voice became tremulous. He wiped some tears from his eyes. "Even as a small youngster, my ambition was to be a doctor. As soon as I learned to read, I got books on the history of medicine, the human body, physiology. I read and I read some more. I went to school in Italy and France. I achieved my goal to become a doctor, to care for patients. What could be loftier than that? I fulfilled my dream and I wanted nothing more than to practice medicine, but I don't have to tell you how all that changed. The Nazis surrounded us and placed all Jews in the ghetto. They took my father and mother out and shot them to death. They asked me who that young lady was in my house. That's my sister, I told them. So what did they do?" He paused—the tears flowed. He wiped them away. "They shot her. They shot her. I should have said she was my wife, than maybe she would be alive today," he wailed and wiped away more tears. "I'm only alive today because they found out I was a doctor. Maybe they'd find a use for me." The others stood by in respectful attention.

When Dr. Atlas regained his composure, he continued, "With those events, my whole life changed. My love of medicine and desire to help people changed. I knew from those moments on that it would all have to take a back seat while I sought another goal—revenge. My whole being would now focus around killing Nazis and their collaborators who killed my family. That is what I will do. That is what I must do. I have wiped away my last tear while I take revenge. People ask me to act as the camp doctor and I'll be busy enough. Let others lead; there are plenty who can, they say. I will be a doctor when I can, but my number one focus will be revenge. That's the way it has to be," he said with an increasing emphasis. He wiped away his last tear.

As Ben, Jozef and Andrei sat spell bound, they each thought. I too have been wiping away tears. It will only stop when the enemy is dead. We can never change the focus of this intense man. Leave him to his revenge. Let him carry out his pact with his family. Andrei expressed these thoughts to Jozef, taking him aside and whispering,

"After listening to that, we'll have to let him do what he wants. He took 120 men from the ghetto and they're in the forest now planning revenge. His men have respect for him. One of them told me that Dr. Atlas told them: Those in my group will not settle down and take things easy. I have plans for revenge. You are welcome as long as you agree that our lives ended in the slaughter when they killed our families. Every day of life that we experience from that point on does not belong to us, but belongs to our murdered families. We must avenge them.

Ah, such a shame. We have plenty of leaders, but not enough doctors. Atlas will do what he wants regardless of what I say, and you know what, Jozef, he'll do a hell of a job," said Andrei. He turned to Dr. Atlas and said, "Go, doctor, and may God be with you. If you need any help, let me know."

"And that goes for me too," said Jozef, overwhelmed by the intensity of Dr. Atlas' rhetoric.

Dr. Atlas and his group went back to the forest, planned and carried out an attack on the Germans killing 127 of them, captured 75 and seized many weapons and munitions. In another attack on a German police unit, he executed 44 over the mass grave of their Jewish victims from the ghetto. The next months, they blew up a train, burned down a strategic bridge and captured a forced-down German plane.

In December of 1942, Dr. Atlas, wounded in battle lay dying. His last words were, "Pay no attention to me. Go on fighting." His Partisan fighters buried him in a grave in the forest and went back to camp to carry out his mandate.

CHAPTER 29
REUNION
EARLY 1943

Jozef was concerned. He went to Dr. Ben and said, "We need to talk, Ben."

"What is it?" Ben asked.

"I need to speak with you in private," answered Jozef.

"Sure, let's step behind Byelorussian Regional Hospital here where we can have plenty of privacy."

Jozef laughed. "I'm glad to see you're still managing a sense of humor."

"We'd all be miserable without one. No sense of humor in these forests would be tough to bare."

When they were alone Jozef said, "I haven't heard from Mikhail in over three weeks. You, I, and Mikhail kept a good secret. Thanks to King Tree and the Knothole our little message passing system we developed has worked well, but the more we do, the more Mikhail could be vulnerable. I hope Mikhail's still alive, but if I were him, I'd get the hell out of there and bring his family to us. A week ago, I left this message at King Tree and the Knothole. The good news is that three days later, he picked it up. I told him that we'd welcome him here just like we've welcomed plenty non-Jews and if he's at all

264

suspicious of a threat to him, come join us." Jozef reflected and said, "He's been the bravest of us all."

"You're right about that, Jozef," said Ben. "He's like a fly in a spider web. What courage; a suicide mission. I hope he gets out soon."

Mikhail did indeed have similar thoughts. He would go to work as unobtrusively as he could, only spoke when spoken to, continued to impress his 'employers,' do great work and wondered why the Nazis hadn't confronted him. After the massacre of the first company of Einsatzgruppe, the two officers left in headquarters were confused, but now that the second company of troops arrived, Mikhail saw little of them because they spent much of their time at meetings. Yes, it was time to leave. He was lucky so far, but how long would it last? He took Jozef's note to heart, brought it to his wife and told her the story of his secret undercover spying insisting all the time that she was never to repeat it to anyone. She was stunned and speechless for moments while she gathered her thoughts. "I suppose I should be proud of you," she said, "but if you leave for work tomorrow, will we ever see you again? The Nazis have to be furious about what's happened to them. We better get out now, tonight. This war is turning and I think in our direction. Look at Jozef and Ben. They've been hiding for a long time now. The three of you deserve a medal for what you've accomplished. I'll tell Val. It'll take us four hours to get ready to go. We'll leave after midnight. Now that I know all this, I can't live wondering every day when you go to work if I'll ever see you again. I cringe when I think of what they're capable of and what they do to people."

Mikhail was nodding his head as his wife spoke. "If they got me, they'd come for you and Val in a minute. It's settled then. We're going."

Sheldon Cohen

Early the next morning the family arrived at Jozef's partisan encampment to a happy reunion of the three planners of resistance toward the hated enemy. Mikhail's family's precious possessions were carried under their arms and on their backs including his grandparent's ancient Jewish artifacts.

CHAPTER 30
THE TURNING POINT
FEBRUARY 1943

The Germans approached Stalingrad confident that it was theirs for the taking. They realized it meant control of the Volga River, the southern front and the Caucusus. Initially there were 40,000 Soviet soldiers within the city, but they were poorly equipped reserves. Even the Soviet leadership knew that they faced disaster unless they could get massive reinforcements under an experienced take-charge do or die commander who would not countenance defeat. Stalin appointed his best man for the job, General Zhukov who along with General Vasily Chuikov pledged to defend the city or die. The Stalingrad Soviet soldiers tried to flee until the new leadership ordered any man found outside the boundary of the city shot on sight. Soviet reinforcements poured in, suffered a high mortality rate, but kept coming and saved the city at its most critical time.

The fighting was close order, a deliberate Soviet strategy to keep German soldiers so close that German aircraft could not bomb the Soviets for fear of risking German soldiers. The closeness of the combat made this battle a sniper and a hand-to-hand war for every building and every room.

Soviet aircraft soon joined the fray, as did Soviet artillery, rockets and mortar stationed east of the Volga out of direct attack reach of the German troops.

Hitler pressed on, bringing all available divisions closer to Stalingrad for one last push never dreaming that the Soviets had enough reserves of men to endanger his flanks. This was his fatal mistake: a mistake that General Zhukov counted on as the onrushing Soviet winter reduced German mobility, observational capability and troop sustainability.

Operation Uranus attacked the Germans about 100 kilometers west of Stalingrad from the north and south in Blitzkrieg fashion easily breaking through German allies positions and trapping the entire German sixth army, cutting off all hope of reinforcements. The German high command at Stalingrad appealed to Hitler who refused to order a retreat. An attempt to supply the German army by air was too little and too late. The Russians, with vastly superior forces now moved in for the kill and slowly but surely decimated the German forces until they lost all combat capability. Recognizing this, General Paulus—now made Field Marshall by Hitler to remind him that no German Field Marshall had ever surrendered—was indeed not willing to die for this great honor and ignored Hitler's orders and surrendered to the Soviets thus ending the deadliest battle of all time.

This victory raised the morale of Russian soldiers who now knew that victory was inevitable, it crippled German morale, boosted American and British morale and destroyed the morale of German civilians and soldiers who now realized that victory was no longer a given. In addition it endangered the German troops further south in the Crimea. The war in the Soviet Union had turned.

CHAPTER 31
KHATYN MASSACRE
MARCH 1942

The 1936 summer Olympic Games, held in Berlin, Germany featured a proud Adolph Hitler watching his German athletes achieve first place amongst the nations of the world. The shot put competition was fiercely competitive as tall, powerful muscular athletes competed for the gold medal. The leading German shot putter was Hans Woellke. Born on February 18, 1911, the five foot ten inch, 231 pound strongman captured the attention of Hitler rocking back and forth in his Olympic stadium seat as he watched the Aryan German Superman step up to the shot put circle for his last attempt to exceed the farthest throw of one of his competitors. A mighty heave put him in first place as Hitler broke into a wide smile. The cheer from the mostly German crowd was deafening as Woellke stepped up to the first place podium to receive the gold.

As was the fate of many of these German Olympians, World War II found former Berlin policeman, Woellke, a Captain of the 118th Schutzmannschaft battalion, a police battalion reinforced by troops made up of Ukranian collaborators, deserters and prisoners of war whose main purpose was to kill partisans. They operated near Minsk in the neighboring small villages. Hans Woelke worked as a Berlin *policeman and served as a captain in the SS. Partisans killed him and others on 22 March 1943 near Khatyn Village. In reprisal, Nazis massacred the Khatyn residents. Woelke's grave is at the Minsk Cemetery (Moscow Street, Grave 28, Row 22, West side).*

A Jewish resident of one of the towns, Shlomo Mishkin, whose relatives met death at the hands of the Nazis and their collaborators, joined Jozef's partisan group and advised him of *Schutzmannshaft* 118 activities and their frequently traveled route through the rural community searching for partisans. With this in mind, Jozef called a meeting of his reliable men and planned to kill *Schutzmannshaft* 118's leaders who made their rounds in a staff car. He appointed David, Abel and two other men to participate in this operation. Armed with machine guns and dressed in make shift camouflage clothing, they positioned themselves with a perfect line of fire. Mishkin would go along to be sure they identified the correct target.

The first two trips met with no success; the targets never showed up. On their third trip, Mishkin, at lookout, excitedly told Jozef that the car in the distance was definitely the target. It approached quickly over the unpaved road, and when it came within ten meters of Jozef and his group, they simultaneously fired and their four victims died in a hail of bullets never knowing the source.

The smiling assassins left the bullet-riddled car and the bloody bodies where they died and fled back to camp congratulating each other on a job well done.

When Hitler heard of Woellke's death, his mind went back to 1936 and a vision of Woellke throwing the shotput in the Berlin stadium surfaced in his mind with the cheers of the stadium crowd in his ears. "You know what to do," he said.

"It has already been done, *mein Fuehrer.*"

That afternoon, the same afternoon that Jozef, David, Abel, Shlomo and the two other partisans killed the four members of *Schutzmannshaft* 118, other members of the same battalion plus new members of Hoffman's Brigade with a fresh entourage of condemned criminals, entered Khatyn village, rounded up all the inhabitants from their homes, marched them into a shed, covered it with straw and set it on fire. Those trapped inside managed to break down the front door of the shed and tried to escape only to succumb to a hail of machinegun fire.

As is occasionally the case in massacres, there are a few survivors. In this case, the Khatyn Massacre, one young boy survived the fire because the dead body of his mother covered and protected him from the flames. Another boy suffering only a leg wound and left for dead, also survived. One burnt adult male recovered consciousness after the Nazis left and found his severely burned son who he tenderly picked up, cradled in his arms and watched him take his last breath. This incident, memorialized by a statue in Khatyn, is a poignant reminder of man's inhumanity to man.

Killed in Khatyn were 149 people including 75 children. The Hoffman killers then looted the entire town and burned it to the ground. This was just one of the 5,295 Byelorussian villages destroyed.

By the end of the war, the Nazis and their allies killed about one quarter of the Byelorussian population, or 2,230,000 people.

The news of the Khatyn massacre hit David hard. His conscience disturbed him because of the deadly reprisals, so he spoke to Abel and the two of them sat down to a conversation as to the rightness or wrongness of what they were doing. Abel, as previously discussed, reiterated his statement that based upon his near death experience when he survived the cold-blooded massacre of the pit, he had no qualms taking reprisals. He suggested that he could understand David's feelings as expected from one who never went through a near-death experience as he had. "It changes you, David. You lose all guilt feeling on taking reprisals when you see the cold-bloodedness of those who want to kill you."

"I'm going to see Jozef. Come with me, Abel. I need to talk."

When Jozef heard David's conscience expressed, he nodded his head and answered, "That's a normal thought, David, we've all thought that way at one time or another, but if we take your thought to its extreme, it would mean that we would have to stop what we're doing. Would that make the Nazis and their allies stop. No way. Never. They would just keep killing us regardless. Do you think, for a minute, the Nazis would stop carrying out Hitler's orders or change their thinking and stop killing Jews or other *Untermenschen*. Do you think they're capable of compromise or reasoning?"

"I don't think so, but my father always stressed the importance of compromise. He would say, 'people should always be able to reason things out together.'"

"David said, "Sure, I agree with that if you're talking about money or property or any other thing not dealing with life or death. But if you're talking about killing Jews, Hitler's burned that philosophy into his brain forever and can't change. It's his mission. He believes he's saving the world against a major threat, or at least saving the master race against pollution by Jews. To him it's easy: a struggle for world domination between Jews and Communists in one breath and Nazis in the other. How do you reason with people who have one thought in their minds, the thought that the Jews must be done away with? How do you compromise with one who wants to see you dead? What is there to compromise—the way you would like them to kill you?

You are dealing with fanatics with a one-track mind, and that one-track mind can never change and that one-track mind calls for your death. Period, pure and simple. These people have weapons in their hands and they aim those weapons and fire at you. There is no time to compromise. One of you will die. Better the other guy"

All the time Jozef was speaking, David listened in rapt attention nodding his head. This was not the first time that his conscience reactivated necessitating a session with Jozef. When Jozef finished, David still kept silent, prompting Jozef to say, "As the leader of this partisan group, and as I've said before, my philosophy is to kill Nazis and I assume that anyone who joins me believes in that philosophy. I hold no gun to anyone's head. The decision to go on any mission I bring up is the decision of the one I ask. It's either a yes or no. Either one I accept on the spot with no hard feelings. I give no orders. I deal only with volunteers, so it's up to you, David. Never forget that."

"I won't," said David. "You have a way of making everything so simple and clearing away the cobwebs in my head. I'm with you all the way."

CHAPTER 32
MALY TROSTENETS
MID 1943

Once Hitler divided Poland with Stalin, he invaded the Soviet Union's portion of Poland and the Soviet Union itself. These actions started the war on the Jews in earnest. Placing Jews in ghettos and killing them piecemeal was inefficient; the sheer volume of Eastern European Jews that Hitler planned to dispose of demanded a better, more organized structure. He birthed the concentration camp system. The top six were:

Auschwitz-Birkenau in Poland, the most notorious of the camps established by the Nazis to implement the Final Solution, initially served as a prison for Poles and Soviet prisoners of war. By 1942, it became a camp for the mass extermination of Jews and Gypsies. Established by the Nazis in 1940 in the suburbs of the town of Osweicim, soon to undergo a name change to Auschwitz, the camp evolved into three main parts: Auschwitz I; Birkenau, known as Auschwitz II; and the Buna subcamp, Auschwitz III. The three complexes became then and remains today the largest cemetery in the world where four million human beings from twenty-four different nationalities were systematically murdered.

Two thousand Soviet prisoners of war built Majdanek concentration camp close to Lublin, Poland. The prisoners lived under the stars, had little food and water, and no toilets. The majority did not survive.

Chelmno concentration camp, built fifty kilometers from Lodz, Poland, had as its purpose a killing field for Jews of the Lodz Ghetto and for Poles, Gypsies, Hungarian Jews and Soviet prisoners of war using experimental methods of mass murder. It served as a learning center for killing methods.

Treblinka concentration camp consisted of two camps Treblinka I and II. The first camp was a forced-labor camp and administrative section where more than half of its inmates worked to their deaths. In the second camp, prisoners died in gas chambers immediately upon their entry.

Belzec concentration camp site, chosen to take advantage of the close and large Jewish populations of Lublin and Galicia, made it geographically convenient to kill the Jews of the neighboring communities. There were so few survivors of this camp that little is known about its operation.

Sobibor, located on the outskirts of Sobibor, Poland, received Jews from Poland, Germany, France, Czechoslovakia and Holland as well as Soviet prisoners of war. Most of them suffered the fate of death by gas chamber fed with engine exhaust (carbon monoxide). In 1943, half of the remaining 600 prisoners revolted, 300 escaped and the Nazis closed the camp.

Escaping early historical review, another extermination camp functioned near Minsk, Byelorussia during the war. At the site of a former Soviet collective farm, this camp in Maly Trostenets, a suburb 12 kilometers from Minsk, had organized killing like the other concentration camps. Those killed were local Jews as well as Jews brought in from Western Europe. Much of the information about this camp was a well-kept secret during the war, but slowly surfaced in the years following.

Mikhail and his family arrived in the forest early morning and sought out Jozef who promptly called Ben. The three of them had a joyous reunion as Jozef unearthed a rare bottle of wine buried for special occasions.

"We were starting to worry about you, Mikhail. We're glad you joined us, so we can fight this war together," said Jozef. Ben agreed, clicking wine glasses with the two of them.

Mikhail answered, "Your last note to me from King Tree and the Knothole was right on the mark, Jozef. I thought my spying days were over. You called it right. The Nazis were getting nervous. Things got tense the more you whipped them especially when the Hoffman Company disappeared. Talk about Nazis going nuts—that did it. They're running around in circles at Minsk headquarters since the war started to turn against them. What a contrast from the cocky days when they first invaded. They acted like superior beings who came from another planet to deal with inferiors, but not any more. Now things are quiet, they have worried looks on their faces and are always looking over their shoulder. All they want to do now is get rid of all the Jews. That seems to be as important to them as winning the war."

"It is, Mikhail."

"I think they're beginning to realize that they bit off more than they can chew and that their leader is insane to think he can take on the world," said Ben.

"Well, let's not get too cocky," said Jozef, "We've got a long hard grind ahead even with the good news coming in, so we better keep our shoulders to the wheel. We can't get complacent because we think the tide has turned. We go after them every opportunity we come up with."

"You got that right," said Ben.

Mikhail and family got themselves situated in the encampment. Val found David and Hannah and renewed their old friendship. "Are you doing any gymnastics here in the forest, David?" asked Val.

"Just some strength exercise, handstands, short tumbling runs on flat land; that's about it."

"Maybe we can add to that," answered Val.

"Let's do it," said David with enthusiasm.

Things remained peaceful for a time until Andrei and several of the other fighters of the Soviet partisans showed up with more explosives enabling Jozef to continue their important task of disrupting rail lines supplying the Nazis with armaments.

"Thanks, Andrei, we were running low," said Jozef.

"Use them in good health, Jozef."

"With pleasure. Who's the new man you brought with you?" asked Jozef.

"I'll tell you as soon as you introduce me to your friend. He's new to me," said Andrei looking at Mikhail.

Jozef nodded. "Sure, Andrei, this is Mikhail Gregov. He just joined us after escaping from the Nazis."

"Escaping? Where was he?" asked Andrei.

"Tell him, Mikhail," said Jozef.

"Yes, sir, I worked at the Minsk Civic Building as the engineer. The Nazis kept me when they captured Minsk."

"Kept you prisoner or kept you working?" asked Andrei.

"Working," answered Mikhail.

Andrei smiled, nodded his head and turned to Jozef. He continued smiling and nodding as his eyes gleamed and he said, "You devil you. Here is the secret of your genius. You had a spy in German headquarters! When this war is over and I tell the army your little secret, you two will become heroes of the Soviet Union and wear a fancy medal on your chest."

Wide-eyed, sly smiling Jozef said nothing.

Andrei laughed. "Never mind you fox. We'll talk about it after the war."

Ben took note of this interplay, smiled knowingly, but did not speak

"So, Andrei, who is the new man you bring today?" asked Jozef.

"This is Sergeant Boris Surdenko of the Soviet army. He is an escaped German prisoner and he has plenty news. I thought you might be interested."

"If he tells me what Nazis to kill, I am interested." Jozef then turned to the Sergeant and looked at this defiant man, tall with slits for eyes, evidence of weight loss with clothes obviously now too big for his large frame, standing about six feet, a deep scar on his right cheek and the corners of his mouth turned down. Jozef said to him, "From where did you escape, Sergeant Surdenko?"

As everyone listened, the sergeant said, "From Maly Trostenets."

Jozef's eyes squinted. "Maly Trostenets? That's a suburb of Minsk."

"You haven't been there lately," stated the Sergeant with certainty.

"I've never been there to be honest. What's there now?"

"It's a concentration camp filled with Jews from Minsk and all over, and Soviet prisoners too. They're organized to shoot Jews and burn them. Andrei thought you'd be interested. Not only that, but the

Nazis gas them in vans—women and children and Russian prisoners
once they've nearly worked them to death."

Jozef asked, "This is a step up for the Nazis, those bastards. First, they took Jews, gypsys and others away, dug pits wherever they could and killed them random fashion. You're telling me that now they have a formal place; a concentration camp something like in Poland?"

"Yes, that's what I tell you. Russian and other Soviet prisoners of war do the dirty work and then they kill us. I was lucky to escape. I'm proud to tell you that I had to kill two of them with my bare hands to get free."

"Bare hands? Ahhh, perfect justice, sergeant. So I assume that the place is fortified?"

"To the teeth. There are tall guard towers in each corner and two layers of barbed wire backed up by machine guns. They are manned twenty-four hours a day."

Jozef turned to Andrei and said, "So a frontal attack is out of the question, Andrei?"

"Only by an organized army with armor," answered Andrei.

"What do you suggest, Andrei?" asked Jozef.

"I'm thinking that this one would be a good one for you, Jozef. You haven't let me down yet. I would like to kill every Nazi that takes over leadership at Maly Trostenets. I'd like to make them so scared to be the boss there that the word will get out that it's a death sentence. We'll confuse them. We'll make them so afraid to take over command that they'll close the place down. Those bastards don't deserve to live. Sergeant Surdenko here tells me that the Colonel in charge now is a Colonel Albert Schultz and I'm offering Sergeant Surdenko to you as the assassin. He's chomping at the bit to kill those bastards; too many of his buddies got bullets in the head. He wants revenge."

"Anyone can understand that." Jozef turned to Mikhail and asked, "Mikhail, do you know that Colonel prick?"

"I met him once at headquarters a month ago. When they come to Minsk, it would be my job to set up a place for them to stay, so I know the exact room where he sleeps. Every morning, he and a group of them would leave in three Schwerer Panzerpahwagen. Those are very heavy armored vehicles and they started using them after we attacked them once. Where they would leave to, I never did know, but it must have been Maly Trostenets if the Sergeant says he's there now. If you want my opinion on the best place to get him, I would say that now that I disappeared from them unexpectedly, I could only guess that they know that I might have been a traitor in their midst, so if they had an ounce of sense, they would switch rooms or get different rooms altogether or even move out of headquarters. Maybe attacking the heavy armored vehicles or dynamiting the road where they travel would be the best approach. I leave that to you experts, except you need to know that ordinary bullets or even explosives may not make much of a dent in those carriers. If you're going to use dynamite, you may need plenty."

Andrei said, "Okay, never anything easy in this business. We all got the message? Jozef, keep Sergeant Surdenko here with you. He'll need some fattening up, so give him plenty of gefilte fish, kugel and knaidloch. Think about whatever you think would be the best way to kill the Colonel and if I can help, don't hesitate to get in touch with me. I'm going back and I've got a nice project to take on with the Russian army. I'll tell you all about it after the war, Jozef. In the meantime, I have some ideas about how you can kill those bastards. Hold for that news."

"Mazel Tov, Andrei. Thanks for the project. We won't disappoint and we wait to hear from you," said Jozef.

He didn't have long to wait. Andrei and two men arrived on horseback two days later carrying long wooden crates tied to the side of each horse. A surprised Jozef said, "I see you're as good as your word, Andrei. What cargo is that?"

"The Nazi bastards are teaching us a thing or two," answered Andrei. "We don't have hand-held anti-tank weapons, but they do and we captured a whole load of them. Any kid can learn to shoot it." He and his men unloaded the crates, placed them on the ground, removed the weapons and lay them down on tarps.

"Behold, Jozef, here's your answer," said Andrei. "These are panzerfausts, and they're used to destroy our tanks, so if they can do that they can destroy the Schwerer Panzerpahwagens which will now become coffins for Colonel Schultz and all. You like?"

"I like," said Jozef with lifted brows and a wide smile on his face.

"Get me the sergeant and one other man, maybe David. He knows his stuff."

"Coming right up, Andrei."

When they all arrived, Andrei showed them the weapons. "As I see it, Jozef, you have one option and that is to attack the armored cars carrying the targets to Maly Trostenets. The panzerfausts should do the job. As I said, if they can blow up tanks, they should be able to blow up the armored cars. Since there are three cars, you'll need three men to aim and shoot simultaneously. There are six panzerfausts, two for each man. You can only fire it once and then you throw away the barrel, get the second weapon and shoot again; two shots for each Nazi armored car. If that doesn't kill them, I don't know what will. One warning you need to know about. Fire and smoke comes out of the rear of the barrel of the Panzerfaust that'll burn a man to a crisp, so no one can be behind it. Understand?"

"I got it," said Jozef with a smile on his face. This looks like a good job for me, the sergeant and David. And I'll bring in Abel as a backup. Right, men?"

Their smile and nods of their heads gave Jozef the answer.

Amdrei said, "Okay, good. I suppose you wonder why I brought Brushka here, Jozef."

"I figured it was none of my business."

"Brushka is your instructor. She'll teach you everything there is to know about the panzerfaust. She is multitalented. The lady can shoot the eye out of a hornet at thirty meters, the range of this weapon. I'll be back for her in about three days. Take good care of her, Jozef."

"We will treat her like Sarah, Abraham's wife," said Jozef as he bowed in her direction.

When David, Sergeant Surdenko, Jozef and Abel were together, Brushka took charge. Mikhail was present as well. Brushka's booming voice was a perfect match for her husky body with clearly delineated forearm musculature that almost looked masculine. She stood a full five feet and ten inches with coal black hair covered by a multicolored babushka. Her hazel, blood shot eyes showed the stress of her hectic life of war and death.

"This is a panzerfaust," she exclaimed as she smiled and, in a show of strength that amazed her audience, she picked up one of the heavy weapons with one hand and held it above her head. "German made, we will kill Nazis with it. Isn't that great? I'll teach you how to handle this simple weapon. It is hand-held and one-shot; use it once and throw it away. The Nazis have been doing a good job with this new weapon. It destroyed many of our tanks, and if it can destroy a tank, I hate to think what it will do to an armored car. The bastards inside will fry. Kill 'em and cremate 'em all with one trigger pull," she said smiling and nodding her head. "You see the warhead in the front attached to the tube? Watch me now. I pick it up, put it on my shoulder, lift up the sight, aim it, pull down the trigger, make sure of the aim and pull the trigger. That's all there is to it. You have to be within 30 meters of the target. Now, see the rear of the tube? It's covered with cardboard that is kept in place even when firing. The cardboard keeps dirt out of the tube. You see this warning on the back top of the tube? It says, Achtung Feuerstrahl, that means Attention Fire Jet. In other words, anyone standing behind the barrel will be fried and blown away; disappear in a puff of fire and smoke. This fire jet can go as far as ten meters behind, so one has to be in an open field with nothing behind him before firing the weapon. Each of you will have two of these weapons. Now let's come up here and see what you can do."

They all handled the weapon, commenting on its simplicity. They spent several hours each repeatedly attempting to aim and pretending to pull the trigger then laying the used weapon down, picking up the second one and pretending to fire again. It soon became automatic.

"Alright, now comes the hard part," said Brushka. She paused, looked around at the man standing before her, and asked, "Where do we get the bastards? Does anyone know the route they take to get from their headquarters to Maly Trostenets?"

Mikhail said, "I know where they leave from and what street they go down, but that's all. They go south and turn right after a few blocks. I never knew where they headed. Now I know. It's to the damn concentration camp."

"How about you, sergeant?"

"There's only one entrance into the camp at Maly, so they have to come in there."

Brushka said, "So we know from where they start and where they arrive, but we don't know the full route. What's the chance of finding that out?"

There was silence as neither Mikhail nor the sergeant spoke.

Brushka said, "I guess that means we have to hit them when they start out or when they arrive at the camp."

Sergeant Surdenko quickly said, "You can forget about getting them at the entrance to the camp. The place is armed all around and with the tall guard posts in each corner they have a good line of sight for almost a few kilometers in every direction."

Abel added, "The roads to Maly Trostenets are all main roads, so they might have some traffic. I'm trying to think of a good place to station ourselves to get the shots off. By the way, Jozef, what's my role here since you've got six panzerfausts, two for each man, you David and the sergeant."

"You're back up, Abel. You'll have a machine gun to finish off anyone the panzerfausts don't kill, or you'll take over a panzerfaust if one of the three of us gets wiped out."

"I got it, Jozef."

Jozef said, "Okay, we got a little problem. Where are we going to get at them? Everybody go and think about it today. Come back tomorrow in the morning at 9 and bring some solutions. This is too important not to get done."

The next morning at the meeting, Abel confidently said, "My mother had a map of Minsk, so I tried to figure out the route that the Germans would take from their headquarters. I drew it on the map here. This is the fastest and best route for them. I know the areas of the city they would drive through and most of it was bombed when the invasion started. There's still some rubble and empty lots standing next to some houses that weren't damaged or only lightly damaged."

He then pinned the map to a tree so all could view it. Jozef, Sergeant Surdenko and David crowded around.

Abel pointed to the map saying, "Where I drew the X is a spot I know. It's a damaged, abandoned house and right next door is an empty lot. There are very few people there anymore. The Germans will drive by the damaged house first and then pass the empty lot. Keep that in mind. Here's what I figure," said Abel pausing to think.

"What?" asked Jozef.

"We get there early in the morning when it's still dark. We hide in the house. If there's no debris on the empty lot we put some there so we can all hide behind it. We station ourselves in the house and wait. As soon as we see the Germans coming down the street, we get out of the house and take up positions on the empty lot. The house will block us from their vision. When they reach the lot we're ready and we, or the three of you I mean, blast them, one...two...three. Two shots each. I mop up if I have to. Then we take off heading south until we hit the woods, circle around, go back home. What does everybody think?"

David said, "Good work, Abel. We'll need luck to get it done without a problem, but I can't think of anything better."

Sergeant Surdenko said, "I don't know anything about that area, but it sounds good to me."

"Jozef said, "I wish we had the luxury of a dry run, but we don't, so we'll just have to risk it. Abel, I think you've given us the best chance. Get plenty of sleep. We meet here tomorrow at 5:00 in the evening. I figure that will get us there about 4:00 or 5:00 in the morning and it'll still be dark. It's not going to be an easy walk for us with two Panzerfausts each on our back. Abel will help carry them if you young pups can't handle the load."

David and the sergeant glanced at each other, both wondering if Jozef was serious or jesting. David said, "Don't worry, old man, the sergeant and I will carry yours."

They all smiled, hoping to insert some levity in a task that could be the last one of their lives.

Mikhail was there the next morning as the four warriors prepared to leave. "God speed, Jozef. I need you all to come back in good health. I've got another idea to talk to you about."

Jozef nodding said, "You got a date, Mikhail, your ideas pay off big. Any chance of a quick preview now?"

"Only that it'll be easy, not dangerous and will pay off big."

"Can't wait," said Jozef. "See you when we get back."

The four of them, led by Abel who was most acquainted with Minsk geography, left on their adventure. It took a slow, fatiguing trip to reach their destination in the dark. It was just as Abel said: a littered empty lot adjacent to a severely damaged uninhabited home left as such by the areas new German masters and the rare individuals who stubbornly still inhabited the area. They immediately entered the house, relieved themselves of their burden and sat down exhausted. Abel said he would take the first watch out of a side window that looks down road to see when the armored vehicles arrive.

Jozef said, "We'll take twenty minute shifts out of this window. The second you see them coming, we go to the empty lot next door and get in position. We'll line up side by side, I aim for the first car, Sergeant you take the second and David the third. I'll shoot first, and the second you hear my shot both of you fire at the second car and the third. Try your best to get off two shots. While the smoke and fire are in the air, we run back into the house, go out the back door and follow Abel back home. I hope it's as simple as I just said it. Abel. You stay in the house and as soon as you hear the first explosion, look

286

out the window and watch. If there's anyone left or anyone that we didn't kill, use your machine gun and wipe them out. I doubt it'll be necessary. Does everybody understand?"

The consensus of the three simultaneous answers delivered from smiling faces was that we got it, we're ready and we can't wait.

I took almost two hours, which seemed like forever, before the armored cars came into view. As soon as David, who was on watch at the time, saw them coming, he signaled and followed Jozef and Sergeant Surdenko out the door, taking well-hidden cover behind their barriers. Jozef and sergeant were lying on their bellies and David kneeled behind a higher barrier.

As soon as Jozef fired the first shot, the sergeant and David joined in. All the armored cars vanished in fire and smoke as the explosions shook the building where Abel was crouched at the ready. They were able to get off the second shot except for David, knocked to the ground from a crouching position. Unhurt, he shook his head, managed to fire off a delayed second shot and ran into the house after Jozef and the sergeant. The four of them ran out the back door and followed Abel to the forest where they sped as fast as they could to get far from the attack site. The arrived at partisan headquarters long after dark.

"The guards at the gate to Maly Trostenets will have a long wait today for their bosses," smiled Sergeant Surdenko.

With this project completed, Jozef, with his one-track mind always thinking of revenge, went on to thoughts of the next project. "Let's see what Mikhail's got on his mind," he exclaimed smiling.

CHAPTER 33
MIKHAIL'S TURN
LATE 1943

Exhilarated after a job well done, the four men returned to camp. "Everyone get a good rest and we'll meet here tomorrow morning at nine," said Jozef. "We need to see what Mikhail's got up his sleeve. I'll bet it's a good one."

The four men gathered at Jozef's hut the next morning. Mikhail was already there engaged in an animated discussion with Jozef as the others arrived.

David said, "By the smile on your face, Jozef, Mikhail must have a hell of an idea."

"It's better than that," said Jozef. Gather around and listen to a winner. First, David, get your father here right away. We might have need of his expert opinion."

Curious as to why Jozef needed his father to hear about a new venture against the Nazis, David said, "Sure, give me five minutes."

As David ran off to retrieve Dr. Ben, Jozef said to Sergeant Surdenko, "Sergeant, David's father is the doctor for our camp. You'll see why we need him as soon as they get back." They engaged in small talk while waiting for David and Ben to return.

When all were present, Jozef said, "Okay, Mikhail, tell them what you told me."

Mikhail said, "First of all for the sergeant here, I want you to know that I worked in the Minsk Civic Building as the engineer for many years before the Nazis came, so I know the building like the back of my hand. The Nazis kept me on and I was able to give Jozef here, some good intelligence about the Nazi plans. Things got hot for me, so I never went back to work one morning, and my family and I came to join Jozef. The Minsk Civic Building is the headquarters for the Minsk Nazi operation against the Jews and all of their "enemies of the state" as they like to call us. I have an idea to stop that operation cold in its tracks." Mikhail paused to be sure that all were listening. "I want to poison the water supply. I know exactly where the water main splits off to supply the building. I need a diamond drill, some poison, and, or as Jozef suggested, some deadly germs to put in the Nazi drinking water." Mikhail paused and stared at four smiling faces and nodding heads.

Jozef said, "For the poison, we're thinking arsenic, and for the deadly germs, what do you think, Ben?"

Ben thought for a few seconds before he said, "The germs I deal with here in the forest like strep germs from sore throats and staph germs from cuts or boils wouldn't do the job. I'm thinking that the germ for Cholera, the vibrio cholerae, if given in a high enough concentration will either make them very sick with diarrhea and dehydration or kill them quickly. We don't have cholera here in the forests because the sanitary measures we put in place prevent it from happening."

Sergeant Surdenko said, "I bet we could get plenty of cholera germs from Nazi prisoner of war camps. God knows we got more prisoners than we know what to do with, and lucky for us, they die like flies."

Jozef added, "That's why when I take the sergeant back to the Soviet partisan camp, I'll talk to Andrei who has a direct line to the Soviet army. If he can get us the arsenic and the germs, we're in business. Meanwhile, Mikhail and the rest of you work on plans on how to get this delicious cocktail into Nazi guts." He paused, a wide smile on his face and then added, "Okay, sergeant, let's you and I get to Andrei and see what he can do for us. Ben, I think we'll need you on this trip because I don't know anything about the cholera germs."

"Sure, Jozef. When do we leave?"

"In two hours. The rest of you, your lips are sealed and I mean tight."

When Jozef, Ben and the sergeant arrived at Andrei's camp. Andrei said, "I heard the good news from Brushka, here. She said you were fast learners and made short work of the Nazis with their own Panzerfausts. Perfect justice, I call that," as Andrei slapped his right hand on his right thigh. Then he turned to sergeant Surdenko and asked, "Did you enjoy it, Sergeant?"

"Perfect is the right word," he said.

Turning to Jozef, Andrei said, "You have a new project, Jozef?" Then he turned to Brushka and said, "When Jozef comes to get help on a new project, we stop everything and sit and listen. The man is a genius."

Ben took note of this camaraderie, and thought back again to the time when his wife recommended Jozef as the perfect commander for the Jewish partisan group. How right she was.

Jozef got right to the point. "We've developed a way of poisoning the water supply to the Nazis at their Minsk headquarters. We need your help."

Andrei stared at Jozef for a few seconds, turned to Brushka and said, "What did I tell you, Brushka. Is he a genius or not?"

"A genius," she answered.

"What kind of help do you need?" asked Andrei.

"We need arsenic and cholera germs and a diamond headed drill to get into the water pipes."

Andrei sat stunned for a few seconds. "Arsenic and cholera germs?" He thought, and added—"A double cocktail." He turned to Brushka laughing and said, "You see how a genius works, Brushka. If the arsenic doesn't kill them, the cholera will make the Nazis shit themselves to death," barely getting out the words before he and Brushka erupted in laughter.

Jozef laughed as well and then Ben said, "If your Soviet doctors can collect cholera germs and put them on agar plates, we'll do the rest, or if they have a better way of transporting them, that will be fine too. We'll need to get them in a large syringe so we can inject them into the water pipes."

"This project of yours is too good to wait," said Andrei. "I'll get right on it. The next time I come to your camp, It'll be with the drill, the arsenic and the germs. When I tell my army friends it is for Jozef so he can kill Nazis, it'll get top priority. They know all about you, Jozef. You are a hero and they say that the army will remember you after the war."

"We'll do our planning while we wait for you. Thank you, Andrei," said Jozef.

Jozef and his four partners trekked back to camp. Jozef, David, and Abel met the next morning around a pitcher of coffee. "Mikhail will tell you what we've worked out," said Jozef.

As everyone listened intently, Mikhail started. "There's a dirt alley in the rear about ten meters behind the Minsk Civic Building .The

Nazis built a cement block fence near the alley on the back-side of the building." He drew a picture on a sheet of cardboard and held it up for all to see. "The fence is about eight feet high and covered with barbed wire on top. There is a copper water pipe in the alley that supplies the neighborhood. I know the exact site where the pipe that supplies the building branches off from the main pipe. It is on the far side of the fence, so I can work there and no one will see me. I figure we come in through the forest in the middle of the night. All of you have machine guns and rifles, and you stay on the edge of the forest hidden behind trees and act as guards, guns at the ready. I dress completely in black clothes, blacken my face, neck and hands with charcoal and crawl to the pipe with the arsenic and cholera germs and diamond drill. I have to dig down about two feet to get the main pipe and find the pipe that branches from the main pipe and supplies the building. It shouldn't take long to hand drill through the top of the branching pipe, inject the poison and the germs and crawl back to the forest. Whoever wakes up the next day in the building and drinks water is in for a surprise. This building will be out of commission. They'll never know what hit them. As soon as we get the supplies from Andrei, we meet with Dr. Ben. He fills the syringes and we're off to the races. Is everything clear?"

"We got it," was the consensus.

"Okay. Let's wait," said Mikhail.

Jozef added, "If I know Andrei, it won't be long,"

It took five days, but Andrei delivered the two necessary ingredients and the diamond drill. Ben stored the arsenic and the cholera cultures and Mikhail took the drill and marveled at its technical perfection and ease of noiseless operation. Andrei didn't settle for second best, he thought.

The day before they planned to leave, they all met and discussed their plans making sure everyone understood. Satisfied, they left at a time to ensure their arrival in the pitch dark of early morning.

On the way there, Jozef, David, Abel and Mikhail engaged in quiet conversation.

"We're winning this war now," said Mikhail, "but we can help by keeping the pressure on right up to the last minute. That's what this is all about, and I can't wait to get this done."

"It'll happen, Mikhail, thanks to you," said Jozef. What's your take on the war now?"

"Well, late last year the Soviets started their counter-offensive around Stalingrad. Hitler didn't retreat and that left us with a great opportunity to surround them and that's just what we did in late 1942 and early 1943. By February it was all over. The Germans surrendered. This was Hitler's first big defeat and turned the tide in my opinion. The Germans must have been worried about it because in January, they withdrew from the Caucusus rather than risk having the Soviets trap them there, plus, I guess they figured that they needed those troops other places. If this doesn't make Hitler realize that his manpower is limited while ours is almost endless, then he doesn't have a military brain in his head. Anyhow in February, we took Kursk and retook Kharkov, which the Germans quickly recaptured, but I doubt they'll be able to hold it."

"So we've still got some back and forth battle it sounds like," said David.

"That's true, but the momentum lies with us, so we keep plugging away. The only time we stop fighting here in Minsk is when we see the Soviets march back to Minsk and head back to Germany from there."

Jozef added, "That's right, Mikhail. That's what we're fighting for. That and to see Hitler swinging on a hangman's noose."

"You'll never get that bastard alive," added David thinking of his father's lecture to him about Hitler when the lived in Germany. "Fanatics like that won't let themselves be captured."

It was a long hike for the four men, but when Mikhail recognized that they were close, he urged complete silence. "We're about a half mile from the building. Not a sound. The three of you will stop before the end of the tree line, lie down and keep an eye on the building."

Mikhail crawled forward to a previously marked destination before the large fence. The day before he made the decision to leave his dangerous work as an agent for the Jewish partisans, he marked the spot where the building water pipe branched off from the main pipe by a buried rock and a mark on the cement block wall. Easy to find, he took his shovel out of a small back pack and dug down slowly and quietly the two feet until he identified the main pipe and the smaller branch pipe feeding the building. It took only a few minutes to drill though the copper branch pipe with his diamond drill and then he injected both 100 cc syringes with their deadly contents into the pipe; first the arsenic and then the cholera germs. When he finished, he thanked God for his progress to this point and then crawled back to Jozef, David and Abel.

"Just follow me," Mikhail said. "Hug the ground until I get up. Then we walk back to the camp. We should have at least three or four hours of darkness. I wish I was a fly on the wall in that building so I could see what happens to those bastards in the next week or so."

What happened was death and illness from both toxins with the symptoms overlapping so that Nazi physicians were confused. Some of the Nazi residents of the building developed severe headache, confusion and disorientation, diarrhea and vomiting followed by convulsions. Those affected in this manner were dead within days. These symptoms were similar to cholera, confusing the physicians who suspected this diagnosis, but there was no cholera in the city of Minsk, so they discarded this possibility until the stool cultures came up positive for the germ. It took three to four days to realize they were victims of sabotage, but how it happened to them remained a mystery. The physicians on the scene never established the arsenic diagnosis until much later in Berlin when their institute of pathology examined pathological and blood samples. Then they realized they were victimized by a double toxic attack; Jews poisoned the water with arsenic and cholera germs. How?

The Nazis buried the victims. They abandoned and boarded up the building. They killed Jews at a faster pace. Maly Trostenets remained as active as ever; much more so when the Nazis agreed that partisans—undoubtedly Jews as they claimed without proof— sabotaged them.

CHAPTER 34

A PROFESSOR'S PERSPECTIVE

MID 1943

Jubilation was the word for Mikhail's success. A festive mood overtook the Jewish partisan camp. When word of the mission's success reached Andrei, he told Brushka and his lieutenants, one of whom was an older advisor, a University of Moscow history professor and a Jew named Leonid Brodsky who insisted on meeting these "Heroes of the Soviet Union," Jozef Askenazy, Mikhail Gregov and Ben Frohman. Andrei sent one of his men on horseback to deliver a note to Jozef to arrange the meeting. It requested that all those who partook of the brilliantly contrived mission be there so that the professor could meet them all—civilian soldiers actively making history.

Jozef informed Dr. Ben and Leah, David, Hannah, Emily, Mikhail, his wife, Sonya, and son Val, and Abel to be there to meet Andrei and Brushka and an admirer, a prominent Jewish-Russian history professor, Leonid Brodsky who was anxious to make their acquaintance.

With the meeting arranged, the three Soviet partisans arrived on horseback and found the Jewish entourage all seated around a tree made table and chairs.

Andrei hugged both Jozef and Mikhail and introduced the professor to all. They took note of a tall, elderly man with a gray beard, salt and pepper hair, what there was left of it, a prominent nose and wide eyes that darted back and forth like a hand adding machine adding up figures, and conveying a brilliance and quick mind that could understand your innermost thoughts. A closed mouth smile completed the picture, bringing them all to attention wondering what pearls of wisdom they would hear.

"It is a pleasure to meet you all," said Professor Brodsky. Andrei has told me much of your good works, so I insisted on meeting you personally to thank you. Efforts such as yours will play a large part in our ultimate victory. Please sit down. I'm honored to meet you all."

David, listening intently, jumped on the words "ultimate victory" and said, "So you are confident we will win the war, sir?"

The professor smiled widely—open mouthed this time—and answered without hesitation, nodding his head. "Yes, we will win it. As a matter of fact, we have won the war. I know it, our soldiers and generals know it and the Nazi generals know it. They knew it as soon as Hitler sacked many of them and took over the leadership himself. Under Hitler's leadership, we can't lose. He has become our best ally." He paused, taking a deep breath before he continued. "Now, I gave you a direct answer. It demands clarification. Does anyone have an idea when the war turned for us?"

David answered, "In the forest here we don't get much news. We do have a radio, but the reception is bad. All we know is that there are still Nazis killing Jews in Minsk and that we have to fight back. We hear about all these battles going on all over the Soviet Union, but don't have the overall picture."

"You have perfectly stated the role of the partisan. Harass, harass and harass some more until you hear from the Soviet army that the war is over. The more you do now as we start winning, the quicker the end will come. Now, in a more detailed answer as to when did I know that the war will end in our favor, let me say that the decisive battle is shaping up around Kursk." We have retaken it, but the Germans have prepared with all their might to take it back and brought up many of their forces. This is no secret. What the Germans don't realize is that we've brought up the most massive defense in armor, weapons and men in the history of warfare. We will defeat them there and they'll never again be able to launch an effective offensive. Our offensive might grows, as now we have unhindered industrial capacity as well as two allies, Britain and the United States who supply us with armaments."

Jozef asked, "So professor, do you think The Nazi's end hinges on this great battle shaping up in Kursk?"

Not really. I believe that going back to Stalingrad, we can see Germany's end. Hitler was determined to take Stalingrad, and his failure to do so guaranteed his defeat. He couldn't stop our pincer movement that surrounded his forces. After that, there was no way they could win as they froze and starved to death and their weapons and machinery didn't work. Stalingrad makes us realize that his fanaticism will do him in. Rather than retreat to fight another day, he was perfectly willing to sacrifice all his men. That became his policy for the entire war. It costs him dearly."

"So you see Stalingrad as the turning point?" asked David.

"Perhaps. How about if I take you back further."

"To when?" asked David.

"To Moscow when he failed to capture the city, or let me take you back even further to when he launched his invasion late and froze before the gates of Moscow and was pushed back. Right at that point one could say that Barbarossa failed. But this type of discussion will occupy historians for fifty years. The point is, Hitler is losing this war, will lose it, and his dream of a breadbasket for his master race with Slavic untermenschen to slave for Germany is a fantasy engendered in a sick mind for which the entire world is forced to pay the price. So, if you want to go back even further than Barbarossa, go to the 1920's when he wrote his Mein Kampf insisting that he must control the Ukraine breadbasket to feed his master race."

Silence ensued until the professor continued on a different vein. "Thank you all for allowing me to get to know you. With your permission, I would like to take a picture of this great group; a picture for posterity. I want a picture to let the world know that not only armies defeat tyrants, but ordinary people do as well."

CHAPTER 35
ASIPOVICHY DIVERSION
MID 1943

"Are you familiar with the town of Asipovichy, Jozef?" asked Andrei.

"Yeah. Never been there, but I know of it. Why?" answered Jozef.

"It's a big railroad hub, and I have it on good authority that a large shipment of new Nazi tanks will be passing through. Whatever we can do to destroy that shipment will play a big part in allowing us to kick Hitler's ass. I think you know what I'm talking about."

"It sounds like you're interested in pulling off a big job there, Andrei, anything I can do to help."

"I would love to do it, but the army gave my whole group a task working with them to help with their planned offensive around Kursk. This is the big one, Jozef. We're fully committed, so I have to pass this one off—and who better than you."

"Tell me what to do. You know I never pass up an opportunity to kill Nazis."

Andrei smiled and said, "Good, good, I knew I could count on you. This may be indirect as far as you're concerned, but you'll make it possible. Asipovichy is about a one or two-day walk southwest of Minsk. There's a big railroad hub there and plenty of Nazi trains go through on the way to the front. We know of a large shipment coming in and we need to destroy those trains."

"You want me to do it, Andrei? You know I would."

"No, not in this case, Jozef. It would be too dangerous. You'd never be able to get through to the station since it's guarded night and day. I have a different plan."

Jozef nodded yes. "Okay, what's the deal?"

"The deal is this. Let me start from the beginning. The Nazis control all the railroad lines and railroad stations in Byelorussia and all over their captured territory. It would be impossible for them to keep the railroads running, so they have to rely on civilian workers. Believe me there are thousands of civilians working on railroads all over the Soviet Union. This is the Nazi's Achilles Heel because not 100 percent of the workers are loyal to the Nazis. Most of them are not, but because they have to provide for their families, they do so biding their time. There are a few who work for them gritting their teeth, but hate the Nazis as much as you do. We're in contact with some of these haters and they're chomping at the bit to do some dirty work. I have one in mind who is waiting for instructions."

"Instructions? You want me to instruct him?" asked Jozef.

Andrei answered quickly and decisively. "Yes, that's it exactly. There is no way you could get into the railroad station. I'm not about to give you a suicide mission. You're too valuable. What I need is a man to give instructions to our contact."

"That I can do, assuming I know the topic of instruction."

"Here's the story, Jozef."

Andrei continued. "I came prepared. Here's a map of Asipovichy, and on the map is a marked route that will take you right to our friend's house about a mile from the railroad station. The name of the street and his address are right on the map here and you'll get there long after dark. Knock on the door—three knocks, a pause, than two knocks. He knows the signal. After he lets you in…"

Jozef interrupted, "What's his name?"

"It doesn't matter. Here is a picture of him so you'll know you have the right man. Once you find that out, destroy the picture. No small talk. Get right down to business, which is to give him these four delayed fuse magnetic mines in wood to avoid the mine detectors, and instruct him in their use. Make certain he knows what to do like the back of his hand."

"He'll do the rest, I suppose."

"You suppose right. Believe me he's as motivated to kill Nazis as you are. I won't go into details, but you can trust me on that. If things go well, we should have an incredible fireworks display. This railroad station has four entering tracks near to each other. Our friend railroad worker knows that you're coming. He knows to put the mines under gasoline filled tank cars, because when they blow up, the gas should also explode and blow up the nearby cars, which have explosives in them and the Nazis new tanks ready to join the Kursk battle. You like that, Jozef"

"I love it, but it's too bad I won't be able to see it. You said new tanks? What's that all about?"

"They're very powerful and could give us some competition, but they don't have nearly as many as we have and the more we can destroy before they get on the field of battle, the better for us. This is important, Jozef. That's why we need you."

"Thanks, Andrei, you've given me another labor of love."

"That's the spirit. And as for you not being there to see it, don't worry, you'll get a full report from me and then you can chalk up another accomplishment on your way to the Hero of the Soviet Union medal."

"My reward will be to learn how many Nazis I helped kill, how many weapons are not in their hands because of what we did and when we drive what's left them back to what's left of Berlin."

"Spoken like a true partisan, Josef, what would we do without you?"

The next morning, Jozef notified David that he would be gone for about four or five days, and David would be in charge.

"Where are you going, Jozef?"

"I may tell you later if I find out that it was a good trip."

"Hmm, I should have known better than to ask."

Jozef arrived on the outskirts of Asipovichy and, guided by the map, found the correct street and address. It was approximately 11:00 pm. When he knocked on the door as instructed, an elderly man opened the door immediately as if he had been ready and expecting him any minute. The man, with a large bushy mustache just like his picture, barely looked at Jozef, stepped back, opened the door wider, nodded his head saying nothing and let Jozef enter. Jozef noted a somber looking man he estimated to be about 60 with slits for eyes visualized through a dim light made by a kerosene lamp on a table adjacent to the wall next to the door. The man pointed to a chair near the lamp and pulled up his own chair. They both sat as the man leaned forward and said one word, "Welcome."

The first thing Jozef did was tear the picture into little pieces hand them to the man and say, Burn these." Jozef got right down to business pulling the four mines out of his backpack and launched into a careful process of instruction gauging his pupil's understanding by a confident nodding of his head as his only response to Jozef's instructions. His slits for eyes, now replaced by wider lids with more white and brown pupils visualized, reflected an expression of intense interest. Here was a man on a mission, thought Jozef and it appears that he had a complete grasp of the low technical aspect of these simple-made bombs. Jozef asked, "Do you understand everything?" The man nodded his head, smiling a closed mouth smile, eyes sparkling. "Thank you, thank you," the man said. They shook hands and Jozef left.

Welcome and thank you, thank you; the only words uttered by this somber and intense man, but Jozef felt confident. He arrived back in camp two days later.

Four days after that, Brushka and two men arrived in camp with a bottle of Andrei's best vodka and a message from Andrei. It read: Mission accomplished beyond our wildest dreams. The fire rages on; our man destroyed the station and the munitions. There will be quite a few less Nazi tanks, shells and bullets to try to take Kursk thanks to you and your new friend. The Soviet Union thanks you, Jozef.

CHAPTER 36
KURSK
MID 1943

In July and August of 1943, ready for the decisive battle, German and Soviet forces faced each other near the City of Kursk, approximately 450 kilometers south of Moscow. Both sides geared up for a struggle that would prove to be the greatest armored and single-day aerial battle in the history of warfare.

The Russians recaptured the city situated in a bulge-like salient that extended out from their north to south line. The Germans hoped to shorten their line by attacking from north and south to choke off the salient, surround and destroy the Soviet army in and around Kursk. For this, they massed armored attack units, artillery and infantry. The Soviets, in a classical example of the importance of military intelligence, learned of Hitler's intentions giving them the opportunity to prepare an excellent defense. In addition, the Germans delayed while they brought up their new and more powerful Tiger and Panther tanks. The delay allowed the Soviets to construct an impenetrable defense wider than any previously constructed and fashioned to force the German attack through minefields, pre-aimed artillery zones, anti-tank obstacles and other obstructions designed to slow the vaunted German Blitzkrieg, an accomplishment that so far escaped German enemies. It would prove to be the most effective defense ever constructed; overkill as it turned out because the Blitzkrieg faltered rapidly.

With the German offense bogged down, the Soviets, in well-planned offensive thrusts, struck with overwhelming force, retook three cities, prevented encirclement, kept Kursk in their powerful grasp and proved that Blitzkrieg could be stopped.

Never again would the Germans be able to launch an effective offensive strike in the Soviet Union.

"You were right, Professor, the war is won. Hitler must be about ready to shoot himself," said Andrei.

"Not yet, Andrei," answered the professor. "That'll happen when our troops are ready to break into where he's holing up in Berlin or the Obersaltzburg in the Alps, or wherever. You can be sure, even if he wanted a negotiated settlement with us, after all the death and destruction he's caused, there would be no chance of that. Unconditional surrender is all he'll ever be offered assuming he stays alive."

"Well, I hope he kills himself to save us the trouble," said Andrei. "What do you think our role will be from this time on?"

"Our role doesn't change. We disrupt supplies and kill and disable as many as we can, concentrating on the high ranking officers even though there is only one high ranking man, Adolph Hitler, who has emasculated his generals. Little did he realize that it would all be to our benefit. Can you get this great victory message to your Jewish friends?" asked the professor.

"I can, but believe me, it won't be necessary." Then Andrei told the professor the story of Jozef Askenazy of Poland, who escaped and witnessed the Nazi killing of forty-nine of his friends in Poland, shot and torched in a Synagogue. "His devotion to the cause is so intense, I think he'll try and follow the German army back to Berlin shooting all the way. He's the perfect partisan. His life revolves around seeking revenge. He's the kind of man we can count on for the tough missions."

CHAPTER 37
OPERATION BAGRATION
1944

The tide turned against the Nazis forcing them to withdraw from Tunisia in Africa in order to reinforce their embattled troops in the Soviet Union. Besides regaining Kursk and beating off the German offensive to retake it in the largest tank battle in history, the Soviets retook Kharkov, only to have to abandon it and recapture it in March, 1943.

The British and Americans invaded Sicily in what would be a successful campaign and the forerunner of an invasion of Italy. Shortly after the Sicily invasion, the Italian fascist government failed and the new government arrested Mussolini. Hitler came to his rescue, recaptured him and reestablished him in power, but this was to be short-lived as Italian partisans assassinated him necessitating that the Nazis take on a solo defense of Italy where they would fight a tough, vicious and lengthy battle against the invading British and American troops. By the last two months of the year, Italy declared war on Germany.

In the early days of the invasion of the Soviet Union, Hitler, not wanting his troops fighting in urban warfare, ordered the city of Leningrad placed under siege. Cut off from supplies and food,

Leningrad became a wasteland. The Soviets did what they could to supply the citizens by truck over frozen Lake Ladoga in winter and evacuate whom they could, but this was inadequate to prevent the starvation and disease that ran rampant throughout the city bombarded on a continuous basis by German artillery. After 900 days of siege, Hitler abandoned Leningrad after the Soviet army broke through. Six-hundred-forty thousand Leningrad citizens died.

Confident of ultimate victory, the Soviets made further plans to end the war.

Only fanatical Nazis continued to have faith in their leader. Most knew that Hitler's dream of a greater German empire was leading them to ruin.

"Jozef, we've had a little dry spell except for the rail lines and roads we dynamite at times, but things will be heating up very soon," said Andrei at a surprise visit.

"We're ready any time. I've got about a dozen men who know how to lay explosives. There's no shortage of rails or roads," replied Jozef.

"Good and keep it up wherever you can," said Andrei. Then he added, "As the Nazi bastards kill more people, there are more partisans than ever now and I've got orders from the army to organize them all to increase their concentration on rail lines and truck roads especially 19, 20 and 21 June non-stop, said Andrei."

Jozef nodded his head and smiled knowingly. "That means the big one is coming."

"Did you ever hear of Petr Ivanovich Bagration, Jozef?"

"Can't say as I have."

"Well, if you grew up in Russia, you would have. He is one of the greatest generals of our history and fought in the Swedish and the

Napoleonic wars. He was an insanely brave man and his superiors made him a general at a young age. He was one of those guys who led from the front, but it finally cost him. He died of a leg wound during the Napoleonic war at age 47. I tell you this because Operation Bagration is the name of the battle that will liberate Byelorussia and get us all the way to Berlin. It starts on June 22. Does that ring a bell, Jozef?"

"Ahh, perfect; three years to the day from the invasion. That must have been Stalin's idea."

"Well, I'm not sure whose idea it was, but it's close to the D-Day landings in France on June 6. We're coming at him from both ends, Jozef. We'll make a Hitler sandwich. Operation Bagration will be the biggest attack in military history. The Americans and British say their invasion of France is the biggest amphibious invasion in history, but I tell you that compared to operation Bagration, it's tiny. This will be the largest battle with the most men in the history of war. There's no way that the Nazis have a chance, especially if we partisans can stop them from getting their tanks and arms. We've got a big job ahead. You'll need plenty more explosives, more than I can deliver, so the army has ordered airdrops that'll come right on your head, so look up at the sky for the next few days. The drop will include plenty of explosives and plenty of small arms, grenades and machine guns. The Nazis will retreat in our direction, so there's the possibility they may invite themselves over for tea. We want all partisans to be ready to oblige. Got it, Jozef?"

"I got it, Andrei. We'll give them a good reception if they do."

Andrei was as good as his word. Within three days, the Jewish partisans heard low flying transport planes overhead. Looking up, they spotted four of them and watched in amazement as wrapped cargo came out of the sides followed by billowing white parachutes, which hit the ground or trees within fifteen seconds. They retrieved them all. Jozef had his dozen men line up in four groups of three apiece and they divided the explosives between the groups and stored the weapons to be at the ready in the event of retreating Nazis coming through. On June 19, they left for their tasks of blowing up chosen rails and burying landmines on well-traveled truck roads. They kept this up for three days of continuous unopposed work.

History would document that many different groups of partisans carried out 9,600 rail demolitions and supply depot raids the first day and 890 rail demolitions the second day completely paralyzing for several days the main source of supply for the Nazi army. On June 22, the Soviets struck with 2.3 million men, thousands of artillery pieces and tanks in what would be the largest allied operation of World War II meant to liberate Russian territory and destroy the Nazis fighting ability once and for all.

At this time, the Soviets faced the Nazis and their Hungarian and Rumanian allies near Ukraine. In the north, three Soviet army groups outnumbered the well dug in Nazis, but it was in the center, in Byelorussia, where the main action took place. Here Hitler had 38 infantry divisions, two air divisions, seven security divisions and one tank division. The disadvantage to the Nazis was that because of the harsh treatment of the Byelorussian people, the killings of a large percentage of the population, the destruction of whole villages, Byelorussians swelled the partisan ranks slowly and surely coming under more organized control from the Soviet army who further directed their activities.

A bulge in the center of the Soviet line caused a lengthening of the Nazi defensive position that created a disadvantage to the Nazis. Because it had the effect of lengthening his defensive position, the

Nazi general in charge requested permission to withdraw in order to shorten the line and prevent a pincer movement against the salient. In keeping with his policy of never retreating, Hitler denied the request.

In addition, although the Nazis had large numbers of troops, many of them were Hungarians, Slovaks, and Germans from occupied territories and security forces. Their method of transport, a throwback from World War I, depended on many slow horse-drawn wagons, disadvantageous compared to the Soviet Communists modern American lend-lease trucks. All this plus Soviet air superiority put the odds in favor of the Soviet forces. They wasted no time pushing this advantage with a massive 724-kilometer wide attack with 1,200,000 troops along with 1,000,000 support troops all supported by massive artillery barrages including Katyusha rockets, or "Stalin's Organs." The attack would include the northern front, the center front including Minsk, and the southern front, all coordinated to trap and decimate the Nazis east of Minsk, isolate Nazi army group north, recapture Ukraine and drive the enemy out of Soviet territories.

Andrei and his second in command, Brushka, made rounds of all the Minsk area partisans to direct their activities in support of the soon to come Operation Bagration. He exuded confidence as he urged continued destruction of Nazi rail and other transport lines supplying their troops. The dynamiting activity continued at an ever increasing pace hindering greatly the Nazi ability to fight.

He and Brushka met with Jozef a few days before the planned offensive. An ever-cautious Jozef did not hesitate to question in detail his bosses and the three of them had a frank discussion, something that Andrei was willing to have based upon his complete confidence in Jozef.

"To listen to you two talk, it seems like the war will be over soon," said Jozef.

Shaking his head and smiling, Andrei said, "No the war won't be over soon, but the war in the Soviet Union might be because they can't stop us now. It wouldn't surprise me if the last Nazi soldier lucky enough to escape what we're going to throw at him stepped back over the Polish border heading back to Germany in a few months. What do you think, Brushka?"

"You speak the truth," she said, "Jozef will have to have plenty of kosher wine for all the toasts."

Jozef watched as the confidence exuded by the two of them flowed out, but being a cautious person and a careful analyst, he needed proof.

"I see your skepticism, Jozef. Don't you believe me?" asked Andrei.

"I want to, but how can you be so confident?"

Andrei laughed and said, You see, Brushka, therein lies the secret of Jozef's success. He wants proof. He studies and studies before he acts." Then Andrei focused his attention on Jozef and said, "I don't have proof, my sterling fighter against tyranny, but let me tell you what I know and then tell me how close to truth I can be once you know the facts that I know. But first get me a more comfortable place to sit, and get me and Brushka some more of your kosher wine, so we can drink a toast to the truth while your God listens to what I say. Is that a deal, Jozef?"

"That's a deal," said Jozef as he reached for the wine bottle.

With wine in hand, Andrei started.

"First of all, Jozef, the German Group Center's front line in the Soviet Union has a large bulge in Byelorussia and Ukraine. We

have watched with interest as we noted that Nazi bulge, which has the effect of increasing their forward line necessitating more arms, equipment and men, all of which are in short supply. Why they haven't withdrawn to shorten their lines is a mystery to some, but I happen to believe that their madman leader can not even contemplate a short retreat even if it means better defense for him. Offense is all that is on his mind, and that is why he has become our ally. His military brain suffers from a superiority complex, but that superiority complex works to our advantage."

"Tell me how, Andrei."

"That I can do, and I do it with pride for our generals have concocted an offensive strategy that is nothing short of brilliant. First of all, what the Nazis have is a large concentration of troops and material. They think it is overwhelming, so we have allowed them to believe that. Do you know how, Jozef?"

Jozef stroked his chin as his mind weighed through the options. "I'm not sure," he said.

Andrei answered, "We have done everything in plain site to let the Nazis believe that we are hard at work preparing a massive defense, constructing fake defenses etc. Plus we no longer attack which also gives the impression that our focus is defense and only defense. More important than that is the fact that we've spread false intelligence that when we do attack we will attack Army Group South in the Ukraine. This is something that our intelligence has told us is what the Nazis expect from us."

"How do you know that they're falling for all these brilliant maneuvers?" asked Jozef.

"You see how you have to convince a genius, Brushka?"

"Yes, hard work for a man with so little brains as you, Andrei," answered Brushka with a smile.

Even serious Jozef laughed at that one.

Andrei just smiled and stared at his friend, and while staring he said, "Anyhow, after that short pause by comedienne Brushka, and as I said before I was so rudely interrupted—he winked at Brushka—we also spread false intelligence that our attack would come through Ukraine against Army Group South, which, as I said, is what the Germans expect. Guess what, Jozef."

"What?"

"The Nazis believed our bullshit so completely that they've removed troops and arms from Army Group Center and put them in northern Ukraine. So when we strike Army Group Center we attack a weaker position. Plus don't forget the Normandy invasion and the Nazi sandwich.

That's why I say the war will be over soon. Now, Jozef, if you don't think the odds are in our favor especially with what is an overwhelming superiority, ten to one about, how can we lose? I think it will be a route, Jozef. We will be teaching them a lesson that they will never forget."

"I have to confess, that's a very convincing strategy, Andrei. You can be sure that my men and I will continue our dynamiting. If what you say is true, I can imagine us having to deal with retreating German troops through the forests. They may flee en mass in their haste to get out of the Soviet Union using ordinary roads. Our planes will have a field day. I pity the poor bastards."

"You're right. Even deserters will not dare to go through the forest especially if they know that Jozef is waiting for them, but they might rather than get strafed to death from our air superiority." He smiled and they all laughed. "But Jozef, we never know, so I want you to assume that they are coming through the forest. Be ready for them. Place your men in defensive positions. Wait. If you see any Nazis coming your way, you'll know what to do.

"It will be automatic. My trigger finger will need no instructions from my brain."

"You see, Brushka, if only we had a thousand like Jozef. This war would have been over a long time ago. Tell your men, Jozef. We go now to visit more partisans and give them the same instructions. We don't want any Nazis who visited us these last three years stepping foot in Germany ever again. This is a big country. We have plenty of room to bury them."

There was a consensus now; this war will be over soon, thought Jozef.

Jozef told his fighters what Andrei's instructions were, preparing them for a final battle if it should come to that. He congratulated them on a job well done. "You will always know that you played a small part in the victory over the hated Nazis. The world has experienced a horror on a scale never before seen in history. The Soviet Union and Poland will soon be free and we and the army will go on until Hitler surrenders or is dead. That's inevitable. Thank you all. I pray that the time is near that we will all be secure to pursue our lives in peace. Now as soon as we know the attack has started, we get ready."

June 22, 1944 found the Soviet army with 1,700,000 troops, 6,000 tanks, and a seven to one aerial supremacy attack in full force. As Andrei predicted, the Nazi army could not cope with such power and their defensive lines crumbled under the onslaught.

It was a route, and it was not long that the forest dwellers heard the explosions in the distance that sounded to them like harp music from heaven.

Jozef rushed to get his troops into position, and just in time, for within two days they spotted a bedraggled appearing small group of Nazi soldiers walking unexpectedly directly toward Jozef's camp. Jozef opened fire and his men joined in immediately. The stunned Nazis did not even attempt to join the battle, rather they attempted to surrender, one of them saying, "I want to live. This war is over." None of the Nazis dropped their guns or put up their hands, however.

As long as the Nazis continued to hold their weapons, Jozef had no choice. "Yes, it is over as far as you and your kind are concerned. I will see to that." With that final statement, he opened fire with his machine gun, saying with a smile, That's for you, my Synagogue friends."

Minsk fell on July 3, eleven days after launching the attack. The Soviets captured 50,000 Nazis and within ten days, they reached the Polish border. Nazi Army Group Center ceased to exist as the Soviets recaptured all of Byelorussia. This action had the second effect of disrupting the Nazi supply lines to Army Group North sealing the fate of the Northern Group Nazis.

Twenty-five days after the onset of operation Bagration, the Soviets launched an offensive in Ukraine, a delayed sister offensive to the Bagration attack which also decimated the Nazis. This successful and secure Ukrainian campaign paved the way for the capture of the Balkans.

For the partisans, the war was over. It was almost like a let down for warrior Jozef, but he took pleasure in the fact that he remained alive, as did his friends, and made a small contribution to the victory that the world would undoubtedly soon celebrate.

CHAPTER 38
THE GUNS ARE SILENT
FINAL MONTHS
1944-1945

The end of partisan warfare in the Minsk region brought relief to some and anxiety to others. Jozef, for instance, with a lifetime of battle so engrained in his mind, could not relax. He spent time speaking with Dr. Ben in counseling sessions geared to developing a mind-set away from the tension of battle. Together they worked on coping mechanisms geared to accepting the reality of peace. How could he best channel one philosophy of mayhem and murder into thoughts of making a living, seeing his children and reordering his life, hopefully the rest of it lived out in relaxing quiet and peaceful purpose.

Most of the partisans from Minsk returned to their homes. They would play a part in rebuilding and restructuring society torn asunder by the Nazi hordes. The great majority of Minsk Jews were dead and those who did return pledged to rebuild Byelorussian society and Jewish life. Many of the partisans joined the Soviet army and continued the march toward Berlin. Some did not return.

Andrei and Brushka met with the Jewish partisan leaders. Jozef, Dr. Ben Frohman and his wife Leah, Emily, David and Hannah, Mikhail, Sonya and their son Val were all there. Abel had gone on with the Russian army to continue the battle, until as Abel put it, "No Nazi is left standing and Hitler and his fellow bastards are all in Nazi hell."

Andrei said, "This may be our final meeting, but I want to be sure that before I finish up my work here and join our troops, you all know that your country is proud of your service. I have submitted a report to my superiors attesting to your brave work. You, Mikhail, are a special case because your work in the building that housed the Nazi leadership puts you under suspicion, and I fear for what may become of you now that our troops are here and they will be likely to take it out on those they feel may have been collaborators. So with that in mind, Mikhail, take and keep this letter. It has the army official seal and I and my commanding general signed it to let them know what you accomplished and the vital part it played in our final victory."

With that, the other attendees broke out in smiles and thunderous applause. Sonya and Val's expression of pride said volumes.

"Thank you, sir," said a humble Mikhail.

Andrei shook Mikhail's hand and said, "Plus I want you all to know that I have submitted the names of the three of you who started your group. Jozef, Mikhail and Ben, I soon hope to see you all with a Hero of the Soviet Union medal around your necks. It will be well deserved."

The three of them stood in silence for a few seconds and then said a feeble, "Thank you, sir."

Andrei continued.

"Now for some of the details of the great progress made by our troops and our allies: The ground war has come to Germany," and as he said this, his face lit up with an ear-to-ear smile. *"Our troops are on the border of East Prussia as I speak. The German*

Army Group Center is no more. We wiped them out in six weeks. Our southern front attack is equally as successful. We have taken Rumania and the Ploesti oil fields. Let's see how well their tanks can go now without oil." He laughed. "Finland is out of the war and they attacked German troops who stayed in their country. Bulgaria quit too. Italy, of course is long gone. The rats have left the sinking ship and Hitler is alone. But this does not mean the war is over. You know what kind of a fanatic he is. I'm sure he will try to mobilize every old man, woman, and child to die in his struggle for the fatherland, which by now he must know is lost. He had two wars actually—the one for world domination and the one against the Jews. I guess history will say that he lost the first war and won the second. But he's killed his last Soviet citizen now and the quicker we eliminate him, the quicker it will all stop.

As far as our allies are concerned, they too are enjoying seeing that bastard and his armies beaten back in Western Europe. I really don't understand how he could even consider continuing his useless struggle as his entire army is kaput. There's nothing left. So the only thing that is keeping this war going is the fact that Hitler is a fanatic who will go on and on until the last German is dead at his feet." He paused before he made a final statement. "Thanks again for your part in this war and now go and have a good life. I hope Brushka and I will have a chance to meet you all again in full peace."

The Ben Frohman and Mikhail Gregov family picked up their lives as best as they could. It was a slow process as they reintegrated into a destroyed society.

Ben and Leah went back to work in the hospital.

David and Hannah restarted their university studies and eventually fulfilled their ambition to practice medicine.

David and Val restarted their gymnastic hobby again.

Emily became an excellent swimmer and when she completed her nursing education, she took up employment at the same hospital where her parents worked.

Mikhail went back to work as engineer for the Minsk Civic building now under new management after seeing to the complete decontamination.

Jozef visited Poland, saw his children and ex-wife and then returned to Minsk since post war Poland, now taken over by the Soviet Union, was an inhospitable place for many returning Jews. Soviet Communism, resisted by many Poles, took over the country. Jozef continued working with Mikhail in the Civic building.

The war in Europe ended May 7, 1945 shortly after Hitler committed suicide in his Berlin bunker.

CHAPTER 39
EPILOGUE
AUTHOR'S NOTE

Much of this chapter is repetition of the historical and other facts interspersed within the book. I put them together here for review.

Although the book has past relevance, in the present era of terrorism and rising anti-Semitism, it has current relevance as well. He who fails to learn the lessons of history is doomed to repeat it.

At this point, I now wish to discuss the fictional characters of this book and whom they represent and the few non-fictional characters.

The Frohmans including Dr. Ben, his wife Leah, their son David and daughter Emily, represent refugees from anti-Semitism, fleeing from country to country in an effort to escape persecution.

In the late 1800's and early 1900's the Jews of Eastern Europe fled to Western Europe, South America, The Middle East, or the United States. In the 1930's the Jews of Germany did the same. If interested in more history, we can go back as far as the 1300's when Western Europeans blamed Jews for the Plague accusing them of "poisoning the wells." Those Jews that survived settled in Eastern Europe, principally Poland.

In my case and fortunately for my family, my grandparents fled from Russian-controlled Poland to the United States in 1904 where they lived in freedom and security and now five generations of Americans have followed.

The Gregov family, Mikhail, Sonya, and Valery represents those non-Jews, free of bigotry, who befriended, collaborated with and in many instances gave shelter and protection to the persecuted Jews of Europe. Many of them are enshrined as righteous gentiles in Israel's Yad Vashem, a world center for holocaust research and education.

Hannah Brunstein represents a young Jew who fell in love with another Jew during a time of great peril. Their trials and tribulations before and during World War II typically faced surviving young Jews during this period.

Miriam Brunstein, wife of Leo and mother of Hannah represents a survivor whose relative fell to the Nazis or their collaborators during the war.

Mr. Brunstein represents those who were shot and buried in pre-dug pits.

Jozef Askenazy undergoes an experience that actually happened after the start of World War II. The S.S. took fifty Jews to repair a bridge in Poland. With the Jews work complete, they then took them to a synagogue where they were all shot and killed. Jozef Askenazy escaped and represents those Jews who witnessed or learned about their friends or relatives death at the hands of the Nazis and/or their collaborators. This prompted in them an intense desire for revenge driving them to join and lead partisans in dedicated anti-Nazi activity.

Abel Stolar represents some few fortunate Jews who fell wounded into the killing pits, feigned death and miraculously escaped.

Andrei Kalemnikoff represents a Soviet army officer left behind the lines by the retreating Soviets after the Nazis invaded the Soviet Union. Their task was to help organize civilian partisan resistance against the Nazis, collaborate with and direct other partisan groups.

Brushka represents military or civilian women of many nationalities who also served as valuable partisans in many roles including combat.

Sergei represents a Soviet army enlisted man who also played a role in partisan resistance.

Colonel Oskar Hoffman represents an actual Nazi Einsatzgruppe leader by the name of Oskar Dirlewanger (1895-1945). In a group famous for barbaric cruelty, Dirlewanger led the pack. An intellectual

PhD in political Science, a rapist who served prison time for molesting young girls, he fought in World War I, then with the Freicorps after that war and in the Spanish Civil War and World War II where he was responsible for destroying many villages including killing women and children in Byelorussia. While recovering from his twelfth wound in Bavaria after the war, he was beaten and tortured to death by Polish guards working for French occupation forces.

Yehezkiel Atlas was an actual young Jewish physician who saw his family wiped out by Nazi forces and dedicated his life to anti-Nazi resistance as a partisan. Wounded in battle, he succumbed to his wounds in December 1942. His partisan comrades buried him in an unmarked grave in the forest. In November 2008, Byelorussian patriots finally brought Dr. Atlas to a traditional Jewish burial when they unearthed his body, provided a religious ceremony and the Byelorussian army performed a gun salute and provided a guard of honor.

Hans Woelke was an actual 1936 Olympic shot put Gold Medal winner. He worked as a Berlin policeman and served as a captain in the SS. Partisans killed him and others on 22 March 1943 near Khatyn Village, Byelorussia. In reprisal, Nazis massacred the Khatyn residents. Woelke's grave is at the Minsk Cemetery (Moscow Street, Grave 28, Row 22, West side).

Luz Long, 1936 Olympic Silver medal long jump winner and competitor and friend of Jessie Owens was wounded in battle in Sicily, died three days later in a British hospital and was buried in the war cemetery of Motta Sant'Anastasia.

Siegfried Eifrig, the 1936 Olympic torchbearer fought for the Nazis in Africa and ended the war in a British prisoner of war camp.

Such was the fate of just three of the famous German Olympians of 1936.

Joseph Schwarzmznn, the German gymnastic triple Gold and double Bronze medal winner of the 1936 Olympics became a paratrooper, fought in Holland where he received a near fatal lung wound, fought on the Island of Crete and on the Soviet front. In March of 1944, his old wound acted up forcing him to spend time in a Munich military hospital. The British kept him as a prisoner of war from May 9 to October 29, 1945. In 1952, he won the Silver medal in the Helsinki Olympic Games at age forty, a remarkable accomplishment. The actual Gold medal winner protested by claiming that Schwarzmznn should have won the Gold, but did not because "he was German." He died in 2000, age 87.

THE END

Printed in the United States
By Bookmasters